A WYATT BOOK for

W

—ST—
MARTIN'S
PRESS

Also by Don Keith

The Forever Season

A WYATT
BOOK *for*

W

— ST. —
MARTIN'S
PRESS

9 January 1997

Dear Dave White:

Here is a finished copy of
Don Keith's WIZARD OF THE
WIND, which has just come
off press. We publish later
this month.

I hope you find Don's book
 of interest and you'll tell
your friends about it.

With all good wishes for the
new year.

Sincerely,

Robert B. Wyatt

A WYATT BOOK *for* ST. MARTIN'S PRESS — 175 Fifth Avenue, New York, N.Y., 10010
Telephone (212) 674-5151 ext. 460   Fax (212) 529-0694

Also 252 West 74ᵀᴴ Street, New York, N.Y., 10023
Telephone (212) 595-8740   Fax (212) 595-4343

Wizard of the Wind

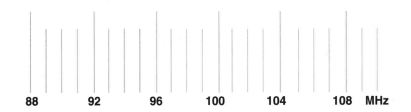

88   92   96   100   104   108 MHz

Don Keith

a wyatt book for st. martin's press

Book design by Gretchen Achilles

Library of Congress Cataloging-in-Publication Data

Keith, Don, date
  Wizard of the wind / Don Keith. —1st ed.
    p.   cm.
  ISBN 0–312–14769–4
  I. Title.
PS3561.E37586W59   1997
813'.54—dc20   96–30527

First edition: January 1997

10 9 8 7 6 5 4 3 2 1

In memory of Clyde, who taught me to listen

This story is dedicated to all radio personalities, those wizards past and present whose banter is their incantation, whose air castles are built with only voices, sound, and music riding on the wind. Among them are:

Casey Kasem, "Brother" Dave White, Denny Ray, "Humble Harve," Kid Red, Robert Murphy, Bob Arthur, Cathy Martindale, Dick Bartley, Hy Lit, Kris Stevens, Robert W. Morgan, Bob and Tom, "Cousin Brucie" Morrow, Wink Martindale, Larry King, Bob Burton, Cat Simon, Charlie Kendall, Dick Biondi, Kris Robbins, Rocky Allen, Bob Costas, Dick Purtan, Catt Stone, "Incredible Magic Christian," Dick Clark, J. Akuhead Pupule, Kurt Kirkpatrick, Rodney Bingenheimer, Bob Dearborn, Charlie Chase, "Kansas Mack" Sanders, Johnny Dolan, Dick Orkin, J. Paul Huddleston, Roger Barkley, Bob "Boogie" Gordon, George Gilbert, Charlie Douglas, "Shotgun Tom" Kelly, J. P. "the Big Bopper" Richardson, Larry Lujack, Ron and Ron, Bob Elliott, Domino, J. P. McCarthy, "The Real" Don Steele, Laura Starling, Ron Chapman, Bob "Wolfman Jack" Smith, Charlie Davis, Don Geronimo, Jack McCoy, Steve Cannon, Lee Abrams, Ron Jacobs, Adrian Cronauer, Don Benson, Jack Thayer, Lee Arnold, Ron Lundy, Bob Glasco, Charlie Tuna, Don Imus, Jan Jeffries, Lee "Baby" Simms, Ron O'Brien, Al Lohman, Bob Grant, Charlie Van Dyke, Don McNeil, Jay Michaels, Ichabod Caine, Lee Logan, Ron Riley, Alan Burns, Bob Kingsley, China Smith, "Dr." Don Rose, Jay Thomas, Lee Michaels, Ross Brittain, Shadoe Stevens, Alan Freed, Bob Mitchell, Chris "Super" Fox, Don Walton, Jaye Albright, Lee Sherwood, Rufus Thomas, Alison Steele, Bob Pittman, Chris King, Mike Murphy, Dr. Demento, Jean Shepherd, Les Turpin, Rush Limbaugh, Arnie "Woo Woo" Ginsberg, Tom Birch, Bob Rivers, Chris Lane, Dr. Dre, Jeff Gonzer, Liz Kiley, Rusty Walker, Art Laboe, Bob Steele, Chuck Blore, "Dr." Johnny Fever, Jeff Pollack, Lon Helton, Sam Riddle, Art Roberts, Bob Wilson, Chuck Buell,

Duke Rumore, Jeff Wyatt, Long John Nebel, Sammy Jackson, Art Schreiber, Bobby Denton, Chuck Dunaway, Art Wander, Dwight Case, Jerry Clifton, Jack Armstrong, Lowell Thomas, Scott Muni, Arthur Godfrey, Bobby Irwin, Chuck Harder, E. Alvin Davis, Mike Oatman, Jerry Damen, "Machine Gun" Kelly, Scott Shannon, Scott Sherwood, Scotty Brink, Bobby Ocean, Chuck Leonard, B. Mitchell Reed, Ed Lambert, Jerry Williams, Mancow Muller, Barry Farber, Bobby Rich, Chuck Logan, Ed McMahon, Jhani Kaye, Marc Chase, Shelley "the Playboy" Stewart, Biff Collie, Brad Riegel, Chuck Nasty, Ed Salamon, Jim Christian, Mark & Brian, Sherm Feller, "Biggie" Nevins, Bruce Vidal, Clark Weber, Elmo Ellis, Jim Bohannon, Mark Driscoll, Sonny Fox, Bruce Williams, Garry Meier, Claude Tomlinson, Elvis Duran, Jim Kerr, Mark St. John, Sonny Laguna, Bill "Birdman" Thomas, Bubba the Love Sponge, Courtney Hayden, Bill Ballance, "Emperor" Bob Hudson, Jim Ladd, Martin Bloch, Sonny Melendrez, Bugsy, Coyote Calhoun, Bill Betts, Eric Rhoads, Jim Morrison, Mary Turner, Stan Freberg, Bumper Morgan, Coyote McCloud, Bill Burkett, Father Tree, Jim Pruett, Mason Dixon, Steve Dahl, Buzz Bennett, Cynthia Fox, Bill "Bubba" Bussey, Frazier Smith, Jim Robinson, Mel Allen, Steve Kingston, Steve Rivers, Mel Leeds, "Captain Midnight," Dan Brennan, Bill Drake, Fred Jacobs, Jim Taber, Mel Karmazin, Sunny Joe White, Steve Norris, Carey Curelop, Dan Ingram, Bill Gardner, Fred Winston, Jim Zippo, Michael L. Carter, Susan Stamberg, Bill Lawson, Carl P. Mayfield, Dan Mason, Gabe Baptiste, William B. Williams, Jimmy Rabbitt, Mike McVay, Symphony Sid, Bill Lowery, John Lander, Dan O'Day, Garrison Keillor, Jimmy Steal, Mike O'Meara, T. Tommy Cutrer, Bill Mack, Dan Vallie, Gary Burbank, Jimmy Vineyard, Moby, Tac Hammer, Bill Tanner, Charlie Cook, Danny Bonaduce, Gary Guthrie, "Red Beard," Joe Bonnadonna, Moon Mullins, "Tall Paul" White, Billy Parker, Dave Donahue, Bob Eubanks, Gary Owens, Joe Niagara, Murray "the K" Kaufman, Ted Atkins, Darrin Wilhite, Gary Stevens, Joe Pyne, Neal Rogers, Terry Dorsey, Dave Letterman, Rick and Suds, Gene Chenault, Joe Rumore, Norm Pattiz, the Greaseman, Dave Logan, Gene Rayburn, Joey Reynolds, Norm Winer, Tim Wall, Todd Storz, Dave Nichols, George Klein, John Boy and Billy, Oedipus, Todd Pettingill, Dave Roddy, George McFly, John Gehron, Orson Welles, Tom Clay, Del Clark, Gerry DeFrancesco, John DeBella, John "Records" Landecker, Paco Lopez, Tom Donahue, Del De Montreaux, Rick Dees, Gerry House, John Bozeman, Pat Clarke, Tom Joyner, Dennis Constantine, Gerry Marshall, John Donovan, Pat St. John, Tom Leykis, Gil Gross, John Ed Willoughby, Patti Wheeler, Tom Reeder, Gordon McClendon, John Rook, Paul Harvey, Tom Rounds, Grant Turner, John "R." Richbourg, Phil "the Bean" Cisneros, Tom Snyder, Greg Bass, John Sebastian, Phil Hunt, Tommy Charles, Guy Zapoleon, Johnny Dark,

Ralph Emery, Trip Reeb, Hairl Hensley, Johnny Davis, Randy Michaels, Trish Hennessey, John A., John R., and John B. Gambling, Harley Drew, Johnny Gray, Ray Goulding, Venus Flytrap, Harold W. Arlin, Johnny Hayes, Red Barber, Vickie Buchannon, Harry Harrison, Jonathan Brandmeier, "Wild Bill" Brock, Regis Philbin, Wally Phillips, Herb Oscar Anderson, Jon Wailin, Rhubarb Jones, Walt "Baby" Love, "Hoss" Allen, Keith Hill, Rich "Brother" Robin, Ken Minyard, Rick Shaw, Ken Dowe, Howard Stern, Richard Belzer, Howie Castle, Kent Burkhart, Kevin Metheney, Rick Burgess, Kevin Weatherly, Kid Leo, Rick Sklar, and the hundreds of others who may be faceless but still touch us every day with their audio alchemy.

—DON KEITH
Indian Springs Village, Alabama

... and they shall seek to the idols, and to the charmers, and to them that have familiar spirits, and to the wizards.

Isaiah 19:3

Incline your ear and come unto me: hear, and your soul shall live. . . .

Isaiah 55:3

A demonstration of wireless communication was given by Nathan Stubblefield in Murray, Kentucky, in 1892. He never capitalized on his invention and died penniless. Patent No. 12039 for communication by electromagnetic waves was granted to Guglielmo Marconi in 1896. He also was the first to participate in a transatlantic transmission and reception. The Morse code letter *S* (di-di-dit) was sent from Cornwall, England, to St. John's, Newfoundland, in 1901.

A radio program called *Rambling with Gambling* has been broadcast regularly on WOR in New York City since March of 1925. Three generations—John B. Gambling; his son, John A. Gambling; and his son, John R. Gambling—have each hosted the program. Over twenty-one thousand shows have been aired to date.

In January 1996, Tampa disc jockey Bubba the Love Sponge received a call on the air from a young girl who was attempting suicide. He was able to keep her on the line until he could get her help and thus saved her life.

The [radio] business is a cruel and shallow money trench, a long plastic hallway where thieves and pimps run free and weak men die like dogs.

—Hunter S. Thompson, who was talking about television. This amended version is often found pinned to radio station bulletin boards

Sign-on

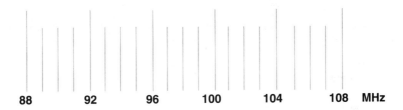

A generic punk band was thumping away on the restaurant's jukebox, with the off-key guitars and sneering vocals seriously out of place in the middle of the breakfast rush. But nobody at that morning's disc jockey "card party" seemed to be paying the music much of a mind. Or the eggs or biscuits either, for that matter.

The get-together was sometimes convened totally by accident at a place called Sadie's, a greasy spoon diner downtown that was a convenient equal distance from each of the town's radio stations that really mattered anymore. Or sometimes a bunch of the disc jockeys would gather at someone's house or apartment with the pretense of watching reruns of *WKRP in Cincinnati* on television. Or the four or five midnight-to-six jocks in town would wander into whatever bar was open at 6:30 A.M. for a cold-beer breakfast and a "card party" meeting of their own.

There was rarely a hand dealt before the radio war stories took over. Everybody knew the *WKRP* episodes by heart by now anyway, and considered the show to be more of a damned documentary than a sitcom. Whether the jocks were hungry or not, breakfast sometimes lasted until lunch. Or until the coffee shop waitress or the manager would tell them to take their cigarette smoke and noise somewhere else.

The subject was always, eventually, sooner than later, radio. The stations, the characters who danced through them, the groupies, the record promotion men, the musical stars who made all the bullshit worth it.

A gray curtain of rain was falling outside Sadie's, and the windows were fogged with steam and conversation. Chick Charles had just stumbled in, ordered his usual four eggs over easy bloodshot with Tabasco, and was now holding court at the row of tables the jocks had slid together in the back of the smoky dining room. Charles had been a legendary deejay on a dozen different stations over twenty years in nine different cities from Jackson to Albuquerque. At that moment, though, he looked more like a bum than a radio star.

"Boys, if I could've just been paid by the word, I'd be a rich mother today," he was saying, his deep-throated voice causing several of the other patrons in Sadie's to look his way. "Instead, I get a dollar a day and all the records I can eat."

Chick Charles was bumping fifty. He was now doing easy listening, 10:00 P.M. till 2:00 A.M., on the lowest-rated FM station in town, along with what few commercial voice-overs he could pick up on the side. But he was still de facto ringmaster of the "card party" circuses simply because he knew more stories than anyone else, or how to cue someone else to tell one of his favorites if he was simply too tired.

"Scotty, tell us about the mule that ate the transmission cable in Shreveport," he'd say, or, "Wild Child, wadn't you in Louisville the night the two old gals set Three Dog Night's hotel room on fire?"

None of the members ever questioned the veracity of the stories. They understood some of them were not even remotely true, that others had the embellishing benefit of time, that key facts often changed more than somewhat. But it didn't matter. They got passed on from jock to jock, market to market, retold like biblical parables.

The common thread was that they were about radio people, mostly from the late fifties and sixties, when the medium was getting reinvented on the fly to stave off television, the latest threat. When the personalities who cracked the mike and created Technicolor images in midair in ten-second bursts became practically as big as the wild new rock-and-roll music they were introducing to a voracious audience of mostly baby-boomers.

The stars of their fables were the disc jockeys, the characters who carried on the tradition of earlier wizards who could make magic on the wind. Arthur Godfrey had been the original Peck's bad boy. Edward R. Murrow was crazy for a story. Martin Block could build a swirling ballroom full of dancers out of ozone and voice and recorded music. They were the stars of the pictureless medium. Kindred spirits with the likes of Wolfman Jack and Rockin' Randy Mathews and John "Records" Landecker and Jerry Diamond and Chick Charles and Larry Lujack and Don Imus and Wink Martindale and Joe Niagara and Jimmy Gill and Dick Clark and Alan Freed and a few hundred others who could bring a laugh or a tear with a word or two, hastily, craftily applied.

Chick Charles was having a coughing fit at the moment so Dr. Don Davis from Q-103 took the floor. He arbitrarily established "death" as the first topic of the morning's meeting and opened the floor for contributions.

"We had a guy working weekends," Cliff Carr from Rock 97 chimed in. "He was having girl trouble, so one night he put on an album and cut both wrists wide open with a razor blade from the production room. The boss was listening and heard him breaking format, tracking the album, came down and caught him bleeding to death. Breaking the format saved the guy's life. But he got fired the next day anyway. I hear the guy is a preacher now, somewhere up in Missouri."

"Speaking of Missouri," Joey Reynolds from the Mix said, "when I worked in Kirksville, we had to have our tower painted so the owner cheaped out and hired two bozos off the street to do it. Well, they had painted their way up to the four-hundred-foot level when the boatswain's chair they had rented broke. Murphy's Law. Stuff on a tower won't break when you're only up twenty feet, you know.

"People said they looked like manhole covers when they were scraped up off the ground. The owner was okay 'cause they had started at the bottom of the tower and painted all but the very top. The old so-and-so never did get the rest of the tower painted."

"You guys remember Rocky Graves?" Jack Ross from WKUY asked the question. "I think you worked with him in Raleigh, Cliff. He was married to a beautiful woman and he was insanely jealous of her. Had good reason, too. He was doing six to ten at night at KJAY in Des Moines. I did middays. He came to work early one night, got himself a reel of tape, went into the production room, and recorded an hour of his show. At eight, he started the tape and drove home.

"Sure enough, there was his lovely wife, doing the horizontal bop with some guy. That was bad enough, but on the nightstand she had a radio playing and Rocky's voice was coming through loud and clear. On the tape, of course. She had figured she was okay to spread her wings as long as she could hear Rocky on the air. Well, he shot both of them to death. And while he was at it, he blew hell out of the radio, too.

"Well, Rocky gets back to the station and it looks like a new doughnut shop just opened up. Cops everywhere. The boss and the station manager, too. Seems the dumbass had grabbed an old reel of tape out of the newsroom to record his alibi and it was full of rotten splices. The tape had lasted halfway through the show, just long enough for the late Mrs. Graves to still be hearing her darling husband on the radio. Then it spilled out onto the control-room floor in a pile.

"The boss heard the dead air, couldn't get an answer on the hot line, so he zoomed down to the station. He figured somebody must have kidnapped Rocky, so he called the law. The neighbors who had the young war back at Rocky's apartment had called the police, too, and they put two and two together.

"Last I heard, Rocky had started a broadcasting class in the state prison. His graduates are better than anybody at stealing records and toilet paper!"

A deep rumble of thunder punctuated Jack Ross's story but no one noticed. It was almost ten in the morning. A few had to leave for midday shifts but they were replaced by a morning-show sidekick or two. Nobody had gotten around to tipping any of the waitresses, so now the jocks were being ignored. Besides the "card party," the only other noises were the busboys setting the salad bar for lunch and the icy rain tapping on the front window of the restaurant.

"J. D. the D.J. died," Mary Midnight from KZ-101 finally said as she exhaled blue smoke and crushed out her latest cigarette in the middle of a bowl of grits.

"Who?"

"Jerry Dobbins. Damn, what was his real name? I think it was Jerry German when he was at the Fox in Baton Rouge."

"Tall, skinny guy? No hair?"

"That's him. Great voice but couldn't ad-lib worth a damn.

Used to have to write down every word he was going to say on the air. Even his own name!"

"Sure! I worked with him in Lubbock. What happened?"

"Liver. He drank more than any six guys I ever saw."

"Imagine that. A jock who drank."

"Who's the biggest druggie or drunk you ever saw in the business?"

That's how the proceedings usually got switched to the next topic. An innocent question, then three hours of stories.

The sleepy crowd around the table was instantly rejuvenated by the fresh subject. Lee Shannon from WCVG got the floor. His was the biggest voice.

"Bruce Kline, hands down. Called himself Cousin Brucie before the real Cousin Brucie up in New York threatened to sue him. Then he was Uncle Brucie. His thing was pills. I told him that I had the sniffles and he brought out five different bottles of stuff, most of them not even on the market yet. We called him the 'staff pharmacist.' "

"I remember that guy," Mary Midnight said. "I worked with him in Birmingham for a while. He ate quaaludes like Life Savers, but he was the sweetest guy. Far as I know, he never dealt or anything like that. Just a 'Dr. Feelgood.' "

"That's the guy. You're right. He was great when he wasn't cross-eyed."

"We had this guy named Rick Richards who nearly burned down the station one day. I drove by the station and saw the fire trucks. The owner was running up the driveway in his bathrobe. He hadn't even taken time to get dressed. Seems old Rick was taking a toke between records. He had flipped a roach into a trash can under the control board. It smoked the whole place, melted the wiring under the console till it was one big gooey mess."

"He's the guy who fell out the window into the alley, isn't he?"

"Yeah! He sure was! I'd forgotten about that! Where was that?"

"At PNP in Pensacola. The station was upstairs, second floor, and the only bathroom was in the far back. Old Rick would put on the longest song we played . . . maybe 'Bridge over Troubled Water' or 'Taxi' . . . and he'd go back to the shitter and lean out the window to smoke a doob.

"One night he was back there getting high and lost his balance and fell right out the window into the alley. If he hadn't been so mellow, the fall probably would have killed him. Scared the bejesus out of a couple of winos in the alley. He just got up, dusted himself off, made sure he had his door key with him, went back upstairs, outroed the song that had been playing, and segued right into the next one. Never missed a beat!"

They were quiet for a moment, some of them thinking of their own close calls.

"Whatever happened to Bruce? He was a great jock when he wasn't goofy on some chemical."

"He had gotten himself together and had a cushy deal, doing all the voice-overs for the Ice Capades and voicing concert spots for a promoter out of Cleveland. Christmas Eve, last year, he was on the way to pick up his kids from one or the other of his ex-wives. It was raining like a son of a bitch. He hydroplaned, crossed the median, and hit a truck head-on. Killed him instantly. And the weird thing? He was straight as an arrow. Cold sober for once and he buys it."

The table was quiet again. Mary Midnight squashed out her latest cigarette.

"Gotta go guys. See you next time."

That was the cue. They all got up and left together, still reluctant to be alone. Chick Charles stopped at the door, hesitated, then waddled back to the table and left a dollar tip under his coffee cup.

"I saved a kid's life tonight."

Jeff Jefferson had been sitting quietly on a couch in the corner of the apartment, sipping a beer, while everybody else pretended to watch the Super Bowl, but they had long since gone into story mode.

Stories about jocks who existed on remote-broadcast hot dogs. Others who made a living selling promotional records and satin jackets, gifts from record companies. And others who lived off payola and had plenty of dope and rooms full of stereo equipment so long as they played the right records.

Jeff had their attention, even though one of the teams had just scored a touchdown and the running back was dancing in mad delight on the screen.

"What happened?"

"The kid called me after he had taken a bottle of pills. He was sinking fast so I segued about ten records, talking to him while I got him some help."

"Damn! Good work, Jeff."

"But you know what? I got hot-lined by the program director. He reamed me good for not talking when I was supposed to. I may get fired yet."

The assembled group hissed and booed lustily. The crowd on the television was doing the same for a bad call by one of the officials.

"That's the way it is," Chick Charles was saying. "We gotta be doctors, preachers, lawyers, drug counselors, sex therapists . . . and it don't pay a dime more."

"I never knew people called in to radio stations, before I started," Jeff said.

"I sure never thought about girls calling," someone else admitted. "Can you imagine how lonely somebody has to be to call up a disc jockey for company?"

"Hey, it's all part of the job. By the thousands over the air or one at a time on the telephone, a living, breathing listener is a living, breathing listener."

"That reminds me of Dick Boyd," Jim Flannigan said. "He was 'Johnny Knight' in Memphis. Everybody who worked seven to ten in the evening was named Johnny Knight because they had so many jocks coming and going that it would cost them a fortune to keep changing the jock-shout jingles. The weekend guy was always 'Jim Holiday.' They even had a gal for a while and she was Jim Holiday, too. I worked with Dick in Knoxville. He hooked up with a gal named Veronica on the request line, and damned if he didn't end up marrying the old gal.

"None of us had the heart to tell him she had gone through the jock staff at every station in town. We figured she probably qualified for the station pension plan considering all the time she put in there. She was really a sweet girl, but man, she had round heels for radio guys!

"Dick fell in love with Veronica and none of us said a word. When they set the date, he made sure we all got invitations to the wedding. Said we were all the family he had and he would appreciate it if we would come to the wedding. He asked me to be his best man. What could I do? Tell Dick about that cute little birthmark on his wife's ass?

"I get to the church and it's packed with all her relatives on one side and nobody but ten radio guys on the other. I'm standing there in my rented tux and Dick has the most ecstatic look on his face. I'm thinking maybe it's my lot to have to take Dick aside and tell him the story before this thing goes any further. I know if I look at one of the other jocks out there in the pews, I'm gonna lose it.

"But then the organist strikes up 'Here Comes the Bride,' and there she is. Miss Veronica. And she is the most beautiful thing I've ever seen, floating down that aisle in her white dress like any other virgin on her wedding day.

"When she gets to the altar, the preacher tells everybody that we should bow our heads and pray. I don't. I just bow my head and look out of the corner of my eye at Veronica. She had lifted her veil and was looking right back at me. Boys, if a face and a pair of eyes could talk, hers were speaking volumes. She was begging me, pleading with me, not to say anything to Dick. I just smiled at her to let her know it was okay. One big tear welled up in each eye and rolled down her cheeks and she smiled right back. It was the most beautiful smile I had ever seen.

"Last I heard, they had three kids and a marriage made in heaven. Dick moved over to sales and is managing a station somewhere in the Carolinas now."

They all applauded the happy ending of Flannigan's story. The television crowd at the Super Bowl was standing, cheering wildly along with them.

The crummy little bar was around the corner from WSFA Radio, two blocks from the Mighty Six-Ninety and a half mile down the road from the Super Q. The top ten scores on the pinball machine were all by disc jockeys at one station or another. The leader on the list had over thirty-seven billion points.

"I hate to be called a damned 'disc jockey,'" Mike McGraw was saying to anyone who might be listening above the noise from the jukebox. "That sounds like all we do is play damn records. Cue 'em up and start 'em spinning. Is that all you do, Chucker?"

"Hell, no! I don't play no records!" The Chucker was wasted. It was almost nine o'clock on a Tuesday night. He had been drinking since before three.

"We are 'broadcast personalities,' ain't we, Chucker?"

"Damn right! Broad-damn-casht person-damn-alities!"

"I don't hear 'em calling Dick Clark no damn disc jockey. Or John 'Records' Landecker up in Chicago. Or Gary Burbank. Or Dr. Don Rose. They're not 'deejays.' They're 'broadcast personalities,' man."

"Who's the best you ever heard, Mike?" one of the jocks asked. Mike had passed through an amazing array of towns in his career and had heard most everybody in the business at some time or another.

"You mean besides me? 'Cause I think I'm the damn best and I listen to myself all the time. Well, sir, Dr. Don's still amazing. He can do three jokes over a ten-second record intro. Then there's the Greaseman. Unbelievably dirty, but he uses made-up words so he can get away with it. I heard Rick Dees when he was in Memphis. He does some great stuff with the telephones and prerecorded bits. Jay Thomas started in Jacksonville where I did, you know, at the 'Big Ape.' He's out on the West Coast now. The more he insults the listeners the more they love him. Scott Shannon's good. He has theater of the mind down pat.

"And I used to love listening to Joe Rumore when I worked in Birmingham. He'd play whatever the hell music he wanted to play . . . country, Top Forty, whatever . . . and he did his show from the basement of his house."

"What?"

"Yeah, he'd go down to a studio in the basement and do his show. He did this contest where if he called you and you answered your telephone by saying 'Joe Rumore' instead of 'hello,' you'd win a new car. My grandmother lived there and until the day she died, every time I called her, she'd answer the telephone 'Joe Rumore.' I think she was always disappointed it was me calling and not old Joe giving her a new car."

"I didn't know you worked in Birmingham, Mike."

"Sixteen months. Longest gig I ever had."

"Well, if you did Birmingham, you probably knew Superbird, too."

"God, yeah! What a character! You wouldn't believe this cat. He was fantastic on the air, too. Always seven to midnight 'cause he worked so well with the kids. A real motormouth. One of the first screamers. And crazy as a loon."

"Is the Macon funeral story true, Mike?"

"Damn straight, it was."

"What is the Macon funeral story?" Rick Stone had only been a jock about a year. He had never heard the Macon funeral story.

"Well, you remember the black group, the Silktones? Their lead singer, Cliffie Dubose, died. Overdose, if I remember right, or choked on his own vomit or something. That's how they all go, ain't it? Anyway, they brought his body back to Macon to bury him. The Bird was working there at the time and he was crazy about their music. Used to use 'Good Night Doesn't Mean Good-bye' as his closing theme song every night. Bird grabbed a couple of guys from the station and went over to crash the funeral, but they weren't letting anybody but family and record company bigwigs into the church.

"Here's the thing, though. Superbird, if he combed his hair just right, looked a little bit like Ringo Starr. He could do a pretty fair English accent, too. Anyway, they get up to the church—the only white faces within six blocks—and a big old burly guard stops them at the door. One of the other jocks with him says, 'Man, don't you know who this is? This is Ringo Starr, the Beatle.' The guard about shits. 'Sorry, Mr. Starr. You and your friends go right on in. So sorry.' Well, before they can even get in and seated, word's spread all over the church that Ringo Starr of the Beatles has shown up at the funeral.

"The Widow Dubose comes back to where other mourners have made room for Superbird and them to settle down in a pew. 'Mr. Ringo, I'm so honored you have come to my husband's funeral. How's George and Paul and John? Cliffie just loved your song 'Backoff Boogaloo.' I'd be so honored if you'd sing it for us today during the service.' Well, Superbird could yell and scream with the best of them, but he couldn't carry a tune in a bucket. 'I'd be delighted,' he told her, 'but I 'ave a 'orrible frog in me throat.' He managed to talk her out of it, but they stayed for the whole funeral and skedaddled afterward before some of the record guys could catch up to them and blow the whole thing."

"Where is Bird now?"

"Out of the business. I think he has a record store or a T-shirt shop in Sarasota or somewhere. Nobody wanted screamers or creative jocks anymore. No more Superbirds or Tom Donahues or Jimmy Gills. Some broadcast consultant decided they needed jocks who would appeal to the adults who had more disposable income, so they wanted only big, bland voices."

"Jimmy Gill? Did you ever hear him when you were in Birmingham? I've heard he was the best. . . ."

"Brother James! Yeah, I worked with him for a day or two."

The jocks who could still sit up straight did.

"You worked with Jimmy Gill? Come on!"

"Yeah, I did. He was only doing overnights then, if you can believe it. I was P.M. drive. Back in the sixties. He had been around already, at a half dozen stations, but he kept getting fired because he was so much better and smarter than the stiffs who hired him. But you could tell the guy was something special. He could open that microphone and make you feel like he was talking with you and nobody else. He didn't tell jokes or do bits, but when he spoke, you wanted to turn up the volume to hear what he was saying."

"Yeah, I've heard tapes. He never worked L.A. or New York either, did he?"

"Naw, I guess Nashville was the biggest market he did."

"Why did he take himself off the air before he made the majors? He might've been bigger than Wolfman Jack and Casey Kasem combined."

"Are you kidding? Once you get to where he was, you don't really have the inclination anymore to play records and talk dirty with fourteen-year-old girls on the request line. Jimmy Gill lived out every one of our dreams. But I bet you one thing. If anybody was born to be on the radio it was Jimmy Gill."

All the heads around the table nodded reverently.

"He'd be out of place now, though. They don't want personalities on the radio. They only want pretty voices that don't care if anybody is listening or not. Hired vocal cords. Audio whores."

"Yeah, guys who can say only what they are programmed to say into a cold microphone."

"Damn big-voiced robots."

"Disc jockeys."

"Yeah, damn disc jockeys."

WROG

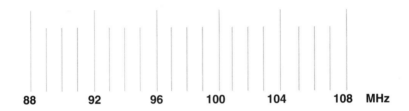

88   92   96   100   104   108   MHz

He was ten years old when he first saw the place where the wizard did his magic. Yes, it changed him. But so did a lot of things that happened. Burying his mother. Meeting Detroit Simmons. The Polanskis. The Georges. Even moving Grandmama and her television set. And rediscovering her old upright Zenith radio.

It was probably a given that Jimmy Gill and his grandmother would be chased from the shack where he had been born. It was the only home he had known except for the impossibly fictional ones that flickered out at them from Grandmama's tiny milky white television screen. With Daddy dead and buried in the little cemetery behind the Holiness church, his mother's final party a fatal one, and Grandmama's Social Security check hardly enough to pay the rent, it was a safe bet they would soon have to move on. Barely a year had passed since his mother's death when his grandmother broke the news to him.

"Your great-aunt Flora down in Birmingham's found us a little house, Jimmy," she cheerily announced one fine spring morning. "Half as much rent as this pile of slabs is costing us, too."

He was busy, getting himself ready for school, trying to iron the wrinkles from the thin overalls he'd already worn twice that week. He pretended not to hear, hoping the notion would die if only he ignored it.

"And mind you turn off that iron or you'll burn down this cow stall before we can get moved out of it."

"When are we gonna move?" Jimmy asked. He was already afraid of the prospects of leaving the few friends he had, the school where he had managed to make the fourth grade, the muddy little river town that was home, no matter how simple and plain it might be.

But Grandmama was gone already, her attention absorbed again by Dave Garroway and his chimpanzee cavorting around inside her television set. The set she had sacrificed and saved up for and had finally bought only a few weeks before Mama died. The old lady had given up snuff and quit smoking for a while to accumulate the fortune it must have cost her. Then she had climbed up on the roof herself in a sleet storm, tying off the pipe that held the antenna to the house and twisting and turning it around to pull in the best picture while Jimmy yelled coordinates to her from inside the house.

For as long as Jimmy could remember, Grandmama had spent most of her waking time sitting in front of her big upright Zenith console radio, totally lost in the soap opera characters and voices and singers that spilled from its booming bass speakers. But then, when she finally got the television set, she was even more a captive of this new medium that dominated one corner of the living room. After his mother died, his grandmother would sit for hours on the sagging living-room couch, rocking back and forth hypnotically, a crossed leg bouncing, a pack of cigarettes and a cup of coffee always within reach. She would be swept away, mesmerized by the wavering picture on the round screen, its swirling, hissing snow reflecting in her eyeglasses. She would talk with the tiny people captured inside the wooden box, fuss at them, argue with them, ask them questions, treat them much the same as she would anyone else she had invited into her house.

Jimmy's spirits plunged at the news of the coming move, but he didn't complain. It was not his way. And there was no one who would listen anyway. He stepped into the hot, sticky overalls, buckled the galluses, tied the laces of his brogans as best he could with their knotty broken strings, and was out the door, slamming it hard behind him to try to cut off any more bad news. But he could still hear Grandmama laughing and talking to the people in the television set as he dodged mud puddles in a mad zigzag run through town to the schoolhouse.

Somehow, she managed to talk Wiley Groves, their nearest next-door neighbor, into bringing over his old pickup truck and helping them move. A few of the men who had worked with Jimmy's father at the sawmill came by to give them a hand, pitching in to help load the few sticks of furniture they had. As the men worked, they talked quietly among themselves about James Gill's death, his trashy widow's craziness, obviously unaware that their boy was close enough to overhear what they were saying.

Jimmy's father's right arm had been severed cleanly one day when he slipped on something and fell into a saw. His blood had been soaked up by the dirt and sawdust as the life flowed out of him in rhythmic spurts. The men remembered him lying there, next to his detached arm, telling each of them good-bye one at a time while they stood idly by, helpless and crying. They mumbled to each other about how his beautiful young wife had done a quick one-eighty after her husband was gone, turning to no-good as quick and sure as a stray bolt of lightning seeking ground.

Then the men apparently caught Jimmy listening and hushed their reminiscing before they got to the rest. About how she came to be floating facedown in the muddy Tennessee River, her hair like blond moss as it billowed about her. Jimmy didn't care what the men said, though. He knew already that his mother didn't exactly have a ticket punched for the promised land when she died.

All his clothes fit into one pillowcase. It seemed as if it took the men only a minute or two to load and stack their few sticks of nicked-up furniture onto the truck bed, and Jimmy was embarrassed that this was all there was to show for Grandmama's years of living, the combined lives of his parents and all their accumulations. A few rickety sticks of furniture, a couple of stained mattresses, a dusty television set, and all of it hardly filling the bed of an old, rust-spotted pickup truck.

Jimmy sat on top of the furniture with the pillowcase on his lap, tucked between the splintered chifforobe and the musty-smelling couch, lodged in next to the truck cab. He refused to cry, no matter how sad it all was. He couldn't. At least he was sitting up high, though. He loved climbing willow trees, scaling sand hills, sitting up as high in the sky as he could get.

When they were ready to go, Grandmama didn't seem sentimental about the situation at all. She swung up onto the running board and into the patched-up passenger seat of the truck like a pioneer woman climbing aboard a Conestoga wagon heading west. Wiley Groves walked around to the driver's side, checking the air in the tires, testing the rope that held the household aboard.

"Sure you got everything, now, Miz Rutherford?" he asked, apparently surprised how small the load had turned out to be. "Don't want to be forgetting anything or we can't be coming back for it."

"Yeah, that's all there is, Wiley. Let's get going so we can get there before night. Hate to be on the highway at night with all the drunks out after dark," she urged, then smiled at a thought. "And maybe we can get there in time to look at some of Ed Sullivan."

From his exhalted seat on top of the load, Jimmy could see through the dusty front window of the house. Grandmama's old Zenith console radio still sat in the living room, all alone and quiet against the back wall, sadly, silently watching them leave.

"The radio, Grandmama! You forgot the radio!" he yelled, just before Wiley ground the truck's starter to life.

"We don't need that old pile of junk since we got the TV set, Jimmy," she answered, motioning impatiently for Wiley to get on the way. They had miles to go and there were television shows to watch.

But Wiley popped open the truck door anyway, climbed back up the shaky porch steps, and wrestled the big brown box outside and down to the truck. He carefully tied it upright on the lowered tailgate with a length of grass rope so it couldn't jump free and escape.

"Might want to listen to the news or some preaching sometimes," he said, red-faced from the exertion of hugging the radio onto the truck. He winked up at the boy. "Might need to wrap some of this rope around you, too, boy, skinny as you are, or you're likely to blow out of the truck between here and Birmingham."

He winked again, took a minute to adjust the ride of his overalls and get himself a pinch of snuff, and then they were off. Jimmy Gill's life to that point disappeared in the blue exhaust smoke of the pickup. The only lasting image left him was the cottony river mist and a squadron of black crows circling above the cemetery behind the Holiness church. He knew there were two cheap grave markers hiding under the elms where his mama and daddy once again lay side by side. Even from his seat high on the back of the truck, he couldn't quite see their tombstones. He doubted if he would ever see them again.

"Bye," he said quietly, his words snatched away by the wind whistling around the truck cab. No matter. He knew they probably weren't listening to him anyway.

By the time they had crossed the river on the rusty old bridge south of Chattanooga, Jimmy Gill had a thumb in his mouth and the music of the rushing wind and the rocking of the truck bed had lulled him to sound sleep.

Chapter 2

Jimmy immediately despised their new home. There were signs that it had once been a nice neighborhood of well-kept wood-frame houses, homes which had once been owned by steelworkers who had prospered during the war and the boom years afterward. But gradually, as their owners moved to suburbs far away from the smelly smoke of the steel mills and the encroachment of the colored people, their homes had been converted into row after row of run-down duplexes. Houses that had once been proudly loved and coddled had now been snapped up by absentee landlords, divided for multiple families, and rented out to those who flooded in from failed farms and dying small towns.

They were hard-luck people desperate to find work in the mills or in the shops and foundries that fed like lichens on the steel plants. Beaten people whose hopes had been slapped down by circumstances or chased from their farms by dirt cheap prices and the inevitable chants of the auctioneers.

A few of the original owners held on, unwilling to move from the plot of ground where they had planted their families years before. People like old Mr. Polanski, who lived two doors down from where Jimmy and his grandmother had moved. He and his quiet wife maintained an oasis in the middle of the weeds and heaped-up garbage. They grew big banana trees that waved in the front yard with the summer breeze, daffodils that boldly announced spring, fragrant hyacinths and rosebushes all decked out in carefully tended beds along the crumpling sidewalk. Their yard itself was a carpet of soft, cool, green zoysia.

But apparently not everybody appreciated the beauty of Mr. Polanski's yard. Several times a week, someone in a loud, angry car would spin across the corner lot and rip up the flowers and bushes and grass, as if their glory were some kind of personal affront. The vandal always managed to steer around the big limestone rocks that lined the edge of the street to try to block such an assault, and he came and went without anyone being able to see who it was or do anything to stop him.

Mr. Polanski would usually be out in his yard later in the day, after his long shift at the mill, trying to salvage what he could before darkness cut off his rescue. He would talk to himself under his breath in a strange, guttural language and occasionally shake his fist in the direction in which he imagined the car that had done such damage might have fled. His wife, who barely spoke English herself, brought him ice water and sat in the shade of a nearby maple, listening as he cursed, allowing him to vent his rage on the dirt clods and severed limbs of his plants. Sometimes she supplied him with the foreign curses that time and anger had made him forget.

The Polanskis were the first people Jimmy met in the neighborhood. He made an instant friend when he walked over and volunteered to help clean up the mess. He suspected Mr. Polanski simply wanted to have someone to talk with, and talk he did. He told Jimmy how it used to be when everyone in the neighborhood did as he still tried to do: kept up their places with pride. Of a recent time when everybody on Wisteria Street knew everybody else. When they held neighborhood picnics and block parties and watched out for mischief while someone was away from home.

"They would never have allowed such as this to happen, Jimmy," he would say. "Together, me and the Angelos and the Kauffmans and Sammy Corkus down there on the corner, we would have stopped such damn foolishness before someone is hurt."

He'd wipe the sweat from his face with a bath towel, take a big drink of water so cold it claimed his breath for a moment, and then look wistfully up and down the street that had been his home for forty years. He told Jimmy how it now seemed to him to be a strange, foreign land out there just beyond his flower beds. An avenue of ill-tempered, unhappy aliens too sullen to speak, too disillusioned to care for much of anything, and especially each other.

And he would talk of his own daughter and son, moved away to Atlanta and California, who only came home on Christmas and called once a month to check on him and their mother and to talk of the grandchildren. They would fuss at him endlessly for not retiring, for not moving away to Florida, for refusing to leave the place that was plenty good enough for them when they were growing up.

Jimmy would be on his knees in the dirt beside the old man, holding the trunks of new replacement azalea plants while he buried their feet in the dark loam, and the man's tears would fall on the fragrant earth like a sudden spring rain. Jimmy would pretend to study the shapes that the clouds spun over their heads to try to keep from embarrassing the old man, to keep from letting him know that he had noticed his crying.

From that first dreary, rainy day when they had unloaded their things into the damp duplex on Wisteria Street, with its musty mildew smell and cold linoleum floors, Jimmy had ached to ride right back up old U.S. Highway 11 in the back of Wiley Groves's coughing pickup truck. Back to his friends, his playground along the Tennessee River, the drafty shack that now seemed a palace in comparison to this dingy place.

The only stream here was the junk-filled ditch that snaked through the vines and weeds just out the back door. He doubted it would be much good for frog gigging or minnow catching. There certainly were no big catfish to catch with a chunk of soap on a hook, no well-worn war trails winding through jungles of honeysuckle and grape vines, no tall trees to climb and claim a lofty limb to cling to and gaze off into the distance. Just dirty cement, cracked asphalt, scrawny trees, and mean, surly people who didn't seem to want to be in this damned place any more than he did.

Jimmy was so lonely he hurt. They had lived in the duplex at least two weeks before he saw any other kids in the neighborhood. It was a steamy hot Saturday afternoon and he sat on the front steps, being careful to stay on his side of the invisibly divided porch.

Neither Grandmama nor he had met any of the loud, dirty people who lived only a paper-thin wall away from them. There was a drawn-looking, skinny woman, a coarse, loud-talking man, and a set of identical twin boys who were probably in their late teens. They were usually locked tightly behind pulled window shades, quiet except for occasional violent explosions from the old man and answering salvos from the boys. Then one or the other or all three would storm and stomp out the doorway and rattle angrily off in one direction or the other in one of their collection of old, loud cars that they kept parked all over the sidewalk and on the muddy front lawn.

The name George had been penciled on a piece of paper Scotch-taped to their mailbox near their front door, but Jimmy couldn't tell if that was a first or a last name. It didn't matter. He had already made up his mind to stay out of their way after his only encounter so far with any of them.

Grandmama rarely slipped far from the television set, so she had not made their acquaintance. The only time Jimmy had tried to be friendly had been on their second or third day there. The frail woman who appeared to be the wife and mother had slipped out her door to throw wet gray sheets over the porch railing to dry. She seemed preoccupied and apparently didn't see Jimmy sitting there in his regular spot, high up on the front steps, where he was enjoying a rare shaft of sunshine.

"Hi, ma'am," he had chirped cheerfully, trying to be friendly, the way he had been taught.

But she was either deaf or chose to ignore his greeting. She finished her task hurriedly and was quickly back inside the house with a dismissing slam of the ripped screen door behind her. It would be a while before he saw her again. And if she and the rest of her family were that unfriendly, then that was fine with Jimmy Gill.

Except for the humid heat, that particular Saturday had turned out to be a nice day. Leaves were finally sprouting on the sycamores that lined Wisteria Street, a full month later than those on the chartreuse ridges that lined up like a collage off into the distance. Mr. Polanski's tulips and azaleas and cannas shouted happily from the corner, a beautiful island of bright colors along the otherwise gray block.

Jimmy almost missed the approaching sounds—the once familiar noises of kids playing, squealing, daring each other, singing, and shouting. Sitting there drowsily in the hot sun, it was so much a sound from his old home, his previous life, that he wasn't at all surprised to hear it.

Then he saw them.

Five or six black kids were spinning around the street like a pack of dwarf circus clowns, darting at and dodging each other on funny, patched-together bikes. Some of the cycles had mismatched tires, one sported handlebars that were cocked at a funny, impossible, crooked angle. The kids were laughing, screaming, doing wheelies, splashing through the ever present mud puddles, obviously carefree and happy.

Jimmy couldn't help himself. He was grinning at them, then laughing out loud at their antics.

One of the kids, the tallest, the one with the wacky handlebars, suddenly spotted Jimmy sitting up high on the steps, as if he were some dignitary on a reviewing stand observing their gleeful parade. And the black kid had caught him laughing at them.

He stood there in the middle of the street and warily eyed this giggling white kid. Jimmy managed to suppress his laughter and stared right back. He had never seen a colored person this close before, let alone one that appeared to be near to his own age. There simply had not been any black people in their little river town, and the school had been segregated. But this kid appeared to be the leader of the band and, furthermore, seemed to pose him no real threat. And they were kids. He desperately wanted somebody, anybody, to play with.

"What's *your* name?" the black kid called out to Jimmy. The way he said it, it almost seemed like some kind of challenge.

"Jimmy Gill," he answered after a pause, seeing no reason not to be truthful. It was the name Mama had given him, after all. "What's yours?"

Jimmy was only being friendly, politely asking the kid his name right back, but his dark face immediately looked suspicious, as if this were some kind of deep personal question to which no one had any business knowing the answer. Slowly, carefully, the kid stepped over the bike's crossbar and pushed it up onto the crumbling sidewalk, inching toward Jimmy's perch on the top step.

The others in his platoon had stopped their playing and backed to the far side of the street, and were watching curiously. They seemed to be on the verge of bolting, apparently afraid of the pale, skinny kid on the steps.

When he got to the bottom of the steps, the boy stopped, looked down at the packed dirt, glanced both ways up and down the street, and, finally, looked boldly, directly at Jimmy.

"Detroit Simmons."

Jimmy couldn't help himself. He laughed out loud at the funny name, the way he had said "*Dee*-troit." The colored kid looked for all the world as if he had been slapped full in the face. He once again dropped his gaze and studied the rotted first step just beyond his bare toes. The others were too far away to know what was so hilarious. They looked at each other sideways.

"Sorry, Dee-troit," Jimmy apologized, but simply saying the name goosed another guffaw from him and he fought to get a straight face. "Where'd you get such a silly name as that? Dee-troit?"

He looked up and grinned. It was like someone had removed a cloud from in front of the sun.

" 'Cause that's where they say my daddy ran off to when he heard I was gonna be borned," he answered. He seemed well practiced in the explanation.

"Well, to tell you the truth," Jimmy reassured, "it's a sight better name than 'Jimmy Fish-gill' anyway."

Detroit Simmons grinned even broader, apparently proud that for once somebody preferred his goofy name over his own.

"Where did you get that name . . . Fish-gill?"

Jimmy explained it was really just Gill and it was the family name, like Simmons was his, and that his mother wanted him to be named Jimmy after his daddy. Detroit listened as if he was actually interested, then pointed to the run-down duplex.

"This your house, Jimmy Gill?"

"Half of it is. At least we rent it from some man. Where do you live at?"

He was wondering why he had not seen Detroit Simmons or his buddies before today. After all, he had spent a lot of time the last few weeks sitting on the top of these front steps, as high above the mud and rain puddles and dirty asphalt as he could get.

"I stay over in Ishkooda, the settlement," Detroit answered, waving a hand generally in a direction Jimmy had not yet strayed in any of his first halfhearted explorations. "Half mile or so over that way."

"Any place to fish over there?" Jimmy was craving catfish or crappie, longing for a tug on a line, the sight of a bobbing float.

Detroit studied hard, a finger to a dark cheek, rocking back and forth from one foot to the other as he thought hard.

"Just Village Creek, but mostly you gonna catch bean cans and whiskey bottles out of there. My grandaddy knows of some lakes down in Bessemer but he ain't never had time to carry me. You might catch something in that ditch over yonder behind your house when it rains and washes some of the fish out of the mill ponds," he said, pointing through the duplex to the tangled bushes in the backyard.

Jimmy had not spent much time near that ditch either, a little afraid of the orange cloud that seemed to hover in the sky in that direction. He was also skittish about the constant lightning that reflected off the colorful smoke every night, and he didn't like the strange smell of the brackish water that trickled along the bottom of the ditch.

"I'll take you over there sometimes," Detroit offered, friendly, helpful, apparently unafraid of the tinted smoke and chemical odor.

"Okay," Jimmy accepted quickly, gratefully, and then pointed toward Detroit's bicycle. "I like your wheel."

Detroit dropped his dark eyes to the grafted-together bike by his side, then back up at Jimmy, obviously concerned that this white boy was making fun of his most prized possession.

"I mean it, Detroit! I ain't never had a bicycle in my whole life!"

"Well all I do is I go over to the city dump and get the pieces and try to plug 'em all together. I can take several junk ones and make one good bike. Maybe we can put you one together. This one turned out real good except for the handlebars. Something heavy ran over it, I expect. Wanna take a ride on it?"

Jimmy was shocked by the friendly offer, embarrassed that he couldn't take him up on it. He had never straddled a bike and would fall flat for certain. But he stood up anyway, aiming to go give Detroit's machine a closer look. And maybe give this dark, friendly boy a closer look at the same time.

Just then, like a surprise clap of thunder from a close stroke of lightning, the neighbor's duplex door flew wide open behind Jimmy and slammed hard back against the wall. The wild-eyed old man who lived there burst through, teeth bared in a vicious snarl, eyes wild as a summer cyclone, waving a double-barreled shotgun in front of him.

The kids in the street scattered and hid. Detroit Simmons stood frozen, eyes like moons. Jimmy Gill hugged the porch support to keep from falling the five feet into the dirt yard.

"Get your ass out of my yard, nigger!" the man screamed, his shrill voice bouncing sharply back off the houses across the street. The echo seemed even more threatening and obscene on its return. The few brave birds in the sycamores along the street stopped singing and fluttered away.

Detroit dropped his bike and danced back a few steps, staring at the shotgun. But then he slowly, deliberately, bravely stepped back to the bicycle, picked it up, showed the crazy man an icy glare of defiance, gave the crooked bike a push, and expertly jumped on board. He peddled as fast as he could into the distance without looking back once, his legs pumping like pistons under the cock-eyed handlebars.

"Boy, you ever see another nigger on this street, you come get old Hector George. I'll make sure they don't come back over here anymore. We don't put a stop to 'em here, they'll take over this whole town," he spewed. Then he spat into the muddy yard where Detroit Simmons had just stood, spun, and stomped back through his door. He slammed it so hard behind him the entire porch shook and a fine dust sifted down from the rafters.

Anger hung in the air like dynamite smoke. Jimmy Gill sat back down in the same spot on the steps but the sun was gone now. It had just started to rain softly and a cold wind had begun to blow.

Chapter 3

It didn't even occur to Jimmy until the next day that he may have seen the last of Detroit Simmons and his friends. He had been sitting on the steps hoping to again hear their happy, carefree laughter when it hit him. No, they wouldn't come back to play on this street. Not after being chased away by the crazy man with the shrill mouth, the wild look in his bloodshot eyes, waving around his double-barreled shotgun.

A long, damp, empty week passed slowly. Nothing to do and nobody to do it with. He listened to the thunder. Watched the rain. Measured the time by the occasional car that splashed its way along Wisteria, or the comings and goings of the shows on Grandmama's television set. He begged for a bluebird to break the boredom, a stroke of lightning to jolt the clock on the kitchen wall into a faster spin. Finally, tedium overcame trepidation. Jimmy sucked up his courage and put aside his hesitancy to venture any distance away from the duplex. He had decided he wanted to see Detroit Simmons and his friends again, no matter what. Maybe he could learn to ride the colored kid's bike, let him lead him to a good fishing spot in Bessemer or somewhere. As soon as the next day's regularly scheduled thundershower had rained itself out, he bravely set out to find the "settlement of Ishkooda."

It was hard for him to believe, but the houses a block or two south of their dismal little duplex were even more ramshackle and decrepit than those on Wisteria Street. The pavement was even more potted and ridged, without the luxury of a sidewalk or curb. And the few solemn elderly people who sat propped up in the shade on their porches seemed too tired and downcast to even acknowledge him. They refused to return his friendly waves and merely stared off into space as if looking desperately for something that had gotten away.

A pair of railroad tracks was set high up on a red-dirt bank, crossing over the street on a narrow trestle. As Jimmy walked closer to the underpass, he heard a deep rumbling, and then a short train, tugging only four or five cars behind a small engine, rolled overhead. It was carrying bloodred iron ore northward to be cooked in the blast furnaces at the mill. A few chunks rained off and bounced along on the pavement as it crossed the street. Jimmy waited until the crimson hailstorm was over and hustled through the short cavern before a car came along and caught him in the tight underpass or before another train could pass overhead. And before he could change his mind.

On the other side of the track, the houses were much better kept. Not bigger or fancier, but neater. Yards were green. Flowers bloomed so brightly they would rival Mr. Polanski's corner. There were no beer cans in the ditch alongside the street, no kudzu creeping up the power poles. Even the wild honeysuckle was trimmed back, carefully shaped, and bloomed fragrantly in the damp air.

He had walked about half a block without seeing anyone. And then he saw a huge black woman, on her knees, pulling wild onions from a patch of grass in the middle of a neat lawn. She looked up and jumped, startled to see Jimmy Gill standing there looking at her.

"What you doing over here, mister?"

She didn't appear friendly at all, but more upset at this kid's presence here in what she must have taken as her territory.

"Looking to find the settlement of Ishkooda, ma'am. Could you kindly direct me?"

With obvious great effort, she slowly rolled over onto her hip on the muddy ground, showing her nylon hosiery rolled halfway up her thick shins. When she got herself comfortable again, Jimmy saw that she was laughing out loud, obviously at him, making a funny cackling noise like a choking hen.

"And what business you got in the settlement of Ishkooda, little mister?"

"I'm trying to find a friend of mine. His name is Dee-troit Simmons. Do you know him?"

That set her to snickering again as if he had somehow turned over her tickle-box. She laughed a big belly laugh that made her shake all over. Jimmy was afraid she was going to lose her breath, collapse backward on the grassy lawn. He wasn't sure he was strong enough to help up such a massive woman.

"You better get on back to the other side of that high line railroad before your mama comes looking for you to blister your behind," she was finally able to say between giggles.

He backed away and the woman suddenly quit laughing and got a serious look on her face.

"Are you thinking Detroit Simmons stole something from ya'll?"

"Oh! No ma'am. I just wanted to play with him is all. He said I could ride his bicycle and he was going to show me some fishing holes."

"Well, mister, let me ask you something. When I see Mr. Detroit Simmons and his pack of rapscallions, who should I say it was that came all the way to Ishkooda looking for them?"

"Jimmy Gill, ma'am."

"All right, 'Jimmy Gill, ma'am.' I'll tell that little ruffian you're looking for him. Now, scat!"

Jimmy double-timed back down the street, through the dark, cool railroad underpass, into the humid stillness on the other side, and then cut through an alley back toward Wisteria. He was still stinging a little from the colored woman's shortness, and he was lost in his own thoughts, his disappointment at not finding his friend. As he approached the corner, something unsightly and out of place caught his eye.

A new set of angry, muddy tire tracks bisected Mr. Polanski's green lawn and left an ugly gash in the row of lavender-blooming azalea bushes. A vehicle had violently uprooted several of the beautiful bushes, apparently in the last few minutes since Jimmy had wandered off in search of Ishkooda.

And there was Mr. Polanski's gray head, popping up above the hedgerow as he worked furiously, down on his hands and knees, trying to salvage what he could from the mess that had been made. Mrs. Polanski stood nearby, in the shade of the porch, wringing her hands, afraid this latest desecration would push her husband to a stroke. He loved his azaleas, nursed them like sick children, talked to them like pets, suffered their loss as much as he might have that of a son or daughter. They bloomed beautifully only a week or so each spring, and now, when they were at their most spectacular, someone had tried to cruelly shut off their glory.

As he got closer, Jimmy could hear the old man muttering vile words to himself. His wife spoke quietly to him, to herself, to God, in whatever throaty language it was that she preferred to use when she was upset.

"What happened, Mr. Polanski?"

"Damn white trash! Damn rednecks!" the old man fumed, a trace of the foreign accent now creeping in to flavor his curses.

"Here, I'll help you," Jimmy offered, falling to his knees in the damp, soft soil next to him. But just then, Grandmama yelled for him from the porch, calling him to supper. "I'll come back directly and we can get this mess fixed," he promised.

"Thank you, boy. I appreciate it," Mr. Polanski spoke, biting off his rage for the kid's benefit.

As he trotted away, Jimmy looked back and could see only the top of the old man's head above the remaining azalea bushes as he furiously worked on. He didn't look up or wave. It seemed as if he had to get the damage fixed before anyone else saw it, as if it would be a battle lost in the war if it were allowed to remain there any longer.

As Jimmy got closer to the duplex, something else ugly and crude fouled the air. The shouts and curses of Hector George next door filled the air like a swarm of angry bees. He scurried up the steps and in his front door before any of the gathering fight could swarm out onto the porch. But the bumping and knocking, the shattering glass and pained screams kept rumbling on like an approaching storm, darkening the warm evening.

Then, as he munched his soda crackers and sardines a few minutes later, Jimmy heard the front door of the duplex next door torn open violently with a splintering of wood. There were more curses and the pained squeals of a woman. Then he saw a dark shadow pass hurriedly in front of their window and heard someone stumbling awkwardly down the front steps.

One of the Georges' old cars coughed angrily to a start, and when he heard the squealing tires, Jimmy ran past Grandmama sitting there, lost, in front of the television, and cautiously stepped out onto the porch. Blue smoke was rolling from the car's tires as Hector George, in his drunken rage, punched more horsepower from the car's screaming engine. As the fishtailing vehicle approached the corner at the end of the street, George jerked the car's front wheels to the right, heading straight across Mr. Polanski's neatly clipped zoysia lawn. He seemed to be following a path exactly parallel to the latest muddy tire scars that defiled the lawn like a profane curse.

Once he had gunned the car across the sidewalk and over the line of sentry rocks, Hector kicked the accelerator anew and sent mud and grass sprigs flying in his wake like a speedboat's rooster tail.

Jesus, no! Jimmy could see exactly where Hector was headed, but there was nothing he could do but gasp in horror and watch the scene play out as if it were in slow motion.

Oh, God! He had the car pointed straight for where Mr. Polanski crouched, head down, behind the four-foot-high azalea plants, cursing and digging and pruning, repairing the latest damage with a vengeance. The old car struck him full force, head-on, the thudding impact not blunted at all by the narrow wall of brilliantly blooming shrubs that he was stooped behind. The collision sent the old man flying crazily, crookedly, ten feet into the air, arms and legs spinning after each other, tumbling upward and over the top of the speeding auto. He landed in a twisted pile directly at the feet of his wife, who looked on in disbelief, first at the body of her husband before her, then at the fleeing car and its angry, drunken driver. Hector George didn't show any sign of being aware that he had hit anything more than a fragrant, beautiful hedgerow, just as he and his twin boys must have done dozens of times before. He never looked back, never checked the rearview mirror to see the damage he had done. He only pushed the car harder, careened around the corner beyond the Polanski house on two wheels, punished the engine cruelly as he roared off, probably headed to some beer joint somewhere to soothe his anger the only way he knew how.

Jimmy could only hold his ears, close his eyes tightly to blot out what was happening, try to erase the image of the poor old man flying through the air like a lifeless rag doll rudely tossed aside by an angry child. He shakily moved to sit on the high steps, trying to fight back the tears. He finally heard the ambulance siren approaching from a distance, pulling into the yard, sliding to a stop on the ruined grass.

But when he dared to look, it was clear it was much too late. Mr. Polanski was gone. There was no hurry in the way the attendants lifted the lifeless mass onto the stretcher and slid it into the back of the ambulance. The men's faces were dark, their voices quiet.

Slowly, Jimmy walked down the steps and along the buckled sidewalk. Carefully, he stepped across the twin set of tire tracks and stood there at the edge of the yard. He watched and listened to what was happening. The sad-eyed policemen tried to talk with Mrs. Polanski, but their frustration with her thick accent and grief finally caused them to give up. They would come back tomorrow, they told her. They didn't notice the kid standing there in the shadows and had no idea anyone had witnessed the tragedy.

Jimmy didn't know what to do. Maybe tomorrow he would come forward and tell them who had done this terrible thing. Or maybe he would just keep quiet to make sure Hector George wouldn't come looking for him with his vile tongue and his double-barreled shotgun.

It was getting dark now, and suddenly, Detroit Simmons was standing a few feet away, his eyes wide as he took in the flashing lights that now retreated into the dusk.

"What happened here, Jimmy Gill?" he asked in a low voice.

Jimmy, still mostly in shock, stammered and stuttered his way through the story. Detroit listened, quiet and still wide-eyed. Then they sidled slowly, sadly, back up the street together and sat side by side in the darkness on the edge of the front porch, their feet dangling into the scrubby hedge, and talked of the horror of it all.

Detroit told of gruesome events he had witnessed or heard about in the settlement, of shootings, cuttings, head-on collisions, sleeping drunks run over as they slept on railroad tracks. Jimmy listened in awe, letting the tales of gore distract him from what he had just seen. He added his own stories of drownings and hunting accidents, but left out his mother and daddy and how they had met their violent ends. He didn't want to talk or think about it.

It was completely dark now, save for the inappropriate smile of a new moon in the western sky. A single dim streetlamp tried to give some light, but it seemed to be losing to the night. Blue, flickering lights in the windows up and down the block marked the houses with television sets.

It had grown quiet, too, along Wisteria. The only noise they could hear was through the open door behind the two boys, where Grandmama was arguing loudly with George Burns and Gracie Allen.

Involved in their stories, neither of the boys noticed the roaring return of Hector George's car until it slid sideways to a screeching stop just beyond Mrs. Polanski's scarred yard. One of its headlights was shining on the damaged lawn; the other one was dark, winking wickedly. George raced the motor, blue smoke billowing up toward the weak streetlight.

Then he popped the clutch and the car jumped forward in a cloud of steam and dust. But he immediately slammed on the brakes, squealed to a stop, forced the gears into reverse with a grinding growl, and peeled backward. Twice more he faked new assaults on the expanse of green grass.

The plants and shrubs and flowers in the yard seemed to stand a bit taller, to mock him and the rest of the dreariness along Wisteria Street with what faint splendor they could muster in the moonlight. Detroit and Jimmy still sat there on the edge of the high porch, frozen in place by the sheer evil of the car's hoarse threats.

Window shades went up a few inches in several nearby houses. Venetian blinds were cautiously parted to see what all the roar and bluster were about. Jimmy jumped. He thought there had been some kind of movement in the moon shadows behind the screen on the Polanskis' front porch. But he couldn't be sure.

Finally, on the fourth run, the drunk old man skewed into the yard with frightening speed, again spewing grass and dirt behind him. Even from half a block away, the boys could see the wild, crazed look on Hector George's face in the glow of the dashboard lights, as intoxicated on this one bit of power in his miserable life as he had ever been on liquor.

He spun in a circle around the lawn, rear end losing traction in the well-watered topsoil. He had just righted the angle of his attack and pointed the car toward the near edge of the yard when the boys saw a flash of some kind from the Polanskis' porch. Then, immediately, there were two more, with sharp cracks that could only be gunshots.

Jimmy and Detroit looked at each other, stunned, then back to see George's car whip suddenly to the left, its weight shifting dangerously, and finally flipping onto its right side, sliding with a clanging thunk into the big water oak that guarded the street corner.

Several men in undershirts, their suspenders flopping, ran from nearby houses to the toppled car. One man climbed to the driver's-side window that now stared blankly upward at the sliver of moon. He waved away steam and smoke, peered inside, and simply shook his head. Another man climbed up next to him and helped him pry open the door, dragging out the lifeless form of Hector George. They handed him down to other neighbors, who laid his body down in the middle of the ruts he had just plowed.

People stood on porches now and others knotted in clumps of three and four along the street, muttering uncomfortably to each other like strangers, as a distant siren once more approached their block. Detroit and Jimmy still sat on the edge of the stoop with their feet in midair, shocked motionless by what they had seen. Grandmama had missed it all. She was still talking back to the television set in the living room.

Then, behind the boys, there was a slight scuff of a shoe on the cold concrete of the porch floor. Jimmy Gill turned his head quickly at the sound. It was the woman, Mrs. George, standing there in the darkness, a bluish glow through the window from Grandmama's television set illuminating a strange smile on her haggard face.

"Thank you, Lord," she said, her voice just audible above the screaming laughter from the television show, the hissing of her husband's car's radiator, the quiet buzzing of the neighbors. "Thank you, sweet Jesus."

Then she turned and floated out of sight into the darkness at the far end of the duplex's porch.

Chapter 4

It rained for two days. A solid, blustery, continuous downpour left rivers in the street and found leaks in the moss-covered roof of the duplex. Grandmama ordered Jimmy to set pots and pans under the more pronounced drips. The music of the dripping kept them both awake at night. She got even more ill when she had to turn the television's sound up loud so she could hear the programs over the constant rhythmic plinking. So she could catch every word that Ralph Kramden and Ed Norton were screaming at each other.

Jimmy had grown tired of playing cowboys and Injuns on the front porch. The soap operas on the television were nothing but the same sad happenings over and over, just as dismal as real life. They certainly offered him no escape. Finally, he moped into the bedroom in search of something to while away the endless rainy hours.

For the first time since the day of their move, he noticed the big Zenith console radio, hiding in a dusty corner where Wiley Groves had slid it out of the way. Its face was against the wall and it was covered with musty sheets and junky bric-a-brac that had not found a better place to live yet.

Carefully, he piled the junk in a corner and wrestled the big cabinet to the center of the room. He almost pulled it over on top of himself when he tried to turn it around to face the dim light that filtered through the raindrops on the window. Finally, though, it stood there, quietly staring back at him.

Even with its dust and scratches, a couple of missing crosspieces on its grill, and a cracked knob or two, it was imposing. Now freed from its corner, it dominated the room with its size and presence.

Grandmama had gotten up during a commercial to shuffle to the kitchen for another pack of cigarettes and another glass of iced tea, and she saw what Jimmy was doing. She stopped at the doorway and watched him for a moment.

"That thing is broke, Jimmy. It won't pull in a thing," she said, and then hurried back to the living room as cascading organ music signaled the resumption of her story. "Mind you don't get yourself electrocuted messin' with that old worthless pile of junk."

The radio's wooden cabinet was a dark crimson mahogany, chipped and peeling and scraped in a few places. But when he wiped at it with a corner of a bedsheet, it shone beautifully in the dim light. Its large circular tuning dial was a smoky tan behind some dark spots of mildew that stained the glass. The row of knobs across its front were labeled cryptically: VOL, TUN, AM, SW, TONE.

The cloth that covered the big speaker in the front of the box was ripped, and a couple of the wooden strips that were supposed to hold it in place had been lost in a prior collision with something. Jimmy could remember a rich, resonant flow of sound from its big speaker when he had listened to it with his mother and father. It had sounded much different, deeper, fuller, more lifelike than the tinny squeaking noise that came from the television's miniature speaker. For some reason, right then and there, he suddenly wanted to hear the sound of the radio again.

The prongs on the plug at the far end of the power cord were bent sideways. That didn't look right, so he twisted them out straight as best he could with his fingers.

A wire that was hooked to a screw in the back of the box was hanging by its rubber insulation only. The screw was labeled ANT, so he figured that was the antenna. Clearly, the inner part of the wire was not making any contact with the radio at all. Jimmy awkwardly backed out the screw with a butter knife and then slid the shiny copper wire underneath it and tightened it down again.

He paused to build up his nerve, then carefully eased the plug into a wall socket, fully expecting an eruption of fire and sparks from the bent plug. Nothing happened.

One of the brown knobs next to the tuning dial was labeled ON/OFF. He took a deep breath and gave it a flick, then jumped away when there was an immediate answering pop from somewhere in the box's insides. But there was still no fire or smoke. Instead, the amber dial light quickly glowed as warmly as a smile.

Almost imperceptibly, a low hum had begun from somewhere behind the cloth-and-wood face. Then there was a crackling sound, a deeper roar, and finally, just as he was sure the big box was going to do nothing but sit there and buzz and hum at him, there was an explosion of noise so powerful it almost knocked him backward onto the hard floor.

Somehow, Jimmy got his fingers on the VOL knob and twisted it until the blaring blast was quieter, identifiable as strange music, unlike anything he had ever heard before. It was a man singing. Drums and guitars beneath his voice pounded out a contagious rhythm.

Grandmama had hurried to the door to make sure all the noise didn't include his electrocution. She switched on a sour face when she saw he wasn't burned to a cinder and heard the song he was listening to.

"You oughta turn off that nigger music," she advised harshly. But she didn't stay to see if he obeyed her. She fled back to the living room and the weepy sadness of *The Guiding Light*.

There was something special about the song the man was singing. The way he phrased the words and slurred them together with such happiness and abandon. The way he told the world that he was "all shook up." The way the instruments and voices flowed through Jimmy's body as he sat there on the cold linoleum floor near the speaker. It all combined to give him a funny feeling in his stomach and made his hair tingle and goose bumps erupt along both arms and up his back.

Then the song ended abruptly with the strum of a guitar. A man with a deep godlike voice jumped on the tail end of the trailing music, his delivery just as frenetic and frenzied as the singer's had been.

"Hey, everybody, that's Elvis Presley and the song that's number one here in Birmingham on our exclusive *Top Forty Hit Parade*. Shoot, folks, it's already number one all over the country on the *Billboard* 'Hot One Hundred.' Even over in England. It's Elvis's first chart topper across the big water, but it's certainly not the last."

The man was speaking English but Jimmy wasn't sure he was

getting it all. The lilt in the man's voice, though, made him smile despite himself, and he forgot the dreary weather and all the tragic things that had happened just two days before. The voice spilling from the big booming speaker hardly paused for a breath, but just kept rattling on at a breakneck pace as if somebody else might take over the radio if he hushed for a second. Jimmy marveled at his energy, could picture the broad smile on the man's face as he preached away, could hear in his voice the joy the talker must be feeling.

"And remember, folks, the rest of the WROG Hit Crew will be joining me at the big sock hop next Saturday night at the National Guard Armory on Graymont Boulevard and we'll have live music from the Favorite Five and I'll be spinnin' records by Fats Domino, Buddy Knox, Pat Boone, the Diamonds, and, of course, Elvis!"

Then a man was singing a silly song about selling cars. Another deep voice talked about a café somewhere that served all the catfish you could eat for a dollar twenty-five. A group of singers harmonized like a church choir as they chanted the letters W-R-O-G. Then another song was pushing beautiful notes and a slight breeze from the speaker next to his ear.

He sat there in awe, captivated by the rapid-fire way the aural parade floated out of the box in the middle of the cold, damp bedroom. He was caught up in the feel-good atmosphere of the radio announcer and the music he sent spinning out into the air like a rainbow that could only be heard, not seen. It was different from anything he had experienced.

The smooth voice of someone with the melodious name of Perry Como gave way next to a raucous piano and the slap of a happy drum, and a liquid-voiced man singing about "Walkin', yes indeed . . ." It was a man named Fats, and Jimmy could picture him bouncing and singing and playing gleefully, just for him.

The hook was set and he spent the rest of that miserable rainy day getting reeled in, mystified by the sounds pouring from the big upright radio. He couldn't believe the way the music and talk made him feel inside. Happy, then sad, like dancing or crying.

Jimmy had listened to the radio before, but it had been different. There had been a sweet-voiced crooner on one of Grandmama's shows, soap operas just like the ones on television except with no pictures, or quiz shows with their boring questions and dull contestants. He also had distant memories of his mother, getting ready to leave them for another night, half listening to the Grand Ole Opry's screeching fiddles and yodeling singers as they barely cut their way through the summer static.

This was different. Something about what he was hearing was vastly different, and he knew somehow that it was touching him in a spot somewhere near his soul. But it was not violation that he felt. It was elation. A feeling that someone somehow knew just the chord to strike to resonate inside him. That whoever sang and played the music knew more about him than he knew about himself. And that they had found a way to pry loose emotions he didn't even know he had.

Jimmy had not noticed night falling outside or that the room was almost completely dark. But suddenly, the man on the radio dumped out of the song that he was playing right in its middle. There was a moment's pause. Then Jimmy heard the opening strains of a band playing the familiar sounds of "Dixie."

"And now, we come to the end of another broadcast day here at WROG," the deep-voiced man spoke, almost reverently. "WROG operates on a frequency of eight hundred twenty kilocycles with a power of five thousand watts, as authorized by the Federal Communications Commission in Washington, D.C."

Five thousand watts! Jimmy was astonished at the image of power that number represented. And the Federal Communications Commission must be some authority just below God and Jesus on the grand hierarchy of things if they authorized the use of such power.

"And now, with thanks to almighty God for the greatest heritage man can possess, the privilege of living under the American flag, this is Rockin' Randy Mathews, saying 'good night' until we resume broadcasting on WROG at six-thirty tomorrow morning."

The martial music quickly died, there was a quiet hum for five seconds, then a cacophony of static, shrill voices speaking staccato foreign languages, and the whines of signals warring with each other for the speaker like distant armies fighting for precious territory. Sadly, Jimmy flipped the power switch off and the noise faded rapidly to nothing but the quiet popping of the wood as the radio's cabinet cooled.

He sat there a moment, feeling elated, disappointed, reborn.

Already, he longed for six-thirty in the morning to come so he could once again lose himself in all those emotional sounds he had been listening to. To once again forget the rain, the loneliness, the grime, the deaths, the orange smoke in the sky, the sad faces of their neighbors on Wisteria Street.

He ate his bologna-sandwich supper in silence, then wandered to the front porch to sit atop the high steps for a while. The rain had finally stopped and the air was clean and cool for a change. A breeze brought the fragrance of gardenias and sweet shrub. He turned to see where it came from.

There was a single sad light in the front window of the Polanski house two doors down, and someone had hung a dark, flowerless wreath on the door. Jimmy suddenly felt as sad as he had ever felt in his life as he tried to imagine the pain there must be in that house.

Behind him, inside the open screen door of their duplex, Ricky Ricardo was yelling something at his silly wife, Lucy. But when Lucy didn't answer immediately, Grandmama volunteered a reply for her.

"She's in the kitchen with Ethel, Ricky!" she screamed. "But you better not go in . . . *aieee!* I warned you, Ricky! Just look at that mess!"

Grandmama had the sound on the set up loud to override Jimmy's radio listening. He was so lost in his own sad thoughts that he failed to hear the door to the other duplex as it opened behind him. Then, before he even had a chance to feel her presence, Hector George's widow was standing there beside him at the top of the steps.

But when he glanced up quickly, startled, he noticed that she looked totally different in the light that filtered out the window from the television set than she had the last time he saw her, different than she had the night of the deaths. He hardly recognized her. Her face was made up so she looked twenty years younger, her hair was fluffed and combed neatly, and she wore a bright flowered dress that showed an almost girlish figure.

"You're Jimmy Gill. I'm Clarice George," she said, and offered her hand, smiling. "I've just recently been set free from the devil and I'm pleased to make your acquaintance, Mr. Gill."

Her words were puzzling and strange, but Jimmy stood politely and took the warm hand. They shook vigorously, sincerely. He couldn't help noticing her sincere smile, the spark of happiness in her eyes as they met his directly, a glow in her face that most certainly wasn't there before.

"I've heard your grandma call you and talk with you, Jimmy. You seem to be a good boy. Kind and obedient," she said. But suddenly, she dropped her smile like a veil. "I'm sorry you had to see the things you saw the other day. I'm sure they must have bothered a good boy like you."

And she was right. They had. Mr. Polanski tumbling and twirling through the air and the lifeless, limp body of Hector George, angry even in death, had broken into his dreams the last two nights like shimmering ghosts. And they had joined the ones that usually played there, the usual black-and-white television shows starring his dead mama and daddy. The images all seemed to stick around for hours as he tossed and turned next to his snoring grandma, and then departed just before the first light of morning like a slow-working burglar.

Jimmy nodded his head.

She reached then to stroke his hair, moved her hand to cup his chin in an affectionate way, and once again broke into a warming smile.

"Some good will come of it all, Jimmy," she said firmly. "You'll see. I can feel it. Some good things will come from all this bad. Now I'm going over to that woman's house and thank her for what she did. Let her know her husband didn't die for nothing."

The woman's strange words still didn't make sense to Jimmy, but he watched her negotiate down the high front steps, sidestep rain puddles in the muddy front yard of the duplex, and make her way to the sad house on the corner. Clarice George marched right up the flower-lined front walk to the Polanski porch steps, paused just a moment to caress the bunch of begonias that already flowered brightly in a pot there, and then gave a knock so firm and sure he could hear it from where he sat.

Mrs. Polanski turned on a dim porch light, timidly opened first the inside door, then the screen door, and stepped outside to see what misery might be visiting her next. There were soft words Jimmy couldn't hear from Mrs. George and a moment's pause from Mrs. Polanski, and then the two women suddenly embraced strongly. The new widows seemed to be drawing something from each other as they stayed in a clinch for a while.

Jimmy Gill could hear their sobs above the roar of an airplane passing overhead, even over the yelling of Ricky and Lucy and Fred and Ethel. Then they turned, arm in arm, and disappeared together inside the house.

Chapter 5

The next day Detroit Simmons talked Jimmy Gill into crossing the ditch behind the duplex. He said he had been dying to see what was on the other side. That meant they would go. Detroit proved to be persuasive.

Jimmy had been awake before five, lying there quietly and still so as not to disturb Grandmama. She was surly if anything woke her up before seven. She usually stayed awake each night until the television stations all signed off at ten or ten-thirty. Then she would roll out of bed at seven in the morning, just in time for "The Star-Spangled Banner" that signified the sign-on and the beginning of *The Today Show*.

As much as he wanted to hear more music from the big upright radio, Jimmy knew not to disturb his grandmother before her first cup of coffee, the first drag on a cigarette, and her first conversations with the fluttery images on the television set. But he had lain there awake that morning as long as he could. Carefully, he rolled off the edge of the bed, gave a quick glance and a wave to the Zenith, standing there, its back against the wall, where he had shoved it the night before. Then he picked up his clothes and worn-out sneakers and tiptoed to the kitchen.

There were a few spoonfuls of peanut butter left in the bottom of a jar. He spread some on bread after the mold had been pinched off, and then he crept quietly out to the porch to eat it as the sun came up.

It was noticeably cooler and less humid than it had been the last few days, and the first brave rays of morning sun felt good when they broke through the new leaves. The sun threw warm light on the other people along the street who had joined him in rising early. Most of them were probably headed for the first shift at the mill. Engines roared to life. There were happy good-byes from some while others left half-finished arguments dangling in the early air. A choir of birds was so happy to see the sun after all the rain that they seemed to be adding something extra to their songs.

Then he saw Detroit Simmons coming through the mist, wheeling his bike around the puddles. The machine was so bent and warped it looked like it was coming down the street sideways. Jimmy laughed at him and again got caught at it, but it didn't seem to bother Detroit this time. He waved, rolled across the sidewalk, propped the bike against the steps, bounded up two at a time, and sat down beside Jimmy as if he had been saving the spot for him.

"You sure are up early this mornin', Jimmy Gill."

"Couldn't sleep. I wanted to listen to the radio but Grandmama's still sleeping."

"You got a radio?" Detroit asked, his eyes showing excitement. "I wanna hear it sometime! My granddaddy's got one on the table next to his bed and he goes to sleep listening to ball games out of St. Louis. But he dares anybody else to mess with it."

Jimmy told Detroit about the songs he had heard Rockin' Randy Mathews play, and tried to describe the feelings that had overwhelmed him as he listened to Elvis and a man called Fats and the Platters and Dean Martin. But Detroit didn't know any of those people or their songs and didn't seem to share Jimmy's enthusiasm.

"Let's go exploring, Jimmy!" he yelled suddenly, and jumped up, ready to take off that instant.

Jimmy sat quietly for a moment. He really preferred to stay home, fire up the Zenith radio again, and listen to the smooth voices and the happy music. He wasn't sure he wanted to plunge into the dense brush under the orange sky anyway. But the way Detroit pleaded with his big dark eyes finally persuaded him to follow his new friend to God-knows-where.

Jimmy stood and Detroit was gone in a flash, disappearing around the corner of the house, wading through the wet knee-high grass and dodging mudholes, diving into the undergrowth as if he knew what awaited them there. Jimmy had to hurry and follow him or be left behind.

It had turned into a glorious morning. All the rain had cleared the air and a cool breeze made the new leaves on the sycamores shiver. The sky was clear and deep blue except for the pastel smudge of smoke hanging over the mills. That was the direction Detroit seemed to be headed, bouncing along boldly. Blindly, Jimmy followed him into a thick wall of honeysuckle, and they were instantly engulfed in a maze of vine caverns.

Jimmy had difficulty keeping up as Detroit scurried through the jungle. When Detroit finally came to a sudden stop, Jimmy almost ran up his back. Detroit simply threw back his head and laughed out loud like a kid possessed.

"Ain't this great? This place is something else, Jimmy Gill! Look! We can build forts and hideouts and everything in here and ain't nobody going to find us if we don't want them to!"

That's what I'm afraid of, Jimmy was thinking, picturing in his mind their skeletons lying here amid the tangle of the brush until some other kids accidentally stumbled over their bones someday. But he didn't have a chance to speak his fears out loud.

Detroit was off again at a trot, and before he could catch his breath, Jimmy was once more slapping vines aside, following obediently, watching as hard as he could for snakes and bears and hornet nests in the deep shadows of the woods that had gobbled them up. And he found himself watching the ground, too, for the bones of other kids who might have gone before.

Suddenly, frighteningly, Detroit stepped through a clump of grapevines and kudzu and disappeared completely with nothing more than a quick yell. He was gone!

Jimmy cautiously eased forward, expecting to see a tiger licking his chops after such a delicious meal or a bear taking apart his friend like pulling a wishbone. The ground dropped away into a small creek, part of the same ditch that wound behind his house. And there was Detroit, standing sheepishly, dripping wet, waist deep in a rivulet of copper-colored water. Cans and trash paper floated lazily by him as he stood there like a black buoy. He looked up at Jimmy, not sure whether to cry or laugh or both.

"You see a water moxican, you sing out, Jimmy Gill," he said as he carefully waded back to the edge of the ditch. Jimmy reached out, grabbed his muddy hand, and helped him up the slippery bank. They wandered downstream a bit to where a huge elm tree had fallen across the ditch. It made an easy bridge to the other side, where the brush looked thinner and the midmorning sun shone down warmly into a clearing.

As Detroit lay back on a soft blanket of sage grass and let the sun dry his overalls, Jimmy sat quietly, leaning back against a tree.

A strange noise caught his attention. At first, he thought it might be Detroit wheezing from all the off-color water he had swallowed. But it seemed to be coming from the other way, toward the far edge of the woods. He stood, then took a few curious steps toward where the sun was brighter, his head cocked, homing in on the noise. He stepped out of the shade into the full, dazzling sunlight, using his hand as a visor.

He saw a low building almost hidden by a row of hedges, and behind it, a towering metal spire that seemed to reach so high it could tickle the belly of heaven. It was the mysterious place where some kind of wizard was apparently working his magic.

His eyes were drawn to the back window of the vine-covered block building, still mostly lost in dark shadows and morning mist. Inside the glass window, an eerie blue glow pulsated to an unheard beat. And he could now clearly hear the ghost voices buzzing at the base of the huge steel arrow that pointed upward into the sky, held to earth and tugged upright by three sets of cables, shimmering with dew. There was a small outbuilding surrounded by a hog-wire fence at the foot of the tower.

To the left of the blue-flickering window, on a grassy mound of dirt, a moss-covered pond made of stone suddenly erupted into a fountain, spraying water and mist fifteen feet into the air. The breeze-blown vapor from the dancing water held captive a brilliant rainbow.

Jimmy's mouth popped open and he gasped at the sudden, unexpected beauty of it all. Detroit must have seen the look on his face, maybe heard him gulp, and he scurried to see what had grabbed his attention. He, too, stood silently as the waters danced, the blue light in the window flashed, and the ghosts sang for salvation at the tower's base.

"What is this place, Jimmy? What do you reckon they do here?"

"Gee, I don't know." He couldn't even begin to guess.

"Well, let's just go over there and take a look and maybe we can figure it out."

"No!"

Jimmy didn't know what the buildings or the tower were, but he suspected, somehow, that they were gazing upon something sacred, a magic place, and he didn't want to rush to unravel the mystery and risk spoiling it. No, he would feel better studying it from a distance for a while, and then, when the time was right, edging close enough to reach out and grasp it.

And he knew at the same time that he could never explain that to Detroit. He wasn't sure he understood it himself.

"Look, Dee, I gotta get on home before my grandmama comes looking for me. I never let her know where I was going," he told him, and it was mostly true. "We can come back sometime later and explore this place. Okay?"

Detroit was obviously disappointed. It was clear to Jimmy that it was his friend's nature to be demandingly and immediately curious about everything he came across. But Detroit, of all people, understood the demands of grandmothers who had accepted the task of raising their children's children.

Jimmy was careful to pay attention to landmarks on the way home so he could find his way back to this sacred ground. The bridge across the stream, a big crooked tree here, a patch of goldenrod there.

The place they had just seen was enchanted, as sure as anything he had seen on *Walt Disney Presents* or *Howdy Doody*. It reminded Jimmy of the man behind the curtain in *The Wizard of Oz* when his mama had taken him to see it at the big theater in downtown Chattanooga.

He kept looking back through the trees, hoping to catch a glimpse of the tower or maybe the wizard himself. But he kept walking. Somehow he knew there would be a better time for them to come back to this place where the sorcerer made the lights flash blue and the spirits hum.

He hoped it would be soon.

Chapter 6

They played soldier up and down Wisteria Street all afternoon
until Detroit reluctantly had to return to Ishkooda. Jimmy Gill half
hated to see him go, but he was tired anyway, his legs aching from
all the running and playing they had done that day. And besides,
he was anxious to get back in front of the mahogany radio.

Finally, with supper in hand, he stood before the big Zenith,
paused for a moment as if saying grace, and then reverently clicked
the switch on. Slowly, the radio came to life with its now familiar
buzz and a few pops from somewhere inside, seemingly waking up
from a deep sleep. He could smell the tubes as they got warm, and
once again felt just a hint of a tickling breeze against his cheek,
kicked up by the bass speaker behind the dusty maroon cloth grille.
And once more he heard the wonderful rock-and-roll beat. The hypnotic, glad-sounding songs. The voices often happy, it seemed, even
when the singer was moaning about terrible pain and loss.

Jimmy Gill was instantly swept up in the continuous flow of
sound from the radio. His sandwich went uneaten as he lay back
on the cool floor and half dozed, lulled to fuzzy sleep by the gentle,
resonant current. He dreamed of captured rainbows and upward-
reaching towers, happy singers and awakening radios, buzzing
ghosts, floating blond hair in muddy water and angry cars spinning
wickedly through flowered yards.

Then he would wake up for a while and listen to the music, the
voices, even the commercials, tapping his foot to the rhythm or
singing along with the ones that were already familiar to him. That
is, until a rare slow ballad would send him back to his dreams
again.

Jimmy had never started school since the move, and it wasn't long until Detroit was out. Summer was there for sure at last. The two boys were able to play their games from first sun until it was too dark to see each other. And they had time to go back several more times to the tree bridge and across the stream to the clearing near the enchanted place. Detroit offered to boldly march right up to the tower, to go knock on the back door at the wizard's house.

"I ain't afraid, Jimmy Gill. Nobody's gonna hurt us. We need to see what kind of place that is over there."

But Jimmy was able to convince him that it was not yet the time for venturing away from the lip of the ditch or the cover of the kudzu and wild grapevines. They would lie there safely hidden among the weeds and watch as the fountain erupted about every fifteen minutes or so like clockwork. Then the spray would suddenly subside, falling back as if at some kind of unseen cue or the wave of the wizard's wand.

The steel spire stood tall, sometimes whistling softly in the wind. The supernatural buzzing at its bottom was almost constant, like a swarm of honeybees. But they still didn't see any magician or enchanter. They saw nobody at all.

Finally, Detroit would tire of the show and wheedle and beg until Jimmy would give in. Then they would dive back into the honeysuckle caverns and make believe that they were hunting dragons, looking for pirates along the "river," or wiping out nests of vicious renegade Indians. Trees became enemy soldiers, bushes were stagecoaches, piles of rocks were buried treasure.

Detroit Simmons was well blessed with imagination. He brought stories from his trips to the movie theater downtown, where he watched the serials and the motion pictures from his seat high in the colored section of the balcony. Jimmy contributed plots and characters from hours of lying at Grandmama's feet as she watched the cowboy shows and space adventures on the television set. They collaborated on scenarios, ran for hours through the dusky darkness of the thick undergrowth, making it all up as they went. The more elaborate and far-fetched, the better. Then they would ultimately fall, near exhaustion, slick-sweaty and almost played out, to lie on their bellies in the pine straw under a grapevine-covered tree to talk.

"How come you don't have no mama or daddy, Jimmy Gill?" Detroit finally asked one bright, sunny day.

The words had poured out of him as if he was simply too curious to hold the question back any longer. Then, satisfied he had finally gotten around to asking, he leaned back against the tree trunk, watched a couple of crows circling overhead, and waited patiently for the answer. Detroit had learned that was the best way to get Jimmy Gill to talk. Let him first be sure that someone would be listening, hush while letting him carefully consider his answer and prudently plan his words, and then he would usually spit it out, filling the dead silence with an answer.

Jimmy told Detroit about the sawmill and his father's accident, the severed right arm, the thick red blood in the sawdust, and the frustration of the quiet, crying men who had gathered helplessly around the dying man.

Then he spoke of the beautiful blond woman, dressed for another night out, but ending up floating gracefully, a bullet hole behind her ear, her long, wavy blond hair tangled with the fishermen's trot lines in the swift, cold Tennessee River's waters. Jimmy surprised himself, talking matter-of-factly and with little hint of the pain the words caused him. He talked much as he might have if he had only been plotting out one of the made-up cowboy-and-Indian stories he and Detroit acted out amid the swampy bushes along the ditch bank.

But Jimmy knew a greater truth that Detroit could only suspect. He was speaking the words out loud for the first time, telling another person something that had been cocooned inside him for so long it had begun to fester. Just saying it all, letting the feelings have their freedom like that, was hurting him like a green-apple bellyache.

But strangely, it made him feel better, too. Made the hurt more bearable, as if he had been purged of something vile. As if having someone listen to him tell the story made it easier to live with somehow. He finally hushed when the lump in his throat grew too big to let the words squeeze by.

Jimmy hoped that Detroit would be satisfied with the answer and consider the story finished. Detroit was quiet, watching the crows dip and dart in the blue sky above them. He must have known. He didn't try to push for more. He seemed to understand how Jimmy felt, finally saying those words, telling the tragic story.

"You never talk about your momma or daddy, Detroit," Jimmy

eventually croaked, turning away, pretending to watch a squirrel zigzag its way crazily between some trees. But it was actually to hide a surprise tear that had sneaked up on him from somewhere.

"Well, Jimmy Gill, I ain't never seen nor heard from my daddy since he ran off up north to Detroit, Michigan. Mama stays over in north Birmingham with a bootlegger. Least, that's what I've heard my grandma and them saying when they don't know I'm listening."

That's all he said and Jimmy had sense enough to follow his example, to not probe for more than his friend was willing to reveal. There was hurt, though, in Detroit's dark brown eyes. Jimmy realized something then. This black boy and he had much more in common than either of them could ever have imagined.

"Let's see what's going on at the mystery place," Jimmy finally suggested.

It seemed like the natural thing to free them from the sudden dark mood that had kidnapped them. And, for some reason, just then the time seemed right to return there. Whooping and dancing, Detroit jumped straight up from his bed of straw. He was ready.

They had dubbed it "the mystery place" because neither of them had been able to figure out exactly what was going on there. But they were sure of one thing. Whatever it was involved magic and some combination of wizards and fairies and ghosts.

The day was already winding down toward darkness when they skinned across the tree over the creek. In the dryness of summer the stream had become a trickle of dank water barely covering slimy green-moss rocks and gravel, with bits of garbage floating in it, but it was still the Mississippi or the Nile or the Amazon to Jimmy and Detroit.

Out of habit, they hesitated a moment in the clearing, considered how late it had gotten, how near dangerous darkness was. But it was time to take a closer look. They looked at each other in the fading sunlight, grinned, shook their double-secret handshake, and pushed bravely into unexplored territory, across the field of saw briers and sassafras bushes, sage grass and short pine saplings, toward the metal spire in the center of the ten-acre clearing. The way the last rays of sun hit the tower's red and white bands gave it a candy-cane look, and that was not threatening at all to the two brave explorers.

But halfway there, something funny happened. The strange buzzing and humming at the bottom of the tower stopped for a second, like a hiccup, then were replaced by something that seemed strangely familiar to Jimmy. The rhythmic throbbing sounded just like the drumbeats that always marked time when WROG played "Dixie" on the big Zenith radio in the middle of his bedroom when the station ended its "broadcast day" every evening just before the sun went down.

He stopped dead still and grabbed Detroit by the shoulder so his shuffling steps through the dry brush wouldn't wipe out the sound. He could almost make out something in the buzzes that sounded like the voice of Rockin' Randy Mathews, reciting his now familiar litany about the American flag and the five thousand watts of power and the authority of the Federal Communications Commission. Then the scratching noises stopped, and the only sound was the hot summer breeze humming eerily through the tower's cross-members and support wires.

Detroit and Jimmy walked closer, until they stood next to the little concrete-block outbuilding, directly under the upward stretch of the tower. They both almost fell over backward as they craned their heads back to look straight up the tower's length toward the orange sky, then looked at each other wide-eyed.

"This thing is a mile high!" Detroit guessed. "No, two miles!"

Jimmy didn't speculate. A wooden ladder was propped against the hog-wire fence, almost hidden by weeds and tangled coils of copper-colored wire. Jimmy didn't know what crazy impulse seized him, what wild urge suddenly possessed him, but he bravely, purposely waded through the weeds, grabbed one end of the ladder, and began to try to drag it over to the tower's base.

"Jimmy Gill?" Detroit, usually the more impulsive of the two, couldn't figure out what his friend was up to, but his expression showed he was worried. "What in the world are you . . . ?"

"Help me prop this ladder against that tall thing," Jimmy ordered, driven by some strange inner force he couldn't account for but was forced to obey.

Two kids their size shouldn't have been able to lift the heavy ladder, but they grunted and strained and sweated and finally managed to lay it against the tower, about ten feet from the ground, forming a bridge over the hog-wire fence. They ignored the signs wired to the enclosure: High Voltage. No Trespassing. Danger!

Detroit looked sideways at Jimmy again, as if he couldn't imagine what crazy thing he was going to do next. Or maybe he was afraid he knew exactly what his blood brother had in mind. Detroit gripped the ladder from underneath to help steady it, and Jimmy, without any hesitation at all, began crab-walking upward, one rung at a time, climbing toward his goal.

"Where the Sam Hill you goin', Jimmy Gill? You're gonna fall inside that fence and you won't be able to get out."

"You'll see. You'll see in a minute."

Detroit obviously felt that something different was going on here. There had been a change in roles. Detroit usually led the way blindly when they ventured into danger. For the first time, Jimmy Gill dived headlong into the dangerous darkness.

Jimmy intended to climb up the ladder until he could reach out and touch the tower. He wanted to see how cool and solid the cross-members might be when his fingertips brushed them, see if he could feel the vibrations, connecting somehow with whatever caused the ghostly buzzing they had heard.

But when his hand first touched the cold steel, he couldn't help himself. Something besides good sense or fear was suddenly in charge of his will. He had to reach out with the other hand, then stretch upward for the next higher grip. Then his feet found an anchor on the tower, much more solid than on the shaky wooden ladder, and without ever consciously intending to do it, he was climbing. Just a foot or two at a time, but he was climbing steadily upward into the warm air.

Thirty feet or more of space stretched out under him before he dared a look back down. Involuntarily, he felt his whole body draw tight, his stomach turn over, his breath leave his lungs. Detroit looked tiny and insignificant down below, gazing upward at his insane buddy, his mouth open in horrified disbelief.

"Jimmy Gill, you can come on back down now. We need to be getting on to supper. It's getting late. You hear me, Jimmy Gill?"

His voice was small, far away.

Jimmy ignored him, turned his face back toward the sky, and resumed climbing. By now, up looked more friendly than down.

Finally, his arms growing tired, trembling from the strain of the climb, he found a grip on a cross-member with each bend of his elbows, locked his calves around a leg of the tower, and stopped there to rest for a while.

Then he found enough nerve to look around himself. What he saw stunned him. He had to fight to catch what was left of his breath.

Jimmy could see the ribbon of the town's main road, the superhighway, as it wound in from the north and disappeared off to the south. Cars already had their headlights turned on as the last of the sun's brightness fled to make way for night. And there was a blanket of lights spread out away from where he rested, stretching in all directions, as far as he could see. Porch lights, kitchen lights, streetlights, stoplights. Millions of fireflies, burning embers, winking colored lightbulbs, all sprinkled among trees, along streets, up the side of Red Mountain, peppered into the sides of buildings downtown, strung along the streets like jeweled necklaces. All those lights were dusted onto the landscape as if they had been tossed out there at random by some great hand.

"Jimmy! Come on now! Hear me? Come on!"

His voice was so far away. Jimmy could hardly hear him.

And over a hill to the northwest was the steel mill, now clearly seen below the orange cloud. Its blast furnace made an angry red-hot wound in the middle of the dusk while several tall needles belched fire amid the smoke and steam that spread out to hug the valley floor like cotton fog.

"Jimmy Gill! Can you hear me? You all right up there?"

And there were people out there. People all over the place. Folks behind the wheels of all those cars, sitting on their front porches, looking out the windows of the kitchens and from the downtown buildings. Maybe there were people glancing up from their labor over at the mill or from where they worked in the filling stations and foundries.

A powerful thought hit Jimmy Gill like a slap in the face. If all those people down there would only look this way, they would have to see him, James Earl Gill, clinging to the side of this tower, still lit by the glow of the sun that had already deserted the earthbound, had left them in the darkness way down there where they were forced to run about in their maze of lights and concrete, ground-locked, shackled by gravity, not hanging freely in the breeze as he was.

From his high perch he was visible to hundreds—no, thousands of people! Maybe even hundreds of thousands! The strange feeling was indescribable. He wanted to shout at all of them down there, wave his arms wildly, scream for them to look up at him as he dangled there, make them see him, listen to him as he laughed and sang. He wanted to make them listen to anything he might feel the need to say.

But he couldn't do that. He dared not release his grip on the cool steel. And he knew, no matter how high he might climb, even if he got all the way to the clouds, to the stars even, the people down below would never hear him.

But somehow, it didn't matter. It was still such a rush! Jimmy had no idea where the euphoria came from, what craziness had laid claim to his senses, but it seized him with a grip so fast, so binding, that he would never lose the wonderful thrill of it for the rest of his life.

"You goddamn brat! Get your damn ass down from there!"

Jimmy looked downward so quickly that it made him dizzy. He almost spun loose from the tower, and had to redouble his grip on the steel to keep from plummeting. In the pinkish glow of the last sunlight of the day, he could just make out a tiny black dot, Detroit's head, parting the brown grass as he wildly fled toward the ditch and into the cover of the honeysuckle.

In the deepening shadows directly below him, at the base of the tower, he could just make out the upturned face of a scrawny little man, the source of all the screaming and spitting that was going on down there. The man's obvious anger was easily reaching up the tower the sixty feet or so that separated them.

"Get your nigger ass down from there before I get my shotgun and shoot you down off there like a goddamn squirrel!"

Jimmy's plight was obvious. There was no way to escape horizontally, and climbing upward would only prolong the inevitable. And who knew? Mad as the little man seemed to be, he might actually start taking shots at him for real.

Jimmy slowly, cautiously started to climb back down. But he

couldn't help pausing for a moment to drink in the vista from the side of the tower one more time. And to again be stunned by all he could see. Maybe one or two people had looked his way after all and had noticed the little lump that was Jimmy Gill dangling up there. Maybe so.

"I said get your ass down! Now!"

There was no other way off the steel column but back across the ladder that spanned the hog-wire fence, and that path led right into the clutches of the glowering little man who was waiting for him there. He knew he would have to take his chances with him now.

"You lamebrain goddamn little idiot! You stupid little bastard!" He was no longer hollering just to be heard but screamed curses out of seething, exasperated fury. "If that goddamn transmitter had still been turned on you would have been cooked blacker than that other little nigger that got away from me! Burned to a goddamn crisp!"

He was no more than five feet tall, wearing horn-rimmed glasses taped together over his nose with black tape, with several days' growth of beard and thinning gray-brown hair, greasy and slicked down with smelly oil. A nest of screwdrivers sprouted from a plastic pouch in his shirt pocket, and odd tools stuck their heads out from his baggy, dirty trousers. It was hard to be afraid of such an odd-looking little man, even as he grabbed Jimmy by the collar and jerked him down roughly off the last rung of the ladder, whipping him around rudely to face him.

"Hell, you ain't even a goddamn nigger after all!" He seemed genuinely surprised by Jimmy's whiteness, but he was still fuming, spewing as if he were about to blow a gasket. "What the hell was you doing climbing my tower, you piece of damn white trash?"

"I just wanted to see what I could see from up there. That's all." Jimmy's voice sounded weak and trembling. He had just wet his pants, too.

"I ought to call the cops on your ass and have 'em put you under the jail right now. Throw you in there with all them rapists and murderers until you rot, or . . . or somethin'," he stammered. The man continued to shake the boy, to curse and rant until he ran out of steam, his white-hot anger finally cooling down. "Look, kid, make for sure that you don't come messing around my radio station again or I will fix you but good."

Jimmy had long since stopped trying to tear loose from the grip the man had on the collar of his shirt. He seemed to be more bluster than danger anyway. And besides, he had just then said the magic words.

"Radio station? This is a radio station here?"

"What'd you think it was, a goddamn playground, with monkey bars for goddamn little monkeys like—"

"Are you the one that plays all the songs and talks on the air? Are you Rockin' Randy?"

Jimmy doubted that this ugly little man could actually be the golden-voiced spirit who had cast such a spell on him from behind the Zenith's speaker grille, but that was the only radio name he knew for sure. The wiry old man stared at him as if this kid were even crazier than he had at first thought, then burst into laughter and lost his grip on the boy's neck as he slapped his thighs and hooted. But Jimmy was going nowhere now. He had questions for this little man.

"Hell, no, I ain't no damned Rockin' Randy," he spat suddenly, cutting off his laughter like a light switch. Suddenly serious, he pulled up his puny chest. That sent the screwdrivers in his pocket pointing in different directions. He was squinting his eyes behind the thick lenses. "I'm Charlie McGee, the chief engineer for radio station WROG, duly licensed by the FCC, and I can put you in the penitentiary right now for messing with this here tower like you did. It's a federal crime to trespass inside that fence!"

"Is that where they talk and play the records and all?" Jimmy asked, stretching to see past this McGee man to the low-slung cinder-block building hiding in the rapidly deepening dusk across the field.

But Charlie McGee was not answering any more questions for this juvenile delinquent.

"Tell me your name and address, brat, so I can have the law come and get you if you ever set foot on my tower again. That is, if you don't get your ass fried by all the radio-frequency current first."

Jimmy really wasn't sure of the address of the duplex, so he stammered something and told him his name. McGee wrote it all down with a stubby, well-chewed pencil on a small notebook he had fished from a back pocket.

"Now then. Let's see here. What's gonna be your punishment for climbing up my radio tower? Risking shorting the whole radio station directly to ground and kicking me off the air? Leaving your goddamn carcass just a greasy place out here for the crows to pick at? Another sorry mess for Charlie McGee to have to clean up like he always does? Opening the door for your goddamn mama and daddy to sue me and WROG and who knows who all for some shit or other?"

He rubbed his bristly chin as he continued to mutter to himself, then rolled his eyes upward. Blinking red lights had just burst forth along the length of the steeple above them. McGee suddenly snapped his bony fingers. He pointed one of them at Jimmy's nose.

"You get your little monkey-climbing butt over here at nine o'clock in the morning and I've got a good day's worth of work for you to do. Trash for you to haul out here to burn and whatever else other goddamn chores I can dream up between now and then."

The little man spun quickly on his heels and double-timed almost out of sight into the weeds and darkness, then stopped suddenly, twirled, and screeched again.

"And if you ain't here, I'll get the sheriff and the police and the FBI on your ass so quick it'll make your head swim," he called back, then walked on, soon becoming invisible in the murky twilight, still muttering about "federal offense" and being "burned to a crisp."

Carefully, Jimmy made his way back across the field. Only a bit of a rising moon and some distant streetlights showed him the way to the tree bridge. It was hard to be frightened by the comical little man, no matter how much he cursed and raged. Besides, Jimmy was too excited about finally being at the place where the magic was made, confirming that it really was sorcery after all that went on in the low block building with the flashing blue lights.

Stopping at the edge of the ditch, he was a little leery of feeling his way across the bridge in the dark and then having to make his way alone through the jungle of vines. But he was still so flushed by the rush of emotion he had found hanging there on the side of the tower that he was sure he could have levitated across the stream!

Once across, Jimmy looked back before diving into the undergrowth. The red lights on the obelisk in the field blinked like a healthy pulse. The North Star had moved to a point behind the tower, and it seemed to mark the spot where he had clung to a place along its length a few minutes before.

A sudden shiver of excitement snuck up on him. He had to tear himself away to head for home. For the moment, he was disappointed that the darkness and the foulmouthed little man were driving him away from this enchanted place.

But never mind. Tomorrow at nine he would be back and would finally see the place where the wizard cast his spells.

Chapter 7

There was a promise of autumn in the breeze the next morning. It must have rained briefly overnight. The air seemed cooler and cleaner, the humidity lower, the view out Jimmy's dingy bedroom window for once not dimmed by mist or haze. The floor was cool to his bare feet so he got a pair of well-worn socks that were twisted together in the chifforobe drawer and then fetched a half-empty bag of stale cookies and a glass of Kool-Aid from the kitchen. He brought his breakfast back to the bedroom to kneel and worship before the radio.

The volume stayed low; Jimmy kept his ear close to the grille cloth so as not to awaken Grandmama. She was still noisily sawing away in the bed across the room, sometimes talking to game-show hosts and soap-opera stars in her sleep.

The night before had brought another batch of miraculous revelations from behind the Zenith's dial. Jimmy had stayed up later than usual, but he had spent only a few minutes in front of the television set with Grandmama. She never noticed when he slipped out of the room to pass several hours in the same spot he occupied that morning, twisting the TUN knob on the big radio until distant voices grew clear, until the music that was being sent out to ride along the wind became distinct and melodic.

And he had listened in awe that often approached disbelief as he heard the rumble-throated announcers rattle off strings of call letters. Some he had heard the night before. Others were new, from even more distant locations. WLW in Cincinnati, WHO in Iowa, WBAP in Ft. Worth, Texas, WWL in New Orleans, WGN and WLS in Chicago, WCKY, WHAS, WNOX, KDKA. There were commercials for stores and restaurants and businesses hundreds of miles away from where he shivered in the darkness, sitting cross-legged on the chilly linoleum in the duplex, and news reports about real people in real cities and towns he had never even heard of.

Then there would be a strange noise that would creep in like some audio tide. Something that sounded like he imagined an ocean wave might sound, though he had never actually heard one. It would rise up out of the sea of static to overtake the signals and eventually wash them away. Even the ones that had been the strongest, the most solid, would fall victim to the surge. He then would have to turn the tuning knob again to search out another clear voice in the night.

Sometimes the voices he discovered spoke a language he couldn't understand, and the music was tinkly, the songs sung in words he didn't know. And then that, too, would fade into the twisting current of static crashes and whines that seemed to rise up and claim what it had allowed to float to the top of the din for a few precious minutes of lucidity. Jimmy could only imagine the exotic foreign locations of those stations, what the view might be from a perch high up on the sides of their red-blinking, candy-striped towers.

"Hav-a-Tampa cigar time is nine-fifty. With studios in the French Quarter at the Roosevelt Hotel, this is WWL, way down yonder in New Orleans."

"This is the air castle of the South, WSM, Nashville, Tennessee. Webb Pierce will be stopping by later. . . ."

"It's fifty-seven degrees on Peachtree, and you're listening to WSB, Atlanta."

"It's the *All-Night Trucker's Show* here on WBAP, with a song going out to John and all the drivers at the Mid-Con Truck Stop up there in North Platte, Nebraska, tonight. Here's ole Hank Williams himself. . . ."

"And now, folks, stay tuned to the *Back to the Bible and Jesus Hour* here on XERF. But first, have you ever thought about how much money you could make raisin' baby chicks right there in your own backyard?"

Most of the stations were only people talking, or bits and pieces of dramas that Jimmy happened to drop into the middle of. He felt as if he were eavesdropping on someone else's conversations. But some of the stations were playing the same songs he had come to know from WROG. And their announcers had the same breakneck spiels, the same joy and excitement that rattled the speakers and slapped a smile on his face.

He carefully tweaked the knob to pull those signals through more clearly. He was disappointed as they inevitably faded away. Then, later, he would locate some of them again on the crest of another wave and could listen to a few songs before they once again plunged beneath the surf noise.

The strain of saving all those drowning signals had finally made him drowsy. He fell into sound sleep right there on the floor, then awoke to the hums and sirens from the radio an hour later, his arms and legs cold and stiff. Grandmama had fallen asleep in her well-worn chair and was snoring louder than the hiss of her television set, now delivering nothing but snow and noise. Jimmy turned the set off and shook her awake.

"What? Restin' my eyes. You eat supper yet?"

She was fumbling for a cigarette from the empty pack but finally realized it was well past ten. She stumbled groggily off to bed.

Now, in the predawn stillness before she woke up and turned on the cyclops in the other room for the day, Jimmy quietly listened to the deep, smooth voice of Jerry Diamond on WROG. He had formed a mind picture of the man who resided each morning inside the radio: in his mid-thirties, broad shouldered, handsome, well dressed, hair dark and wavy and combed straight back, casually smoking a cigarette, sipping hot coffee between sentences, as he spoke to Jimmy and the thousands of others who were coming to life to the sound of his friendly morning chatter.

Finally, Jimmy rinsed out his milk glass in the red-stained kitchen sink, slipped on his worn sneakers, and eased quietly out the front door. He didn't want to risk Grandmama waking up and remembering some chore that might delay his sentence at the radio station. And he didn't doubt for a second that Charlie McGee would, indeed, have the FBI come after him if he failed to show up for tower-climbing penance.

Detroit Simmons was already sitting on the front steps, his back to the door, waiting for him. He jumped as if he had been shot when Jimmy opened it.

"Jimmy Gill?"

"Morning," he said, the word clipped and short, with an intentional bit of gruffness in his voice.

"Boy! I thought for sure that old man had done shot you or put you in jail last night!"

"He threatened to do both."

"Jimmy, you are crazy, man. What do you mean, climbing up that thing like that? What if you fell off? What if they had started shooting at you?"

Jimmy was glad he had been worried, but he'd never admit it to Detroit. He was still irritated, remembering the way his best friend had run away and left him at the mercy of the station's livid engineer.

"You sure took off lickety-split when he came up," Jimmy reminded him.

Detroit's face fell and it was obvious he was ashamed he had left him to fall or get captured.

"Listen," he said, sincerely. "Let me promise you one thing, Jimmy Gill. I won't ever leave you like that again. It don't matter what, I won't ever leave you again. Do you believe me?"

"Yeah, Dee. I do. Don't worry about it anyhow. I'd have probably done the same thing yesterday myself."

That made Detroit brighten a little. Finally, he broke into a big smile. They shook one of their other secret handshakes, an Indian one that Detroit had seen in a Roy Rogers picture.

"Tell you what, Jimmy, let's go build a fort today. We can find some tree limbs and build it on the ditch bank and play like . . ."

He stopped midplan. He must have sensed that Jimmy wasn't going to be joining him in this particular adventure.

"I gotta go back to the radio station and work or the man said he'd have the FBI out after me," Jimmy explained.

"Radio station?"

He told Detroit what had happened after his swift retreat the evening before, and that the place with the strange flashing lights, the tall tower, and the spirit-buzzes had turned out to be the WROG radio station. Then they walked along together through the woods, as far as their tree bridge. Detroit stood in the clearing as Jimmy made his way toward the rear of the radio building. He stayed there, watching almost sadly until they lost sight of each other through the tall grass. Before he let Jimmy go, though, Detroit made it clear that he was still leery of this strange place, still not sure if its witchcraft was good or bad.

Jimmy wasn't so sure either, but his curiosity about this place was stronger than any fear he had. The humming at the base of the tower was just as eerie as ever as he walked past it. Wires strung on poles stretched back from the tower to the low brick building, and he followed their trail. The undergrowth was shorter and thinner in their wake.

A back door to the building was propped open by a big square chunk of metal with a nest of multicolored, twisted wires at its crown. Cool air was being sucked in around him as he stepped carefully around the door prop and into a dark hallway. He remembered Charlie McGee's warning about being cooked alive by the power of the station. Maybe he wouldn't get skewered if he stayed on tiptoes.

There was a strange smell inside the building, something like he remembered from the time lightning had run into their old house and burned up Grandmama's stove—a sharp electric smell. A big fan roared overhead and pulled air down the hallway. This thick air was much warmer than the cool morning breeze he had just left outside.

And there was the familiar flashing blue-hued light, pulsing at him from behind a dusty glass panel on his left. Several bulbous cylinders with cables sprouting from their tops throbbed to some unheard, hypnotic beat.

As his eyes grew accustomed to the darkness, he noticed the knobs and buttons and huge, oversize on-off switches that pushed through metal panels in the wall. Meters danced and swung across cryptic numbers and notches and symbols that were printed on their faces. If a wizard with a magic wand had suddenly appeared in a shower of light at the far end of the hallway and called his name, Jimmy Gill would not have been one bit surprised.

Cautiously he moved past more smudged windows that looked in on other glass jars with glowing embers captured inside them. They were all tied together with tangles of gray and black and red wires. Slowly he made his way toward a dim light that beckoned from a doorway at the end of the hall.

Around the corner and through the opening, he spied the back of Charlie McGee's head. The little man was sitting at a desk piled high with books and papers and tools and junk. He held a magazine close to his nose, carefully examining pictures of women with no clothes on. He was so intent on his reading that he apparently didn't hear Jimmy's footsteps above the roar of rushing air and the growling of all the equipment held in big racks all around where he sat.

"I'm here, Mr. McGee," Jimmy spoke, loudly enough to overcome the noise of the fans and the pounding of the music that gushed from a huge speaker in the corner of the junk-filled room.

It looked as if someone had suddenly turned on a jolt of electricity to the man's chair. He jumped straight up, sent the magazine flying like a freed pigeon, cracked his knee hard on the desk with the wet sound of bone on metal, and let loose a stream of curses and oaths that seemed to leave the air smoky and charred. The little man danced and hobbled and swore some more, and then, still pale with pain, he sat down in the middle of the desktop amid the electrical parts and dusty books, rubbing his knee.

"What are you sneakin' up on me for, you goddamn little yard monkey?"

His glasses had been knocked crooked by his injured jig, and his leg was bony and white when he rolled up a pants leg to check the damage. But the hair on his head had not moved. It was plastered in place with grease.

"I'm sorry, Mr. McGee. I really am."

He tried to look as apologetic as he could and McGee must have seen that it was sincere. He finally straightened his spectacles, rolled down his pants, stood and tested the leg, and then motioned for him to come closer.

"You're a goddamn hour early anyhow. Shit. Well, come on in here and let me put your tower-climbing ass to work before you cause anybody else any more trouble."

He hopped around the room, still favoring his left leg, checked the big chunk of black-banded watch on his wrist, and then led Jimmy back down the long hallway next to the blue-glowing bottles. He stopped at one of the glass windows and looked lovingly at the pulsating electronic display behind it.

"Five hundred volts at ten amps of current. Five thousand watts of pure power. That's enough to tickle aerials in five states, boy. And this here's Big Beulah. She was homemade from the ground up. Ain't but one or two more like her anywhere else in the whole world. Doherty modulation. Water-cooled from stem to stern. A feller's got to be as much a plumber as an electronics man to keep this old bitch in heat. That spray pond out back keeps the water cool so we can keep Big Beulah bathed and beautiful. And them big pumps along the wall back yonder keeps the water circulatin'. Else this whole thing would melt into a big copper junk pile in just a few minutes."

Jimmy didn't understand much of what Charlie McGee was saying but he remembered the "five thousand watts" from the station sign-off and promised he would ask somebody about it sometime. And at least he could now tell Detroit what the fountain behind the building was for. They stopped at a collection of fifty-five-gallon drums filled with trash and papers.

"Finally got around to my spring cleaning last week. You're gonna tote all this shit out to the trash pile at the far end of the field so we can burn it," he ordered, and waved vaguely toward where the tower stood. "And then come on back up to my office when you're finished with that and I'll have some more things for you to do. And make sure you don't be slippin' up on me again or I may yet throw your little juvenile delinquent ass in the high-voltage cage and fry you like a chicken."

He didn't care what Charlie McGee said, or what work he made him do. He was so proud to be a part of the radio station that he gladly did the dirty work.

Once the barrels were emptied, he made his way again past Big Beulah, stomping and kicking up as much of a warning noise as he could. He saw Charlie hastily slide the naked-girl magazine under a stack of papers when he heard him coming; then the little man stood carefully on his injured leg and motioned for Jimmy to once again follow him.

This time, they went the other way out of the engineering office, through a heavy door onto carpeted floors and down a narrow hall. Then they made a quick left into a tiny cramped room with a small glass window in the door. A red On Air light above the door warned them to stay out, but Charlie McGee ignored it and led Jimmy right on into the musty darkness.

A big upright panel filled with knobs and switches and meters stared back at them along the far wall of the room. Stacks of 45 rpm records seemed to cover every flat surface that wasn't already filled with foot-high piles of ragged yellow paper covered with purple typing.

A skinny man with bad teeth sat before the control panel and spoke into a mesh-covered box, his voice deep and booming as he told a tilted glass window in front of him that Fats Domino was coming up next on WROG. The walls of the room seemed to vibrate with the force and resonance of his words. He hit a switch on the panel in front of him, a turntable at his right elbow spun into motion, and he flipped another couple of switches, all seemingly in the same motion.

There was a sudden explosion of noise from a speaker that was as tall as Jimmy and stood in the far corner of the room. The noise was deafening, and Jimmy covered both ears. The skinny man sitting behind the panel angrily jerked the headphones off his head and slammed them down hard onto the desk in front of him. He ignored the stack of records he had knocked over. Red-faced, he twisted around in the chair toward the two intruders while reaching awkardly behind him to spin some kind of a knob. The song's volume fell to only a murmur.

"Damn it, Charlie! How many goddamn times have I told you not to barge in here when I'm talkin' on the air."

Jimmy couldn't believe it. The man's voice that had just been so mellow and strong was now high-pitched and nasal as he whined and spat at Charlie McGee. He couldn't have weighed more than a hundred pounds, had ratty hair twisted in all directions by the headset he had been wearing, sweat rings under the arms of his black T-shirt, and several days' growth of beard covering his snarl.

"Jerry Diamond, this is my slave," Charlie introduced Jimmy, paying no attention at all to the skinny man's anger.

"What's your name, slave?"

The skinny man had suddenly lost his mad-on. He accidentally knocked over another stack of records as he stood. He extended his hand, ignoring the discs as they crashed noisily to the floor.

"Jimmy Gill," he said, shaking the man's bony fingers.

Jerry Diamond? Had Charlie said "Jerry Diamond"?

"Well, I'm pleased to meet you, Jimmy," he said, dropping his speech an octave closer to his familiar radio voice. "Welcome to WROG Radio."

"Lulu's so damned afraid to come in here with you disc-jockey animals and she won't get within a hundred feet of the transmitters," Charlie was saying, "so I'm gonna let old Jimmy do some cleaning up for me. He'll get all this Teletype paper crap outta your way so you can have an easier time getting one of your women spread-eagled up here on this desk."

"Don't pay no attention to this old fart, Jimmy. You the young'un that was doin' the Tarzan bit off the tower yesterday?" Jerry asked, his voice unconsciously drifting back higher and thinner.

"More like Cheetah, if you ask me," Charlie answered for Jimmy. "Goddamn monkey-ass!"

Diamond suddenly spun around as if he had been signaled from somewhere by someone that Jimmy couldn't see. He plopped back down hard into the ragged chair, cranked the big knob on the panel clockwise until the final strains of the song were again blasting painfully throughout the room, and slapped a switch which instantly muted the music completely and simultaneously set afire a brilliant red lightbulb in front of him. He coughed brutally three or four times. It sounded as if a piece of lung might follow. Then he twisted another knob on the panel and retrieved his deepest voice from somewhere in that emaciated little body.

As the words flowed smoothly from him, he dug blindly into a stack of 45 rpm records that had been near his elbow. He found one and held it up so he could read the label in the red glow of the lightbulb. Gracefully, he sailed the disc onto another turntable to his left that had been spinning away empty. He lifted the phono arm until the needle fell onto the lip of the disc and caught hold. He did all this without missing a beat in the continuous, melodious speech he had been making into the microphone.

". . . and here's a new one from another great young artist you'll be hearing a lot about . . . from Memphis, just like Elvis Presley is . . . it's Jerry . . . Lee . . . Lewis!"

The switch was flipped, and screaming, manic piano music filled the tiny room. Jerry Diamond danced in his chair, waving his arms over his head, singing along with the lyrics at the top of his lungs for a few words. But then he quickly hushed, dropped his shoulders, and quietly watched the two meters in front of him wiggle wildly. It was almost as if he was ashamed for having lost his cool for a while, for allowing himself to get carried away by the music with an audience looking on.

After a moment, he turned and winked at Jimmy, then reached underneath the spinning turntable and pulled out a filthy trash can. He dragged it over to the edge of the desk and raked into it a pile of yellow paper, brown lunch sacks, cigarette packs, a paper cup half full of coffee, the dried-up rind of an orange, and some other unidentifiable garbage. Then he dumped in two ashtrays full of cigarette butts and an old cigar or two. Diamond stood and packed the mess down with a sneakered foot. He sneezed several times as the dust kicked back at him and then pushed the trash can over toward Jimmy with the foot.

He spoke in his fullest, deepest, window-rattling disc-jockey voice.

"Mr. Jimmy Gill, let me be the first to welcome you to the exciting, fast-paced world of radio broadcasting."

Chapter 8

Jimmy never figured out where punishment for climbing the tower ended and a part-time job with WROG began, and he didn't care. After Jimmy had hauled out drums filled with junk and bags of garbage and old electronic gizmos for two full days, Charlie next had him stripping ivy from the back wall of the building and slapping on new paint. Then he put Jimmy to hacking down the weeds in the trail from the station to the building at the tower's base.

After a week or so of that, Charlie presented him with a bucket and a squeegee and told him to wash the glass windows that looked in on various rooms inside the station, including both the filthy window that shielded the transmitter named Big Beulah, and the smaller slanting pane that looked into the room where Jerry Diamond and the other deejays played their wonderful rock-and-roll records.

Charlie McGee usually shooed the boy on home by eleven o'clock or so each morning, but after two weeks of meting out the punishment, he handed Jimmy a crisp, new one-dollar bill. He told Jimmy to go on home before the wage-an-hour people crawled all over his ass, and he gruffly disappeared back into the darkness and noise of Big Beulah's den.

It was the first money Jimmy Gill had ever earned. He stood there for a while and looked at the new dollar bill, felt its texture, smelled it, carefully folded it, and put it into his overall bib pocket. Later, he searched through the chifforobe drawers until he found a mateless sock without a hole in it and put the dollar in that. He would keep each of the dollar bills Charlie McGee would give him from then on. He hid the sock in the bottom of the radio, behind the big speaker and underneath the electronic chassis.

School was to start the next Monday and Charlie winced when Jimmy told him he would have to cut back on the job some, maybe only coming in the afternoons for a little while from now on. McGee told him to come by a couple of days a week, after he had gotten home from class, and he'd find plenty of work for him to do.

Jimmy was not looking forward to school. It took away his play and radio-station work time. And it would be difficult getting back into the habit, considering that he had not been in class since they had moved to Birmingham back in the early spring. Even then, school had never thrilled him. The teachers wanted to do all the talking and not listen at all. He knew, too, that he would be behind on all those hated lessons, and everyone there would be a stranger. He still didn't know a soul of school age except Detroit Simmons.

And Detroit didn't count. He would be bused ten miles across town to the colored school while Jimmy walked the six blocks over to Potter-Finley Middle School. It was a dreary dark-brick dungeon with a tall chain-link prison fence that separated the forboding building from anything resembling brightness or happiness or freedom.

On the first day in class, Jimmy found it wasn't only the building that was depressing. The convoluted arithmetic, arid Alabama history, and incessant English lessons dragged on and on endlessly. The view out the window and through the fence of bright blue sky and emerald green grass made the torture even worse.

Miss Claudia Cleveland, his fifth-grade teacher, was so old, dry, and dusty, it seemed she was on the verge of disintegrating into a sudden cloud if a stray breeze found its way into their tomb of a classroom. Even her voice cracked and snapped like pine kindling when she spoke. No matter how warm the early fall days were, she wore gray or dark brown sweaters draped over her bony shoulders, wool skirts that swept the oiled floors of their stifling classroom, and heavy shoes fit for any workingman at the mills. She stubbornly refused to open the windows to let in even a gulp of fresh air, no matter how boiling hot it became in the classroom. The only green plant on her desk was a spiny cactus and it thrived in the dry heat while the kids sat and wilted.

It seemed that they were doomed to sit stiffly and swelter as they endured her droning lectures, the maddening popping of her dentures as she spoke, the audible creaking and cracking of her knees each time she rose from her desk. Little things kept them awake, like the accidental squeak of a piece of chalk on the blackboard as Miss Cleveland furiously reduced fractions. Someone might fall asleep and tumble noisily from a desk. Or some poor inmate would accidentally break wind and send the whole cellblock into hysterics. Such simple distractions always drew cheers and made whoever did it into a temporary celebrity.

The highlight of the school year came two weeks into the torture, and it was Jimmy Gill who did it. He found a bluebird at recess, the poor thing waddling crazily near a chinaberry tree on the tiny playground. It had obviously been eating the fermented berries that had fallen from the tree and was staggering drunk.

There was no plan for mischief on his part. It all just happened. For some reason, he put the lush-bird in his overall pocket and took it back when Miss Cleveland summoned them all to return to class. While they reluctantly filed in, the old woman stepped to the cloakroom for another sweater, obviously chilled from her brief trip to the doorway to revoke their precious moments of recess parole. Jimmy was afraid the bird might come to its senses and start making noise, so he stepped quickly to the teacher's desk and put it in the top middle drawer for safekeeping. There was no other place, and the windows, he knew, were nailed closed. He'd get the thing out of the desk and set it free after school.

Two hours later, Miss Cleveland was busily diagramming sentences on the chalkboard while the class fought sleep. Her piece of chalk broke with a loud snap and Jimmy sank deeply into his seat when he saw what was about to happen as Miss Cleveland reached to open the desk drawer for another piece of chalk.

Please, he prayed, still be drunk on your butt, bird. Let it please be asleep. But nobody heard his prayer. The bluebird, now completely revived and probably irritable from its chinaberry hangover, suddenly flew up directly into the teacher's shocked face.

The woman shrieked wildly, slapping at the confused bird, using language not fit for fifth-grade ears. The class was instantly wide awake, watching the whole thing play out in front of them like a good television show. Jimmy cringed.

Miss Cleveland lapped the room twice, still screaming and slapping and cursing so loudly she could probably be heard throughout the entire school building. The poor bird had somehow gotten itself tangled in the old woman's hair bun and was flapping its wings as hard as it could to escape. That just made Miss Cleveland scream and slap and curse harder.

Finally she found the room's door, managed to tear it open, and made it halfway down the hallway before she fainted dead away. The hungover bird managed to get free and fluttered down the short stairwell, past a surprised janitor, and outside to blessed freedom. The entire class had followed their teacher out the door, thrilled with the unexpected entertainment that had been dropped so wonderfully into their day.

Jimmy Gill, the skinny new kid, was an instant hero to all but Principal Cornelius Fagan. He definitely was not amused. For a horrible moment, as he sat in Fagan's superheated office, Jimmy was afraid he was about to be expelled from school for good.

"Son, I'm at a loss," the huge old man spoke from behind his cluttered desk. He was looking down on Jimmy through a set of bushy eyebrows. Jimmy was sitting low, in a tiny chair more fit for first graders than someone going on eleven years old. "This irresponsible stunt could have seriously injured one of our finest teachers. And a dear friend of mine, I might mention."

The principal stood then and began pacing in tight circles around Jimmy.

"Perhaps if I required that you stay after school for the remainder of the term . . ."

Jimmy's stomach fell and so did his jaw. Getting free from that prison each day, running through the jungle with Detroit, crawling over the tree bridge to WROG, or hurrying home, sitting before the Zenith, and pulling in distant rock-and-roll music were his only salvations.

He even passed time in class each day by writing down the call letters and locations of the stations he heard each afternoon after school, finding the cities on the big map that hung behind Miss Cleveland's desk, or listing on the blue lines in his St. Joe spiral-bound notebook the artists and songs the stations played. If that was taken away from him, he might as well be shot dead right then and there.

"No, please! I have . . ."

"Yes, young man?"

"I have a job after school."

Principal Fagan stopped pacing and looked at him incredulously. Even in that deprived neighborhood in which it was his misfortune to be employed as an educator, it was uncommon for a fifth grader to work after school.

"Yes, and exactly what kind of job is it, young man? Bird trainer?"

The old bag of wind laughed softly at his own joke, bent forward at his ample waist, opened his eyes wide in disbelief, and stared down at Jimmy through the underbrush of his eyebrows.

"No sir. I work at WROG. The radio station."

The principal laughed again and resumed his circular pacing.

"I suppose you are a radio announcer, then. Maybe you play the piano. Yes, that's it. You play the piano on the radio. And I suppose 'Bird of Paradise' is your favorite number."

He fairly giggled out loud.

"No sir. I take out the trash and do odd jobs for the engineer there, Mr. McGee. You can call him and ask him about it if you like."

But Jimmy was secretly hoping he wouldn't do that. Charlie McGee would be just as likely to tell Fagan he had never heard of the "little bastard" as to confirm his employment. Charlie was like that sometimes.

The principal had again stopped strutting around the office.

"Do you know Jerry Diamond?"

"Yes sir, I do."

Jimmy guessed Diamond had seen him around the station enough to confirm that he worked there. At least, he hoped so.

"He is a former student of mine, you know. When I had the high school, that is. An excellent student. On our debate team. I listen to him often in the mornings. Not as much now as I did before they began to play all that rocking rolling jive Negro music. Can't stand that. Makes me nervous."

"Yes sir. Me, too."

Jimmy would have confirmed black was white if it would get him out of having to stay after school.

"Well, Mr."—he glanced at the folder on his desk—"Mr. Gill. Stand up and bend over. I'll give you ten whacks with the Enforcer and expect no more of these shenanigans from you from this moment forward. And you tell Jerry Diamond that Mr. Fagan said hello and to play me a nice Glen Miller selection. Or maybe some Guy Lombardo music. I do dearly love Guy Lombardo."

After every second or third whack from the huge wooden paddle, Mr. Fagan thought of other bands he would like Jerry Diamond to play for him. Jimmy Gill didn't care. He had avoided detention and could make the trek to WROG or curl up in front of the Zenith instead of serving his sentence at the school prison.

He was out the door of the school and halfway home before he realized a truism: Plenty of other people were as fascinated with and curious about radio as he had been. The kids in his class were always asking him about songs and deejays since they had found out he worked at WROG. Even his grandmother was mildly interested in what he did and who he saw at the job. She'd sometimes give him a minute's attention before something moving about on the television screen would jerk her interest back to the box.

He stored the thought away. Who knows? Maybe it would be of some use to him someday.

Chapter 9

It was usually near dark when Detroit would arrive at Jimmy's house. The days were growing shorter, so their play time was cut, their adventures curtailed by nightfall. And Jimmy could only spend an hour or so doing chores for Charlie McGee before the station signed off for the night and he had to feel his way back through the woods to get home. Grandmama didn't seem to care where he spent his time as long as he checked in periodically, changed the channels for her when she didn't feel like getting up, or brought her a pack of cigarettes from the kitchen cabinet. She seemed to know more about the daily activities of the Mousketeers and the Little Rascals than she did of her grandson's comings and goings.

One afternoon, Charlie told him to go ahead and get the scrap Teletype paper out of the control room because he had to leave early on important business. So far, Jimmy had pointedly stayed out of that tiny room since the morning he had met Jerry Diamond. He didn't want to risk riling the disc jockeys, the stars of the station. Charlie had been setting out their trash in the hallway so Jimmy could get to it without risking intruding on the shows.

That day, Jimmy nervously waited for the On Air light to fade out, then opened the heavy door and slipped inside as quietly and inconspicuously as he could. The biggest man he had ever seen was squeezed impossibly into the narrow space between the two turntables. Massive folds of flesh draped over almost onto each of them, and the man could barely reach the switches he toyed with on the console because of the grotesque belly that stretched down and away from a jiggling set of triple chins. The swivel chair underneath him bent dangerously under his incredible mass. The telephone receiver was almost lost, tucked between a dumpy shoulder and an ear that was nearly hidden by wads of flesh.

"Baby, you know I wanna meet you so bad," he was saying to the phone's mouthpiece, his voice raspy and clipped and short of breath. "You sound so-o-o sexy to me. You really do, sweetheart!"

"Mister?"

Jimmy didn't know whether to interrupt or not, but he needed to get the trash can and be gone before it got any later and darker outside. There was no way he was going to get it out from under the desk past this mountain of a man without bothering him, though.

"Hold it, sweetie, and don't let it get cold," he said to the phone, and made a couple of kissing sounds. Then slowly, with obvious effort, he twisted his body around in the chair as it screeched its resistance. He had to raise his elbows to keep from knocking the tonearms off the records resting on each turntable. He stretched the coiled phone cable until it was straight and threatening to snap.

"Whatcha need, midget?"

"Trash? I need to get all that paper and stuff out from under there," Jimmy said, pointing to the trash can piled full of used Teletype paper and the other garbage.

The man threw a stack of paper toward Jimmy and shoved another pile off the edge of the desk in the direction of the trash can, the phone still hiding somewhere there in the pillow of his shoulder. He had no neck, just rolls of fat up to a brush of oily hair on top of his head.

Risking a crushing, Jimmy reached under his chair for the purple-splashed paper and stuffed it into the overflowing trash can, while the massive man turned back to his bank of switches and dancing meters. He cranked up the music on the control room's speaker and talked quieter so Jimmy couldn't hear what he was saying to whoever it was on the other end of the telephone.

Then, just as Jimmy started to open the door to drag out the trash can, the first strains of "Dixie" punched their way out of the studio speaker. The red bulb filled the room with bloody crimson light, the music hushed, and he heard the huge man's voice go low and smooth and so familiar that he got goose bumps.

"And so, we come to the end of another broadcast day. . . ."

Jimmy's lips moved along with Rockin' Randy's litany as he waited for the end. He started to go back and speak to him, to tell him how much he enjoyed listening to his show. But when the music died, Randy was once again cooing to the woman on the telephone, rocking slowly from side to side, the chair beneath his bulk squealing in agony.

Somehow, he had pictured Rockin' Randy's hair wavy blond, combed fashionably in a cowlick, a golden version of Elvis Presley's famous black mane. Maybe he had a Clark Gable mustache, and his necktie was slightly loosened at the throat as he smiled with perfect teeth and spoke deeply into the microphone, one hand cupped to his ear the way the announcers on television did it. He never imagined a mountain of flesh, sweating and straining for breath as his program took a backseat to some woman he was trying to sweet-talk on the other end of a telephone line.

The tower lights had come on by the time he dumped all the trash at the burning cage behind the station building. The moon lit the way back to the edge of the field, but it was almost too dark to see under the kudzu and honeysuckle. Jimmy felt relief when he finally popped out of the bushes into the knee-high weeds in the backyard of the duplex. The lone working streetlight at the corner of Wisteria was the only illumination, but he immediately noticed that there was something else that lit the still night air. Something ugly and sinister.

It was an eerie red glow beyond the house, back toward the highline underpass he had run through to Ishkooda. At first he ignored the red smudge in the sky and climbed up the back steps. But the strange light bounced off the house next door, and for some reason, he felt drawn to it.

Maybe it was a house on fire over there. Maybe a stand of grass had been ignited by a stray spark from a train. Or, God forbid, the Russians had finally dropped the A-bomb.

But there were no sirens. No conelrad warning on the television's sound that sifted out at him through the back-door screen. Just the quiet of the early evening, when most folks on Wisteria Street were at supper, watching the news, working second shift at the mill. Or the laughter and banter of *I've Got a Secret* and Grandmama trying as usual to outguess the panelists.

In a matter of minutes, Jimmy was back down the steps and

on the street that cut under the highline railroad. Now he could see the source of the scarlet light, high up on the railroad bank, near the underpass that led to the neat homes where he had gone looking for Detroit Simmons.

A huge cross burned with a bright fire and black, billowing smoke. The smell of singed rags and kerosene filled the deathly silent air. Small groups of people from nearby houses stood in the street. Hands in their pockets, they watched without comment as the fiery light flickered off their slightly upturned faces.

Slowly, Jimmy's eyes were drawn to a movement in the dark shadows. An old red pickup truck backed from its parking place along the dirt bank, then eased past those standing along the street watching. Two men with hoods over their heads sat in the front and two more, also hooded, sat behind them in the truck's bed.

Jimmy Gill shivered, although the dusky air was gentle and warm. The hooded men didn't look back to the flaming cross, nor to the left or right as they passed the people gathered there. But one of the figures in the back of the truck raised his hand in a familiar gesture, the same one Jimmy had seen in movies on television about World War II: arm straight at the elbow, palm flat, fingers toward the sky. The Nazi salute. A flash of light from the fire glinted on a chunky wristwatch with a black band that also looked familiar somehow.

And there, through the tunnel, like a dim picture on a huge television screen, he could see other upturned faces lit by the embers. Faces just like theirs, only darker. And those faces showed more fear than curiosity, more anger than casual interest.

A mother held close a scared, clinging toddler. A man used his hands to try to shield the eyes of a small boy who struggled to see what view was being denied him. And the woman Jimmy had met the day he had gone in search of Ishkooda and Detroit Simmons was in the crowd, too. From where he stood, Jimmy thought he could make out the jut of her defiant jaw.

The crowd on both sides of the track quickly melted away as the fire burned out. When Jimmy got home and told Grandmama about what he had seen, she said it had been on the news all evening. The Ku Klux Klan had burned over fifty crosses all around Birmingham that night.

"The niggers have all been harping on integrating the schools," she said. "Even the old Supreme Court says they got to go ahead and let them mix. So the Klan wanted to show them not to get too uppity just yet. They're gonna make sure them niggers stay in their place! Reach over there and turn that to channel thirteen, Jimmy. It's nearly time for Dinah Shore."

For some reason, Jimmy Gill didn't feel like listening to the radio that night. The air was still warm outside, so he sat on the front porch, on the high top step, nibbling on some hot dogs he had boiled. He watched the occasional car ease along the street as a few men arrived home from overtime at the mill.

He had a feeling in his stomach he had never felt before. He was only eleven years old, but he was worried. About Detroit. About their friendship. About what might happen if the troubles between the races got any worse, as they were threatening to do.

There was no doubt in his mind. He loved Detroit Simmons as deeply as he might have a brother if he had had one. He didn't care about his race. Not a bit. Why should anybody else? He would love to have Detroit going to the same school as he did. Why would anybody be against that?

A soft breeze played with the turning leaves on the water oaks near the Polanski house. Noisily it scattered the first ones that had already turned to gold, giving up their grip on the highest branches. The breeze also brought him the aroma of something delicious cooking somewhere along the block, the perfume of honeysuckle, and of Mrs. Polanski's rosebushes on the corner.

But then, before he could block it out, the same wind brought the stench of kerosene, of singed rags, of black smoke, fear, and hate.

Chapter 10

The leaves had turned to glorious oranges and yellows and scarlets, painting the distant hills the same colors Jimmy figured the NBC peacock might show if Grandmama's television set had not had a dim black-and-white picture tube. But the leaves on the trees along Wisteria Street simply went from dull green to gone. They were washed into soggy mounds by the rain, clogging gutters and building dams, creating muddy, stagnant lakes that had to be skirted and hopped.

The trail through the woods to the radio station had grown slick and treacherous, mossy and slimy. More than once Jimmy had come home with mud caked on his overall knees or with the seat of his britches sodden from a sudden slip or slide.

Grandmama gave him what-for and a whack on the butt, but he simply rinsed the clothes out in the bathtub and hung them up to dry for the next day's school. She didn't have time for such. She spent her afternoons with cartoons and western serials, laughing out loud at the simple jokes the kids in the local studio audience would tell the clown-host.

"You oughta be watchin' this show, Jimmy. Spin and Marty are gonna be on the *Mickey Mouse Club* today. They get into the funniest messes on that old dude ranch. They may have *Zorro*, too."

"I need to do some homework, Grandmama."

"And then we can switch it over in a minute and see Roy Rogers and that feller with the Jeep on *Channel 6 Rodeo*."

"If I can finish this arithmetic, I'll come look."

But he rarely did. The big Zenith radio was his only release.

October looked like January already, but on a rare warm, sunny day he escaped out the front door of the school building, breathed the clean, fresh air like he had been holding his breath all day, and ran the entire way home as if on a mission. He had stayed up late the night before, twisting the Zenith's knobs, and then slept too late to have time to fix his lunch that morning. That helped make him an even bigger hit in class that day in a round-about sort of way.

Loud stomach growls started about two that afternoon. Growls so boisterous that they provided welcome entertainment for the kids sitting anywhere near him. All their merriment and giggles inevitably got them into trouble with Miss Cleveland, and Jimmy and several buddies were left standing the rest of the day with their noses in chalk circles drawn on the blackboard. But even that was better than the mind-numbing boredom of sitting in the schoolroom all afternoon.

Jimmy seemed to have been accepted by his new classmates. Anybody with a gut that loud, and who worked at a real, live radio station, was all right with them!

As he ran past the Polanski house on his way home, he spotted Mrs. Polanski and Clarice George sitting on the sunny end of the porch, enjoying the rare remaining remnants of warmth before damp winter swept in for good. They excitedly waved him over for a glass of iced tea and a talk. Jimmy only hoped there would be tea cakes, too. He could put up with the old-woman talk if there were only some of the wonderful cookies.

The cold tea was sweetly wonderful, especially as thirsty as he was from the arid dryness of Miss Cleveland's class. And there were some frosted tea cakes and a generous slice of pecan pie. He tried not to make a pig of himself.

The two women had become inseparable since the day their husbands died. Clarice George had, for all practical purposes, moved in with Greta Polanski, taking care of the older woman. Both of them kept each other company. Jimmy would often see them sitting on the porch, coming and going in Mrs. Polanski's car, or working in the front yard or the rose garden in back. The duplex next door to Jimmy and Grandmama had apparently been surrendered completely to the two twin boys. The only time Jimmy even knew they were there was when they would bump home, obviously loud drunk, in the wee hours of the morning, returning from some adventure he could only try to imagine. They must have slept away their days because it usually stayed quiet over there then. There was no indication that they worked or did anything constructive. The only exception was when they would tinker at one of the old cars they kept parked helter-skelter in front of the house.

The women asked about his grandmother, and then politely inquired about school. Then they listened with nodding attention as Jimmy hemmed and hawed and tried to avoid the truth about the hell it had become for him.

"Yes ma'am, I spent a good part of this afternoon at the blackboard, working out a problem for the class."

"Why that's so wonderful, Jimmy," Clarice George said. "My own boys never cared much for school and Hector didn't help me encourage them at all. I'm so glad you are paying attention to your studies."

"Young ones so need their education to be successful in life," Mrs. Polanski added. "Education . . . so taken for granted in this country . . ."

"And I've been working some at the radio station over yonder," he added quickly, trying to change the subject. He waved a cookie in the general direction of WROG's tower.

"Oh, Jimmy, at the radio station? How wonderful! What do you do there? Sing?" Mrs. George gushed.

She seemed excited to be talking to someone from the media. Mrs. Polanski did, too. She leaned forward in her rocker, listening for his answer as she shoved the glass plate of tea cakes toward him again. Jimmy took two more, a chocolate one for now, a lemon one to slide into his overall bib pocket for supper.

"No'm. I just help take out the trash and do odd jobs and stuff."

But the truth about his thrilling job in show business didn't seem to diminish their interest. They pushed for more information about the radio station, insisting on knowing what famous people he had met so far. They asked if he personally knew any of the people who "talked on the wind," as Mrs. George put it. Had he seen any of the singing stars in the flesh? They named several people he had never heard of—Mitch Miller, Kay Starr, the McGuire Sisters—and a man he had seen on television named Tennessee Ernie Ford.

Apparently the two women assumed all the people who performed on the radio were alive, in person, waiting right there inside the station, crammed into a studio of some kind until it was their turn. That Perez Prado dragged his orchestra into the little concrete block building on the superhighway each time the station wanted to play "Cherry Pink and Apple Blossom White," then hustled them all out quickly so Roger Williams could wheel in his piano for another rendition of "Autumn Leaves."

They pumped him, asking excited questions, most of which he couldn't come close to answering. Then, when Jimmy rose from his seat on the chaise lounge to start for home, the ladies begged him to get the autographs of all the stars he undoubtedly met every day, and urged him to tell Jerry Diamond, their favorite announcer, hello for them. They both loved him, they said. The smooth way he talked, his beautiful, deep voice. But Jimmy dodged their questions about what he looked like, what sort of person he really was one-to-one.

"And be careful you don't get electrocuted working around all that juice, Jimmy," Mrs. Polanski called out to him as he cut through the gap in the row of azaleas in her front yard.

He merely waved back an okay. Everyone who found out that he had started the job at WROG was instantly fascinated by the personalities who "talked on the wind," and most usually weren't afraid to ask for favors. Even the kids at school wanted him to get autographs from Elvis and Tab Hunter and Pat Boone, or to see if he could steal some records for them. He acted smug about it, but he secretly loved it when they wanted to know about the station. And especially when they actually listened to him when he talked about it.

Jimmy was almost to the open front door of the duplex, still munching his cookie, when he heard an unusual sound from inside. Grandmama had squealed loudly. That was a sound usually reserved only for the biggest winner on *The $64,000 Question* or *Twenty-one*. Or maybe the sudden, unexpected death of one of her soap opera favorites when he had been written out of a part, killed off so he could show up on another show. He rushed inside to find her sitting on the edge of the sunken couch, hand to mouth, eyes wide and disbelieving, an ash about to drop from the end of a neglected cigarette that trembled between her yellowed fingers.

"Oh, God. Oh, dear Lord."

"Grandmama, what is it?"

The look on her face was awful. They must have finished off Townsend Faulkner on *The Secret Storm*. No other character's demise would cause such abject panic.

"It's the Russians, honey. They just broke in on one of my stories with a news bulletin, Jimmy. The Russians have put up some kind of a space satellite."

Jimmy was perplexed. He wasn't certain what a space satellite was, but it sounded like something from *Captain Midnite,* "presented by Ovaltine."

But he did know one thing. Whatever the Russians did meant worry and fear. His class at school actually enjoyed the monthly atomic-bomb drills because they meant a few minutes of giggling under their desks instead of fighting sleep while sitting in them, a quarter hour without having to listen to Miss Cleveland's drone while they filed outside to check the damage caused by the nuclear blast.

But there was always something else lurking there on their A-bomb larks: the underlying fear that one day the wailing sirens would weep for real. Their simple wooden desks with their murals of carved initials, curse words, and phallic art would offer little protection from the hellish hot wind and flesh-melting radiation.

They had seen the films of tests in the desert somewhere out west, and heard the breathless descriptions on television by those who would ban the bomb for everyone. But Grandmama always cussed viciously when the whine of the conelrad test tone interrupted her shows.

"That damn whining is hurtin' my ears," she'd say. "Where's *Truth or Consequences?*"

But there was always the thought that one day, the announcer behind the civil defense logo on-screen would say the horrible words, "This is *not* a test."

Now Jimmy Gill sat on the cold linoleum floor, absentmindedly eating the last of the tea cake, and listened to the sad-eyed newsman on the television, half afraid of what strange new threat he might be about to report.

". . . and the small capsule has been called *Sputnik* by the Soviets. It will continue to orbit the earth and send back a weak radio signal until its battery runs out. Neither President Eisenhower nor Pentagon spokesmen had any comment about this major space breakthrough by the Russians, but critics of the administration said it is a major blow to . . ."

"Lord, Jimmy! What if they can send down a atom bomb from that thing? Or if they can launch rockets at us like they do on them shows you watch on Saturday mornings?"

She seemed to be on the verge of tears, still shaken, as she slid back into the depths of the couch and took a deep drag on her cigarette. But her panic lasted only until the special bulletin had finished. She immediately locked back into the show interrupted by the newsman. The mushroom cloud left her consciousness immediately as she became lost in yet another tale of misery and pain to be rewarded with furniture and appliances on *Queen for a Day*.

Slowly, Jimmy rose from the floor, dusted the cookie crumbs off his lap, and went outside to his favorite high front step, where he sat and then leaned back on his elbows to get the fullest view possible of the darkening late-afternoon sky. He searched as deeply as he could for the tiniest of lights in the blue going to purple overhead, looking for a glint, a glimmer of something that might be the Russian *Sputnik* satellite as it sped overhead in a path that might carry it directly above Wisteria Street.

He wasn't even sure what he was looking for up there, or that he would know it if he saw it. But he knew that this thing that had happened that day was somehow momentous. The ability to hurl an object into space was stunning, even if it was only a small, practically hollow metal ball. Then, to follow it with tracking equipment as it whisked around the earth almost faster than the eye could see.

Man! It was nothing short of a miracle. The *Buck Rogers* movie serials Detroit and he had mimicked in the woods behind the house were suddenly, instantly, not so far-fetched after all.

Jimmy suddenly jumped. Red lights and a loud roar zoomed across the northern sky above him. But he realized immediately that it was only a Southern Airways plane banking for a landing at the airport across town. Then he caught his breath when he noticed a faint, winking gleam in the middle of the airplane's arc across the sky. But he knew that was only Venus making its regular nightly appearance behind the veil of the orange smoke from the steel mills.

It was getting chilly quickly now, and the stars were popping through the fabric of the sky everywhere while he watched. Somewhere a dog was starting to bark loudly with its first peek at a full moon on the horizon.

A shiver tickled Jimmy Gill's spine.

Up there, so high above his head that he couldn't even see it, something made by the hands of humans was being whipped across the dusky sky by a combination of man's thrust and complicated natural physics. Anyone on the globe with a telescope or the right radio receiver and antenna could see it or hear it. Were it just a bit bigger or brighter, anyone on the face of the planet could look up in the night sky and lock their eyes on the ball.

And just imagine the wonder of it! From the satellite's view at the edge of the pull of the planet, it could look down on all that walked and worked and slept and moved and fought and loved and lived and died way down there below it.

The thought was almost overwhelming to Jimmy. That little ball of shiny steel had the wonderful ability to reach and touch so many from its perch on the highest rung of God's tower.

Chapter 11

So you're the little skinny rascal that's tryin' to steal my job!"

Her black face in the dark hall outside the control room was stern, angry. Then it cracked in half and she erupted into the same cackling laughter Jimmy Gill had heard that afternoon when he had gone in search of Detroit and Ishkooda. It was the woman who had been weeding her yard that day, the one who had chased him back home. And now here she was, confronting him in the hallway at WROG.

But she suddenly seemed friendly enough. She offered him her hand and he took it and shook it.

"I'm Lulu Dooley," she said. "Did you ever find that scoundrel of a nephew of mine you was lookin' for?"

"Nephew?"

"Yeah, Mr. Detroit Simmons. I'm his aunt Lulu. Surely he's been bragging to you about me."

Jimmy was struck by what a small world it could sometimes turn out to be. Lulu Dooley, the maid at WROG who was afraid of the deejays and the transmitter, was Detroit Simmons's aunt.

"No ma'am, I never did find Ishkooda. But me and Detroit play together all the time. We're best buddies, I guess."

"Well, it may be best that you didn't try to find Ishkooda anyway, little mister. You're way too pink and blue-eyed for that neck of the woods!" And she cackled again, then shut it off with a big hand when the On Air light popped alive just above their heads. She waited for it to die out, then turned her head sideways, exactly the way Detroit would do, and pried a little more. "What they pay you to work here, anyhow?"

Lulu looked at him defiantly, daring him not to answer her

nosy question, and he could see even more of Detroit Simmons in that expression.

"Mostly Charlie just gives me old records they don't want, or copies of fan magazines. Maybe a dollar every once in a while. But I don't mind."

Jimmy and Detroit had retrieved a couple of discarded record players from the city dump and Detroit had somehow managed to get them both back into working order. When Jimmy wasn't pulling in stations on the Zenith, he would drag the two turntables to the middle of the bedroom floor, sit down between them, and play disc jockey, just like Jerry Diamond and Rockin' Randy. He wrapped an old sock around a Vienna sausage can and taped it to the end of a broomstick for a microphone. Since Detroit wasn't able to come into Jimmy's house, he would sit under the bedroom window and listen to the songs and Jimmy's high-pitched deejay patter until he would finally get tired and slip on back home to listen to the old radio he had salvaged from the dump and fixed up for himself.

Jimmy Gill rarely noticed that his one-kid listening audience had tuned him out. He'd just keep on spinning the discarded records and gabbing into the sausage can mike and pretending to talk with girls on a make-believe telephone.

"Come on with me," Lulu was saying, "and I'll find you a thing or two to help me. Then I'll give you something better than them old nasty rock-and-roll records." She twirled in her tracks and dusted both sides of the narrow hallway with her bulky hips as she charged back toward the front lobby of the station building. "Skinny as you are, young Mr. Gill, you look like you could use some cat-head biscuits and fried chicken and apple pie for your trouble."

Well, she certainly had his full attention there. He had no choice but to follow her.

In the four months Jimmy had spent time at the station, he had never once been past Big Beulah, the transmitter, Charlie's junky engineering office, or the on-air studio. He noticed that the hallway opened to several offices on the right. Through a large picture window on the left side he could see a large open studio filled with rows of folding chairs, a big square microphone on a stand, and an upright piano.

In one of the offices, an older man that he had seen a time or two in Charlie's office was sitting at a cluttered desk talking on the telephone. He had his shoes off and his stocking feet propped up on stacks of papers that covered the top of the desk. His toupee had slid to one side of a perfectly bald head and he idly scratched his dome as he talked—". . . and that little old station we had in Tuscaloosa had such low power we couldn't be heard more than a couple of miles away. We told sponsors the reason we were weak was because so many folks was tuning in to us that it was sucking all the signal out of the air. . . ."

The next office held one desk, covered with flowers, strands of twisting ivy, an amazing collection of bric-a-brac, souvenirs, and knickknacks, and dozens of framed photos of dark-haired children. There was barely room for the big electric typewriter that hummed and ground away as if in agony. The woman who sat behind the desk pounded the groaning machine wildly and chewed busily a mouthful of gum. She was tiny, almost hidden behind the typewriter and all the junk on her desk. The little woman was sitting high up on a stack of pillows that allowed her to be able to reach the keyboard. She danced in her seat to the music that was playing on the air, piped through a speaker in the corner of the office.

Lulu didn't take time to introduce Jimmy to either of the people in the offices. She must have assumed he knew them, or that he simply didn't need to, and she kept bumping along down the hallway until she came to a stop at a closet at the far end. Her bulk seemed to plug that entire end of the corridor. She pulled open the closet door and dragged out snakelike tubing to attach to a big canister vacuum cleaner.

"My rheumatiz has got me so stove up I can't hardly push and pull this old contraption around no more. Been after Miz Clancy to get me another one but that woman is so tight with money that she squeaks when she walks," Lulu rambled on, more to herself than to Jimmy. "That old biddy has got the first penny she ever made, I swear. She squeezes a dollar so hard that you can hear old President Washington holler."

Jimmy knew who Mrs. Gloria Clancy was. She was the station owner who had inherited WROG outright when her husband, Clarence, had passed away several years before. The woman was well past eighty years old herself, still spry, but in the grip of senility that sometimes bordered on daffiness.

When she made her daily pilgrimage to the station, all speakers were immediately turned down by the first person who spotted her coming. Mrs. Clancy was the only person in the state of Alabama who didn't know what kind of music WROG was playing those days. And the staff wanted to keep it that way.

The old woman assumed it was still the big-band records, the soap operas and quiz shows from the old Blue Network. Or maybe the daily shows with hillbilly music singers and the preachers on Sundays, all originating live from the big studio he had just passed. The shows that had been the bulk of the programming when Clarence Clancy had been alive and ran the station with an iron hand.

Amazingly, Mrs. Clancy didn't seem to notice the rock and roll throbbing from the speakers when she popped her head into the control room every morning at 7:30. She never failed to say hello to Jerry Diamond. If Jerry was in the middle of a live commercial or reading a news report on the air and couldn't return her greeting instantly, she would take a tightly rolled up copy of the *Birmingham Post-Herald* newspaper and whack him hard in the back of the head until he stopped reading to the vast audience and responded to her.

Nowadays, no matter what he was doing, when the boss lady came into his studio, he stopped in the middle of whatever was going on, said a smiling "Good morning, Miz Clancy," and then picked up where he had left off. It had become a regular part of his show, something the listeners actually looked forward to.

"Good morning, Miz Clancy!" It became his trademark, and later it even showed up on T-shirts and bumper stickers and coffee mugs.

"Here, Mr. Jimmy Gill. You can start earning your biscuits by running this vacuum cleaner around in the lobby and then in yonder in the big studio," Lulu was ordering. "Mind you get all them needles that's been falling off the Christmas decorations."

"Yes'm," he acknowledged, happy that he was finally getting a look at the rest of the station, and that some good food might be his eventual reward. He knew, too, that doing more work gave him job security.

The lobby was a big room with a metal desk near the front-door entrance. A bleached-blond woman sat behind the desk and answered the constantly ringing telephone, filing her nails without missing a stroke as she tucked the phone between her head and shoulder and stabbed the buttons with a long red-nailed finger. There were a couple of sagging couches and a table or two lined up along the wall under a bank of windows. The tables were littered with mimeographed WROG station survey sheets that listed the top songs for that particular week in the order of their popularity and featured photos of Jerry Diamond and Rockin' Randy and the other disc jockeys.

Dying cedar limbs and a strand of weak, blinking lights had been hastily tacked to the windowsills in deference to the season, and over in the far corner, a scrawny Christmas tree with a few broken ornaments tilted precariously to the north. Someone had wrapped empty boxes in gaudy paper to simulate real presents under the tree, but they didn't fool Jimmy or anybody else.

He worked vigorously to impress Lulu Dooley and managed to suck up most of the brown, dry cedar needles from the floor. Then he captured a bunch of dust bunnies from under the couch, got the contents of several overflowing ashtrays on the tables, and finally switched off the roar of the vacuum.

He was standing there, proudly surveying the excellent job he had done, already tasting Lulu's fried chicken, when the station's front door flew open behind him with a noisy rush of wind and traffic noise from the superhighway. Someone was in a big hurry to break into the radio station. Two young men, dressed identically in dark pants and black leather jackets over white T-shirts, each with his hair slicked back and cowlicked in the exact same direction, marched inside in tandem. They pivoted on the balls of their feet and quickly canvassed the lobby, as if looking for some kind of trouble that might be awaiting them at WROG.

Apparently satisfied that neither the skinny kid tangled in a nest of vacuum cleaner hoses nor the bleached-blond receptionist with the jangling telephone attached to her ear posed any serious threat to them, they turned back to the door in unison, pushed it open, and motioned to someone outside that the coast was clear, that it was safe to come on inside.

The blond receptionist watched the men's choreographed moves, her eyes huge, and allowed the phone to temporarily go unanswered. Jimmy knew he probably looked as stunned as she did, standing there tied up in the vacuum's hoses, his mouth wide open.

The man who next burst through the door was the skinniest man Jimmy had ever seen. His tight pistol-legged black pants clung to his legs and their bottoms were shoved down into black motorcycle boots that boasted flashy stainless-steel studs. His shirt was black, also, but with colorful embroidered designs criss-crossing its front, and he had a black motorcycle jacket thrown casually across his shoulders.

Jimmy was struck at once by the sharpness of the man's angular features, his high forehead, and the mass of wavy blond hair that was heavily greased and combed back to an arrowhead of a ducktail. Electricity seemed to crackle around him as he moved into the lobby.

He looked around quickly, swaggered to the desk, obviously recognizing and enjoying the effect his presence was having on the blond receptionist. He lifted the telephone receiver from her shoulder, looked at it hard, as if it had insulted him somehow, and then dropped it heavily back into its cradle. That seemed to kill the incessant ringing for the moment.

Then he bent toward the woman and boldly kissed her on her forehead. He said something to her that Jimmy couldn't quite hear over the music from a corner speaker.

It seemed for sure that the woman was going to faint dead away. She turned crimson, her hands clutched together at her breast as if she didn't trust them to behave otherwise. The man held up a hand blindly while he looked into the woman's worshiping eyes. One of the two men behind him read his mind and slipped a ballpoint pen between his fingers. He wrote something with a flourish on the first page of the woman's telephone message pad, then winked at her. She turned even redder and seemed now to be having trouble breathing.

The skinny man turned and spied Jimmy Gill, standing there in the middle of the radio station lobby, apparently being attacked by the boa constrictor vacuum cleaner hoses.

"Hey there, whippersnapper!"

He strode over to Jimmy with a cocky walk, casually reaching for a comb from his back pocket and running it down each side of his head as he approached. Jimmy didn't know whether to run or stand his ground. It was odd. The man seemed so friendly and likable, and yet so threatening and dangerous. And all of it at the same time.

"I guess you'll be wantin' an autograph from old Jerry Lee, too."

Jimmy smelled beer and cigarettes. The skinny man reached to shake his hand and a spark of static electricity leaped from his hand across space to Jimmy's. His grip was firm and confident, but the look in his eyes was just a shade away from animal wild.

It suddenly dawned on Jimmy who this man was. Jerry Lee Lewis. The young challenger to Elvis Presley who, like "the King," also came from Memphis, Tennessee. A rising star who was already dominating the charts and radio airwaves with his manic kind of hillbilly-rooted rock and roll. He reached to thin air again and one of the men immediately produced a glossy photograph from an inside jacket pocket and handed it to him.

"What's your name, whistle-britches?"

"Jimmy," he stammered, but then had a sudden thought. "And could you do one for Mrs. Polanski and Mrs. George? They're my neighbors."

He signed Jimmy's picture, then two more, the handwriting so cockeyed that the names were impossible to read, but Jimmy didn't care. He held the photos at a distance, not wanting to smear the ink before it had time to dry. The pictures were of Jerry Lee, semi-crouched at the front of a stage with a band playing behind him, his blond hair pitched forward over his face, lips seductively close to a huge microphone that he held in both hands, almost as if he were caressing it lovingly. His mouth was set in a snarl revealing blazing white teeth, while girls in the audience below struggled to reach him, to grab him, to claim him as their very own.

Lewis suddenly turned and bolted toward the door to the studio as if someone in there had called out his name.

"Boys, there's a pee-anno in here! Come on!"

And they were after him as he shot through the doorway. The blond receptionist and Jimmy Gill were close behind.

"Goddamn, I've missed playing music while we've been doing all this handshaking and picture-autographing stuff," he yelled to the ceiling, limbering his fingers, doing a quick dance step and a twirl on his toes, then laughing crazily, like a mad scientist about to unleash his self-created monster.

He stepped to the piano that had been placed in the studio for the preachers and gospel singers who still did their Sunday morning shows live on WROG. He sat down on the bench reverently, ran his fingers lovingly along the length of the keyboard, and smiled a dangerous smile. He tickled one of the keys with one finger, doing something that even Jimmy Gill recognized as a caress that implied pure sexuality.

Lightning flashed in his eyes. Quietly, then louder, he began to stroke several of the keys at once, and the sound poured out of the instrument like a flood that wouldn't be dammed up any longer.

Lewis soon was banging the keys violently, stomping the pedals, bouncing on the bench in what appeared to be a fit of ecstasy that bordered on religious fervor. But it was not noise that he was coaxing from the piano with all his wild pounding and foot stomping and crazy gyrations.

It was pure rock and roll. Primal thunder. Sex with shaped notes.

Jimmy couldn't believe how fast Jerry Lee's fingers flew, how he threw his head from side to side with sheer joy and abandon, and then finally kicked the bench away and stood in a crouch, all without missing a beat. He started to sing, a smile still on his face, a tear in one eye.

It was "Great Balls of Fire," even more frenetic and powerful than the record they had all heard so many times already, the version that Jimmy had spun on the twin record players on his bedroom floor. The boy had to sit down quickly in one of the metal folding chairs, the emotion of the moment almost too great for him. For a few seconds, he was sure he would faint dead away. The receptionist was leaning against the wall, fighting a faint herself, still flushed from her kiss from Jerry Lee Lewis.

Rockin' Randy was behind the glass in the control room, bouncing dangerously in the already overtaxed chair, his fat lips open in a wide grin, holding on to his earphones as if they would pop off his head from the sheer force of the music. The On Air light over the studio window was burning hotly. That meant that Randy had opened the studio microphone and was broadcasting Jerry Lee's impromptu concert live to the audience lucky enough to be tuned in to WROG at that magical moment. The torrid licks and the soulful singing were vibrating at 820 kilocycles, pushed out by five thousand watts of signal power all over the southeastern United States.

After another frantic verse and a chorus, Jerry Lee whipped the keyboard lengthwise with his fingers another couple of times, banged the keys mercilessly again, then threw his head back, his blond hair flying, and laughed that maniacal laugh once more.

"Goddamn, this son of a bitch can rock, can't he?"

He screamed it to the studio ceiling, to all gathered in the room, to God, to the uncounted thousands of radio listeners who were eavesdropping.

Randy slapped wildly at the switches on the control-room board, then held his huge head in his hands, glowing red with embarrassment.

Just then, as if on cue, a short, bald man wearing a plaid coat and striped trousers burst through the studio door, arms waving, spit flying, face crimson with anger.

"Damn it, Jerry Lee, we were supposed to meet at WBMH two hours ago! They're the station that's sponsoring this concert tonight, not WROG, and they're fit to be tied already. And then I hear you on the air over here, and we got a sound check at the auditorium in ten minutes."

Lewis slammed down the keyboard cover, gave the man a withering go-to-hell look, and stood menacingly straight out of his crouch, clenching and unclenching his fists. Jimmy thought Lewis was going to hit the little man in the face right then and there. But suddenly, he just looked in Jimmy's direction, grinned, and gave him a sly wink. Then he stepped to where the blond receptionist still leaned against the wall for support and kissed her again, this time square on her red lips. She struggled to keep from collapsing.

"Looky here, boys and girls. We got the music that can make the blind see and the crippled walk, but we got to put up with bastards like these just to let people hear it," he said quietly, to no one in particular. Then he strutted out the door, his bodyguards and the loud little man in the funny clothes close behind them.

Charlie McGee, Lulu Dooley, the tiny woman from the office with the typewriter, and the man with the cockeyed toupee had all stood at the studio window and watched wide-eyed as the scene played out in the sound-deadened room. Except for the slight lingering smell of beer and cigarettes, there was no evidence at all that Jerry Lee Lewis had even been there. That any rock-and-roll magic had just happened right there in front of them.

But when Jimmy Gill glanced over at the old, dusty piano, it seemed to almost still be quivering. Then, almost imperceptibly, it actually did move, the piano's leg on the left rear corner giving way, and it settled at an odd angle. When it hit the floor, the impact of the frame on hard cement coaxed one more soft, melodic note from the instrument's strings.

It was almost as if Jerry Lee's spirit were still in the studio, longing for just one more chord, one more precious stab of pure rock and roll.

Chapter 12

As usual, Christmas Eve was shaping up as no big deal that year. Jimmy had made Grandmama a present, a coaster for her iced-tea glass, carved from a piece of cypress with some cork glued on. Detroit gave him the idea and helped him make it. It had been raggedly wrapped and placed under the tiny cedar tree Jimmy sawed down with a butcher knife out behind the house. They had no ornaments for the tree, so he cut paper strips from the newspaper and made a chain out of them for a garland, and then he found an old forgotten set of colored bulbs in the bottom of a dresser drawer. Only a half dozen of them still burned, but they were the red, yellow, and orange ones, the ones Mama had always thought were the prettiest. He wrapped them around the limbs of the cedar and plugged them into the wall socket.

He almost cried. It might look a tiny bit like Christmas in the duplex on Wisteria after all.

Somehow, Grandmama had been able to afford to buy him a new pair of tennis shoes for school. He had a couple of other packages under the tree that felt suspiciously like a pair of socks and some underwear. She also told him Mrs. Polanski had sent over some ham and dressing and Mrs. George had brought by a fruitcake. Lulu Dooley had given him a pumpkin pie that smelled wonderful through its waxed-paper covering. But he half lied and only told Grandmama that one of the ladies at the station had sent it. Not that it was a colored woman. That way, she would allow them to eat it.

The weather was crisp and dry. Detroit and Jimmy played most of the morning along the highline bank, shooting savage Indians off passing ore trains with stick rifles, or defending the underpass from the onslaught of German soldiers marching in from occupied territory in Ishkooda. But Dee had to leave early for a Christmas Eve get-together with kinfolk down in Bessemer, so the wars had to end by noon.

Grandmama was the only kinfolk Jimmy had, but he didn't want to sit there with her and watch the soaps awkwardly weave the holiday into their sad plots. The lavishly decorated backdrops on the quiz-show sets depressed him, too. All the stations on the big Zenith radio had been given over to Christmas songs and he had grown tired of them a week ago.

Finally, he decided to leave. There was no guilt. He doubted Grandmama would miss him before he came back.

He dove into the bushes in the backyard and headed for the radio station. Charlie had not asked him to work that day, but there was simply nothing for him to do. No other place to go. No one else for him to spend Christmas Eve with.

The back door at WROG was closed against the cold wind but not locked, so he went on in, wishing Big Beulah, the transmitter, a good holiday as he passed her humming, pulsing chamber. The warm red glow inside her huge electronic tubes did bear just a hint of holiday cheer as they winked back at him with what looked like sincere wishes.

Charlie McGee was leaned back in his chair, legs propped up on the desk, sound asleep. Empty, tipped-over Dixie cups were strewn among the junk on the desk. They smelled of well-spiked eggnog, just like Jimmy's mother had celebrated the holiday season with during her last Christmas on earth. The familiar smell made him sad.

Charlie snorted, snored, belched, and then slumbered deeply again. It looked as if Rockin' Randy would have to turn off Big Beulah's high voltage after he played "Dixie" tonight. Charlie McGee usually did that chore, but he was dead to the world.

Jimmy ambled into the hallway, checked the On Air light by habit, and then turned into the control room to wish Randy Mathews a merry Christmas. Lately, when he wasn't on the telephone with a girl, the huge man had begun to invite Jimmy to come on into the control room, to sit down for a while, and to talk with him between records. They had almost become friends.

Sometimes the huge man almost desperately insisted on the

company. Jimmy figured it was only because he was so young that they could be pals. Maybe that was why Randy was able to open up to him, tell him things he was unable to say to the other disc jockeys. They would have almost certainly laughed and made fun. It never occurred to Jimmy Gill to make fun of him. He was glad to be a good listener, honored Randy wanted to confide in him.

And Jimmy had learned a lot about Rockin' Randy during their little talks. He was a hopelessly lonely man, desperately looking for someone, anyone, who would accept his grotesque physique.

He had told Jimmy how badly it hurt to have people attracted to him by his radio voice, his on-air persona, only to be quickly, rudely rejected when the women finally saw him. How the women had been so willing, so anxious, then would laugh or ridicule him cruelly when he showed up in person. Or how others had actually turned and run away in disgust when they eventually met in a bar or café somewhere.

"I lie my ass off to them, Jimmy," he would say. "I tell them I'm six-two, one seventy-five. I even lie about the color of my eyes and I don't even know why that would matter. Shit, I know they'll eventually see me, see how fat I am, but it's good to have them want me for a little while. It'd really be something to have somebody feel the same way about me once she saw what I looked like."

Then he'd laugh and say, "Oh, hell. I guess I just got the perfect face for radio, Jimmy, my boy."

Or he'd slap the counter and promise, "One day I'm gonna lose me some weight and go through all them women like Sherman went through Georgia."

But the hurt would still be in his eyes until the next time he turned on the microphone and spoke. Then it would fade away for a while. Rockin' Randy wasn't one bit repulsive on the radio.

The smell of liquor was almost overpowering when Jimmy pushed open the control-room door that day. More Dixie cups littered the floor. The countertop was covered with paper plates, bits of food, gnawed bones, half-full cups of eggnog and punch.

Jimmy shook his head wearily. It would be his job to clean up most of this mess the day after Christmas.

Randy was swigging more of something green and foamy when he walked into the control room. He belched loudly, then noticed that he had company.

"Hello, Jimmy Gill!" His words were slurred and liquid, his eyes glassy. Grease stains pocked his shirt, and Jimmy couldn't even see the control board in front of the man because of the pile of remnants from the party. "Merry Christmas all over you, you little son of a bitch!"

Through the glass, Jimmy could see that all the metal chairs in the studio had been folded up and leaned against the walls and a table had been erected from a couple of Charlie's sawhorses and sheets of plywood. The final morsels of a Christmas feast littered plastic drop cloths that covered the makeshift banquet table.

There was apparently nobody else at the station. Everyone had gone home to spend Christmas with family. Or maybe to sleep off the party.

From the looks of him, Randy Mathews wasn't going to make it the last twenty minutes before sundown and sign-off, much less to home.

"You okay, Randy?" Jimmy asked.

He didn't seem to hear the boy or even to understand the question, but from force of habit, he somehow managed to cue up another Christmas record on the turntable and send its music spinning out into the cold December air. It was quite a talent to be so damned dexterous when he was so drunk.

"Another Christmas by myself, Jimmy," he finally said between slurps of punch. "Nobody wants no fat-ass hanging around, you know. Hell, I'm too big to even play damn Santa Claus!"

He belched again sourly, made a terrible face, rubbed his chest as if in pain, then reached for some other unidentifiable bit of food amid the heap of rubbish mounded up in front of him. Something from the stack of food fell over onto the turntable where the Christmas song was playing and sent the tonearm skipping with a screech of noise. It didn't faze Randy. He quickly grabbed another disc, centered it on the other spinning table, dropped the needle onto the first groove, and slapped on the mike.

"Here's another song of the season just for you . . . 'White Christmas' . . . Bing Crosby . . . on eight-twenty . . . WROG," he spoke, without a trace of a slur. He had expertly ended his introduction just as the mellow-voiced Crosby started singing about his snowy fantasy. Maybe the man would be able to make it until sign-off after all.

But then Randy stood up suddenly, as if something had prodded him. He seemed more wobbly than normal, his knees cracking loudly as he struggled to stretch upright and get out from between the turntables without tipping them over. Jimmy stepped back quickly to give him room as he squeezed through the doorway, a moving mountain of human flesh staggering to the rest room across the hall.

"That damned record is two minutes and five seconds long. I'll be back, Mr. Gill. I'll be back once I . . ." The door to the rest room slammed shut on his smeared words.

Jimmy wanted to help, but all he could do was hold the control-room door open for Randy's eventual return. It was sure to be a hasty one, and Randy seemed to be having a hard time doing anything hastily this Christmas Eve. Just opening the control-room door might be too tough a task.

He seemed to stay in the rest room forever. For a moment, Jimmy was afraid he might have passed out drunk and wouldn't make it back before Bing Crosby finished the song. But just then, the latch popped and Randy clumsily pushed open the door and tried to get turned to the proper angle to squeeze his bulk back out into the hallway.

He seemed lost, not sure where he was at all. His huge, custom-made jeans were still unfastened, threatening to fall down around his ankles and trip him up, but he managed to grip them with one meaty hand and take a few staggering steps out of the men's room and into the hall, filling it completely with his foul-smelling mass.

Bing Crosby was, by then, on the last verse of the song.

"Better hurry, Randy," Jimmy urged. "The song's about . . ."

But then he noticed the glassy look in the man's heavy-lidded eyes. The sick gray pallor of his pitted, scarred face. The eerie blue tint of his thick lips.

"I don't feel so good, Jimmy," Rockin' Randy said in an odd, pinched voice.

Then Jimmy was afraid the deejay was going to throw up, so he took a step backward, into the control studio, out of range of anything that might happen. But instead of vomiting, Rockin' Randy suddenly pitched forward like a falling radio tower and landed hard, flat on his face. His whole massive body quivered once, twice, and then was deathly still.

Jimmy ran the only direction he could figure to run, through the door into Charlie McGee's office. He desperately tried to shake the drunk engineer awake. But McGee was unconscious, no help at all.

He ran back to where Randy lay and tried to feel his pulse like he had seen the people on television do. At the neck, among the rolls of fat. Nothing. On one huge wrist. There was nothing there either. He listened for his breathing. There had never been a problem hearing Randy's rasping, wheezing breathing before. Now, it was completely silent.

There was no doubt about it. Rockin' Randy Mathews was dead.

Jimmy was in shock. Once again, he had witnessed a man's death right there in front of him. But strangely, only one thought dominated his mind at that awful moment. The monitor speaker on the bathroom wall no longer sounded music. It only clucked a rhythmic, repetitive, clicking sound: the pop of the turntable needle striking the label of the Bing Crosby record over and over as it spun around and around, long since played out.

Five thousand watts of the worst possible thing in radio: dead air!

In a daze, he stepped around Randy's still body on the hallway floor and into the control room. Quickly, he located another Christmas record from a stack of discs next to the mixing board. He dusted the garbage off the other turntable, centered the disk quickly but carefully, laid the needle on the outer edge of it, and turned up the knob marked TT 1 until there was music gushing from the speakers.

Church bells. Violins. A chorus humming peacefully about mangers and stars and wise men.

Then the voice of Perry Como filled the filthy room, and Jimmy turned it up loud, trying to blot out the last few minutes from his mind with the words of "Silent Night." His hands shook violently on the controls and he was near tears. But then something hit him like a punch in the gut.

He was "on the wind"!

He was sitting there in front of the control board, playing songs for God knows how many thousands of people who had tuned in to WROG that late Christmas Eve afternoon. People on the highway trying to get home. People still working, the radio cranked up loud to give them any kind of holiday flavor they could find. People at home, cooking, decorating, wrapping presents, using the station as background for whatever they were doing at that magic moment.

For a few minutes, he completely forgot about the dead man already growing cold on the hallway floor a mere ten feet away. He set up another record, turned the knob on the control board down until it clicked into the cue position, then spun the disc around with his finger until the first note of music roared in the tinny cue speaker under the desk. Then he backed the record up a quarter turn. He waited patiently and hit the switch to kick it off just as Perry Como finished his song.

Seamless. The songs mixed together as if they were meant to be that way. And chills ran all over Jimmy Gill.

He played several more Christmas records. Somehow, he accidentally started one at 78 rpm and blushed as if everyone out there in radioland knew it was Jimmy Gill who had messed up the song, made it sound like a bunch of mice singing instead of the Mormon Tabernacle Choir. He backed one up too far when he cued it and fifteen or twenty seconds went by with no music on the air while it slowly twirled around to the beginning of the song. It seemed like an hour to him! And again, he blushed with embarrassment over his dumb error.

Then the clock above the control board said 4:45. Sundown in December. Time to sign off. Time to play "Dixie." Time to do the speech. Time to go back and put Big Beulah to sleep for the night.

The disc of "Dixie" was hiding under a pile of crumbled cookies and divinity fudge and empty eggnog cups. He wiped it off as best he could on his shirtsleeve and cued it up to its beginning. Then, when the final holiday record faded with a flurry of sleigh bells, he hit the switch on the other turntable and turned up the music. Without hesitating, he flipped the button that opened the microphone, turned the music back down halfway, and spoke the words from memory into the birdcage mike at his lips.

"And so we come to the end of another broadcast day. . . ."

He tried to make his eleven-year-old voice go deep and resonant as Randy and Jerry and the others always did. But there was only the shrill, high-pitched whine of a kid. Somehow, he got through the whole thing with only a stumble or two, raised the music level back up until the needles in front of him danced over into the red zone, let the music play out, then shut down both the turntables.

Only then did he pause for a breath. He was dizzy with a strange exhilaration that flooded through him.

Finally, he remembered why it was that he had been forced to go on the air in the first place. Randy. He had to call for help. He reached for the telephone on its hook at his hip, placed it to his ear, and searched for the rotary dial to call someone, anyone.

There was one problem. He had never used a telephone before in his life, so he really didn't know that there was supposed to be a dial tone there when he put it to his ear. But before he could figure that part out, there was a voice there instead. A sultry, low female voice that tickled his ear and sent chills down his backbone.

"Hello? Anybody there? Who is this?"

"Uh. This is Jimmy Gill."

"Well, Jimmy Gill, huh? I've never heard you on the radio before, Jimmy. But I tell you one thing. You sure do have a sexy voice! What do you look like, darling?"

Jimmy dropped the phone as if it were radioactive, bolted through the doorway, tripped over the mound that had recently been Rockin' Randy Mathews, struggled to his feet again, and ran the length of the hallway to the front door of the station. Its dead bolt was locked and he had no key to open it.

Charlie McGee was even deeper asleep than before when he tried to shake him awake again. He didn't even groan this time.

Then an idea hit him.

Jimmy trotted back toward the control room, hopped over Randy, once again snapped on the main microphone switch, put his lips against the coolness of its metal grille, and begged for someone to help, pleaded for anybody listening to please send an ambulance, to call the police.

Days later, he heard that calls had come in to the Birmingham Police Department from six states and twelve different counties in Alabama, urging them to send help over to WROG.

But having done the only thing he knew to do, and now crying softly, Jimmy made his way to the back steps of the radio station and sat outside in the frigid December air to wait for the help to arrive. The first star of the night flicked on as if its switch had just been thrown by an unseen hand. The tower lights, driven by an automatic timer, suddenly popped to life with their own blinking Christmas Eve display. There were holiday firecrackers snapping away in the distance. He could hear the squeals of kids in the trailer park across the highway from the station. They were obviously excited at the fireworks and about the imminent arrival of Santa Claus.

And just beyond the line of trees, past the pulsing tower beacons, roman candles shot happily into the night sky, scattering the darkness, rending the ether with hot colored fire. They looked to Jimmy just like a human soul might, climbing hard, burning brightly, then sputtering earthward, dying.

Chapter 13

Rockin' Randy Mathews was buried five days after Christmas, a piano crate for a coffin, in the cemetery a few blocks down the superhighway from the WROG studios. It took four men two days to dig the grave by hand. It was carved from two separate plots that had been intended to one day be the resting place for both Randy and his sister.

There were fourteen pallbearers who strained mightily to haul the crate from the back of a flatbed truck to the edge of the grave. The group included Charlie McGee, Jerry Diamond, and the man from the radio-station office with the bad hairpiece. The rest were men who worked in the cemetery. A small crane was brought in to lower the makeshift coffin into the gaping hole in the cold, muddy ground.

Jerry Lee Lewis, Pat Boone, Elvis Presley, and other singing stars had sent notes and flower arrangements. So had dozens of record companies and concert promoters and simple fans of the man's radio show. Most of the cards were addressed to "Rockin' Randy, c/o WROG." Few knew his last name, and those who did misspelled it. The massive bank of flowers was piled in a horseshoe shape around the grave, but they would be snatched up immediately after the funeral service, swiped by souvenir hunters.

Jimmy almost skipped the funeral, since he was sure he had been to too many of the things already. But he went anyway because he felt he owed Randy at least that much. He stood at a distance, though, far from the few family members and the crowd of curiosity seekers who pushed and shoved for a better view of the show. He had trouble hearing the preacher's words as the cold wind snapped them up and carried them away, but somehow, he doubted he was missing much. Those in the crowd didn't seem to be listening to him either as they stretched and stumbled, trying to see the famous names on the flower arrangements.

Then an odd thought entered Jimmy's mind completely uninvited. Some of the women who stood there at the edge of the muddy grave, all black-veiled and sniffling, might have been some of the ones Randy had talked with on the telephone. Maybe the same ones he had arranged to meet and who had fled from the pitiful sight of the real Rockin' Randy. He wondered how they felt then, standing there, watching the rough crate about to be lowered into the earth forever. Did they regret the hurt they had caused? Did they wish they had been more tolerant, that they had given the poor man a chance? He was growing angry, and took a few more steps backward to keep from blurting out something to one of them.

The short service ended with a quick prayer and the cranking up of the crane's smoky diesel engine. Just then, as the crowd was turning away and the chain attached to the crate was drawing taut, a bit of cold light from the late-December sun finally escaped from behind dark clouds that had held it prisoner all day. It was trying to brighten the sad scene that had been playing out under the leafless elms. But something massive and powerful got in the sun's way, throwing a thick shadow across the grave site. Something seemed to be defying the sun, scolding it for finally shining on this man now, when it would do him so little good. Jimmy Gill turned to see what it might be.

It was the bulk of the WROG transmitting tower.

Jimmy decided that Rockin' Randy Mathews would have liked that.

Chapter 14

Jimmy Gill soon learned something important. People have to take their breaks in life where they happen to fall, and there's no point in looking back and wondering why. And he learned that that's especially true in the radio business. The two best ways to advance in the broadcasting industry are to be in the right place at the right time or to have pictures of the boss with a donkey. At least that's what Jerry Diamond had told him one day. Either way, you prosper at someone else's misfortune. And if you don't, someone else will.

When Rockin' Randy Mathews pitched over onto his face and died in the hallway at WROG on Christmas Eve, Scotty Bowman got the big break. He was shifted up from his part-time weekend job and moved right into the afternoon drive-time show where Randy had been. Everybody knew he was ready, and he was instantly a star there.

That put Charlie McGee on the hot seat. He was afraid he was going to be stuck with a dreaded weekend chore that Scotty had always done, and he wanted no part of it. So, out of self-interest, and not because he wanted Jimmy Gill to get his own big break in radio, Charlie talked the manager into letting the kid do it.

He would have to come in early on Sunday mornings and rack up the taped programs of the Holy Roller preachers, watching the tapes as they spooled off on the big recorders in the control room, making certain they didn't break or run out too soon. He would also have to ride the volume controls on the one black quartet and the several ministers who still showed up and did their shows live on the station each weekend.

Charlie knew the kid would always show up and do exactly

what he was told to do. He knew there was no chance of him making a mess or getting drunk or screwing any women in the bushes out back of the building when he was supposed to be cueing up tapes and collecting cash money and writing the preachers their receipts.

Jimmy immediately felt like a radio professional, even though his pay had not changed. He still received a few throwaway records or an occasional gimmick from a record-company promotional campaign. And he still wasn't allowed to turn on the microphone and say anything on the air. They had tapes made to cover every possible emergency, and he was ordered, in no uncertain terms, to use those if anything happened.

"You say anything on the goddamn radio, it better be something like: 'The Russians have just launched the damn missiles so kiss your ass good-bye,' " Charlie warned. "Otherwise, it's your ass that's gonna be gone."

But Jimmy wasn't complaining. He figured he had to be the first twelve-year-old disc jockey in the world.

Most of the time there was only Jimmy and Clifford Snodgrass, the weekend engineer at the station, pulling the Sunday morning shift. Clifford usually slept off the previous night's drunk on a cot set up near Big Beulah's warmth while Jimmy handled the tapes and controls and the money. The old man would only get up from his resting place once or twice each Sunday, for a trip to the bathroom and to fake the meter readings on the transmitter log he was required to keep.

Then, after a month or two, Detroit started tagging along to the station with Jimmy. He would wait out back in the bushes until the gray-haired old engineer would get settled down next to the transmitter. Then, when Clifford would start snoring as loudly as Big Beulah's exhaust fans, Detroit would quietly sneak in the back door, past the cot, and into the studio.

Detroit would spend the time each week keeping Jimmy company or leafing through the Sunday paper. But after a while, he began wandering back to Charlie McGee's engineering office. He liked to fool around with the tools and electronic parts and test equipment that were kept there, and to read the books that were piled on the desk and shelved in a shaky bookcase in a corner. After a few Sundays had passed, Detroit would only make a quick appearance in the control room and then, as soon as he could, he would disappear, headed back to what he called "the shop."

"What the Sam Hill are you doing back there, Dee?" Jimmy finally asked him one morning.

"Nothing."

That wasn't like Detroit Simmons. Usually, a question like that led to a long discourse on the subject at hand.

"Well, you just make sure you don't leave anything out of place, or Charlie McGee will know somebody's been messing with his stuff and he'll come looking for me."

"There's no rhyme or reason for anything back there, Jimmy. I've been arranging everything the way they ought to be for a month now and he hasn't said anything to you yet, has he?"

Jimmy cringed. He could see his budding broadcast career slapped down rudely by the bewhiskered, ill-tempered engineer.

"He'll lynch you if he finds out you're messing around back there! He doesn't care much for nig . . . uh, colored people, you know."

"I'm helping him and he doesn't even know it. Like this morning. I've been matching up all his resistors by their color code so he can find them a lot easier. Then I'm gonna put all the capacitors in boxes, sorted by their values, and put new labels on all those audio transformers."

Jimmy couldn't imagine what a color code or a resistor or the value of a capacitor was. He was mightily impressed that Detroit did.

"You just don't mess up my job for me, Detroit Simmons. That's all I got to say on the matter."

But Detroit was about the most stubborn person Jimmy had ever seen. And he seemed to love his Sunday mornings spent in "the shop." He looked forward to it every week and babbled on and on about all the things he was doing back there, the things he was learning.

Jimmy sometimes left the tapes running and walked back to Charlie McGee's desk, merely to check on him. Detroit would be stringing together the rainbow-coded resistors and flat yellow capacitors and tiny lightbulbs and buzzers on sheets of aluminum or squares of brown perf board, making them blink and flash and hum in some predetermined order. His knack for melding junkyard flotsam together into something useful had led him naturally to his electrical experiments with the circuits in the radio station's back room. Jimmy continued to be amazed and impressed with what Detroit was learning and doing all by himself.

When he wasn't tinkering, Dee seemed to be soaking up all he could read in the electronic books and shop manuals Charlie had left lying about. He devoured pages of schematics and diagrams, and cooked up funny, odd boxes that sometimes smoked and sparked, or burped and beeped, and always had questionable purposes.

One Sunday morning, he appeared in the control-room door, proudly carrying a black metal box. It had a single red button on its face. A piece of plastic label above the button clearly ordered: Do Not Push.

"Whoops. I think I left the soldering iron on. Be right back," he said, and trotted back out of the room. He left the black box lying on the counter, three feet from where Jimmy sat, preparing to switch from a taped show to a live one. Only a half minute passed before curiosity got the best of Jimmy. He dragged the box closer, examined it, shook it, listened to it, read the warning label again, chose to ignore it, and pushed the forbidden button.

A piercing siren inside the box tore open the control room and nothing Jimmy did could make it hush. No matter how hard he pounded the button or slammed the box on the floor or called the thing the few foul names he had learned hanging around the disc jockeys at the station, it only continued its ear-numbing squealing and warbling.

Sister Phoebe Richards and her gospel-singing sidekick, Ralph, were in the big studio getting tuned up for the next show. When they heard the squalling siren, they jumped up in a panic, looking wild-eyed around the studio for the source of the racket. Then they looked at each other and immediately fell to their knees on the studio floor, crying and praying, absolutely certain that the Lord was coming back that very instant with the blaring of angelic trumpets.

Jimmy couldn't silence the beast by beating it to death, so he ran to the bathroom, tossed the noise box into the toilet, closed the lid, and flushed. Only then did the wail give way to the wicked laughter of Detroit Simmons, in the hallway behind him. All the noise, though, had brought back to life the painfully hungover Clifford Snodgrass. He burst through the swinging door in a full charge, stomping and grumbling and cussing whatever it was that had broken his slumber.

"What the hell is that? What's broke? What's on fire?"

Detroit ducked into the toilet to hide, just ahead of Clifford's appearance, but his sniggers almost gave him away.

"What the hell was that noise, kid?"

"I don't have any idea, Clifford. I heard it myself and came looking for it out here."

"Well, it hadda be something."

"Yeah, it sure did."

"Shit! I guess it'll go off again if it was something important, won't it? I feel so bad with this flu that I ain't even got the strength to look for whatever the hell it was."

"And I got another show to get on the air in a second."

"Mind you watch for smoke. Don't let this goddamn place burn down on top of us if that was some kind of fire alarm or something."

"I will, Clifford."

And he was gone, grumbling, back to his sickbed next to the purring Big Beulah.

About a year after he had started his first big job in the broadcasting business, Jimmy found out how much knowledge Detroit had picked up in his experiments in the station's back room. It was a blustery Sunday morning. The two boys had peddled full speed to the station through wind-driven rain and stinging hail.

Thank goodness, Detroit and he had saved up odds and ends and pieces from the junkyard until they could finally put a bike together for Jimmy. He was proud of the bicycle, even though the frame was bent at an odd angle so it looked as if the thing was always traveling down the road sideways. He was especially glad he had it to ride that stormy Sunday morning. Fierce lightning bounced off the boiling clouds and thunder grumbled just as irritably as Charlie McGee and Clifford Snodgrass combined.

Even Big Beulah balked when Clifford goosed her high-voltage button to get her started that morning. Only on the third try did her big contactor switch finally stick and the current begin to flow through her multicolored veins. Her roar and hum rattled the windows, almost as if the old woman were defying the electrical storm that raged outside, daring to challenge her signal with its static.

"Look kid, I gotta go to the store and get me some medicine," Clifford told Jimmy wearily, once he was assured the transmitter was going to stay on the air. "I feel like I'm fixing to die back here. This weather's got my bones achin' like hell. I'll be back directly."

Snodgrass knew it was illegal to leave the transmitter unattended by a licensed engineer, but Jimmy figured the crusty old man must need his anesthetic badly, so he didn't say anything. Surely no Federal Communications Commission inspector would be out and about so early on a Sunday morning. Surely not out inspecting radio stations in such bad weather.

Detroit was glad that Clifford was leaving the station for a while. He could leave his damp hiding place under the back steps sooner and come inside, where it was warm and dry.

They were five minutes into the first religious show of the morning, the tape-recorded *Full Gospel and Holiness Hour* program. Suddenly, all hell broke loose throughout the building. A blinding flash of brilliant lightning scurried up the hallway. There was a sharp crack and a sizzle and then an instant explosion of thunder that threatened to shatter the control room's double-paned windows and knock Jimmy Gill right out of the chair. The headphones hopped right off his head, but he hurriedly felt himself and seemed to all still be there.

Somehow, the lights in the studio only flickered, managing to stay lit through some kind of miracle. But the speakers that should have been rattling with fire-and-brimstone preaching and fevered gospel singing now only spit staccato static crashes and an ominous frying noise.

Big Beulah had obviously been severely injured by the lightning strike.

Detroit had left Jimmy's side and gone to the back room only a few seconds before the lightning bolt's visit. He wanted to get to work on one of his projects while Clifford was gone. But when Jimmy burst through the engineering-office door to check on him, Dee was nowhere to be seen. Smelly black smoke hung in the air everywhere. The atmosphere was electrically charged, saturated with the stench of burning wiring and ozone.

Oh, my God! Jimmy's first horrible thought was that Detroit had been vaporized by the lightning. Completely gobbled up!

But then he noticed the usually locked door to Beulah's cage was open, and he heard Detroit banging around somewhere inside her, talking to the old transmitter the way he did his bicycles while they were under construction and the projects on the workbench as he wired them together.

"Detroit, you stupid so-and-so!" He was relieved to see his friend alive and not a pile of ashes, but at the same time he was furious at finding him in a place where all logic told him he didn't belong. "God help us, Dee! You're gonna get yourself fried to a crisp in there!"

"Aw, the lightning just took out the filament transformer is all," he assured Jimmy. "I can switch it to another winding and get you back on before that old drunk Clifford even knows you're off the air."

"But Dee . . . there's electricity and high voltage all over the place in there and it's still lightning outside like crazy. . . ."

Then Detroit stepped out of the cage, slammed the door hard behind him to set the interlock switch, reached as high as he could reach, and flipped up a huge circuit breaker in a box on the wall, and once again punched the high-voltage button on Beulah's breast. She spat once, balked and bitched a bit, but then finally made up her mind to go ahead and work again. The old woman hummed and purred as if she had been rejuvenated by the jolt of heaven-sent lightning she had just taken.

Jimmy Gill stood in the middle of the engineering office, his mouth open in awe. Detroit Simmons sat back down at Charlie McGee's desk and calmly resumed soldering a mess of twisted wires into a metal chassis as if nothing had happened at all.

The Full Gospel and Holiness Hour Choir happily sang its praise and thanks from the big corner speakers.

Chapter 15

Jimmy knew it was inevitable that Detroit's tinkering and experimenting and hanging around the station would eventually lead to trouble. It led to big trouble. It got Jimmy fired from his Sunday morning job, his first radio job, and got him banished from WROG for good. And it came dangerously close to getting them both shot.

Jimmy had sensed all along that Charlie McGee was suspicious about what was happening in his department at WROG. There was no way he could not know that someone was coming to the station on the weekends, and that whoever it was was using his tools and parts to build things. But he never said anything to Jimmy about it, or mentioned it to anyone else for that matter, as far as the boys knew.

Either he was afraid he would have to start coming to the station on Sundays himself and putting up with the quirky preachers, or he was thankful for what was getting done there in his domain, with or without his permission.

After a couple of years, the station had begun to pay Jimmy Gill a few dollars an hour for his labors. The manager even told him how pleased he was with the way he kept the preacher programs tight together with no dead air. He praised Jimmy for always racking up and playing the correct ones instead of accidentally replaying the same one that ran the last week. He thanked him for cutting off the preachers when their program time was up so they wouldn't run over into somebody else's time, no matter how fervently they were involved in electronically saving souls at the moment. And he was especially pleased with Jimmy for always making sure to collect the cash money before allowing the ministers on the air, and then giving receipts to those preach-

ers who were live and who paid for their segments of time each
week with wrinkled, wadded-up listener-contributed one-dollar
bills.

But Jimmy was growing tired of the dull sameness of it all, of
never getting to play the rock-and-roll records that he loved or to
talk again into the microphone. He did take advantage of the dead
time during the taped programs to flip some of the console's
switches to AUDITION. That gave him a chance to spin records and
do his own "show." But of course nobody could hear it except him
or Dee when he took a break from his mysterious project-building
and sat in the control room with him.

But at least it gave Jimmy the chance to practice lowering his
changing, cracking voice to as much of a baritone as he could muster, to work on his delivery and clever patter until it sounded as
much like Jerry Diamond and the others as he could, and to practice talking over the music at the beginning of records right up to
the point where the singing began the way the pros did it.

Detroit used his time wisely, too, hungrily learning all he could
about the intricacies of the broadcasting and electronic equipment
and the rules of the Federal Communications Commission. He borrowed books and brought them back the next Sunday morning, and
no one seemed to notice them missing. He also continued to use
Charlie's tools and parts to build contraptions and curious boxes.
But he left the workbench and tools so neat and orderly that they
were better organized than before he was there.

Detroit even began to rewire some of the gear in the studio
where the station's commercials were recorded. Years of abuse and
neglect had left them a mess of jury-rigged wiring and makeshift
parts, and all the jocks complained of static and hum and distortion
when they tried to record there. Detroit also cleaned up the rat's
nest of old brittle wiring in the transmitter's control circuits and
redid the heavy cables that delivered power to Big Beulah and
Little Bertha, the one-thousand-watt standby transmitter.

If anyone ever noticed the work getting done, nothing was said.
The station engineers never noticed that things looked neater,
sounded better, worked more dependably. Finally, Detroit even
began leaving Charlie McGee neat schematic drawings of what he
had done, along with carefully lettered notes telling him exactly
what changes had been made, documenting the improvements.

Anyone would have known it couldn't have been the work of Clifford Snodgrass or the other part-time engineers. But still, Charlie McGee said nothing to Jimmy about it, or ever let on that he noticed anything at all going on.

That wasn't unusual, though. Charlie didn't say much to anybody about anything. All along, he had seemed to grow more distant. He was always irritable or preoccupied, even more so than before. And he was gone from the station instantly each night at sunset after the power to Big Beulah had been cut.

One afternoon, Jimmy caught Charlie reading a newspaper that he quickly dropped and tried to hide when he heard him coming, just as he once had his books with pictures of naked women inside. But this paper did not feature unclothed girls. Jimmy saw a fiery cross sketched on its front page, a hooded man holding a sword skyward on the back. The headlines screamed something ugly and angry in bloodred letters that he couldn't quite read before Charlie hid it away.

Just that quick glance at the newspaper reminded Jimmy of the night the crosses were burned on the railroad highline. Just then, and for the first time, he made the connection between Charlie McGee and the man with the chunky wristwatch, the hooded man who had made the sinister salute as he rode away in the pickup truck bed, leaving the flaming cross behind. Charlie caught him staring at him, at his watch, and gave Jimmy a quick, aggravated wave of dismissal. He muttered something about having to do some paperwork and to get the hell out of his way.

It was an odd time, a time of strange feelings for Jimmy Gill. He was so busy trying to avoid schoolwork, hanging out at the radio station, cooking and cleaning for Grandmama and himself, that he hardly noticed the change that hung in the air like the orange smoke from the mills.

It was happening all around him. All over Birmingham. All over the South. The status quo was reeling under the strain of conflict, a clash of ways of life that had torn things right down the middle. But Jimmy Gill spent most of his efforts merely trying to pass ninth-grade math and trying to make his voice go deep and his segues on AUDITION smooth and professional-sounding.

Eventually, he and Detroit talked about what was going on. It frightened him. He was afraid that all that was happening would somehow get in the way of their friendship. And Dee Simmons was the only friend Jimmy Gill had in the world. He didn't know what he would do if something happened to end it.

Jimmy knew better than to discuss such weighty matters as race relations with Grandmama or anyone at WROG. She had her head in a picture tube all the time. The people at the station were wrapped up in the music, sock hops, and selling commercials.

The George twins were about the only other people he had anything to do with and there was little doubt where they stood on the subject of race relations. Jimmy and Detroit had gotten to know Clarice George's boys well since the night their father was killed. The twins usually worked on one of the collection of cars they kept parked in front of the duplex. It was hard to avoid running into them.

Jimmy was especially surprised that Hector George's sons took to the colored boy so readily. Maybe it was because Detroit seemed to know more about the mechanics of their old ragged cars than they did, or because he seemed always to be able to find the exact part they needed or to jury-rig something else if he couldn't. That impressed the hell out of the twins.

Duane and DeWayne were also fascinated by Jimmy Gill's attachment to the radio business. They asked him endless questions about the celebrities and songs and the disc jockeys they listened to. Soon Jimmy was bringing them sacks full of giveaway eight-track tapes and junk records. They loved the rock-and-roll music and played it loudly on the powerful car stereo systems Detroit had put together and sold to them.

In exchange, the twins took Detroit and Jimmy wherever they wanted to go and sometimes let them climb behind the wheels of the cars and drive themselves. Or they shared a can of beer or a cigarette with the boys while they told amazing stories about the girls they had met and conquered in all their exploits.

Lately the twins had not been around so much anymore. Sometimes they would be gone from home for weeks at a time, only showing up to take their mother or Detroit and Jimmy for rides in their ever newer, sleeker, fancier automobiles. Mrs. George proudly told Jimmy that her boys were doing well in their new jobs. That they were running a "transportation co-op" for truck farmers and small businesses around the state.

Jimmy later learned their transportation consisted of rented panel trucks, and the crops they hauled to market for the farmers weren't exactly legal. Their drivers made runs to secluded mountain coves in north Alabama and Georgia, to out-of-the-way bayous around Mobile Bay and east of Pensacola, to sloughs along the Biloxi River on the Mississippi coast, bringing in loads of commodities by the dark of night for a very demanding marketplace.

They were still good for the occasional ride and Jimmy wanted to take advantage when the twins were home. Detroit seemed to have lost interest in hanging around with Duane and DeWayne much anymore. He always had something else to do when they offered him a lift, so Jimmy would stay behind, too. That meant he spent more and more time hanging around WROG, listening to the music, practicing his show in the production room.

That's what he was doing one Saturday afternoon when Charlie McGee finally broke his surly silence to ask Jimmy to help him paint the outbuilding at the base of the tower. He promised him five dollars cash. Jimmy jumped at the chance since he was already saving money for an old car of some kind to replace his warped bicycle.

As they worked that afternoon, the sour little man began to talk to him as he had never done before. He started talking about football. Of how things were going straight to hell at the University of Alabama with the coloreds wanting to go to school there.

"Next thing, old Bear Bryant is going to have to take in a young buck down there. And that'll be the end of it, boy. The end of it all."

Charlie looked frightened; a sad cast moved across his eyes as he viciously swiped white paint against the blackness of the mildewed concrete blocks.

"We got to put a stop to all this uppity nigger stuff, boy," he said loudly, to overcome the demon buzzing of the coils inside the tower building. There was a cold meanness in the man's eyes. A stony evil Jimmy Gill had seen only once before in his life: in the eyes of Hector George the day he chased Detroit Simmons away from the duplex. "It's gonna get real ugly before it's over, boy. Only way to show them is to hurt some of them. Only way to stop them is to kill some of them and show them we're serious. That'll put an end to it once and for all."

The tone of his voice scared Jimmy even more. He pretended to stop painting to wipe the sweat from his eyes. Then, slowly, he worked his way around to the opposite side of the building, as far from Charlie's bitterness and angry raving as he could get.

It didn't matter. The man was determined to have his say. He followed Jimmy around the shack, completely forgetting to paint any more, but continuing his preaching.

"I'd advise you of one thing, Jimmy. Stand clear. When the shooting starts, them that's friendly with the niggers are gonna get shot just as full of holes and get blown up into just as many bits by the dynamite as the coons are. You know what I mean, boy?"

McGee had backed away, watching Jimmy, and he stood there trembling with emotion in the knee-high grass as his brush dripped paint. Jimmy let the arcing and hissing of the transmitting coils serve as his only answer and kept vigorously swiping his brush across the cement blocks.

They had made quick work of the paint job. Almost finished, Jimmy was anxious to get his five dollars and deposit it in the sock in his bedroom. And he didn't want to hear any more of Charlie's dark words.

The sun had dipped below the trees at the far edge of the field and darkness was threatening to catch them. Just then, the first fuzzy drumbeats of "Dixie" signaled it was sign-off time, and its buzz drowned out any other warnings the old man might want to spew at him.

As they gathered up their buckets and brushes, the last of the noise from inside the outbuilding faded away. "Dixie" was over. The transmitter would be turned off momentarily.

Suddenly, though, Charlie McGee stopped his work, cocked his head to one side, and cupped his paint-splattered hand to an ear. He seemed to be listening to the breeze droning through the tower supports and guy wires that stretched high above their heads.

"What the hell was that, Jimmy?"

He had not heard anything but a couple of crows fussing as they played across the field from them. He told him so.

"You don't hear that squeakin' and squawkin' in the matching coils?"

"No, Charlie, I don't. . . ."

But the engineer had taken off toward the station building at a full gallop. Weighted down by the buckets and brushes, Jimmy had to trot to try to keep up. Charlie burst through the back door of the station, almost running over the part-time engineer who was about to pull the main power switch on Big Beulah. He stomped through the door and down the hallway for the control room, now dark, quiet, and deserted, the "broadcast day" done.

"Dixie" had recently been recorded on one of the new continuous-loop tape cartridges. The old scratchy disc recording of the song had been put away on a shelf. The tape machines had been an important development for radio stations. The song or commercial announcement was always cued to the beginning, ready to play instantly when a button was pushed on the new tape players. Charlie had tried to install them, but their sound had been muddy and distorted at first. Detroit had done the job correctly the next Sunday morning and they had worked well ever since.

Charlie McGee jerked the tape cartridge from the rack where it lived in the control room and slammed it into one of the machines stacked on the counter. He cranked up the knob on the control console, slapped the machine's start button hard with the punch of a fist, then listened as the band instantly played loudly, happily, all the way through. Trombones, fifes, and snare drums bounced off the carpeted walls of the tiny room. Jimmy couldn't help it. He tapped his foot on the floor to the happy beat.

Then the music ended with a flourish of flutes, and there was only the hiss of tape and the slight rumble and pop of the needle in the record's groove, just as it had been recorded on the cartridge.

"Bloop-bleep-bleep-blonk-bleepity-bloop-squeak-squeak!"

Jesus! The sudden loud series of tones almost deafened them both. Charlie's eyes lit up like coals of fire. He jerked the plastic tape cartridge from its slot in the playback machine the instant it stopped and rushed back out the control room door. Jimmy followed him again, now even more confused. He had never before noticed the noise on the tape after "Dixie."

Charlie stood at his desk and held a small black box in his hands, twisting and turning it around as he studied it intently. Jimmy couldn't imagine what he was looking for.

"You ever seen this contraption before?"

Jimmy shook his head. He said, "Never saw it before."

It was one of Detroit's experimental projects, just like the screaming black box that had to be flushed to silence it. Jimmy knew that. He had seen him working on it and several more just like it.

"I found this box under some stuff on that shelf over there the other day. First I thought it was something Clifford might be working on, but that old drunk ain't got the sense to do any work this pretty. The goddamn solder joints are perfect. Holes in the chassis are punched out just right. And whoever did it used some new components I don't even know what are yet. Solid-state goddamn Japanese transistor shit. I got me an idea, though. . . ."

He spun quickly and dashed into the production studio, then plugged the cord attached to the strange box into a power socket and set it down on the shelf in front of a speaker. He gave it a few seconds to warm up, then shoved the "Dixie" tape cartridge into a player on the shelf and punched it off. When the music finished and the squeaks and squeals on the end of the tape rattled the speaker, something strange happened to Detroit's black box. A series of letters and numbers in a window on the front of the thing suddenly began flipping over with each squeak and squeal, one at a time, in perfect order, as if riffled by an unseen finger.

They read "300315N."

Charlie held the box out to show it to Jimmy. His hands were shaking. He had developed a twitch in his right cheek.

"It's that damn nigger, ain't it, Jimmy? That damn nigger buddy of yours. What's the little bastard been doing here in my shop?"

He was quietly livid, the maddest Jimmy had seen him since the day he had chased him off the tower. He grabbed up the black box, ripped its cord from the wall socket, turned suddenly, and trotted toward the back door of the station.

Sure enough, Detroit was there, waiting in the dark shadows of the building for Jimmy to finish washing his paintbrushes and ride home with him. Somehow, Charlie had known he would be there. Before Detroit could hide, the old man threw the box at him hard, well aimed, and only a quick duck and a dodge kept Detroit from getting hit square in his stomach.

"What the goddamn hell are you doing with my radio station, you little black bastard?"

Charlie fairly spat the question, stomping his feet with each of the words. Jimmy was afraid the dirty little man's head was going to explode like a cherry bomb in a watermelon.

Detroit stepped bravely from the shadows. He obviously saw McGee had nothing else to throw at him and no gun to shoot him. There was an odd, defiant look on his face, in his eyes. Jimmy had seen it the day Hector George had appeared on the porch with the shotgun.

He wanted to warn his friend, to scream at him to run, to get on home to Ishkooda before Charlie fetched the nickel-plated revolver Jimmy knew he kept in his middle desk drawer in his office. The old man seemed, at that very moment, just mad enough to use it. But before Jimmy could squeak out a word, Detroit was answering the question.

"There's one of those boxes sitting right next to the radios in a dozen houses all around Birmingham. The houses belong to colored ministers. They are the preachers who are leading the protest marches for Dr. Martin Luther King."

Detroit was speaking calmly, deliberately, his voice so low, so different from any tone Jimmy had ever heard from him that he could hardly make out what he was saying.

"The tones on the tape control the numbers and letters on the display on the front of the box. They let the ministers know exactly where and when the marches are going to be held so they can tell their congregations. The colored stations announce it, too, but their frequencies are so bad and their power is so low, some can't hear them. I record the stuff on the tail end of the sign-off tape cartridge so it can play after 'Dixie' and before the transmitter switch is pulled. Three in the afternoon, Third Avenue and Fifteenth Street North. That's what that one said that you have there. Everybody in town will know where the march is tomorrow, thanks to WROG."

Jimmy was stunned, amazed Detroit had hatched such a plot without him even knowing about it. Maybe he was a little hurt that he had been left out of the scheme. But at that very moment, he was mostly afraid that Charlie McGee was going to shoot or strangle Detroit right there behind the radio station.

The skinny old man surprised him, though. He just sank back down to sit on the step, his head in his hands, disbelieving, and

Jimmy took advantage of the chance to scoot around him, grab Detroit, and try to make their getaway.

They jerked up their bikes, jumped on them in a full run, and pointed them up the drive and toward escape along the highway. They only turned back to look when Charlie McGee screamed at them in a voice that sounded like metal on metal.

"Either of you ever come back around here again, I'll string y'all up my own damn self!"

He shook his fist, then reached down for handfuls of gravel from the drive and hurled them toward the fleeing boys, stomping around the backyard of WROG in a blind rage.

The next time Jimmy Gill saw Charlie McGee's face, it was only a grainy black-and-white photo, glaring out at him from the front page of the *Birmingham News*. The dim eyes and face full of whiskers were just under a headline proclaiming arrests in connection with the bombing of several houses in North Birmingham. In a place called "Dynamite Hill." In a city dubbed "Bombingham."

Jimmy fussed at Detroit for not telling him about what he was doing. But it was hard to stay mad at him when he saw the pride in his face every time he talked about it.

It had been his aunt, Lulu Dooley, who had first talked with Detroit about the scheme. She knew how inventive he had become, how knowledgeable he was with the electronic mysteries in the radio-station shop. The ministers were looking for a way to efficiently notify everyone where the marches would begin without Bull Conner and his police or the Klan finding out beforehand. If they found out, they could barricade the street or gather a crowd of ruffians to try to disrupt the demonstration.

Of course, neither of the boys told anyone about Lulu's role in the whole thing. She continued to work at WROG. But Jimmy was finished there. He had been fired from a radio job for the first time at fourteen years old.

And it didn't discourage him. It only strengthened his resolve, aimed him like the pointer on a radio dial toward where he had to go. He knew what he wanted to do now. No, what he *had* to do.

Jimmy Gill had vowed to himself that he would one day reach the point where he could control his own destiny. That he would arrive at the place where he could truly touch people with his voice and a blend of songs. Have them listen to him. Hang on his words.

After the showdown with Charlie McGee, Jimmy would spend long nights in front of the Zenith, his schoolbooks practically untouched. And there, with the music pounding and the announcers talking, he began to lay his plans and dream his dreams.

It was no different from chasing the signals on the radio as they drifted in and out, up and down the broadcast band.

WBMH

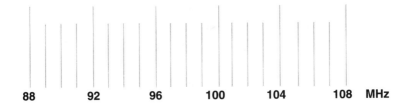

88   92   96   100   104   108   MHz

Damn it! You're either the damn stupidest black man or the damn blackest stupid man I've ever seen, Detroit Simmons!"

The cuss fit didn't seem to be bothering Detroit at all. He kept on tinkering at some project spread out before him on the workbench, a tongue of smoke from his soldering iron curling around his head like a halo, as he completely ignored Jimmy Gill's frustrated fussing. Jimmy stood there for a moment, angrily clenching and unclenching his fists, then spun around quickly and left Dee sitting there.

He didn't have time to stay and try to do any more convincing at that very moment. The Monkees were involved in the last screams of "I'm a Believer," and even the insomniacs who might be awake at 4:30 in the morning didn't appreciate it when their music stopped cold and wasn't followed up immediately by something just as inane and juvenile.

For his part, Dee wasn't sure he was up to hearing any more wild schemes from Jimmy. Not when the modulation monitor needed calibrating and the newsroom headset amplifier was on the fritz.

"Home of the Good Guys . . . ninety-seven B-M-H . . . Jimmy Steele here with Question Mark and the Mysterians!"

His own voice in the headphones sounded high-pitched, strained, and syrupy. He immediately dropped the silly grin on his face like a heavy load as soon as the mike was killed. But that's what they insisted on at WBMH. A smile in the voice. Excitement in every word. Scream! Yell! Push! Never be down or subdued. Never sound natural or conversational. Heavens no! And God forbid that you sounded at all like a normal human being talking one-on-one to another normal human being. Jimmy angrily twisted up the volume on the inept organ riff at the start of the song but just as quickly spun down the monitor control so he didn't have to hear the damn song for the fourth damn time since his damn shift had started at damn midnight.

He was really getting fed up with teenybopper radio. With bubblegum music. With teenage girls and drug addicts on the telephone all night. People who didn't give a shit what music he was spinning, as long as it was noise in the nighttime to keep them company in their miserable existence.

When Jimmy looked up, Detroit stood in the studio doorway, a twisted link of solder in the corner of his mouth. He was still shaking his head in wonder at what Jimmy had been telling him before he had to rush off to the studio to catch the song's ending. He had decided to humor Jimmy. Why not?

"Where in hell do you get all these crazy ideas, Jimmy Gill?"

"It's not crazy, Detroit. We can do it. We can get that Nashville FM license, and there are lots of people out there who would listen to a radio station that played something besides this shit. Damn good music! There's money to be made and it might just as well be us that make it."

"But what makes you think you can get a radio-station license, Jimmy? You're just a skinny, longhaired midnight-to-six jock, barely twenty-six years old. And here you are talking about putting a damn radio station on the air!"

"Yeah, but I know what I'm doing. I've got a plan, Dee. And it will work. You'll see!"

The revelation of his surefire plan was interrupted again by the fadeaway ending of the song, a screeching jingle on a tape cart and the segue into a Herman's Hermits record on the back turntable. And by the agitated arrival of Wacky Jack Bruno, the morning newsman.

Jack was tall and thin, with a voice like God, but, as usual, he didn't notice Jimmy or Detroit when he burst into the control room like an Old Spice–scented cyclone. His pants were unzipped, his shirtsleeves were unbuttoned and flapping like wings, a screaming paisley necktie was draped around a flipped-up collar, and his shoes on sockless feet were untied, the laces threatening to send him sprawling as he exploded into the room. A comb was still stuck in a partial part in his long, thick gray hair, and a dab of shaving cream clung stubbornly to his cheek. As he staggered into the control room, he dropped a twisted pair of headphones near the small desk where he would deliver the news twice per hour during the morning drive-time show, then kicked off his shoes.

He had a sheaf of Teletype paper ripped from the machine down the hall wadded under one arm, and, as he did every morning, weather permitting, Jack stumbled groggily over to the lone control-room window, lifted it, and climbed outside onto the twelve-inch-wide ledge. He always preferred sitting on the ledge in the cool predawn air, bare feet dangling seventeen floors over downtown Birmingham, as he culled stories to use on his newscasts. As he edited, he allowed the rest of the rejected wire copy to drift down like huge yellow snowflakes to the streets below. As he worked, he reached for doughnuts and sweet rolls he kept hidden away in various pants or coat pockets and sipped steaming coffee from a paper cup. He would alternate bass-voiced belches while trying out the news stories aloud, reading them to the pigeons who joined him on the ledge to hear the latest news of the day and to share his pastry.

Sometimes he got a notion to stand up and wander along the ledge, to take a piss off the side, to dance to music that only he could hear. He would often yell at janitors and early arrivers in adjoining buildings or at the morning disc jockey at WBMH, Doug Dempsey, as he parked his car in the lot directly but far down below him. Doug would yell back, angrily shake his fist up at the loony newsman, and Jack would sail a cruller down at him with practiced accuracy and a maniacal laugh.

No one ever questioned how Wacky Jack got his name, but someone said he had actually calmed down since he quit jocking and became a newsreader.

Jimmy had been doing the overnight shift at WBMH for a couple of years by then. After WROG, he had finally given up on his education, quitting that school foolishness altogether while halfway through the eleventh grade. Then he had worked mowing grass at the cemetery for a while and as a gofer at a foundry. A tiny radio station south of town let him do a few shows on the weekend for no pay and another one twenty miles farther down the highway hired him to mow the lawn, take out the trash, and do an occasional on-air shift.

Then he got a full-time overnight job at a station in Montgomery. He was Jim Gilbreath. He made enough money to send Grandmama a few dollars to supplement her Social Security. That job led to a 10 P.M. to 2 A.M. show in Augusta, where he was Jim McGill, but he soon got fired from there when a new program director told him he talked too much and he wanted to bring in his own man. He landed a weekend job in Pensacola that barely paid his flophouse rent, then took a seven-to-midnight shift in Jackson. He was Jim Gilroy there and made enough money to buy an old car and Grandmama a birthday present. But it only lasted until the station was sold and the new people told him he was an egomaniac and the format changed to country and western with a whole new lineup of announcers brought in over a weekend, all while no one noticed. His severance had been a free trade-out pizza from a local restaurant, an oil change from a car dealership, and a "Thanks . . . good luck." He worked several other stations, from overnights to afternoon drive time. The story was always the same.

"You don't take direction, Gill. Good-bye."

"We don't need somebody who can't follow the format, kid."

"You'd be a great jock if you'd learn the music is what they listen for and not you running your mouth."

Fate or blind luck had finally brought him to WBMH after two months "on the beach." He spent most of that dead time watching television with Grandmama or visiting with Duane and DeWayne George the rare times they were home.

He had had a good time at each of the stations, but he still missed something he had never actually had. Being "on the big wind." Missed it as badly as he might have breathing or eating. The puny jobs in Montgomery and Augusta and Jackson had each been on shows late at night, when the little AM stations' power had been lowered to protect some other weakling halfway across the country, or the signal had been aimed narrowly directional in deference to the Canadian or Mexican border. None of the stations were important, the ones with the big "numbers" and thousands of listeners and megadollars of advertising on their air.

He had longed for the strength of the more powerful stations.

The Number Ones. He had hungered for any chance to sate his radio appetite, the craving that had only been whetted with the parade of also-ran stations he had graced with his presence and who had lacked the vision to let him help them to the top.

Then a chance came. The overnight guy quit WBMH to begin a career preaching in a Holiness church. BMH was now the top-rated Top 40 station in town, full-time, with high nighttime power and a nondirectional signal. WROG, with its daytime-only broadcast day, had long since been left in the dust and was an also-ran. Jimmy figured he must have been the only one who had wanted the terrible hours and minuscule pay of overnight radio, but he leaped at the chance to get back on the air in his hometown with a station that mattered—even if his show was on the air at a time when only a few shift workers and the various drunks and burglars and night crawlers made up his entire audience. At least they could hear him. And at least he had his foot in the door. He could eventually move to seven-to-midnight. Then middays. Then, God willing, drive time. But the long hours also gave Jimmy time to think, to scheme, to plan. And to develop an idea.

In a roundabout way, Detroit Simmons had come along with him to WBMH. The timing was perfect because the Federal Communications Commission, the agency that regulates radio stations, had finally started pushing for more minorities to be given a chance to break into the business. Detroit had quit school when he turned sixteen, about the same time as Jimmy, but he attended classes at a technical school in nearby Bessemer, where he taught the staff there a few things about electronics and got his first-class engineer's license. Until then, no one in radio wanted to hire him. He had been working as an electrician's helper at minimum wage. As soon as Jimmy heard the station needed another engineer, he told them about Detroit. WBMH was glad for the chance to have a colored engineer sit there and watch the transmitter meters overnight, filling a quiet quota for little pay.

Detroit used the long, empty hours to good advantage as he learned to design and build more black boxes and blinking circuit boards. He devoured every book and equipment manual and FCC rule book in the station, and was soon rebuilding everything in sight as he had at WROG. As long as the stuff worked and didn't make their jobs any harder, the other engineers didn't give a damn.

Jimmy was happy to be working again with his best friend. They had kept in touch while Jimmy made the southern radio circuit and Detroit soaked up all the electronics he could hold. But Jimmy had plans he needed to share and he was impatient, anxious to finally tell Detroit how crucially he figured in the whole scheme.

Everything was falling into place and he couldn't wait to talk about it. But it was proving impossible to do while he was on the air. The Top 40 songs he played at WBMH were short, so he had to rip off a line of clever patter or punch a series of buttons to play jingles, sound effects, and commercials after every single one. It required concentration, even from somebody like Jimmy who could do the whole routine by rote.

Then Leon called just as he was about to approach Dee again. God, why had he answered the telephone? Other than the fact that the program director threatened to fire them if they didn't pick up the request line by the third ring.

Leon was an older black man who had begun calling shortly after Jimmy started at the station. He always began his conversations with praise for how Jimmy ran his show, how much pleasure Leon got from listening to his "wonderful voice." Then he would quickly move to offers of "presents," money or whiskey or his wife's home cooking, if Jimmy would come by and pick them up.

"Mr. Steele?" he would say. "I just wanted to let you know how much I appreciate your fine program. I've got you a little gift to let you know how much I appreciate your beautiful voice and all the happy music you send out. Can you run by the house?"

"I can't talk this morning, Leon. Thanks for calling."

He knew Leon was only trying to hit on him, and he had to talk with Detroit. Jimmy rudely hung up the telephone before Leon could say more.

And then Doug Dempsey stumbled into the control room. He was in a foul mood as usual, cursing Wacky Jack Bruno, the goddamn elevator, the goddamn air-conditioning in the goddamn studio, the goddamn bitter-ass coffee. It had always been a mystery to Jimmy how Doug Dempsey could be so stunningly happy and naturally funny when he was on the air yet instantly become so dismally, perpetually unpleasant when he wasn't.

No matter. Dempsey's tenure was to be short-lived at WBMH. His career was soon to be redirected by management when his ratings dipped for two Hooper surveys in a row. The man found out about his firing when the security guard in the bank lobby downstairs refused to allow him to get onto the elevator one morning. That's how WBMH usually informed employees that their talents no longer fit into the long-range plans of the radio station. Dempsey went on to work at stations in Jackson, Houston, Dallas, Oklahoma City, Tulsa, and Tupelo, and then dropped out of sight, his career the typical bell-shaped curve of radio success.

When it became clear to Jimmy that he would not have a chance to make his case, he finally ordered Detroit to meet him in the doughnut shop a half block away when he got off his engineering shift at seven. Jimmy promised he would lay out the program for him then, and swore that once he heard the whole story, he'd be as excited as Jimmy was. Somehow, Jimmy would have to transfer his confidence and his enthusiasm to Detroit. He was a major cog in the machine. Dee was the conservative one, more interested in tinkering in the shop than in building empires. He would be a tough sell. But Jimmy thought Detroit Simmons would be the first of many.

"Jimmy, you know I got to get to my other job by eight. I can't live on what folks in radio pay me."

"Dee, listen to me. It will be worth your while. Trust me!"

"It damn well better be. If I call in sick . . ."

Jimmy grinned and tripped a switch that sent yet another record spinning, opened the mike and screamed the artist's name and the song's title and some inanity that almost made him sick just speaking it.

Detroit was almost seven-thirty arriving at the doughnut shop, but he had a unique pair of excuses. Any other business and they would have been too far-fetched to believe. Not in radio, though.

It seems Miss Nude America had shown up to appear on the morning show and had stripped to her birthday suit in the middle of the control room while Doug and Wacky Jack breathlessly described the whole thing to their audience. Dee had suddenly found some transmitter logs that needed checking or some trumped-up chore to keep him there until the buxom young woman had put her clothes back on.

Then, three members of Paul Revere and the Raiders were in the bank lobby downstairs with an entourage of girls, trying to convince the guard they should let them all on the elevator up to the radio station. Dee waded through the riot to get out of the building and found Jimmy rehearsing the sales pitch to his cup of coffee and his jelly doughnut.

The two men ignored the bird-eyed stares of the denim-clad rednecks and the double-breasted lawyers and the jabbering store clerks perched all around them in the Krispy Kreme. They gawked and clucked curiously at the skinny, longhaired white guy in his Allman Brothers T-shirt, wearing an earring, talking to his food. They clucked at the muscular young black man with the pronounced Afro who joined him in the booth. Detroit and Jimmy were used to it. They knew they made an odd pair.

As he talked, Jimmy munched lemon-filled doughnuts and gulped scalding coffee, while Detroit kept his head down and listened quietly, forming pyramids with sugar packets and grunting occasionally as the plan was laid out for him.

"The FM license in Nashville is up for grabs, Dee. There's only one other applicant who is going to try for it. He's some old guy who owns a store where he sells radios and stereos. He wants to use the station to sell records and hi-fi systems, sort of like a live demonstration thing. He thinks people will buy equipment to hear what he's going to put on the air. You ought to see the programming plan he's filed, Dee. He's just gonna play jazz and classical music all day and run ten minutes of news every hour from the network and sign the son of a bitch off at five o'clock every afternoon. It won't even be on the air on weekends at all! He's not even applying for full power or antenna height!"

Detroit was busily building the largest existing sugar-packet pyramid in the free world. He had not looked up since Jimmy had begun his pitch. There was no indication he had heard a word so far except for the way he chewed on his lower lip.

"Nobody thinks FM is going to do anything, Dee. They all think it's a wasted hunk of frequency spectrum, just for audiophiles and the like. But by God, it will! Think of all the great music that's out there and how fantastic it would sound in stereo, as crystal clear as any record or tape player! No static at all, not even in the summertime! Not even in the middle of a damn thunderstorm!"

Jimmy knew the technical stuff would draw in Detroit. It always did. Dee believed in FM's future already. Hell, he was the one who had first convinced Jimmy it would one day be as viable as AM. Maybe even more popular than AM radio, he had said, once people heard how much better it sounded, how much fuller and more lifelike the stereo imaging made the music, how the signal didn't drop away to a buzz when the car passed under power lines.

"I've been out there, Dee. I know what people want to hear. I've had to sit there on the request line and tell them I couldn't play it for them. There's a whole other world of music that isn't making its way to the air. The Allman Brothers, Jimi Hendrix, the Rolling Stones, the Beatles songs that weren't big hits . . . great stuff that nobody is playing on AM Top Forty radio. None of this teenybopper crap! Led Zeppelin, the Animals, Bob Dylan, the Who! Damn, there's so much great rock and roll out there that nobody gets to hear unless they buy the records! We can do it, Dee! We can do it!"

Jimmy realized that he was almost yelling, pounding the table with his empty coffee cup. The waitress was giving him a scowling, worried look. She probably thought this was another drunk or druggie on the verge of freaking out right there in the middle of her shop.

Detroit glanced up but didn't look Jimmy directly in the eye. Instead, he watched a spot somewhere over his right shoulder when he spoke.

"Where the hell are you going to get the money to file for the license? Or to pay for all the legal stuff and the engineering work? And then, where are you going to get the money to actually build the station if, by some freak accident, you do get the license grant? Who'd run the thing? Who would handle sales? And look at yourself, Jimmy Gill. You're not exactly corporate America, you know. No offense, but you are a freak, man. What makes you think that you, of all people, can even get a radio-station license? Then run the damn thing if you did?"

Those were the easy questions. Jimmy smiled.

"Because I have you, Dee. And you are a black man, in case you haven't noticed lately!"

Detroit gave Jimmy a look then that he had come to know so well. The one usually followed by: "You are as crazy as a bessie bug!" He finally looked Jimmy in the eye and grinned crookedly at him.

"What the hell have you been smoking?" To Detroit, that was the only explanation for such carryings-on.

"Congratulations, Mr. Simmons! I'm surprised you haven't heard already. The board of directors just yesterday named you the president of Wizard Broadcasting Company, Incorporated."

Detroit sat back in the booth quickly, knocking over his towering, sweet pyramid, and stared, wide-eyed and openmouthed. A red-faced construction worker in the booth behind him twisted around, glared, and grumbled when the sudden bump caused him to spill his coffee.

"We're sure to get the license when our top corporate officer is a bona fide, full-blooded, certified Negro. You know the FCC is very partial to minority ownership these days. And just to make double-damn sure, your aunt Lulu Dooley is already on our board of directors. And Mrs. Polanski and Mrs. George are voting members, too. They are both putting up some of their own money. A few dollars each, for sure, but that's not the point. With all of them, that gives us a board made up of a black man, two women, and one director that's both female and black! It's in the damn bag, Dee!"

Jimmy thought Detroit was going to keel over face first into the white pile of spilled sugar packets. He seemed to be gasping for air, like a man awakened in the middle of a dream. The construction worker was cocking an ear their way now, trying to hear, while an elderly couple in the next booth stared disapprovingly at all the commotion and arm waving Jimmy was doing. But they tried to eavesdrop, too.

"You still won't have enough money to get it going," Dee finally stammered. "Not from that bunch of folks. They don't have the kind of money it will take. A tower, transmitters, studios, operating capital, real estate. You would need a quarter million dollars or more just to start, and lots more to make a payroll, utility deposits . . . you know."

He seemed to have suddenly run out of steam just thinking about the financial mountain they would face climbing with such a venture.

"We actually need a half million to seven hundred thousand to do it right, I figure, but I got it all covered. You can do all the engineering. We can lease most of the equipment. Cash flow will certainly take care of the salaries in a few months unless I'm totally wrong about the potential. And I'm not. We can safely guarantee enough rating points to sell a ton of spots out of the chute, and before you know it, we'll be making our nut and have the whole thing into the black . . . so to speak." Jimmy paused and took a deep breath, then plowed on before Detroit could sense that the next part was being spoken with a little less enthusiasm, spit out hurriedly to blunt the effect. "And we have one more ace in the hole. Duane and DeWayne George have agreed to bankroll us, no matter what it ends up costing. We've got a blank check from them, Dee."

Detroit Simmons stood up so abruptly, so violently, that he jarred the construction worker behind him hard, sending his just-refilled coffee mug and his half-eaten sweet roll skidding off the table and into his lap. The old man at the table next to them was so surprised by the sudden movement that he choked on his doughnut. His wife jumped up and began pounding him on his back before he could choke to death. The waitress behind the glass case made a move toward the pay phone on the back wall, set to call the law if the two freaky-looking men started to fight.

By then, Detroit had twisted out of the booth and stormed out the door. The waitress watched him wide-eyed, relieved that the troublemakers might be leaving, taking their scuffle out into the street.

Jimmy ignored the construction worker's threatening looks, left a dollar tip on the table, and sprinted after Dee, but he was taking such big steps that he was a half block away before Jimmy could even get out the door and onto the crowded sidewalk. Jimmy ran hard to catch up, calling his name, shoving aside window-shoppers and office workers who got in his way.

Damn! He should have found a better way to bring up the involvement of the George twins. He should have set the hook deeper before he tried to reel Dee in, not just blurted it out like that. He should have known what Detroit's first reaction would be.

When their mother casually mentioned to Duane and De-Wayne about Jimmy Gill's plans to put a radio station on the air in Nashville, they immediately told her of their need to "invest"

some money for "tax reasons." They sent word to Jimmy that they
would be willing to put in all the money that was needed, no questions asked. The only stipulation was that they eventually be paid
back with generous interest as the business improved, but only by
check, and those checks would have to be drawn on a different
bank than the one where the original money was deposited. They
would establish the operating account with stacks of cash in small
bills deposited over a long period of time. The exact source of that
investment capital would, of course, have to remain confidential.
The Georges wished to remain the most silent of silent partners.

Jimmy wasn't naive. He knew the drill and the reasons for the
odd requirements of his investors. But it was the only way to accomplish this thing that he had only been able to dream about up
until then. He would have to ignore the shadiness of it all. After
all, the George twins' money would spend like anybody else's. And
they seemed to have plenty of it to contribute to the cause.

But now the most important part of the entire Wizard Broadcasting plan was stomping his way angrily down Twentieth Street,
sending early-arriving office workers dodging in all directions.
When Jimmy finally caught up to him and grabbed his arm, he
stopped but refused to look at him. He talked to a streetlamp post
instead.

"There's nothing but trouble getting messed up with those boys
and their dirty drug money, Jimmy," he sputtered. "I don't want
any part of it. No part of any illegal dope money!"

Two cops walking their beat nearby looked at them curiously
but kept moving, completely losing interest when a gaggle of sec-
retaries in short dresses passed in front of them.

"Look at me, Detroit Simmons! We just need their money to
get this thing started and then we can buy them out. Pay them
back and tell them to kiss off. They really have nothing to do with
us and the station. They are just making us a loan. That's all.
Nothing more. Nothing less. Nobody else even needs to know
they're bankrolling us. It's the only way people like you and me
are going to be able to pull off something like this," Jimmy pleaded.
"Look, I've tried the bank, the Small Business Administration. You
name it. They take one look at me, at our background, and they
fall all over themselves to tell me that there's no goddamn way."

Dee spoke now to a corner stop sign that he was leaning against for support.

"Look, Jimmy. You are right as rain about what FM radio is going to do someday. And you're right about the music, too. Somebody's going to do it and be successful if they do it right. And as stupid as it sounds, unless you really screw it up, somebody like you could find himself a gold mine up there. But what do you know about running a radio station, Jimmy? What makes you think you can make a go of it?"

"Look. You come back to the house with me and I'll show you exactly how we'll do it. Give me fifteen minutes. That's all. Okay?"

They didn't say a word to each other all the way back to the west side. Detroit punched buttons on the car radio he had sutured together from scraps of other radios that had long since been abandoned. And as he dialed around, he kept muttering under his breath about how bad all the stations sounded to him. He flipped a button and then twisted the dial between the only two FM stations in town. One was playing the same thing as its AM sister station, but the music sounded squashed and tinny. It was probably only a radio parked in front of a microphone somewhere. The other FM station was simply broadcasting a whining test tone. It wouldn't begin transmitting its easy-listening music until noon.

That morning, for the first time ever, Jimmy Gill invited Detroit Simmons to come into his home. They walked right past Grandmama, in the living room in front of her new RCA color television set. Jimmy had bought it for her when her old set finally went out with a pop and a sizzle and a smoky finale one day. He had taken the old set to Detroit to look at, and Detroit agreed it had been worn completely out and was not fixable.

Grandmama didn't seem to notice Jimmy or his houseguest. She merely half waved at them and kept on fussing at the green-faced soap-opera characters on the dusty screen.

Jimmy retrieved a big leather satchel from under his bed, then returned to sit at the cheap dining-room table. He pushed aside Grandmama's dirty breakfast dishes and produced a pile of paperwork from inside the bag.

It was time. Time to actually show Detroit Simmons that he could really accomplish something major without his help, without him even knowing what he was doing. But time to sell the man on the idea or lose him altogether.

Thankfully, Detroit seemed impressed already with the volume of work Jimmy was stacking on the table in front of him.

"I've been talking with the engineering consultant who was working for the old codger in Nashville. The one who's trying to get the license. The consultant was willing to sell me all the old guy's studies because the bastard hasn't gotten around to paying him for the work yet. And Duane and DeWayne introduced me to one of their lawyers here in town. He drew up the incorporation papers for Wizard and helped me with the application for the station license. The Georges paid for it all. The lawyer here has a good friend who practices communications law before the FCC in Washington, D.C. It seems that this particular attorney has a fondness for smokin' Alabama-grown."

A cloud passed over Detroit's face. He was distracted as he looked in amazement at the mountain of documents on the table, touched the piles of exhibits and papers, and thumbed through some of the bound volumes, trying to read some of them upside down.

"Dee, you only need to sign your name in several places . . . here where it says 'president' . . . in front of a notary public, and we'll have the application for a construction permit on file with the FCC in three days. Grover—that's our attorney in Washington— says the license should be granted within three months. Depending on how quickly we can nail down the real estate for the transmitter and the studios and offices and you can get the equipment together and the studios built, we can maybe have the station on the air within six months after that. Within a year, tops. Then, we'll be covering Nashville like the dew!"

For a second, he thought Detroit was going to jump to his feet again, maybe storm out of the house, stomp away again in anger down Wisteria Street all the way back to Ishkooda. Or maybe he would flee in fear at the momentous project that was being proposed. His hands on the edge of the table gripped so tightly that Jimmy was afraid he was about to flip it over, sending his carefully laid plans flying all over the kitchen along with the dirty dishes.

But suddenly, Dee seemed to relax, and began thumbing through the bound books of engineering exhibits, tracing with his fingers their swirling drawings of towers and their tables of cryptic figures and sweeping coverage maps with circles and measurements filling the pages like strange hieroglyphics. His lips moved as he unconsciously calculated power and height above average sea level and microvolts per meter of signal, and Jimmy knew then, for the first time, that it was a done deal. Detroit Simmons was in his element. He was sucked into the scheme, head over heels, totally engulfed.

Wizard Broadcasting had its figurehead. The plan was complete. Soon, Jimmy Gill would, at last, have himself a signal in a medium that would allow him to blanket the landscape farther than the eye could see. A signal that would fan out at the speed of light. A one-hundred-thousand-watt way to tickle the ears of all who cared to tune his way.

And if they did try him, he would make sure they listened. All of them. No doubt about that. Finally, everyone would have to listen to Jimmy Gill.

Chapter 17

It was obvious Jimmy Gill was pushing his "mutt" of a car much
too hard. But he had to. There was too much business that had to
get done to take it easy with the car. He and Detroit Simmons were
in a damned big hurry to get to Nashville and get to work. They
were businessmen with important business to do. And that was
what they were talking about all the way up U.S. 31.

When they drove over the bridge across the Tennessee River
at Decatur, Jimmy felt a quick twinge near his heart. All it took
was a short lull in the big talking they were doing, a quick glance
down at the swirling, muddy river water below the bridge. A door
opened for an instant's memory to sneak into his head of his
mother floating in the brackish backwaters upstream a hundred
miles from where they were crossing that morning.

He shook his head and tried to concentrate on budget and game
plan. He shoved the old heap's accelerator harder. The heater hose
couldn't take it, gave up the struggle, and ruptured with a spray
of white steam and rusty water. They pulled to the side of the
roadway, climbed under the car, and wrapped the hose back together with Detroit's ever present roll of duct tape. Then they
climbed up and down the brushy riverbank, bringing water to refill
the thirsty radiator in a couple of Pepsi bottles.

The car's thermostat went next. It stuck fast just south of
Franklin and they had to get out, raise the hood, take loose some
hoses, and poke a hole in the thing with a screwdriver. This time,
they made many trips up and down the chalky bank of the Duck
River, bringing Pepsi bottles full of water to refill the radiator.

As they sat down to rest in the shade of the bridge, they turned
to look at each other, and laughed like a couple of drunks at the

picture they must have made. Two high-powered media executives, nursing and patching together their old jalopy all the way to the scene of their coming broadcasting triumph. They changed into their new suits under the bridge while the car cooled down enough to nurse it on to Nashville.

The completed station license application required that they go to Nashville and conduct interviews with community leaders and government officials. This was supposed to force the licensee to determine how the new station would best serve the interest of the public with its programming. It was just a formality because the programming had long since been decided. They were going to play lots of rock-and-roll music and sell as many commercials as they could.

Grover White, their attorney in Washington, had explained to them that they had to go through the motions of doing the interviews and filing all the legal papers in a timely fashion to make absolutely certain that they would receive the license. The strength of their integrated ownership and management and the fact that the two of them were going to relocate to the city of license and run the station made it almost a sure thing. Another applicant, totally unaware anybody else was slipping in on him, had filed a weak application.

But there was no sense taking any chances that another last-minute applicant might pop up and throw a wrench into the works.

"Dotting the t's and crossing the i's on this paperwork shit makes it a damn lock for us," Grover had said with a conspiratorial laugh. And Jimmy could hear him over the telephone line, taking another toke and lapsing into an unending coughing fit.

At a phone booth beside the highway somewhere south of Nashville they began confirming appointments, feeding dimes to the phone, closing the door against the passing traffic, and dropping their voices to try to sound older, more businesslike and serious. Detroit would take the black people. Jimmy got the white guys.

The mayor gave Jimmy three minutes, the city council president four at the most. When they first saw him, each of them seemed instantly put off by his age, his ponytail, and the cheap, baggy suit. It could have been worse. He had taken out the earring and shaved off the beard for the trip.

They seemed unimpressed with his plans for an FM station.

"I generally only listen to WSM," the mayor said. "Y'all ain't gonna make much of a showing against them, I don't reckon. But more power to you for giving it a try."

Jimmy didn't argue. Get the license and then they'd see. He got his stock answers scribbled down on a writing tablet to send to Grover for transcribing.

Detroit got a better reception from the president of the local NAACP chapter, a crowd of ministers, and other black leaders. They were proud a brother would be president of a company that was putting a new radio station on the air in their town. They gave him page after page of suggestions about the kind of programming the community needed. Church services, discussion programs, special musical shows, lots of jazz and gospel. But they were confused about what FM was. And they were concerned that it had no chance against the long-established AM stations.

Detroit didn't argue. He dutifully wrote down every word they said, read it back to them, nodded a lot, smiled, and promised nothing.

While Detroit finished up the last of his interviews, Jimmy drove to the foot of a tall gray building downtown, circled the block several times until he could find a meter with time on it and out of sight of the lobby, and then parked. It was important no one saw his "mutt" car.

He checked his watch. He couldn't put this off any longer.

Carefully, almost as if it might explode if he mishandled it, he retrieved a wrinkled brown paper bag from the spare-tire well in the old car's dusty trunk. Then he waited patiently inside the immaculate twentieth-floor office of a Union Bank vice president. The receptionist watched him curiously as he nervously unfolded and refolded the top of the paper sack and shifted from one butt cheek to the other. He smiled at her. She quickly went back to her typing.

"Mr. Gill?"

He jumped at the voice but hesitated for a second. No one had ever called him "Mr. Gill" before. The older man in the conservative blue suit seemed surprised when he saw Jimmy sitting there in his office with the paper bag on his lap. He must have expected another kind of person. But in Nashville, some millionaires didn't look as if they had two dimes to rub together. He'd at least give this rough kid a moment.

"You are Mr. Gill?"

"Yes sir."

"Uh . . . come on into my office, son . . . uh, sir."

His voice was cold, his manner gruff. He spun and went back through his door, almost daring Jimmy to follow.

Jimmy tried to stop his hands from shaking when he handed the heavy sack across the massive desk to the frozen-faced banker. The man turned white around the mouth and caught his breath sharply when he saw the stacks of bills inside. His eyes were wide in amazement when he emptied the money onto the desk.

"This will establish Wizard Broadcasting's operating account, Mr. Lawrence," Jimmy told him, as authoritatively as he could manage. "I hope you will tell your bank's advertising agency that we have chosen Union as our exclusive bank of record. And please, if you will, convey to them how grateful you are for our business and how thankful we will be for yours."

The banker was suddenly very friendly as he smiled and nodded and shoved forward a stack of counter checks and papers to be signed. He came around the desk and pounded Jimmy on the back. Then he offered him a cup of coffee. Perhaps he would like something a bit stronger to properly seal their promising new relationship?

Jimmy repeated the procedure at three other banks within three blocks of each other. Three more wrinkled brown paper sacks filled with money, but with no bills larger than a fifty. Three more promises that the banks' advertising people would know of Wizard Broadcasting's "exclusive" commitment to their institutions.

Then he picked up Detroit in front of a black church in north Nashville and they drove back downtown to the Hyatt. They took an envelope full of bills and checked into the hotel. After cleaning up, they rode the glass elevator to the revolving restaurant at the top of the building. As they ate, they could watch the lights coming on across the city, the tugboats throbbing up the Cumberland River, the lines of cars fleeing downtown for the suburbs.

Jimmy loved the view. Detroit kept trying to figure out how the revolving restaurant platform worked.

They spent as much for dinner and drinks that night as either had made in salary for a week's worth of work at WBMH. They felt high-volume guilt at the extravagance, but the prime rib and two bottles of wine helped fade it quickly.

Later, they walked off the huge meal along the streets of Lower Broadway, dodging the strange looks of tourists and a few cops walking their beat. They passed in front of a dark redbrick building that looked like a church. But a sign told them it was the old Ryman Auditorium, where the Grand Ole Opry broadcast originated each Friday and Saturday night until its upcoming move to a new home at Opryland. That was the same show that the old Zenith radio once snatched out of the air. The place was a shrine for radio history, and both of them were duly impressed as they stood there reverently.

It was the first time they had stayed a night in the same room together. They were too excited to sleep, still half-drunk from the wine at dinner. They talked in the darkness for hours until fatigue finally claimed them. Then Detroit woke Jimmy up at six to tell him that he snored like a sawmill and that he had just called out for his mother in a whimper so pitiful that Detroit had to shake him out of his nightmare.

Jimmy ignored Detroit. He reached for the telephone and ordered a huge room-service breakfast with a meal befitting two entrepreneurs about to set Nashville radio on its ear.

They both had to pull their midnight shifts that evening. They started back south to Birmingham before noon. They were rested, well fed, excited, full of talk about all the huge tasks ahead of them and of all their glorious plans to conquer the radio dial in Music City like a horde of Huns.

A few miles south of town, Detroit told Jimmy to pull over, a knowing grin on his face. He produced one of the engineering maps that he seemed to always have handy for studying.

"Take the next right turn, Jimmy," he ordered.

The winding blacktop road carried them off U.S. Highway 31 for a mile or so, and then Detroit pointed to the right again, up a rugged gravel road. It led to the top of a knobby mountain, to near where Channel 9's huge steel television tower seemed to be getting in the way of vectoring airplanes and galloping clouds. They abandoned the car a quarter mile short of the spire's base because of a locked chain-link gate. Skirting the gate through the woods, they walked up the steep grade quickly, panting as much from excitement as from effort.

Detroit pointed to a spot near the top of the candy-striped tower, just under the spiky television aerial.

"That's the place where our antenna will be hanging," he said. "And you see the far corner of that cement-block building? That's where the transmitter will sit in a few months. The transmission line will come right out the side there and go up the north face of the tower."

Channel 9 had fallen on hard times. They had happily welcomed the offer of tower rent money when Wizard's consulting engineer approached them with a nice deposit. But it was unreal and abstract to Jimmy until that moment. It had only been stacks of papers to sign, circles drawn on maps for Detroit Simmons to study, bodiless voices on the other end of a telephone line to negotiate with. Now it was real steel standing tall and straight in the cool air.

Beyond the squatty building and the tower's base, through the pine trees and honeysuckle, Jimmy saw the entire city below, cradled in a bowl of green mountains. The Cumberland River snaked through its middle, and sunlight flashed off the windshields of thousands of cars.

He fought the impulse to scurry over the fence that protected the tower and start a climb up its side, just as he had done years before at WROG. He longed to feel the cold steel, the slight trembling of the mast as the wind set off vibrations along its length.

Soon it would be his transmitter conjuring the magic electromagnetic waves inside its enchanted chamber. His transmission line conducting the pulsing current to a pretzel of copper strapped to the side of the tower near its crest. His voice modulating the signal that would spread out all over a million acres.

On the way back toward Birmingham, they twisted the radio's tuning knob and listened to the terrible small-town, hick radio stations whose weak signals barely circumvented the hills. They giggled like schoolkids on a field trip, made mocking fun of the stations, imitated the amateurish announcers and the poorly done commercials.

They changed a flat tire after a blowout near Tullahoma. The spare was almost as flat, but it didn't matter. While they worked, and again as they drove on, they talked and planned and schemed. Promised each other that they would build a station the whole industry would talk about. Invent a sound that the world would come to Nashville to listen to and study and take back to wherever and duplicate. Turn on a revolutionary format on a virgin radio band that would soon be discovered by others who were just like they were: pioneering people who held the medium and the music in such reverence that it had become almost a religion to them.

Tired and talked out, they listened to eight-track tapes of the artists they would play and imagined how they would sound on their air. Jimmy did his best disc-jockey introductions to each song, smoothly ad-libbing a joke or two into the gearshift-lever microphone. And they laughed and listened and sang along, the car's windows rolled down, the sun bright, the air cool and crisp as it whistled in. Jimmy was so deep in the joy of it all, he didn't even notice when they crossed the Tennessee River bridge. It was almost as if they were high on some exotic narcotic only they knew about.

They both were aware of the reality of it all and of how little they really knew about the deep water into which they were diving. They agreed that their ignorance only made the adventure all the more exciting. It was like when they were kids, playing together in the jungle along the ditch between the duplex and the mysterious radio station, living Detroit's movie-theater upper-balcony adventures as they plunged blindly but bravely through the thicket of dense honeysuckle vines and snatching saw briars.

They had ignored the sinkholes, dodged the hornets' nests, and refused to worry about any lurking rattlesnakes or hidden pitfalls they might encounter. They had invented their fantasies as they went and found happiness in their smallest discoveries.

The way had opened magically and all their thrashing about had thrown them into a clearing near the wizard's place, a spot where the sun was warm. They had lain together on their bellies in the smooth grass and watched the blue flashing lights and listened to the mysterious buzzing. The place had changed them and showed them the way to something they could never have dreamed about.

The River

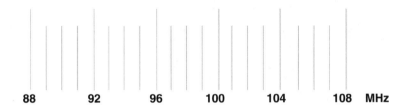

88   92   96   100   104   108 MHz

Chapter 18

Jimmy, it's that Golberg man from the bank again."

"Goddamn it, Sam, how many times . . . ?"

Jesus! Didn't she ever listen to what he told her? He had ordered Sammie Criswell, the receptionist, not to buzz him when he was doing his show on the air. And especially if it was this particular loud-talking banker from Boston, trying his damnedest to get to Jimmy for more than a week now.

He merely sighed, bit his tongue to keep from yelling at her any more, hit the button on the console that started the back turntable and Crosby, Stills and Nash's song "Suite: Judy Blue Eyes" filled the control room with its pulsing acoustic guitars and elastic-tight harmonies. The seven-minute track would give him a chance to handle some business and get the next record cued up and ready to play at the same time.

"Okay, Sam. I'm sorry. What line did you say?"

"Two. And Jimmy Buffett's out here in the lobby with his tapes again."

"Tell him to just leave them, please, hon. I'll listen to them when I get a chance."

To Jimmy's credit, he would later take the time to listen to Buffett's songs and put a couple of the tracks right on the air, even though nobody had heard of the kid yet. After all, his name was Jimmy and he was from Alabama, too.

"Bro . . . uh . . . James Gill," he said into the telephone. He had almost stumbled and said "Brother James," the on-air name he had adopted since starting on the air in Nashville. When he was in the control room, he was Brother James. When he was in the front office, he was James Gill, senior vice president of Wizard Broadcasting, Incorporated.

"Mr. Gill? Sol Golberg at BankMass in Boston. Howyadoin'?"

"Fine as frog hair, Sol," he answered, intentionally launching into his best slow-as-a-slug, Spanish-moss-and-magnolia southern drawl. He had managed to excise traces of the South from his on-air delivery, but the accent could sometimes be useful. It put certain people, and especially Yankees, completely off guard. The slower, the more like a character off *Hee Haw,* the better. "How y'all doin' by now?"

"Good. Good. Now, have you had a chance to look over those figures I sent down to you on the Atlanta property? Gold mine. A damn gold mine, Gill, and with the price at ten times cash flow, it's an out-and-out steal for you guys. But you got to get off the pot or piss. We got lots of tire kickers. Somebody's gonna beat you to this thing if you don't do something soon."

He shot the words down the phone line at Jimmy like hot shrapnel, his voice abrupt, nasal, completely in command. Jimmy smiled.

The alleged cash flow on the stations in question is actually next to zilch, he was thinking to himself. And the stockholders of BankMass are on the verge of taking a cold, cold bath in Boston Harbor unless they can find a greater fool than the trio of New York doctors they underwrote on the original deal three years before. Jimmy Gill knew the score much better than Sol Golberg could ever suspect.

The headphones lying next to his elbow were pumping out Crosby, Stills and Nash's wonderful harmonies so loud he was afraid they might feed through onto the telephone. He slid down their volume control some more, paused a deliberate beat, lowered his voice, and gave Golberg his well-rehearsed speech.

"Sol, y'all know that thang is a dry well and that pack of Park Avenue sawbones would druther pull the plug before dark tonight than keep pouring more good money after bad. It's worth a third what yer tryin' to hold me up for and you know it."

The digital countdown timer Detroit had built and mounted on the console showed two minutes were left on the record spinning away on the turntable behind him. He checked the needles kicking wildly in the center of the control board and wiped away a thin sheen of sweat from his upper lip.

"Mr. Gill, I . . ." Golberg's voice was hesitant now, raspy and quivering with suppressed anger. "Look, why don't you and your folks come on down to Atlanta Friday and look this thing over in person? Maybe we can find some common ground if we can get face-to-face."

Both Jimmy and Sol Golberg knew that Wizard Broadcasting was about the only minority-owned group with the wherewithal to close a deal as dirty as this one had become and that the whole Atlanta operation was teetering on the brink of being belly-up, so near default Golberg could feel the icy wind blowing through his thirtieth-floor office suite up there in Bean Town.

What Golberg didn't know was that it would be hard for BankMass to blow smoke up his ass. The George twins had the connections to give Jimmy more information on the station's health than Dunn and Bradstreet could. He knew the Atlanta station's books as well as he did their own. And he knew that it was one sick puppy.

Golberg was aware that every troubled radio station in the South had approached Jimmy since Wizard Broadcasting's success in Nashville. The phone messages were piling up. Jimmy Gill had become a must-call anytime anybody wanted to liquidate a weak property.

"Well, Sol, we got our fourth-anniversary party comin' up this Friday evenin' and I cain't miss that blowout, ya know," he drawled, laying it on thick as ribbon-cane syrup. He resisted the impulse to mention the availability of grits and okra and a bowl of chitlins at the party. "We'll be in there at the crack of dawn Saturday mornin', and we'll meet with y'all then. That is, if it's okay with y'all."

If Golberg wanted some relief from the heavy weight that was crushing him, he'd do it on Jimmy's terms and at Wizard's bidding. Jimmy was talking from a position of strength. He knew it. So, now, did Sol Golberg.

Checking the minute's worth of groove left on the record, Jimmy went for one more dig to let Golberg know he was aware of exactly how strong his bargaining chip was.

"You orter just hop on a airplane and come on down to Nashville and help us celebrate all our success, Sol."

"You guys are the talk of the business, all right, Jim," Golberg admitted, but it sounded as if he were about to chew on the telephone mouthpiece as he said it. "Damned good job you have done down there."

"Why, thanky, Sol. 'Preciate them kind words. I better run. I got a meetin' that's a-waitin' on me to git goin'. See y'all Saturday mornin' about ten. Y'all keep warm up there. Bye-bye!"

Jimmy was panting and sweating as if he had just run a race, but there was a big grin on the reflection of his face in the double-paned control-room window.

Perfect timing. The Crosby, Stills and Nash record was in its last throes, the guitars thumping toward the cold ending to the song. He had practically closed the deal for Wizard's first acquisition in the seven minutes it took the group to sing the song. This was a story for his memoirs.

Quickly, Brother James slid the *Yes* album onto the near turntable, dropped the needle on the fourth track, and just as "Suite: Judy Blue Eyes" died abruptly, the a cappella harmonies of the British band's "I Hear All Good People" kicked in in a perfect, seamless segue, as if the show had been taped and carefully spliced together. Over the first guitar break after the vocal opening, Jimmy found he couldn't restrain himself. He reached and flipped the microphone on, laughing out loud with the exhilaration left over from the deal making and the sheer beauty of the music.

"Ain't life great? You got rock and roll in stereo, free for the taking on Nashville's WRIV . . . the River . . . one-oh-four-point-one. Turn it up now for Yessss!"

The headphone gain was on 10, the speakers on the wall above him cranked up so high they threatened to jump off their hooks. Jimmy had his head back, laughing and singing along with the music, ignoring the puzzled stares from the junior high school class field trip now passing the studio window. If they didn't feel the power of the music now, they soon would. Feel it all the way to their adolescent little souls.

And Jimmy knew for certain that once it had a grip on them, it would never let go.

Chapter 19

Jimmy Gill had the car seat reared back as far as it would go. He was trying for as much sleep as he could before the session with the moneymen and the owners at the Atlanta station. Detroit drove smoothly and, for once, wasn't constantly punching the buttons on the Buick's radio, criticizing signals and formats and audio processing. He was so quiet, in fact, that Jimmy opened one eye every so often to look over at him, to make sure he wasn't dozing at the wheel.

In the glow of the first rays of sun through the windshield, it was clear that Detroit was wide awake, apparently deep in thought. When Jimmy looked at him, he was struck at how Dee had suddenly become a man. How serious the lines in his forehead had become. How his dark brown eyes had become even deeper and carried more practical intelligence than anyone else he had ever known. How distinguished he looked in his navy pin-striped suit, pastel button-down shirt, and paisley tie.

The party the night before had been a late-night hoot that almost ended disastrously. Detroit Simmons saved the day, as usual.

He had been in the background so long at WRIV, it was Jimmy's pleasure to finally introduce the president of the company to everyone who counted. This had been the first chance to acknowledge what Detroit had contributed to the technical side of the business. All night, advertising execs and representatives of WRIV's sponsors sought him out, grabbed his callused hand, and congratulated him. He soaked it all up like warm sunshine. Jimmy had hoped all night that Detroit wouldn't start spouting off about wavelengths and transistors and vector currents in front of someone important.

The station's sales manager, Jerry Morrow, moved through the crowd easily, pounding backs, shaking hands. He had been a god-send, coming over to WRIV merely on "blue sky." He had quit the town's number one station and signed up with Jimmy and Detroit before WRIV aired its first test transmission. He loved their con-cept and maybe he simply craved the risk and danger, and the possible rewards, of a start-up station in an untried format on an untapped broadcast band.

He had brought with him instant credibility for a salt-and-pepper pair of too-young-to-be-true owners. He had also brought an account list that had WRIV billing in the black months ahead of Jimmy's most optimistic projections. And he had also brought with him Nashville's largest accumulation of exotic-animal-skin cowboy boots.

Lulu Dooley was at home at the party, sampling everything on the buffet tables and chiding the hotel help when they let a chafing dish go empty for too long.

"I could teach these pecker-heads a thing or two about biscuit makin'," she told Jimmy as she swept past him and back down the serving line to fill another paper plate. She stopped back by and thanked him for the tenth time for her bus ticket and the room he had arranged for her upstairs in the King of the Road Hotel. Jimmy thanked her in return, but she just shushed him.

"But you're a part of all this, Lulu," he reminded her. "You helped make it happen."

She only waved and danced away.

Greta Polanski and Clarice George emerged from a bus tour that wound past the homes of the country music stars. They told Jimmy and Detroit about Webb Pierce's guitar-shaped swimming pool and Little Jimmy Dickens's musical-note mailbox. Jimmy merely smiled and hoped the music business bigwigs and station sponsors didn't overhear the members of the board of directors of Wizard Broadcasting gush like simple tourists from Paducah.

The women finally caught up with Detroit and Lulu at a table in a corner of the banquet hall. Jimmy once again marveled at what good friends this odd assemblage of people had all become through this venture he had put together from nothing but a dream. At the same time, he was relieved they were temporarily out of circulation. He wanted them somewhere they would be less likely to do or say something inappropriate.

The room had been packed early. Some of the invitees were drawn only by the free food and drinks. Most knew the necessity of being seen at this get-together and the importance of being identified with WRIV and Wizard Broadcasting.

Later, Jimmy turned from a fawning group of ad people and almost collided with a couple of identical shaggy characters. The two had ridiculously long, oily hair and wore dirty bell-bottom jeans and tie-dyed T-shirts. Amid all the suits and party dresses, Jimmy thought, these two stood out like June bugs in the punch bowl. They were hovering at the side of the bar and fishing beers from a garbage pail full of ice.

Then Jimmy recognized his scraggly guests: Duane and DeWayne George.

"Jimmy! Jimmy Gill. This here is one damn fine party," the one on the left burped.

"How much is all this costing us?" the one on the right asked gruffly, nodding toward the piles of shrimp cocktail and roast beef on nearby tables.

Jimmy knew then which was which. The first was Duane, the simpleminded one. The other was DeWayne, the ill-tempered one who sometimes scared the hell out of Jimmy.

"Not a thing, boys. All trade-out. We'll just run them some commercials somewhere between midnight and six in the morning until we get it all paid for. Enjoy!"

Jimmy had not taken a dime from the twins in three years. He had repaid every cent of the original seed money with generous interest. But in the last year, he had sniffed a hint of curiosity on DeWayne's part, as if he might want to be more than a silent partner in such a profitable, legitimate business. Especially since it was "show" business.

Against his better judgment, Jimmy was going to have to tap the twins' tainted money supply one more time in order to pull off the Atlanta deal without putting WRIV in hock. Detroit and Jimmy had already fought that battle with each other. Jimmy had won. But barely. Now he could only hope their party guests would mistake these two characters for rock stars or disc jockeys or a couple of weirdos who had wandered in off the street. It could not be known that they were the benefactors who had provided initial financial backing for Wizard Broadcasting.

"I need to see you before the night's up, DeWayne," he half whispered, hoping no one would see him spending time with someone like the Georges. "I think I have an idea that would cinch the deal in Atlanta tomorrow."

DeWayne grunted and swallowed most of a bottle of beer in one noisy gulp.

Distracted by the twins, Jimmy almost didn't notice someone else who was coming his way, the crowd parting for her. Then he saw her. Blond hair long and straight. Red dress fitted as if she were born to it. And a presence about her that captured the attention of everyone in the room. Yet, her manner was such that she seemed unaware of the stir she was causing. Jimmy rudely turned his back to the Georges and admired the woman as she approached, hoping she was headed for him. She was.

Her handshake was cold and damp from the drink she had just shifted to her other hand, but it quickly warmed as she lingered.

"Cleo Michaels," she sang. "Brother James, I'm a big fan of yours."

"So am I. Of yours . . . I mean you . . . you and yours."

She laughed loudly, naturally, in a nice kind of way, and it sounded like perfectly shaped piano notes. He tried to avoid her grabbing gaze, to look past her to Detroit Simmons and the bunch gathered at the corner table, but she kept him captive.

"No, really. I've listened since you first went on the air. I write and sing country music, but I sure love the rock and roll you play on the River. And I love your voice, too."

Cleo Michaels was one of the biggest names in country music. Maybe the biggest female star. Jimmy didn't have to be a fan to know who she was, but he was a fan. She had boldly taken the gimmicks out of female country songs, writing and singing strong lyrics that spoke of far more than keeping her man at home and satisfied. Jimmy had several of her albums next to the stereo system in his new home. They were welcome relief from his constant diet of rock and roll.

"Listen, I don't want to tie you up, but I'd love to have lunch with you one day next week," she said. Her amazing eyes never left his. "I don't know how much longer this music ride's gonna last and I've got a chance to buy into a radio station in Dallas. I'd appreciate some advice from an expert like you."

Her smile seemed to dim the lights in the hotel banquet hall. But Jimmy suddenly realized the lights had actually flickered in the room, and then they went out entirely for a second, followed by a quick clap of thunder from outside.

"Is that okay with you, Brother James?" she was asking.

"Sure! Call me a give. I mean give me a call one day and let's do it," he yelled over the quick burst of noise from the startled crowd. Her hand released his, her gaze fled, and she floated out of sight, disappearing into the throng.

Before he could recover from the wonderful presence of Cleo Michaels, there was quick movement of some other kind to his right. Detroit was sprinting toward the exit.

"We got that balloon floating two hundred feet up and this storm will blow it all the way to Kentucky in a minute!"

They had bought a huge helium balloon with the station's logo painted on its side for station promotions. The party was its debut. Detroit had it tied to a portable trailer sign in the hotel parking lot as a guide for guests to the ballroom.

When Jimmy got to the door, curtains of rain and hail were blowing across the entrance, and a wicked stroke of orange lightning licked at a flagpole across the lot. Through the deluge he saw the dark form of Detroit Simmons chasing the portable sign as it rolled crazily away across the asphalt. He was wading in water up to his knees. His new gray suit was already soaked.

The two-thousand-dollar balloon with "The River" emblazoned across its sides bounced happily along in the windstorm, right in the middle of Murfreesboro Road, the city's busiest stretch of highway. Cars were backed up in all directions, horns bleating over the pounding rain and roaring thunder. Thank God there had apparently not been an accident yet. Jimmy had no idea if there was insurance coverage for such a thing, but he doubted it.

A blue-lighted police car had pulled up close to the bouncing balloon. The cop in his yellow slicker looked as if he were contemplating shooting the balloon to death, if he only knew where he needed to aim to kill it quickly.

Jimmy hesitated for only a moment, then dived into the downpour himself, chasing Detroit and the scurrying, escaping portable sign. There was no choice. He had to help. The guests and the party would simply have to get by on their own.

Together, they were able to run down the sign and stop its mad progress across the lot before it rammed into somebody's car or crashed through the chain-link fence and onto the main highway. Then they began wrapping the balloon's tether around the sign base as they tugged it slowly back out of the traffic and away from the murderous cop. The gusting wind tried to pull the massive thing away from them. They both expected another bolt of lightning to strike them dead any second. Their arms ached but they kept wrapping and pulling, wrapping and pulling, slowly bringing the bouncing blimp closer and closer.

When the balloon was near, Detroit pulled it downward until he could reach the valve and let the helium spew out and mingle with the rain and fog. The flat, wet heaviness no longer caught the wind. It lay depleted, covered by the water at their feet, the station logo wrinkled and crushed.

The rain had slackened, the lightning and thunder had grown more distant. Jimmy and Detroit looked at each other as they leaned, exhausted, against the sign. Their new dress clothes were soaked. Their faces were filthy. They were panting like a pair of coon dogs.

"Man, that was a trip," Detroit said.

"Sure as hell was!"

Their voices were munchkin-tight and high-pitched from inhaling the helium from the balloon.

Suddenly they broke into wild laughter, like two silly kids.

The president of the country's most successful radio station and Nashville's number one radio personality stood in the middle of a downpour, sounding like the Chipmunks and looking exactly like a couple of drowning gophers.

Chapter 20

The situation with the Atlanta AM and FM stations was what Jimmy Gill and Detroit Simmons had expected. The high-powered AM station carried the bulk of the commercial billing with its middle-of-the-road music and an expensive-to-maintain news department. The FM had a big, beautiful signal but few commercials amid its mishmash of big-band and easy-listening music and pre-recorded preachers' programs. All the programming came from huge, impersonal reels of audiotape, racked up and played back on a bank of machines hidden away in a dusty back closet at the AM studios.

The receptionist answered the telephone with the AM call letters only. The big sign out front of the run-down building had only the AM call letters on it. The FM was a well-kept secret.

The Boston banker, Sol Golberg, turned out to be a foot shorter than Jimmy, three times as big around, bald, a chain smoker, and maddeningly fidgety. The station's general manager was a senile old engineer who treated his properties like a couple of ham radio stations, on the air for his own amusement and constant tinkering. He had a difficult time even remembering the names of the New York physicians whose depleted money contributions kept the stations on the air.

They all walked along together through a dark maze of hallways, past racks of ancient equipment and haphazard sales offices, and through dingy, muffled studios that smelled of cigarette smoke and mildew. The staff on duty that morning nodded curtly at them, knowing what was up, though they had been told these were only new investors, not potential new owners.

Then they all climbed into Detroit's car, grabbed hamburgers

at the Varsity, and rode to the tower site east of town where the
FM leased space for its transmitter and antenna. The studio building was leased also, the equipment practically worthless. As
Jimmy already knew, the only real estate the station owned was
a few acres of swampland where the AM tower sprouted from the
middle of frog ponds and cattails.

"Two-fifty for the FM alone."

After the tour, Jimmy spoke abruptly, cutting through the
bullshit chatter, as soon as they sat in the manager's office.

Golberg blanched, his mouth flying open, his cigarette landing
in what there was of his lap. The old general manager dropped his
cigarette on the carpet. It burned there for a while as he stared at
this brash, longhaired young man as if he must be from some other
planet.

"We assumed . . . that is, we thought . . . it would be a package
deal, both of them . . . but surely the AM station, James," the
banker sputtered. He looked as if he had swallowed something
bitter and vile.

"AM's going to be a dead duck by the end of the decade, Sol.
We would only be interested in the FM. And we know it's bleeding
badly now. You want me to cite some figures for you. There are no
accounts receivable at all, so that's a moot issue. The equipment's
not worth squat, except maybe to the Museum of Broadcasting.
The stick value couldn't be more than a hundred thousand, and
that's on a good day with the wind blowing right. We could help
stop the hemorrhaging for you and your partners and get us an
FM signal in Atlanta at the same time. You know as well as we do
that you'll never get the whole investment back, but we can help
you cut your losses and get the hell out of town. That's a good deal
for all concerned. And we are prepared to make the deal right now.
What do you gentlemen say?"

Jimmy wished Detroit would quit staring at him in such obvious disbelief before the other two men noticed. They had already
agreed between themselves that they could pay a half million for
the FM station, with the George twins' help. The signal and the
old transmitting equipment were worth at least five hundred thousand and they would need to invest another quarter million in
upgrading the facility. And they had no interest whatsoever in the
dinosaur of an AM station.

"Mr. Simmons . . ." Golberg turned to Detroit, hoping for a life preserver from him.

"That's our offer, gentlemen," Detroit said, quickly dropping the telltale incredulous look he had worn for the last fifteen seconds.

Then Detroit carefully removed a brown paper sack from his new leather briefcase with his initials embossed on the top. With agonizing slowness for maximum effect, he counted out bundled bills worth fifty thousand dollars in cash onto the manager's dusty, cluttered desk. Both men gaped.

"Earnest money?"

Jimmy noticed just a slight crack in Detroit's voice, but the others apparently didn't.

The sight and smell and power of the new bills turned the trick. Suddenly they were all talking receipt, contract terms, approximate closing dates, all while the stack of cash money provided by the Georges created a screaming distraction in the middle of the desk.

They had pulled it off! And saved a quarter of a million dollars in the process! Enough to do the equipment upgrade without having to borrow more from Duane and DeWayne.

On the ride back out of Atlanta, Detroit and Jimmy scanned the FM band like fishermen searching for a school of red snapper. They heard nothing on the air similar to what they planned to do with the new station.

Along the new multilane freeways, they stared at the germinating office parks, the skeletons of skyscrapers erupting from city blocks. Atlanta was booming. The FM radio dial was empty but fertile. And the other operators in town were leaving it all to Wizard Broadcasting to cultivate for what amounted to seed money!

Finally, the two men settled into their own silent thoughts. Jimmy drove. Detroit was apparently near a doze. They were almost in Dalton, near the Tennessee state line, before Detroit spoke again.

"Jimmy, where did you learn to be such a hard-ass like that?"

"Don't know, Dee. I guess I just figure I've got to ask for what I want if I'm going to make anybody listen to me. And if I've got the facts on my side and if I do my homework, I'll get it. I can get anything I want if I want it bad enough."

"Well, sometimes you scare me just a little bit. That's all."

Then he was quiet for a while, the roar of the highway under the tires the only sound. Ten miles farther along, he turned to Jimmy and spoke again.

"Did you see that big old FM tower today?"

"Damn right! I can't wait to climb that mother!"

And they laughed for five more miles.

The sun was disappearing over the nose of Lookout Mountain as Jimmy flipped the radio on near Chattanooga, and, for some reason, switched to the AM band. He knew the sky wave would be bouncing back distant signals soon, and he still loved the magic of it all.

He punched up WLAC in Nashville at 1510 and there was a delicious, throbbing blues song pumping out of the dashboard speakers. Then he hit 650 for the "Mother Church of Country Music," WSM. Hank Snow was just opening the first segment of the Saturday night Grand Ole Opry. It sounded as if he and Dee were sitting in the front row until the ionosphere shifted slightly and let the signal drift away from them. But at 770, WABC was bursting through the static from Manhattan, with its frenetic deejay frothing at the mouth, it seemed, and the thumping songs he spun sounding just a shade this side of musical anarchy. A commercial for a truck stop in Utah boiled out of Fort Worth on WBAP. And when Jimmy dialed down to the high numbers at the right side of the band, a gravelly voiced preacher was wailing away, gasping for breath and salvation, on one of the high-powered Mexican border stations.

When Jimmy twisted the knob back to the left, the AM station in Atlanta they had passed on buying just a few hours before filled the Buick with sound. A newscaster took them to an anti–Vietnam War rally in Washington, and the audio perfectly captured the anger of the speaker, the shouts of the crowd, the distant sirens of police cars. Then the station switched to Europe for a satellite feed on the peace talks going on there, and to a reporter in the suburbs for an on-the-scene report at a local antiwar demonstration. Another man checked in from a golf tournament in town, interviewing players and spectators. A happy-voiced disc jockey spun a couple of up-tempo records. Then, finally, with a flourish of music and the roar of an excited crowd, the station took them to a Georgia Tech football game for all the play-by-play.

The signal never wavered, even as they passed through the girders of the Tennessee River bridge. It easily overrode the ambient nighttime static, blanketing the countryside across forty states and most of the Caribbean.

Jimmy looked at Detroit's face in the dim light from the radio dial. He was looking right back at him. They read each other's mind.

"Okay, okay. I'll call Golberg first thing Monday morning and do a deal for the AM, too."

The big signal rode with them all the way back to Nashville.

Chapter 21

There had never before been anyone in Jimmy Gill's life like Cleo Michaels. He was nervous as a schoolboy driving out Franklin Road to the massive iron gate that blocked intruders from entering her estate. The long, snaking driveway gave him a quick glimpse or two of her low-slung mansion, of acres of ponds and shrubs and towering trees.

He had spoken to her briefly on the phone on Monday, then again over the speaker that was mounted on a pole at the entrance gate. Her voice had left him numb and stunned both times. And now she was coming out the front door of the mansion to greet him, wearing faded jeans and a sloppy plaid shirt. She was all smiles as she hugged him like a long-lost friend, then grabbed his hand and led him back inside into her huge living room.

She sat down on the couch next to him, turning to face him, all smiles, welcoming. Again, he was breathless from her beauty, disarmed by her natural manner.

"Thank you for coming! Do I call you Brother or James or what?"

"Well, do I call you Hester or Miz Cudsworth?"

She just grinned, amazed that somehow he had found out something she had always tried to keep secret: her real name.

"Cleo, for God's sake," she said, "and don't tell anybody what my mama did to me at birth or I'll have to have you killed! How'd you know that name? I've spent more money than I care to think of to try to keep it buried."

But he wasn't revealing his sources.

"And I'm Jimmy, please. A very nervous Jimmy, I might add."

"But why?" She seemed genuinely surprised.

"Meeting you. Being here."

She laughed softly and looked embarrassed for an instant.

"And I was afraid to admit that I was nervous meeting you," she said. "I meant what I said the other night. I really am a fan of the station and especially your show."

"Me, too. Of yours. Oh, God! Don't let me do that number again."

This time they both laughed.

"Coffee? Iced tea? A beer?"

He declined and surveyed the auditorium-sized room, its massive furniture, and the paintings under spotlights on the fabric-covered walls. She excused herself and darted into another room, then returned with her own cup of something hot and smoking. She shoved a shiny-wood guitar aside and curled her legs under her as she again sank into the sofa next to where he sat, almost swallowed up by its plushness.

"Jimmy, I really appreciate your time," she started after one sip, getting right to business, again holding his eyes with hers with the most direct gaze he had ever seen. And especially from a woman. "I can only imagine how busy you must be, but I really don't know of anyone else to ask about this sort of thing."

She blew on the coffee to cool it, shifted slightly, dropped her eyes, and talked on as he leaned forward to show he was actually interested.

"I'm almost thirty years old. The last two albums sold half as many units as the couple before them did. We're already getting booked into the second tier of halls and clubs. They're starting to talk about us as an opening act again. And to top it off, I haven't had a cut on any of the songs I've written . . . at least a cut by a major artist . . . in almost a year, mostly because I have not had time to pitch them but partly because there are newer, hotter writers sleeping in offices all over Music Row, cranking them out like cans of beans."

She paused for another sip of the coffee, and he was surprised that these realities she was ticking off so matter-of-factly didn't really seem to be bothering her. Again she looked up at him, and her eyes bore into him, checking his interest.

"The ultimate signal came last week. My manager's negotiating to put together a 'greatest hits' cheapie collection for marketing on television. That's the sure sign that the sun's setting, Jimmy!"

"God, Cleo, you're the freshest thing going in country music. Any kind of music for that matter. You're the only one doing straight-ahead stuff without all the strings and syrup they're putting out now. And your lyrics are phenomenal."

He meant exactly what he was saying.

"That's what they want now, you know. Big production, lots of violins, adult-contemporary sound, smarmy ballads. Words aren't what they are looking for at all. You don't want the audience to have to think, for God's sake. Nothing acoustic or traditional-sounding is selling now either. Country stations say country music is too country for them to play, if you can imagine that. Tammy Wynette, Barbara Fairchild, Loretta Lynn . . . they can't get a song on the radio anymore. And I can't sing at all when they lay all that orchestral stuff on so thick. It's like it chokes me."

Cleo broke eye contact, looking off into the distance through a crimson-draped, floor-to-ceiling window. Beyond the glass, he could see a corner of swimming pool and, beyond that, a fenced tennis court.

"It'll come back around someday. It always does. But I'm realistic enough to know that I'll be way too old to ride that horse by then. That's why I wanted to talk with you, Jimmy."

She shifted her legs and leaned closer, setting the coffee cup on the table and using her hands for emphasis as she talked. Her every movement looked as if it was choreographed for effect, as if for a stage show, but it seemed natural. He was enjoying watching her dance.

"I'm listening, Cleo."

She smiled. The morning sunlight streaming through the window dimmed in comparison.

"I've made some money and I've had the good sense to carefully plant it where it could grow. I don't ever want to be as poor as I was growing up in Jasper, Texas. So hungry that a mess of poke salat was a banquet for us. And I think I see a way to make sure I don't ever have to chop another row of cotton to live, no matter what happens with this music thing.

"About the only good thing I remember growing up was listen-

ing to our old Crosley table-model radio. When the electricity
hadn't been turned off, that is. We could get the Grand Ole Opry
from Nashville, the 'Barn Dance' from Chicago on WLS and another 'Barn Dance' from Knoxville on WNOX, and all the country
music and big band shows from Dallas and Houston and San An-
tonio. Daddy bought me a Sears and Roebuck guitar when he was
working at the sugarcane mill, and I learned to chord listening
every night to an old guy named Boots Crockett on WGOJ in Jasper. He'd pick and sing on his show and call out the chords when
he forgot the words. Which was regularly, because old Boots apparently did love to drink."

Her eyes were now moist with the remembering, and Jimmy
was afraid he was about to tear up a bit himself. Of all things, he
had found a kindred spirit here in the living room of a mansion on
Franklin Road in Nashville. Another soul raised on the magic of
radio! When she paused for another swallow of coffee, he launched
into his own story, telling of his hours spent on the cold linoleum
floor dragging in any signal he could find, surfing the tide of radio
waves that floated in and out on the ether.

"Somehow, I knew you would understand," she said. "I can
hear the love for the music, the passion you have for radio when
you talk into that microphone at The River. It's not just a job for
you, Jimmy. Certainly not just another investment like a hamburger stand or a filling station or some kind of dull old franchise
would be. They've tried to sell me on 'Cleo's Chicken Shack' and a
dozen other ideas just as stupid."

Then she told him of her dream, and he was struck by how
similar it was to the one he was only then realizing himself. Of
how she wanted to put country music on the emerging FM band,
where its clean melodies and from-the-heart picking could shine
through without all the static.

"You know for yourself how great our music sounds on a good
record player, Jimmy. You wouldn't believe how great it is in the
studio," she said, and he nodded. "Folks need to hear it without
the noise and in stereo. The producers here in Nashville are all old
rock and roll guys and the production values are as good as anything ever put on disc, no matter the kind of music. Country music
desperately needs a medium that can do it some justice. I think
FM will do it just fine, and when people really hear it, when there's

something there worth listening to, they'll come over to it in droves."

Conventional wisdom had it that no one would listen to anything as hokey as country music on FM. They had said the same thing about the brashness of rock and roll. That the FM band was only good for classical music and Mantovani.

"A disc jockey I got to know in Dallas told me about an AM and FM station that is up for sale out there, and I sort of got excited about it for a minute and a half. My manager, Gene Cooper, threw a bucket of cold water on the whole thing, though. He thinks I'm off my rocker. Says I don't know doodly-squat about broadcasting and he's right, of course. He usually is. But you do, Jimmy. Want to be partners?"

"Uh . . . well . . ."

Cleo Michaels could be as straight and abrupt as her gaze, it appeared.

"You don't have to answer me now. I'll give you . . . oh . . . twelve minutes."

She mimicked looking at a watch on her bare arm and they laughed again. Then Jimmy told her he would appreciate a cup of that coffee after all. It smelled wonderful.

A woman so direct put him totally off balance. He had caught himself nodding positively with only her excitement to base it on. Sure, he agreed with her about country music's possibilities on the new band. And when she told him the legendary call letters of the AM station she was talking about, he filled her in about his own ideas for the Atlanta AM station they had just reached the agreement on. She listened to him intently, as if he was singing the world's most beautiful song.

For the next hour, they were like a couple of drunks pouring each other shots of rye whiskey. She sang him a few of the songs she was working on for the next album. He told her of his dreams for the River and the new stations in Atlanta.

He finally had to stand and tell her point blank that he had to go. Bankers, clients, the sales staff, and a lobby full of record promoters awaited him back at the River. She saw him to the door and kissed him bye on the cheek. It was a totally natural act, completely lacking in pretense.

As he steered back down the twisting drive away from her, he knew, somewhere deep inside, that he was completely, undeniably, irretrievably in love with this woman with the direct eyes and the enchanting voice and the love for radio that came so damned close to matching his own.

Chapter 22

It took Detroit Simmons about ten seconds to throw a bucket of icy cold water on his hot, hot fire.

"Jimmy Gill! There's no doubt at all now that you've lost your ever-lovin' mind! We got a tiger by the tail here in Nashville, we're borrowing more bloody drug money from the Georges to jump into a snake pit down there in Atlanta, and now you're about to tie up with a hillbilly singer and risk everything we've built, all for another station you've never even heard in a town that you've never even been to!"

Detroit was so mad he turned his back to Jimmy and stared out his shop window at the traffic zipping past on the street outside. Then he cursed loudly, picked up the chassis of some dingus he was working on, and slammed it back down on the workbench so violently that several tools danced off the edge and rattled noisily on the hard floor. Jimmy had put his ideas into logical sequence on the drive back into town from Cleo's. He had just begun laying out the facts in exactly the way he knew Detroit couldn't resist, no matter how skeptical he might be, when the man had suddenly blown a gasket.

Jimmy stood there, shocked at Detroit's anger. He was about to turn and leave, saving the rest of the scenario for a time when Detroit might be more in a mood to listen. He was going to do the deal. He didn't need Detroit Simmons for that. It was only a courtesy mentioning it to him in the first place. But then, Detroit spun around suddenly and blasted Jimmy with a cold stare he had rarely seen on his friend's face.

An ugly thought slipped up on Detroit and he spoke before he meant to.

"Are you tapping that woman?"

"What?"

"You sleeping with her?"

"Frankly, it's none of your goddamn business."

Jimmy almost went further, came frighteningly close to calling Detroit a "stupid nigger," or maybe even bouncing across the office and hitting him. But he realized immediately that he loved him too much for that. Instead, he only bit his tongue and turned abruptly to stomp down the hallway to his office. He slammed his door behind him so hard it dislodged two framed gold records hanging on the wall and sent them crashing to the floor.

Detroit heard the commotion, but he didn't follow. He wanted to say more, something profound to try to keep Jimmy Gill from blundering into the unknown blinded by the beauty of this woman he had only just met. Why couldn't Jimmy ever think things through, line up the pros and cons on each side of a ledger and balance the decision on cold, hard facts instead of raw, wild emotion? Detroit tried to lose himself in a schematic that unfolded over the entire workbench, but the lines kept merging and the symbols blurred.

Jimmy sat, reared back in his big office chair, studying the patterns of the ceiling tile over his head. He had spent two hours with Cleo Michaels and, once past the initial stun of her beauty, he had been so lost in their talk of radio signals and music that lust had not cropped up again at all. And he had meant exactly what he had growled to Detroit. It was none of his business who he was doing what to or when or why.

And if he wanted to buy half the radio stations in Texas, it was none of Detroit's business, regardless of what expedient, made-up legal title he might have in front of his silly name on the top of a piece of letterhead. He could wire radio equipment together all right and keep a transmitter humming on spit and tinfoil, but he better keep his nose out of the rest of the business that he didn't know jack about.

Jimmy knew it was Detroit's weak knock at his door ten minutes later. He let him try three more times, though, before he grunted a reluctant "Come on in." That fifteen seconds gave Jimmy Gill all the time he needed to reload his weapons.

"Look, Jimmy. I'm sorry," Detroit said, obviously pulling the apology from somewhere deep inside himself. "It's just that we both have worked so hard on building up these stations and I can't stand to see us risk it all for some hillbilly—"

"Dee, you gotta trust me! Hear me out for once without jumping to conclusions!" Jimmy was practically yelling at his only friend, but he wanted to do more. He wanted to actually slam him down viciously in a chair and force him to listen to what he had to say. Detroit fought to stay cool himself, standing there a full, quiet half minute, shifting from foot to foot, uncomfortable as he always was when the two of them suffered through such disagreements. He wanted to make sure whatever he said and however he said it wouldn't send Jimmy storming away again before they could make things right between them. They always had before. And now more was riding on it than ever before.

"Jimmy, I just want to make sure you're not grabbing hold of some high voltage you can't let go of," Detroit finally said to the carpet, and then sank tiredly into the chair across from Jimmy before his feet betrayed him and he fled back to the sanctuary of his shop. "I know what it's like to fall for somebody. I haven't been the same since I started dating Rachel."

Jimmy continued to dissect the ceiling, but he had relaxed now. It was clear that Dee would be okay. He let him keep talking.

"Jim, you know how many shysters and con artists there are running around Music Row trying to siphon off all the money they can. All these wanna-bes and never-wases trying to cash in on somebody else's talent or ideas. How many crooks there are out there who would love to jump on board with us for the ride. I just want to make sure—"

"Where's the nearest satellite uplink?"

Detroit was stopped cold in midsentence. He looked at Jimmy sideways once more with that familiar puzzled look of his, as if he seriously suspected that Brother James had gone stone crazy. Lord knows, he should have been used to such questions by now.

"The Grand Ole Opry House out at Opryland is building an uplink for all the network television specials and the like. Why?"

"Do you know anybody over there?"

"I know everybody over there. I helped them wire up the new mixing suite in the auditorium. It's the world's biggest radio studio, you know."

Jimmy obviously didn't care about the trivia. He rattled on.

"Is it true you can put audio piggyback on the television signal when it goes up to the satellites?"

"Sure you can. They have plenty of subcarriers," Detroit said, impressed that Jimmy knew as much about a technical topic as he apparently did. "They mostly use it for backhaul and talk-back and cue for the production crews on programs and stuff like that, but, yeah, they could be EQ'd to twenty-five K I think. Plenty enough frequency response for FM radio."

Jimmy didn't understand all that gibberish but he nodded as if he understood perfectly and let it pass as if that, too, was useless information. Detroit had given the right answer, "Sure you can," and Jimmy had obviously succeeded in arousing his interest. He was sniffing the bait.

"How about see what they would charge us to put a couple of stereo channels up, twenty-four hours a day, seven days a week?"

"Okay. You gonna make me guess what the hell you are talking about?" Dee nibbled.

"We're fixing to put up a progressive rock-and-roll radio station in Atlanta, Georgia, aren't we? And we'll be playing exactly the same music that we play here in Nashville already. With the same type jocks, the same contests, the same everything else. Only the commercials and call letters will be different between here and there, right?"

Detroit nodded, not following where the explanation was going at all, but biting the barb anyway.

"What if we sent the River's programming down to Atlanta on satellite, and just played the local commercials from there? Any ideas how we could do that, Dee?"

The man was hooked solid. He twisted in his chair a few seconds, reeling himself in, lost in thought. He suddenly brightened.

"Sure! Audio tones. Just like my black box that got us canned at WROG that time. Different dedicated tape machines and special tones to fire off jingles, use automation carousels for the commercials with a simple ASCII routine to rack them up from a file we could import directly off the traffic system computer—"

Detroit Simmons was mentally spinning wonderful webs, pulling cable, wiring circuit boards, even while he still sat right there in the chair in Jimmy's office. But then he stopped suddenly, remembering something.

"Wait. You said two stereo channels?"

"Picture this, Dee. A station that plays country music, with the biggest stars in the music business stopping by all the time to bring their latest records, do interviews, be guest deejays, sorta like they do on WSM here. The only place in the world you could do that sort of stuff is right here in Nashville. But what if the radio station in question happens unfortunately to be located in Dallas, Texas, nine hundred miles away?"

Dee slapped his knees with both hands and cackled. It was suddenly clear to him.

"Damn! We gotta have an on-air studio somewhere and it might as well be here as out there in Texas!"

"Right. And I don't see why we can't eventually put a lot of the stuff we are going to do on the AM stations up on the satellite and cut some more of our programming costs, too. Just don't tell the folks at Opryland what we're up to. They'll steal our idea in a minute."

Jimmy began to spin his plan, to make the two AM stations true community bulletin boards, each like a giant fifty-thousand-watt party line, with remote units popping in all the time with man-on-the-street interviews or direct reports from anything happening in town. Talk-show hosts could generate excitement and controversy and pull common folk into the debates on the turbulent times in which they found themselves as millions eavesdropped. And there could be heavy involvement with sports in games-crazy Atlanta and Dallas, from play-by-play to sports talk shows. Music on AM would be dying a slow but sure death over the next few years as the better fidelity of FM claimed more and more of the available listeners, Jimmy explained. But no other medium could offer the immediacy and flexibility and broad coverage that made AM radio a natural for information and one-to-one communication. Most of the programming would have to originate locally to capture the feeling he wanted to achieve, but there was plenty of what Jimmy called "glue," the stuff that held the formats together, that would be common to both markets that could be done by satellite from one or the other location.

But before Jimmy could preach him the rest of that sermon,

Detroit decided that he had heard enough. He jumped to his feet and sprinted toward his shop to start making calls and drawing schematics for all the notions he had conjured up already. But three minutes later, he was back at Jimmy's office door, hopping with excitement until he could get him off a telephone conversation.

"Yeah? What you got Dee?"

"Footprints!"

Now it was Jimmy Gill's turn to look sideways at him, baffled. "What?"

"Footprints, man! Satellites have big footprints. The area down on earth that the satellite's signals cover from space. Anybody with a satellite receiving dish at a station inside that footprint could pick up the stuff we put on the uplink. We could sell our programming to stations all over the country. Doesn't matter if we have two or two thousand stations that want to do it, it wouldn't cost us a penny more to put the music and stuff up there for them to tap into."

Jimmy's mouth fell open as he jumped to his feet, dashed around the desk, and danced arm in arm with Detroit. They waltzed out into the lobby, frightening two job applicants, a couple of salesmen, and three singers waiting to push their songs.

Jimmy was amazed that he had not thought of such a natural extension of his original idea. He was ecstatic that Detroit had. A few of the station's salespeople stuck heads from their cubbyholes and looked on in shock as their president and the station manager did handstands and a wild square dance in the lobby. Sammie Criswell shielded the phone with her hand to keep a caller from hearing their maniacal screams and gales of wild laughter.

Suddenly, just that quickly, Jimmy Gill and Detroit Simmons were dangling from the side of a tower so tall it touched the ionosphere. And before anyone else knew it, the two of them could be yelling to the wind, waving at the horizon.

Chapter 23

Several more weeks passed before Jimmy and Cleo's relationship had enough time and opportunity to flourish the way they both had suspected it would. It was no surprise to either of them when it did.

James Gill was crushed under the weight of all that was going on around him. The sudden roller coaster of business stopped and started and climbed and fell with such force it seemed to always be robbing him of breath. He spent every waking moment putting the complicated Atlanta deal together, checking out the information from DeWayne and Duane's sources on the condition of the Dallas stations, working with Detroit on the plans for the satellite feeds, running the programming and sales departments for the River, and still doing a three-hour show on the radio every morning. The show required that he get up at four-thirty each day to be at the station and prepared to entertain an eager audience by six o'clock.

He would vow to himself to finally give up the on-air program, especially when he dozed in important meetings or slurped gallons of black coffee to try to stay alert enough so nothing got past him. But then he would argue with himself viciously because his ego craved the air shift. Sometimes he thought he would probably stop breathing, that his body's metabolism would grind to an abrupt halt, if he didn't have that connection every day. No, he couldn't give up being on the radio. Maybe he'd find something else, some other piddling duty that he could better delegate to someone else. Maybe he could turn loose another hot potato once he had put everything in motion.

Soon. Soon he'd be able to step back and ease up and begin to concentrate only on the big picture.

When Cleo and Jimmy did have a chance to see each other, it was always in one or the other's office, with her abrasive manager there, and Jimmy's pit bull lawyer, too. The two men's personalities clashed from the outset, and Cleo and Jimmy spent as much time refereeing ego prizefights as they did talking business. And there were always teams of bankers and their attorneys, and, of course, the attorneys had their own attorneys along, too.

Usually it was clear that the assembled money and legal people's only goal was to spend most of their time and effort firing fusillades, trying to shoot holes in what Cleo and Jimmy were attempting to put together. It was as if they used their collective skills and knowledge to find dozens of reasons why the deal would never work. The two of them had to spend all of their time and effort deflecting the bullets, repairing the damage, binding their wounds.

Cleo Michaels had incorporated dozens of different ways, a convoluted complex of companies that fanned out into a mishmash of expensive confusion, when all the unraveling began. Wizard Broadcasting, on the other hand, had been put together loose and free, legally structured on the fly with spit and baling wire, a lick and a promise, just to get it going in a hurry. It all combined to cause the tidy legal minds fits as they tried to match the square peg and the round hole. Meantime, the bankers turned dispeptic watching the money flow off in all directions with nothing but piles of paperwork to show for it. And Jimmy and Cleo grew more and more frustrated with all the trouble it was taking to consummate their hopeful union.

"We ought to just shake hands on the thing and close this deal by ourselves," he told her one day.

"Shoot, we could just get married and it would all be done with a couple of 'I do's!'" she said with a laugh.

They were driving, alone at last, to a little meat-and-three restaurant not far from Music Row. The morning's meeting at her office on a side street near the Vanderbilt University campus had dragged sluggishly along throughout the day, creeping and staggering until well past lunchtime. Jimmy had been fighting sleep, but mostly losing the battle, after his usual early wake-up. Cleo had been pacing and pawing like a pastured pony, dying to run free outside the confines of the office fence.

Then, finally, they stood up together at some unseen and unheard cue and simply fled the room, leaving the suits to argue incorporation language, cure periods, and default clauses, and to draw up reams more of paperwork for the two of them to later pretend to read, then blindly sign. Cleo, out of the blue, had interrupted a hot discussion about the board of directors structure, mentioning how long it had been since she had tasted good fried okra. The attorneys looked at her as if she had spoken a few words to them in some exotic foreign language. Jimmy smiled and told her that Maggie's Diner had the best in town, with fresh sliced tomatoes on the side and hot buttered corn bread.

That did it. They immediately slipped out of the office without anyone noticing they were gone.

"Or maybe we oughta just make a double-secret Injun blood pact and that would settle it all once and for all," she said, and reached over, cranking the River to 10 on the car radio's volume control.

"Aw, we'll get it done soon!" he yelled over the frantic, bluesy rock and roll that was rattling the speakers under the car's rear window. They rolled out of the parking space in her Mercedes. Once in the traffic along the street, he reached to turn the music down slightly so they could talk.

"The trouble is that the bankers and lawyers and accountants are squeezing the life out of the broadcasting business. It's just not as much fun as it used to be, Cleo."

He knew he sounded like some old fart lamenting the long-lost good old days, but that was exactly the way he felt sometimes.

"Same thing in the music business. You gotta have a guitar player, a drummer, and a team of accountants before you can record a song now."

He glanced over at her and her beauty almost stole his breath away the way it always did. Her lips moved as she mouthed the words along with the singer on the radio while she danced in the seat to the Allman Brothers song Jimmy's station was playing at that moment. A truck driver stopped at the light next to them and did a double take when he recognized the beautiful driver behind the wheel of the rich red car. Jimmy knew exactly how the trucker felt. He couldn't believe he was sitting next to Cleo Michaels either.

"That's one thing I always loved about radio," he said to her when they were moving again and the song's instrumental bridge stopped her singing. "You don't need a meeting of the board of directors to do something fresh and creative. Just open the microphone and say something clever, or cross-fade a couple of records that fit together perfectly, or spend ten minutes with a razor blade in the tape-editing room, and you can create some magic right then and there. You can really touch somebody with what you're able to do with only a little creativity and imagination. I've had people tell me I've made them laugh or cry, fall in love, break up a relationship . . . all simply by something I've done on the air."

"Yeah, I know what you mean, Jimmy. The best stuff ever committed to vinyl was off-the-cuff when some old boys were just goofing around in the studio. Nowadays, you need a memo from some vice president on the West Coast just to make a chord change!"

Then they turned to each other at the same instant and laughed in unison, aware again of how closely in tune their thoughts so often turned out to be.

They had stopped alongside the same truck at the next light and the driver again looked over at them, singing along with the radio, laughing at each other like a couple of loons. The trucker had no doubts at all. These show-business types were already into some heavy drugs, right there in the middle of the damn day! He was shaking his head as he drove on, while Cleo peeled the Mercedes away and into the crowded parking lot at Maggie's.

The okra was fresh and crisp, as delicious as Jimmy had promised, the corn bread hot and smoking, the iced tea perfectly presweetened and icy cold, the lemon icebox pie obviously homemade. They ate and laughed and talked like a couple of teenagers on prom night. Even the autograph seekers were cool for once and didn't come over to bother them.

There was never any conscious decision on either of their parts to drive back to his house. It simply happened. Going back to the legal wars was not an option. There was never any hesitation on her part to follow him to the door and inside. She did it without need for an invitation. He wasn't even aware of being embarrassed by the mess of albums and tapes strewn around the floor, or the suit coats and slacks and ties and underwear slung haphazardly across his new furniture.

As the door closed behind them, she came to him as naturally, as easily as a warm summer rain. Their faces instinctively turned at exactly the proper angle, as if premeasured and calculated so that everything fit perfectly. Their lips met softly in the beginning, then more imperatively, with the urgency of thunder. He felt her body against his own, at first as flitting as a cool breeze, then as emphatic and demanding as a hot wind.

Somehow, they each anticipated the other's moves, responded to the other's touches like a choreographed ballet. It was as if they had rehearsed the moves beforehand so they could be accomplished without awkwardness or fear. There was no hesitation, no holding back.

And later, there was no self-consciousness either when she hopped from his bed to run and sit Indian-style in the middle of the living room, searching through the records to find something for the turntable. He joined her, helped her turn the correct knobs on the stereo system to fill the room with the opening sounds of a Grateful Dead song.

And then he held her closely again, stroked her gently, and listened as she sang along with the music, surprised she knew the words, that she could sing the perfect harmony parts in a voice so beautiful he hurt inside when he heard it. Then, when they made love again, she sang softly into his ear. He loved the way her song grew more urgent, her voice breathier and huskier until she was no longer singing but moaning, laughing, and crying a wonderful melody.

They were in tune, in harmony, in love.

Of course, they eventually had to return to their damned meeting. The lawyers and moneymen either hid their thoughts well or never missed them at all. They presented both of them with massive stacks of legalese, hot off the Xerox machine, and tried to explain the ins and outs of their deal. Their minds weren't on the corporation, though. They only wanted to sign what needed to be signed and get on with it.

On their own, they had already managed to complete the merger, just as they had vowed to do from the very beginning. They had no doubt that it would be a wonderful partnership.

Wizard
Broadcasting
Network

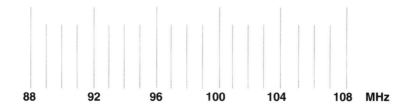

88　　　92　　　96　　　100　　　104　　　108　　MHz

Chapter 24

Jimmy Gill sandbagged for all he was worth. He deliberately stalled the closing of the sale on the Atlanta stations while Detroit pulled every string he could to get the satellite transmission deal put together, the equipment built and tested. And Jimmy searched for the perfect captain to pilot the strange ship they would be floating down there in Georgia. It was Jerry Morrow who brought him Vester Green. Once the two men met and compared notes on all the call letters they could remember from the fifties, the stations they had each grown up listening to, Jimmy knew for certain that the man would fit perfectly into Wizard Broadcasting's expansion plans.

And Green turned out to be a good hire, immediately taking pressure off Jimmy as he began solving convoluted logistical puzzles, bending bureaucratic rules like so much electrical conduit, and even managing to understand most of Detroit's engineering jargon.

The Georges came through with the cash as they always had, but there was one curve thrown at him in the last minutes. DeWayne George hinted strongly that he would like to be at the closing to see his money change hands. Jimmy did his best tap dance, convincing him he didn't really want to be there among all the suits and stuffed shirts. Duane had wanted to go to Atlanta simply so he could hit the striptease clubs and cruise Underground, but that was headed off, too. Besides, as it happened, they had pressing business of their own suddenly pop up somewhere else. Jimmy didn't ask for details.

Later he wished he could have gotten a photo of the faces of the bankers and lawyers when he made the entire down payment in cash, pulling it all from the usual wrinkled brown grocery sack, piling the bundled stacks of bills ceremoniously in the middle of the conference table. Sol Golberg and the old engineer–general manager merely puffed their cigarettes and smiled knowingly while the others at the table turned white and dropped their jaws at the sight of so much legal tender.

Duane and DeWayne were excited about Wizard Broadcasting getting into the Dallas stations. It seemed that they had just established a "working relationship" with some colleagues there, and business was already booming. Thanks to Cleo Michaels and her money, Jimmy only needed a small amount of their tainted cash to finish wrapping up the deal. He tried to ignore the implications of the Georges' alliances in Texas and hoped it would all go away when the cash flow was such that he could pay them off again, finally and completely.

And that would be that. No more loans from the twins. No more dealings at all.

Thankfully, they had just enough time to test Detroit's mystical electronic systems before airdate in Atlanta. The people there could only stand by and scratch their heads as they watched all the flashing lights blink crazily and listened to the rumbling tones that tripped the equipment that had been lined up in row after row of racks into spasms of usefulness.

Detroit was good for far more, too. Jimmy realized more than ever how much he needed his almost mathematical voice of ordered reason.

"If we lease the equipment, we can amortize, but if we finance we can write off the interest and depreciate. We need to see which would be best," he would suddenly say over a quick hamburger at the Varsity or while they drove from Nashville to Atlanta. They might be talking about the weather or the food or whatever, and Detroit would suddenly offer an observation that would stop Jimmy midbite with his face screwed up or twist him around in the car seat.

"Dee, how the hell do you know this stuff? Last time I checked, you were building bikes out of scrap iron and swinging on vines over the creek."

"I don't know. I'm just curious and I suck up a lot of information, I guess. Hey, here's something else. I'm thinking we might

want to someday start our own company, buy the equipment outright and lease it back to ourselves and other stations, too. That
way . . ."

Detroit would go on and on while Jimmy pretended to understand what he was saying. Instead he was listening to whatever
song was on the jukebox or the car radio while managing to nod
at the appropriate times.

The Atlanta advertising agencies already knew Wizard Broadcasting well. They had done business with them in Nashville. That
meant they were able to presign massive commercial business,
guaranteeing the sponsors and their agencies that the station's
ratings would be above a five share in the first ratings book, an
eight share by spring, and even better in the target demographics.
That was optimistic by the agencies' standards. Jimmy was sure
it could be done. It was no gamble at all on his part.

He and Detroit continued the search for people. That was the
hard part. Fortunately, the reputation Wizard Broadcasting was
winning in the industry was leading the best to seek out Jimmy
and Dee. They found a former ABC Radio Network news director
named Lem Loxley, who quickly convinced Jimmy that he shared
his vision for the future of AM radio. Once Loxley was safely hired
and under contract, Jimmy mentioned his satellite idea to him.

"Let's do a news wheel," Lem said immediately, his sonorous
voice rattling loose items on Jimmy's desk. Jimmy replied with
only a vacant expression.

"We'll put continuous newscasts on a satellite channel. Then
our client stations can hop aboard anytime they need to. Or drop
out for local programming and news. We'll leave windows for local
commercials. Here's the good part. We can sell spot announcements on the entire network, charge the stations for the part they
carry from us, and even sell long-form programming overnights
and on weekends. Here's a thought, Mr. Gill. We could have another whole dedicated channel for nothing but long-form shows.
Maybe another with nothing but coast-to-coast two-way talk. Yet
another for sports. Sports talk as well as sports play-by-play. Hell,
man, the possibilities are endless. Give me a satellite!"

Jimmy loved the way the man's mind had taken off! Since the
AM was halfway where they all wanted it to be already, the tran-
sition was a breeze, the pieces falling together even better than

they could have hoped. It sounded like a constant audio merry-go-round, informing, entertaining, amazing those who dialed in, but never leaving them bored. The object was to make the listener afraid he would miss something if he tuned away to a competitor. Advertiser reaction was brisk, since it was a natural buy for the older audience it was already delivering.

A few technical glitches plagued the FM, and Jimmy was afraid Detroit or the engineers he had hired in Atlanta were going to have a stroke before they got the gremlins out. But two days before air-date, Dee came to Jimmy's office, grinning, obviously pleased that he had been able to pull the whole thing off with no model or prototype. The whole system had been concocted inside his head, just like his pieced-together bicycles and the black, flashing gadget boxes he had once built for fun.

The key was that it was all still a hell of a lot of fun for Detroit Simmons.

The programming formula was an instant hit, too, giving the city its first taste of a radio station that played the best of the previous fifteen years of rock and roll without the bubblegum and kid stuff and the incessantly chattering deejays they had grown so weary of on Top 40 AM radio. It was positioned as antiradio radio. The personalities, the "sweetening" that held the record sets together like glue, a never-a-dull-moment audio smorgasbord, the constant aural rainbow they had strung together was unlike anything the listeners had heard before. Unless they had been to Nashville and tuned in to the River.

No one even suspected the disc jockey he or she was hearing on the radio was sitting in a studio on the west bank of the Cumberland River, 250 miles away, giving the time from a clock with only one hand. It was "twenty minutes past the hour," never more exact because of the time-zone difference.

The Dallas station debuted with a frenzy, once they got a staff together and ironed out some kinks in the satellite uplink. Then Detroit wired up a couple of old army surplus facsimile machines and they used them to send commercial copy and program logs back and forth between Atlanta and Texas and Tennessee.

"Someday, everybody will be using these things," he predicted when he finally got the facsimile machines working. Jimmy never doubted him for a second.

It was time for stunting in Dallas. Doing something to create curiosity and street talk about the new station. They preceded the changeover to country music with a week of nothing but ocean sounds on the radio, seagulls chirping, waves crashing against the shore. Even with only the few FM radios that were available then, it caused quite a stir and lots of speculation, including in the newspapers, which usually only mentioned radio when it was bad news.

Then they played a country song called "Fadin' In, Fadin' Out" by Tommy Overstreet. Not only once, but over and over, continuously, for one full day. The song was about a girl's fickle affection coming and going like an AM radio signal that was constantly getting lost in the static. Its lyrics fit KBDC's needs perfectly. The message was that AM was on the wane. FM was the future for country music.

Then, when the format finally started for real, they gave away $102 every 102 minutes to the 102nd caller. The telephone company made them pull the plug on the contest by midafternoon the first day, when the whole exchange locked up and emergency calls couldn't even get through, just as Dee had predicted. Somehow, a lot of people in Dallas, Texas, had found themselves an FM radio to listen to.

No one in Dallas noticed the announcers being so far away either, but they sure enjoyed Ronnie Milsap bringing in a tape of his latest recording, coming directly from the studio to try it out on the air. Or Mel Tillis stopping by for an interview on the way to the lake and a fishing trip. When Loretta Lynn took calls directly on the air over the toll-free number, the announcer had to limit each caller to one minute to accommodate the thousands who tried to get in.

Jimmy Gill was in awe, too. His morning show was now being piped to a potential seven-figure audience each day. He had to start spinning the records an hour early to hit the Georgians who were just crawling from slumber and craved something to get them going.

But even that was not enough. He couldn't resist the impulse to reach an even bigger audience. A couple of times, he used the name "Jimmy Gee" and pulled a weekend shift on the Dallas station. He needed to feel the rush as all seven incoming WATS lines stayed lit, brightly blinking to the beat of the country music he was sending up to space from Nashville and then back down to eager Texas ears.

And he even broke format and played more of Cleo Michael's records than the playlist said that he was supposed to. Hell, he figured, the boss has some privileges!

Then the radio-television critic for one of the Dallas papers, Christopher Julian, wrote a scathing front-page article about KBDC . . . Big D Country. He was frothing about Wizard Broadcasting riding into town like a Texas tornado and replacing the fifteen-year-old classical-and-jazz format with "caterwauling and cow calling of the worst ilk." He fussed about the "sticky-sweet-voiced 'talking heads' who ramble and rant about the hillbilly songs they play over and over ad nauseam," and even hinted that Cleo's partial ownership of the station was just a way to salvage a fading singing career by giving her a personal one-hundred-kilowatt jukebox. Except for Jimmy's few appearances on the weekends, everyone had carefully avoided favoring her songs, but Jimmy could tell she was stung by the charge when he showed her the column over supper that night.

"Don't play any of my songs on the station," she said bluntly.

"Then we can't play any of Waylon Jennings' or Willie Nelson's songs, either."

"Sure we can! Just don't play—"

She had paused midthought. God, she was even beautiful when she was mad, too! Then she relaxed and smiled at him.

"I'm sorry, Jimmy. I sound like a crybaby, don't I? Shoot, I've had my share of bad reviews. Why does this one make me so goofy?"

"Because you know it's not true. If you sing flat or don't work hard at a show, that's one thing. This jerk is just mad at us because we took 'his' station off the air. And I'll bet you a dollar he never even listened to it. A damn critic's got to criticize or he's got no job. It'll all shake out. You'll see."

Jimmy's opinion had always been that any publicity was great, so long as they spelled the call letters right. He had even hung the scathing article on the "Dallas" control-room wall for grins. The disc jockeys seized the moment and gave Christopher Julian a hard time all the next day on the air. They even dedicated the hokiest few songs they played on the station especially to him.

Jimmy was relieved. He had been right. It had all blown over.

The Dallas newspapers were flown to Nashville each day so the on-air personalities could talk on the air about the important things that were going on in town and act as if they were actually sitting in the middle of Dallas. Detroit had found them a college student intern from Middle Tennessee State University whose primary daily job it was to retrieve the paper from the airport and place it in the disc-jockey lounge.

A couple of days after the appearance of the critic's column, the intern tapped timidly on Jimmy's door.

"You better check out today's paper first, Mr. Gill. Before the jocks see it," the kid said. He tossed the paper on Jimmy's desk like a grenade and fled before it exploded.

"Staffer Serious After Attack," the front-page headline screeched. Jimmy held his breath as he read. Someone had snatched Christopher Julian as he parked his car near his apartment the night before and proceeded to beat the holy hell out of him. Whoever did the job knew exactly what he was doing, inflicting just enough punishment to put Julian out of commission for a while but not enough damage to permanently cripple or kill him. And the attacker had left no clues at all.

There were a couple of things, though. The attacker didn't bother taking his victim's wallet. It obviously was not robbery. He did, however, take the time to spray-paint the call letters KBDC in blaring black writing all over Julian's automobile. Julian only recalled seeing a shadowy figure and hearing muttered threats that were hard to remember. There was plenty of blood and pain.

Jimmy Gill felt dizzy until he realized he was still holding his breath. Then the anger took over.

He tracked down DeWayne George on his car telephone, driving somewhere in southern Mississippi. When he answered, he sounded either half-asleep or half-stoned through the scratchy static.

"I've been reading my morning paper, DeWayne. There's an article in there about a newspaper guy in Dallas who had something of a rough night last night," Jimmy told him right off, skipping any pleasantries, fighting the irate quaver that threatened to take over his voice.

"Yeah?"

"You know who did it?"

"Sumbitch deserved worse. Betcha he leaves us alone from now on."

"Damn, DeWayne! He didn't hurt us. He probably did us a big favor. And he damn sure didn't hurt *you*. You can't be doing stuff like this—"

"Hey, we don't know who's listenin' in on this mobile phone, man," DeWayne interrupted. "We'll talk later."

He obviously did not want to discuss it. Jimmy could hear him gunning the car's engine, cursing under his breath, just before the crazy bastard slammed the phone back into its cradle.

Jimmy had to fall back into damage-control mode. He fought a feeling of dread as he began to return the stack of calls from the Dallas media that he had been pointedly ignoring all morning. He had assumed until he read the newspaper story that they were merely asking about KBDC and its new format. Not that they would be inquiring about attempted murder against one of their own.

It was a fact. Newspapers loved to jump on radio stations any chance they got. They were competitors for some of the same advertising dollars, after all. DeWayne George's mess presented a ribbon-wrapped opportunity for them to do just that.

Jimmy Gill knew he could put it off no longer. He had to tell them something. He fought back a sudden attack of the dry-mouth, lifted the phone off the hook as if it were a hundred-pound weight, and prepared to lie his ass off.

Chapter 25

Cleo tried not to show her disappointment, but it was clearly there when Jimmy had to beg off supper for three nights running. She had promised him she would cook a huge, authentic country dinner especially for him, a dinner better than any his mother had ever cooked. He didn't tell her he couldn't remember his mother ever cooking a dinner. He was sorry. He told her so. But the fact was that he simply didn't have the time right then. In a few days though, for sure.

That same week, Lulu Dooley had driven up from Birmingham to visit Detroit and his girlfriend, Rachel. Lulu had wanted to treat them all to a meal at her favorite soul-food place in north Nashville—the only place in town that cooked fit to eat, she had said. It was to be a special occasion besides, to celebrate her resignation as cleaning lady at WROG. After all, by then she was making more money in a week from her tiny investment in Wizard Broadcasting, Incorporated, than WROG was paying her in a month's salary. But Jimmy had to ask Dee to please make excuses for him. He had meetings late into each night. Paperwork piled to the ceiling seemed to be mating and birthing more paperwork. And he had more contracts to read when he got home.

"Jimmy, you need to take a little while and unwind with us," Detroit had said.

"Maybe I can catch up with you later. I need to—"

But he had been interrupted by the bleating of the telephone. Detroit intended to further make his point, but when it became clear this would be a long call, he quietly backed out the office door, shaking his head, and went off to meet Lulu.

Sammie Criswell had given Jimmy several messages from

Grandmama but he seemed always to be tied up when she tried to reach him. And something always came up that had to be taken care of, so he never got the chance to call her back. He did want to hear from her, he kept telling himself. He wanted to tell her all the exciting things that were happening with the stations. Somehow, before he realized it, more than two months had passed since she had last managed to get in touch with him and since they had actually talked with each other.

It was an awfully busy time, and he felt bad about it, but Cleo Michaels and Detroit Simmons and Lulu Dooley and Grandmama would simply have to understand if he couldn't always match up his schedule with whatever it was that they had in mind for him. He had conference calls with the sales staff in Atlanta to make sure he kept them on quota. He had to review the promotion and advertising plans for the fall rating book with the Nashville management team. This sweep was a crucial one. They had a shot at being number one in all the key demographics for the first time. A possible clean sweep. And the engineer's union had held a vote and was already in the door in the Dallas stations before Jimmy or Detroit knew anything was happening. They wanted to talk contract immediately. Jimmy vowed loudly to chop off some managers' heads for not seeing it all coming and giving him fair warning. He also gave Detroit public grief for not anticipating such a thing.

Sometimes, when Jimmy allowed himself the luxury of stopping to think, he felt as if he were drowning, floating facedown in a swift current that swirled wildly about him. But he was always buoyed by the drive to do more and do it better than anybody else had ever done it before. To fulfill the craving he had to put on the best-sounding radio stations he could, making audio magic.

He often seemed on the verge of being pulled under by the demands on him and his time. He was weighted down by his concern for the growing number of people who depended on him for their careers, their livelihood, their creative inspiration; smothered by the prospects of making a growing payroll every two weeks. But he was always saved by seeing the success that so many people were enjoying under his leadership.

Winning made it all worthwhile; winning had become everything.

Something eventually had to give, though. One morning during his show, he put his head down on the control board for a moment, only to collect his thoughts, to relieve the pounding of the lack-of-sleep-and-too-much-coffee headache that was making him half-blind. Before he knew it, he had fallen into a deep sleep. Ten minutes later he awoke with a start to find the turntable three tracks deep into the album from which he had been playing a song. And the number that was then being broadcast featured language not usually heard on the radio. A quick cross-fade to another turntable got him out of the mess, but his face was burning with hot embarrassment. He felt intense shame, but no one else could see. Only Jimmy Gill saw his reflection in the dark control-room window.

The wild eyes and scraggly hair stared back at him with hollow eyes, almost lost in a pasty, lined face, beneath a rat's nest of uncombed hair.

"You, Brother James, are a goddamn mess."

Even his own voice in his ears was tired and raspy. Burned and wasted.

Jimmy decided he would reluctantly begin the search for his replacement as soon as the shift was over, if he lived that long. He had finally realized in that one sleepy, defining moment that he couldn't allow the on-air product of the stations to suffer due to his own inattention. Or to stroke his own ego and need to be heard.

The stations had to be the best. Brother James was no longer the best on-air talent there was. No one else was going to tell him that, of course. He would have to fire himself.

He desperately missed being on the air even before that day's shift was done.

Suddenly, money was everywhere. Jimmy had never paid himself much of a salary. Instead, he had traded commercial time for groceries, clothes, apartments, gasoline, even the cars he and Detroit drove. He didn't need much, he kept telling himself, and anything at all was certainly more than he had been raised with.

But then, because of his position, because of expectations from those he dealt with, it became necessary for him to drive bigger cars and wear nicer suits, to buy clients' lunches and dinners in better restaurants than before, to have his hair styled at a salon instead of cut at a walk-in shop. Jerry Morrow had been the first to suggest that they needed their own airplane so they could hop to Atlanta and Dallas and back to Nashville as quickly as possible. Jerry was a licensed pilot, so Jimmy told him to go look for a plane. He and Dee found one in two days and the deal was done. Then Jimmy was making plans to take flying lessons himself in his spare time. Detroit was flying like an experienced ace the first time he took the stick.

On some level, Jimmy Gill knew that he missed Detroit Simmons. They saw each other in the hallway, but only to speak. When he had a question, he had to get Sammie to dial the extension because he couldn't remember the number. When he saw Rachel in the lobby one day, he couldn't recall her name. He couldn't even recall what brand or color of automobile his best friend was driving.

Time was finite, and it seemed that their only chances to talk were limited to the essentials of getting their technical bases covered. Sometimes Detroit would walk by Jimmy's office, catch him off the phone for once, and drop into a chair to touch bases. Invariably, they would just begin catching up, speaking of something besides business, and the damned telephone would rudely butt in. Or someone in the throes of a major crisis would burst with waving arms and wild eyes into the office. Eventually, after he had sat waiting patiently, Detroit would realize that he had some things that probably needed doing, and he would wander on back to his office.

A few times, Detroit hit Jimmy broadside with his qualms about the way things were going. He always had doubts that they could actually pull everything off, was afraid of the risks they were having to take to give life to their dreams.

"Jimmy, have you really thought this network thing all the way through?"

"Of course I have, Dee," and Jimmy shot him a pained look over the tops of his new tinted reading glasses. It was an expression that questioned Dee's sanity for even suggesting that James Gill couldn't do anything he set his mind to do.

"I was just wondering. Think about this," Detroit plunged on. "You get the River format on a hundred radio stations. Say that each station averages having five disc jockeys on their staffs before they start carrying our satellite programming. They'll only need one man after they go on-line with us. That puts four hundred people on the dole right there. And that's with just one format. You're already talking about putting up three more formats. Don't you see? We are going to be responsible for cutting lots of disc jockeys' throats, Jimmy Gill."

Jimmy grimaced, pulled off the glasses, and spoke to Dee in a tone he might use with someone addled or simpleminded.

"But the owners will love us! And remember, they are the ones who have the money and they are the ones who will write us those nice, big, fat checks every month. Not the deejays. What the satellite format programming is going to do is keep some of these operators from shutting the doors and pulling the big Off switch for good and turning the damned places into liquor stores and filling stations. At least we can keep the sales staffs working. Make the investors and the owners happy. Get them high ratings in the market with minimum cash outlay. And make us happy and rich at the same time, I might add."

Detroit slapped his thigh hard.

"Most of those idiots shouldn't be radio-station owners in the first place, Jimmy. Bankers, doctors, lawyers, silent partners, investment trusts, mezzanine financiers, stock offerings . . . shit, these people don't even know what frequency their radio stations are transmitting on! What the format is! Most of them don't even listen to their own stations. Couldn't find them on the radio dial if they tried. They just stop by on the way to the golf course to check out their precious bottom line or fly in every couple of months to hack away some more from the heart of the station. They take and take and don't put anything back into the station or the market. Excuse me! Town! Not market! Listeners! Not rating numbers! Radio stations are not like a damn shopping mall, Jimmy! All most of these bastards want to do is build up some cash flow by cutting overhead, throw some more money at quick promotions to spike the ratings, then sell the stations for umpteen times cash flow, take an obscene profit, and then let some other sucker take a bath when it all crashes after they've flown the coop. And then the next vulture swoops in and buys it cheap and the whole cycle starts over again. It takes heart and soul to own and operate a station the way it should be run. People like us who love it. Or like we used to be anyway. Jimmy, we can't let money be the only thing that matters. Where did the magic go?"

Detroit had stood and was pacing around the office by that time, flapping his arms in frustration. Jimmy had never heard him say so much at one time and with so much emotion. He must have been rehearsing that speech for a long time, waiting to get it all out of his craw. Why didn't the phone ring now?

"Dee, why don't you go on back to your little shop, twist some pretty-colored wires together, and make something nice that sparks and smokes," Jimmy said, abruptly cutting him off before he could get even more worked up and continue his sermon. "The radio business is the way it is and we're going to be here to make money on it. Times are changing. Remember, if we don't do this, somebody else will. And we can do it a damn sight better than anybody else can because we do love the business of broadcasting. We'll give them good programming. Let them do with it what they will. That's not our concern."

Then Detroit gave him that squint-eyed look of his, turned on his heels, and left the office, slapping the door facing angrily on the way out. He retired to his shop, turned the speaker on the back wall up high to drown out his own muttering, and stabbed the workbench with a screwdriver.

Damn! Jimmy Gill could be so dense sometimes! It was as if he wasn't really interested in listening to what Dee had to say anymore. As if he wasn't listening at all to anybody. Even Cleo had mentioned to Dee that Jimmy seemed distracted, distant, as if his mind was far, far away, off somewhere in the ozone.

Okay, he thought. I'll give it a day or so and hit him from another angle. I'll make him slow down and take stock before he crashes and burns.

It would be at least two weeks before they said more than "Good morning" to each other again.

Cleo Michaels was, of course, far more than merely another distraction for Jimmy. Against his better judgment, and try as he might to fight it, he had fallen even more deeply in love with her. And she had obviously fallen for him, too. At least she told him she had. But it was not an easy relationship to maintain for either of them.

She still followed a dizzying tour schedule, crisscrossing the country for weeks at a time, playing bars, dance halls, state fairs, early-morning television shows. But she called Jimmy every night without fail from her Silver Eagle bus, usually parked in some stump-water stop somewhere along the road or whisking past a mile marker between exits on an interstate highway as it cut a swath through an endless prairie.

She had given up trying to call him at home or trying to anticipate his erratic schedule. Since he was no longer on the air, she could not count on catching him on the hot line, assured of his being trapped in the studio during those three hours. And if she depended on him to call her, to track her down at whatever truck stop parking lot she was hibernating in, then she knew they would rarely if ever talk with each other.

She usually had the best luck by calling every fifteen minutes until she forced him to interrupt one of his crisis calls to talk with her, or by dialing his private office number after eight or nine o'clock at night, when everyone else had gone home, and finding him still at his desk, still neck deep in toil, and answering the call because he assumed it was one of the managers.

When Cleo did get through to him, she fussed at him for working so hard, told him how much she missed him, how badly she wanted to see him and hold him and make love with him. Then, all that said, she would listen patiently to his tales of carnage and bloodshed in the broadcast wars.

He rarely thought to ask how things were with her or how the tour was going. But she didn't seem to mind. It was just good to hear his voice, she always told him. And she knew it was good for him to hear hers, whether he remembered to tell her or not.

When she found her way back home for a few days between shows, they stole precious time with each other, time squeezed from her studio recording sessions and songwriting, from his hours spent stomping out fires and constructing kingdoms. When they managed to converge, to finally shut out everything and everybody else, it was ultimately worth all the trouble.

She was instantly renewed. He was completely revived. Their love was totally rekindled.

It was one of those rare times for them, curled closely together on the thick, soft rug in front of her massive gray stone fireplace. They had spent most of the night involved in wonderful lovemaking, until the flames on the fireplace grate were only smoldering embers. There had been no time for conversation. It seemed, as

usual, as if they had to get to know each other all over again, a
step at a time. Somehow, and again as usual, their bodies were the
first things that needed to be reexplored.

The first blush of a Tennessee dawn dusted them with precious
soft light through the big windows of her living room. He was
awake already, lying as still as he could. Although he tried not to,
he couldn't help composing memos that needed to have been written a while ago. A couple of key management positions should have
been filled yesterday, and he kept running over the candidates in
his mind.

All the while, Cleo breathed softly, sleeping peacefully against
his chest. It felt wonderful, but he needed to get up, make a few
calls, wake some people up in Atlanta and get some tails moving
before the competition's day got started.

But for once he simply couldn't move just then. He didn't want
to wake her. He didn't want to move away from her warmth.

Earlier that week, Jimmy had flown from brutal budget meetings in Dallas directly to New York City to talk with a syndicator
about marketing the programming network. He had also held
meetings with people from a representative firm who would sell
commercials on the web for them, and taken a pack of potential
sponsors to dinner at the Four Seasons. Then, those tasks finished,
he had wrapped everything up several hours before he had anticipated, had managed to commandeer a taxi in midtown Manhattan, had bribed a cabbie with a fifty-buck tip to hurry like hell, and
had somehow managed to get the last seat on the final flight out
of La Guardia that night. Sitting there in New York, arguing
across the desk with the syndicator, he had suddenly missed Cleo
Michaels so badly that it had physically hurt, almost as painfully
as the major ulcer he was culturing. That's when he decided to cut
the deal with the bastard as it stood and run like hell, just on the
off chance that he would be able to capture a few hours alone with
her.

They must have been on the same wavelength again. She had
finished a leg of her tour the day before in St. Louis with an entire
two days off before the next date in Louisville. But the band voted,
and instead of spending one more night on the road than they
absolutely had to, they had instead pointed the Silver Eagle toward Nashville and home. She had dropped the band off at each

of their houses, then driven the bus to her place herself, ready for a few hours of rest and some home cooking.

She had not expected Jimmy back from New York for another day. She knew from experience that matching her schedule with his was like trying to catch mercury with tweezers.

The look on her face when she met him at the door had made all the hustling worthwhile for Jimmy. So had the whole night spent making up for lost time. So much lost time that they didn't want to waste any more getting to the bedroom. They had only made it as far as the oriental rug on her living room floor in front of the fireplace. He couldn't imagine making love could be any better than it was with Cleo Michaels. He learned more about her every time they made love, and he loved it all. Lying there with her soft breath warm on his skin, he vowed he would do better by her, give her the attention she deserved, the caring that he knew she needed.

He grinned and softly kissed her forehead. Who the hell was he kidding? He was honest enough with himself to know he was only telling himself another lie. Maybe soon he could make it all up to her and start giving instead of taking.

Then Jimmy tried to put work out of his mind for a few more minutes, to enjoy her closeness, and he had almost drifted back to welcome sleep when the phone on the end table across the room rang like a coarse Klaxon. Cleo jumped but acted as if she had no intention of getting up to answer the shrill bell. She only groaned and lay there and tried to ignore it as it continued to rudely splinter their dark peace and calm.

Jimmy made a move to go after it himself, mostly out of habit. A ringing telephone usually meant some crisis was going unresolved. But Cleo had him pinned with an arm and a leg and he couldn't move to get it without dumping her. When the thing wouldn't hush, though, she finally raised up on one elbow, her hair beautiful in its after-love tangle, and gave the phone a go-to-hell look. Even that, Jimmy noticed, was breathtakingly lovely in the soft pink light of dawn. She threw a throw pillow at the screeching instrument, then fussed at it when she missed.

"No, no, no, no, no! Shut up, you damned old telephone! Don't bother us now. Go away! Git! Leave us be!"

The she rolled over completely on top of him, straddled him, settled down on him. He marveled again at how well, how naturally, they fit together. Thanks to her, Jimmy Gill was about to forget memos and hirings and firings and the screaming telephone, no matter that the damn thing refused to take a hint and stop ringing. He was quickly getting lost in her again and he knew everything else would be washed away for a precious little while.

"Aw, shit! I better get it, Jimmy," she finally said through a kiss, and reluctantly pulled away from him. The room instantly became ice cold without her. "It's usually something important when it rings this many times this loud this time of day. One of the guys or something."

He tried to pull her back down but she pushed him away playfully and walked to where the phone threatened to jump off the table in its urgency. He wanted her back on the rug with him so badly it hurt.

"Hmm? Yes, he's here. Just a minute."

She ignored Jimmy's futile head-shaking and his fierce scowl and held out the telephone like a threat until he was forced to crawl off the rug, stand up, and take it from her. He kissed her first. Let his hands wander. And he almost put the phone back on the hook without saying a word to whoever it was that had had the gall to interrupt something so special. But the look in her eyes finally made him place the damned thing next to his ear and speak.

"Yeah?" he answered grumpily, hoping whoever had tracked him down would take the hint and leave them alone until he got to the office. Until he could fire him or her properly.

"Jimmy? Detroit said we'd probably find you there. We tried to get hold of you in New York City but we missed you."

Well, Detroit Simmons would have to answer for giving someone this number. That would be agenda item number one. Jimmy couldn't immediately recognize the hesitant female voice on the line since it was so low that it was almost lost in the long-distance hum. But the odd lilt of its foreign accent was eerily familiar.

"Okay. You've found me. What gives? Who is this?"

"Greta Polanski, Jimmy. I'm so sorry. We tried to get to you in Dallas, but you'd left. Then Clarice tried to reach you in New York all day yesterday, but we got the wrong number for a while, and then you were gone again last night."

A numbness began somewhere deep in his gut.

"It's your grandmother, Jimmy. They found her day before yesterday evening. She had been gone a day or so already, they think, sitting up so natural in front of her TV set. They say it was her heart. It just quit."

The numbness spread all over him. He had to concentrate hard to hold on to the phone. Cleo watched him, frightened by the expression on his chalky face, questioning him with her eyes.

"When is the funeral, Mrs. Polanski?"

"I'm so sorry. We couldn't get in touch with you, Jimmy. They had to bury her yesterday. In the cemetery down the superhighway from the radio station. They couldn't wait any longer, you see. She had been gone so long already. I am so sorry, Jimmy, to have to bring you such sad news."

He had seen his grandmother once in the past year. He had actually talked with her three or four times on the telephone. Each time she had ranted on so much about her health, convinced she had every disease that she saw being treated by Dr. Casey and Dr. Kildare each week. He had sent her money for food and clothes but Mrs. Polanski and Mrs. George reported that she had spent it on cigarettes and fan magazines, a new television set and an outside antenna. And then she had spent the money to put in the new cable television system so she could get ten channels instead of two. Since then, they had seen even less of her.

She had never really understood what her grandson did for a living these days. Sure, she had listened to him on the radio a few times, pulling the FM signal in from Atlanta on the big upright Zenith, but she rarely went to the trouble because it took away precious time from her television watching.

When they did talk, she always asked Jimmy if he had run into Pat Boone or Ed Sullivan or Arthur Godfrey lately, or how Elvis Presley was doing. He didn't try to explain anything to her, but told her yes, he had seen them all, and that they were all fine. And once, during one of their last telephone conversations, she announced casually that she had heard from his mother. That she and his father were doing very well and that they sent their love and would look forward to seeing him at Christmas. He had humored her, thanked her for relaying the messages from the ghosts and hung up as abruptly as he had dared.

Now she was gone, too.

He carefully placed the telephone back down, then walked to Cleo's huge picture window. He stood there before the rising sun as it painted pastel streaks in the eastern sky with a sure, broad brush. New leaves were still thin on the tall maples that surrounded the dew-covered lawn, and, even through the glass, he could hear a couple of mourning doves calling sadly to each other.

He didn't mean to, he wasn't looking for it, but he couldn't help seeing it. In the misty distance, perched on a ridge overlooking the valley, there were the series of scarlet lights along the tall, straight tower that held high the antenna for his radio station. They were blinking hypnotically in a soothing, comforting pattern, assuring him that all was still well with that one part of the world that really mattered most to him.

But then, as he watched the tower, the first shaft of sunlight peeked over the distant hills and struck a sensor along the spire's flank, and it tripped a relay, just as it was supposed to do. The blinking lights died suddenly, causing the tower to become lost completely in the soupy morning haze.

The glass of the picture window was cool against his forehead, but the single tear that suddenly cut a path down his cheek was hot and scalding.

Chapter 26

The idea was so obvious that Jimmy Gill couldn't believe he had not thought of it before. But one night, there it was, right in front of him, burning brighter than a bonfire in the corner of the living room. Jesus! Maybe he had been working too hard after all. Or all those radio frequency magnetic waves that had been swirling around his head the last twenty years might have caused some brain damage after all.

He and Cleo had gone to dinner, spent a wonderful, precious few minutes together at her place, and then kissed good-bye. Then her tour bus had pulled up in front of the mansion, the band members yelling and blowing the horn for her to climb on board so they could get started for God only knew where. He had wandered back inside, not the least bit tired but lonesome for her already. Jimmy was still half wired from some pills DeWayne George had given him. Something small and colorful to help keep him functioning through the final stages of launching the radio programming network. Trailblazing could sometimes be nerve-racking.

The television set kept a bright night-light and a steady babble of noise going in the living room. That was good. He didn't want to be alone yet. He stepped to Cleo's kitchen and made another urn of coffee. Then he fished into his briefcase for a bundle of paperwork he had to finish reading before an early-morning breakfast meeting with some important, impatient people.

The past year had been a swirl of papers, lawyers, equipment, bankers, buildings, faces, problems . . . no, not problems . . . opportunities to succeed. That's what he tried to call them now. Got to be positive. Got to keep moving forward or die.

In just over a year, Wizard Broadcasting had added to the

chain with new radio stations in Houston and Louisville. Now
Jimmy Gill was on the verge of closing the sale on WROG in Birmingham and the new FM that the owners there had recently
signed on the air.

They had paid too much money for WROG. Far more than the
cash flow or the station's shabby real estate would justify. He
would admit that fact to anyone who might raise the point, if anyone dared. But there were other factors the bankers couldn't cal-
culate and the accountants couldn't tally. The studios were still
located in the same old cement-block building, a few blocks from
the cemetery where Rockin' Randy Mathews and Grandmama
rested only a few yards from each other. The halls in that old building could definitely tell some tales.

Jimmy had already promised himself he would have to walk
through the building one more time before they bulldozed it all
and moved to new offices and studios in a marble monolith that
hung precariously on the side of Red Mountain. Maybe, if he could
find the time, Detroit Simmons might want to explore the building,
too. Jimmy promised himself he would try to remember to mention
it to him the next time he saw him.

And maybe, Jimmy thought, he'd take a minute and get by the
cemetery, too. He thought he could still locate the spot in the
shadow of the tower where Rockin' Randy's piano-crate coffin had
been lowered into the cold ground. Someone might be able to point
out to him exactly where his grandmother's grave was, too. He'd
tried to find it when he came down to take care of his grandmother's things, including the old Zenith radio.

The Wizard Networks were already going through dry runs on
the air. What little he had heard sounded fine. They would be
broadcasting from the new state-of-the-art studios Detroit had designed and wired together on the top floor of a high-rise bank building in Nashville's Lower Broadway district. Jimmy already had
several dozen signed contracts on his desk from client stations.
They couldn't wait to begin carrying the music, news, and commercials that would be beamed up to the satellite twenty-four
hours a day, hurled to the sky from a huge dish on the bank building's roof.

Wizard Networks was making it possible for some of the stations to move to profitability, to even stay on the air. They would be able to run their stations on a shoestring, pocketing the money that had gone to the on-air personalities before. And without living, breathing people, there would be no worries about labor unions, vacations, sick days, pregnant wives, and guys getting arrested or not showing up.

But this particular night, Jimmy Gill was too restless to work anymore. He brought his steaming coffee mug into the living room, loosened his tie, kicked off his dress shoes, sank into Cleo's plush couch, and drank in the smell of her that still lingered in the room. He missed her badly any time she was out of sight, longed for her soft touch, healing voice, wise words. He needed her for the way she seemed to listen to what he had to say, and the way she always understood him. She did so much to keep him on an even keel, to help stave off the insanity into which the breakneck pace was threatening to shove him headforemost.

There was still a part of him, though, that resisted loving her so much. He knew what it was because he had admitted it to himself already. He wanted to keep her from getting too deep inside him so that he wouldn't be totally destroyed when she eventually abandoned him. And he knew with firm certainty that no matter how much she loved him now, or how much he loved and needed her, she would leave him someday.

He picked up her Gibson guitar and held it close to him, strummed its strings and felt its wood vibrating against his chest. He had to do a better job of staying on guard. He could not let her get so close that her eventual leaving would kill him.

Just then, he thought of a question he had needed to ask Detroit Simmons earlier in the day. Something about another control tone he thought they might need to fire off yet another set of jingles at all their network affiliate stations. That's how his thoughts came these days. Zooming in out of the ozone like some kind of misaimed comet. And if he didn't act on them immediately, they sometimes left him forever, burned up in the jumble of all that he had to think about.

Instinctively he grabbed the telephone and had most of Detroit's number dialed before he realized it was, by then, probably after three o'clock in the morning. He and Dee had had a blowup two or three days before about something so insignificant he couldn't even remember what it had been. They had only spoken curtly with each other a time or two since.

Damn it, Detroit had become so stubborn, such a brick wall to all Jimmy was trying to do lately. Only when he was presented with some kind of impossible technical mountain to climb did he brighten and become the old Dee for a while. He still loved to lose himself in a mound of circuit boards and wiring harness, to produce some kind of complicated, blinking, bleeping black box that accomplished a task so convoluted that only he knew what it was doing and why.

Jimmy put the phone back down and sat alone in the darkness. Then, for an instant, he almost rose from the couch and went to his grandmother's old Zenith radio. It now sat in a prominent place in the corner of Cleo's living room after Jimmy had rescued it from the duplex. He had brought it back carefully in the trunk of his Caddy to Nashville. Cleo had insisted he bring it to her place. She loved the old box immediately.

She scrounged all over town for new tubes for the thing, finally having to get them from an antique-radio dealer somewhere up north. Then she refinished and polished the mahogany cabinet until it might have passed for new. Detroit replaced the dead filter capacitors in the power supply and then had to build some of the other dying components from scratch because they were not available any longer.

When they got it working, Cleo wrapped it in a red ribbon and made it her gift to Jimmy, commemorating the second anniversary of their relationship. He had forgotten the significance of the day altogether, but when he got to the office he postponed an important conference long enough to instruct Sammie to order Cleo some flowers. Expensive flowers. And he asked her to go to a department store and pick out something nice and frilly and sexy and have it sent over to Cleo, and to please fake his signature on the card.

Cleo loved the way the radio sounded, with its deep-toned, throaty, rumbling bass and the sparkling crispness of its high frequencies. She listened to it constantly when she was in town. Jimmy never had the time. He had not even listened to the River, his own station, for more than a few moments in the last several months. It seemed he was always on the telephone or in a meeting too big or too deep to interrupt to simply listen to music or waste time seeing what was happening on the radio.

He didn't move from the couch, but only continued to sit there in the darkness. He'd listen to the Zenith some other time. He was still wide awake. DeWayne's medicine was doing its job too damn well. It promised to be another night with only minimal sleep.

Then, for some reason, the flickering of the television set in the corner caught his attention. He couldn't remember the last time he had watched an entire show on the thing. Maybe an appearance by Cleo and her band on *The Tonight Show*. Or half watching the late news on occasion while he worked away at something else.

Now, some fat man in a flowered shirt and a tall chef's hat was demonstrating a set of steak knives on the tube. On an impulse, and since he always kept the phone nearby wherever he was, he dialed the number that was flashing insistently, begging at the bottom of the screen.

Busy signal.

Jimmy watched the man slice meat with one of the knives, then shrimp, an old automobile tire, a tin can, while the studio audience clapped and cheered as if he were accomplishing some kind of magical illusion. He tried out the number on the telephone's dial again.

Still busy. Damn.

Three more times over the next ten minutes he tried to dial the steak knife ordering number. It was continually busy. Almost three o'clock on Thursday morning and people were flooding a phone bank somewhere to buy goddamn steak knives!

Jimmy Gill fell to his knees in front of the television set and twisted the channel knob, dialing up the other stations that were still telecasting. The other two local network affiliates were off the air already. One only showed snow, the other a complicated test pattern with a squealing tone for the only sound. The movie channel on the cable was spinning an old black-and-white foreign picture with subtitles almost lost in the blur at the bottom of the screen.

Those were all the choices at his disposal.

Twelve VHF and seventy-four UHF channels on the television set, a cable converter box that went all the way up to fifty more channels, and there was nothing on the air but a man peddling steak knives! The potential power, the latent reach, the room for

creativity in this medium were massive! But the vacuum of programming was almost suffocating!

Something momentous clicked inside his brain. Something he
couldn't believe he had overlooked thus far.

Jimmy dove back to the couch and twisted out Detroit Simmons's number on the telephone's rotary dial.

"Hello . . . yes?"

It was his girlfriend. What was her name? Rachel? Yes, Rachel.
After ten rings. She was confused, still asleep.

"Rachel? Is Detroit there, please, honey?"

"Hmm? Uh, yeah. Just a minute."

The phone clattered noisily to the floor where she had dropped
it. He could hear Detroit whispering questions and curses to her.
He probably assumed the station was on fire. Or worse. Off the
air.

"What is it, damn it?"

"How many channels can they send at the same time on a cable
television wire?"

Jimmy could almost see him, shaking the cobwebs from his
head, deciding whether or not to even reply to this latest and sil-
liest out-of-the-blue question. But then, Jimmy knew, he would be
thinking about it despite himself, actually trying to pull the answer from a memory bank somewhere. There was only a five-
second pause while the wheels turned.

"I guess dozens, maybe fifty or more. The wire can carry plenty
but they need the converter boxes to decode the signals."

He could hear Rachel in the background, questioning Detroit
about who it was and what the hell was going on. Detroit ignored
her. He was awake already, involved, thinking, wondering already
what Jimmy was up to now.

"Fifty, you say?"

"Jimmy, what are you thinking about now? What time is it
anyway?"

"Turn on your television right now and just look. There's nothing on the thing but lame, silly programming. Garbage they throw
on there just to fill the time between the commercials. Just like
radio was before FM took off. Look, cable TV's going in everywhere,
and people are going to want more choices than the networks and
the few movie channels are giving them now. It's going to be niche

programming, narrowcasting, boutique formats, just like radio's gone to already. Just like magazines have been for twenty years. No more *Saturday Evening Post* or *Life* or *Look*. Imagine it! Fifty, sixty channels, all different. Nothing needs to be mass appeal anymore. Give them something for a specific demographic, deliver what the advertiser needs to reach his target, and they don't give a shit about raw numbers at all. Deliver them an audience of left-handed midgets between eighteen and twenty-four years old if that's who they need to reach. Narrowcasting! Targeting! It's the logical extension of the television medium. Just like radio! Just like damned radio!"

As he talked, Jimmy unconsciously reached for the pill bottle that was resting on the coffee table. He shook out three of the capsules, downed them, and chased them with a swallow of the strong, cold coffee. He suddenly had another castle to build in his burgeoning empire, and sleep would simply have to wait.

"Let me guess. You are going to supply the programming."

"We are, Dee. Wizard Cable is! Think about the possibilities, man! I can see a home-shopping channel that costs next to nothing to run and the friends and neighbors out there in televisionland keeping the telephone lines hot, tripping all over themselves to give us their credit card numbers and we take a cut of every damn thing that we sell. Oh, and how about this? A channel that does nothing but broadcast the news all day, and another one for just the weather, twenty-four hours a damn day! Shit, man, we could put the audio from the channels up on our radio networks, tie them all together, and get double duty out of everybody. Oh, and how about a preacher channel . . . just one damned religious show after another? And we sell the time to them, just like we used to do on Sunday mornings at WROG. Cash business. Pay in advance. Give them a receipt. Hustle to the bank. Beautiful! Damn beautiful!"

On the blinking screen in front of him, the man with the knives had made way for a sweating, stalking preacher who pounded his Bible and screamed at an auditorium full of writhing people. His telephone numbers for prayer and donations constantly scrolled across the bottom of the picture. The donation number was huge and outlined in rainbow colors. The prayer number was tiny and almost lost on the bottom of the screen.

"Cable systems are even poorer than radio stations, Jimmy.

They're not going to want to pay anybody like us for programming when they can rebroadcast the local television stations for nothing."

"No! That's the beauty of it! First we teach them how to sell their own commercials locally and insert them in the shows themselves. Then we've got a shock for them. We pay them . . . so much for each home, let's say . . . to carry our shows. Then we make all the money on advertising and the stuff we sell and what the preachers pay us. Hell, we'll even furnish them the satellite dish, the receiving equipment, the whole kit and caboodle. All they got to do is wire us to their system and collect the dollars. How much you figure something like all that will cost us?"

For a few seconds Detroit actually thought about it, then realized he didn't have any idea.

"Hell, Jimmy, I don't know! But I'll bet you want me to find out. And probably before breakfast, too."

"Nah! By lunchtime will be fine."

He laughed out loud, the first time he had done that in weeks, and he loved the sound of Dee's chuckle coming back at him through the phone. Their differences were forgotten for the moment. They had found a new challenge to attack and conquer together. A new toy to wire together from scrap.

"Damn," Detroit said, "I might've known you'd want to take on television before it was all over. Television! Damn chewing gum for the eyes!"

"Just radio with pictures, Dee. That's all she is. Shoot, man, if we don't do it, somebody else will."

"And somebody's going to build a rocket ship and go to Mars, too. I hope you're not planning on tackling that one."

"Well, now that you mention it . . ."

And then they talked and laughed some more until Rachel screeched and prodded and finally convinced Dee to hush and go back to sleep.

" 'Night, Mr. Dee-troit."

" 'Night, Jimmy Gill."

But Jimmy didn't go to bed. He took two more pills, spent a good hour making notes, hurriedly read over the contracts from his briefcase, ran through the shower, dressed, and headed directly for the station. It would be seven o'clock before he got there now. Middle of the day!

He had to hustle. He had a whole new world to explore. He didn't want to take the risk of having someone else beating him to paydirt while he rested, wasting precious time.

Chapter 27

One of the jocks stopped him in the hall and hit him with the news the instant he walked in the door. Somebody named De-Wayne George, claiming to be one of the investors in the company, was waiting for him in his office. The jock apologized for letting him in, but what could he do? The guy seemed convincing enough and he had seen him around before so he figured it would be okay.

Jimmy told him it was fine, and to get on back to the booth and do a great show. Then he swallowed hard, checked the front desk, and found he also had messages in his box from four different attorneys, two accountants, the engineers union shop steward in Dallas, the landlord for the studio building in Houston, and two record company promotion men who were mad enough to murder him because he hadn't added a couple of their records to any of the network playlists yet.

It was a typical day at the office at Wizard Broadcasting.

Damn it! He had a hot idea he wanted to set aboil instantly. He didn't have time to deal with all the bullshit! And especially with the slithery likes of DeWayne George.

The more he had thought about the cable television idea in the shower and in the car on the way in, the more excited he had become. He hardly remembered showering, wasn't even sure he had brushed his teeth, and he had made three wrong turns driving in, as if he had somehow forgotten the way to the office. He was ready, primed to get things moving before the plan got cold.

DeWayne sat there behind Jimmy's desk as if it were his own, brazenly examining confidential papers that were stacked there. He didn't even flinch when Jimmy walked in but kept reading whatever it was he was looking at until he had finished it, or was simply good and ready to look up at him.

Jimmy closed the door behind him, locked it from the inside, vowed he would keep it locked from now on when he was out of the office, and then stood there for an awkward minute while DeWayne finished his snooping. The grubby man didn't offer Jimmy his own chair, not even when he finally raised his eyes to look at him. Then he only sat there, staring through his slitted eyes, obviously waiting for Jimmy to speak first. It must be some kind of territorial thing, Jimmy figured. First one to speak is the weaker.

"What do you need, DeWayne?"

"And a gracious good mornin' to you, too, Brother James," he said, turning on a crooked grin. "Fine time of the day to be coming to the office. I figured you'd be here by five-thirty. Since when do you keep such bankers' hours?"

Jimmy finally took the chair across the desk from him. De-Wayne George had lately taken to wearing his black hair slicked straight back from his forehead and tied in the back in a long, dangling ponytail. He also had a beard that he kept clipped to the length of about three days' growth. He had recently abandoned his jeans and tie-dyed T-shirts, too, and now dressed in expensive suits, his tieless pastel shirt collar buttoned tightly at the neck.

He could have played a dope dealer in the movies or on television with no wardrobe changes.

It had been a long time since Jimmy had seen Duane, the twin brother. It seemed he was usually away somewhere, running some mysterious operation in an isolated, exotic, unspecified location in a far corner of the southern United States or in the Caribbean or Central America. The job seemed to always require him to keep late hours and drive fast vehicles and be unavailable and out of touch for prolonged periods of time.

"It's only seven o'clock and I'll be here till ten tonight."

Lord. Why did he feel the need to respond to the fool?

"Duane sends his love, Brother James," DeWayne hissed, now flashing him a snake's smile.

"Well, tell him I send the same sentiment right back at him."

"I was passing through town and I just wanted to stop in for a minute and get a little state-of-the-stations report from you, buddy," DeWayne said through his frightening smirk. "How's it all going these days anyhow?"

"Everything's peachy, DeWayne. Every property is well ahead of projection except Houston. That'll be a tough nut to crack. We've got some serious competition from some big group owners down there."

"Who's giving us the most trouble, then? K-Rock?"

Once again, the twin glanced down to a ledger sheet on the desk in front of him, as if he could actually make sense of all the columns and rows and endless figures.

Jimmy still resented DeWayne and Duane using "us," including themselves in any way with Wizard Broadcasting. As much as he appreciated their seed money, and the risk the twins had taken early on, he desperately wanted a divorce from them now. Wizard had repaid the twins completely. The company was making it on its own, had been self-sufficient and turning profits for several years. Every borrowed penny since the Dallas purchase had come from actual banks. Clean money from respected lending institutions with loan committees and buildings and vaults and daytime office hours.

"Yeah, K-Rock for sure will be the toughest competition we've faced anywhere. They're a good station and they've got a war chest to fight us with. But we're going to do it right. We've commissioned a strategic research project to find some chinks in their armor. We'll put a plan together and attack them with both barrels. We'll get them eventually, but it'll take some time and money. But hell, that's the fun part. Beating good competition. And we've got the war chest to do it."

Might as well let him know that Wizard had money now, that there was no need for his dirty stuff anymore. But there was no indication that DeWayne had heard a word of his answer. He blatantly continued to read the correspondence on the desk, nodding only slightly at Jimmy's words. Then, when he was once again ready, he finally looked up and spoke.

"Did you know that I can drive just about anywhere I wanna go and still not get out of range of at least one of our stations. It sure makes me proud to know me and my brother and my mama had a little bitty bit to do with the success of it all."

Jimmy blinked once and swallowed hard.

"You know we appreciate what you and Duane did for us," Jimmy offered. He was still of the opinion it was best to humor DeWayne George. He didn't doubt for a moment that he could be a very dangerous man if he got the impression he was being slighted. "We're at a very sensitive time right now. We are a major player in the business, and we'll have plenty of other groups taking potshots at us since we started up the networks. We're going to make some enemies and you can bet on that. We've got to walk a fine line or the government could come poking around, too. I don't need them riding in, questioning our financing or how much Lulu Dooley or Greta Polanski or your mama . . . or even Detroit Simmons, for that matter . . . really have to do with running this whole shebang. We've come a long way on 'integration of ownership and management.' If they decide all those folks are just figureheads, the feds could throw a wrench in the gears in no time flat."

"Yeah, yeah. But me and Duane, we feel like we took some big risks backin' you and the nigger when you was gettin' all this shit started," DeWayne went on, again seeming to ignore Jimmy and his cautions. The man obviously had something he wanted to spit out.

He suddenly uncoiled and jumped to his feet so quickly he startled Jimmy. The taps on the heels of his snakeskin cowboy boots clattered loudly as he turned his back and strode to the window. He stopped there and stared outside. From that window, he could see the new bank skyscraper downtown with the studios inside and the huge satellite dish on top. If the humidity was low enough, the broadcasting tower for the River was even visible from there, beyond the city, on the mountaintop.

"If you boys had gone bust, we'd have lost ourselves a lot of cash money for sure. Cash money me and Duane worked awful hard and took some powerful risks to accumulate, you understand. And there wouldn't have been any way to sue you and the nigger or take you to court or nothin' to get it back if you-all had gone belly-up. Our names weren't on any piece of paper or a promissory note nowhere. But we put it all right there on the line for y'all, didn't we, Brother James? Me and Duane? We were there for you when you needed us, weren't we?"

He seemed to be asking the panes of window glass the questions, but the answers came from Jimmy Gill.

"Like I said, Dee and I appreciate what you guys have done. And we paid you every cent back plus fifty percent interest, too, DeWayne. Good clean money that you could put in any bank and spend just like you came by it all perfectly on the up and up."

"Yeah, we scratched one another's backs didn't we, Brother James? We make a helluva team."

And then there was silence for a bit, broken only by the slight squeaking of the hardwood floor as George shifted his weight from one foot to the other.

"Okay, DeWayne, what do you want?"

Jimmy couldn't stand the fencing anymore. He let his impatience show.

The twin turned abruptly from the window, eyes squinted, teeth clenched, as if he were about to strike out at something or somebody.

"You got any idea how big me and Duane's business is? How much cash we get and the volume of the commodities that we move? How many people we got working for us now?"

He virtually hissed the words, spit flying.

"No, and I sure as hell don't want to know either, to be perfectly—"

"Well, we're a damn sight bigger in what we do than you and the nigger are in the radio business. We're so big now, in fact, that we're attracting attention from some folks we don't necessarily want to mess with just yet. And I ain't talking about the law, neither."

Jimmy couldn't figure where this was all heading. It had been a long time since he had seen DeWayne so worked up. Finally Jimmy stood up from the chair, circled the desk, and claimed his own executive's seat. He felt better there. More familiar. More at home. More in control. Then he began reshuffling the papers on the desk, carefully placing the ones the twin had touched into their own pile, as if in quarantine.

"Well, DeWayne, I'm really happy that there are enough idiots out there who want to get swimmy-headed and messed up that they can keep you boys in business. I hope you can keep on making money as fast as the mint can print the stuff. More power to you.

But, DeWayne, tell me. What's all this got to do with me or Wizard Broadcasting?"

DeWayne's eyes narrowed. He walked back to the office chair Jimmy had just vacated and sat down heavily.

"We wanna grow our business, Brother James. That's what it's all about. Just like you want to own every goddamn radio station on the planet. It's time for us to expand into South Florida and make a move up the East Coast. Probably into New Orleans and spread out into more of Texas, too. Cocaine's the next big thing. It's worth more money than smoke by far, and not nearly as much trouble as heroin. We can sell the shit by the boxcar, just as fast as we can import it. But there is a basic law of marketing that's getting in our way, Brother James. I'm sure you will understand perfectly. We got to already physically be in them places to make it worth the risk. We can't do a deal with the suppliers in South America if we don't have the franchises and the organizations already set up. Trouble is, they got some mean sumbitches where we are goin' that don't cotton to any kind of competition a'tall. The only way we can bust in is by bein' legit first. Have us some front to work out of that's legal. We could go in as a trucking company or something like that. But the competition is already wired into the unions like nobody's business, and they'd know what we were up to, know we were pissing in their pot, in a New York minute."

He stood again, walked over and sat on the edge of the desk, then bent to within six inches of Jimmy's face. Seven-fifteen in the morning and his breath carried the smell of whiskey already.

"I've been watching the way you do things, Brother James. You are one impressive bastard, you know that? And there's a way you can put some of that skill to work for me and old Duane. Just to show how much you appreciate what we did for you. There's plenty of those little pissant, low-power AM radio stations in every one of the places where we plan to expand. What we need to do is quietly buy some of them, get our asses in there, and set up business without anybody being none the wiser. Poor as them stations are nowadays, nobody would pay us any mind at all."

"DeWayne, I still don't get it."

"You are going to help us buy 'em and get the licenses for 'em."

Jimmy was stunned. The last thing he needed now was to be in bed with a couple of cocaine cowboys.

"Damn, DeWayne. You don't need me! Just go on to wherever you want to go and buy the damn things. Your pothead lawyer buddy in D.C. can get you filed and granted in his sleep."

Jimmy had fired Grover years before. He hoped no one would ever have to know he had once represented Wizard Broadcasting.

"Well, there's one little crimp in that plan, buddy. Me and Duane both got a few black marks on our record. A drug conviction apiece, possession with intent to distribute. It didn't cost us much time, but it put something of a stain on our otherwise stellar credentials. You know we can't be a radio-station licensee with a felony conviction."

Jimmy felt sick. His ulcer screamed just below his breastbone, and massaging it wasn't helping at all. He should have eaten something for breakfast. He was always forgetting to eat unless Cleo was there to remind him.

"Look, there are probably plenty of people out there who would front for you for the easy money. Why me?"

"You've already proved that you can get things like this through the FCC without a hitch. Having the niggers involved and all oughta help, too. Nobody's gonna look too hard at you when you go buyin' some more stations. And God knows, me and my brother can't afford to have anybody lookin' too deep into our little business operations just now."

"No, DeWayne. Not just no. Hell, no! Even if I was willing to do this, I can't legally buy but three more AMs. We've got four already. You can only have seven, total. We're right now negotiating to go into some bigger markets, and to do it we'll have to take some AM/FM combos to make the financing work, to put the deals together. We can't afford to get boxed in like that. No! No way!"

Slowly, DeWayne drew back from Jimmy's face, his anger appearing to be a smoldering fire somewhere deep inside. He dropped his cold stare, eased off the corner of the desk, and clanged back to the office window. Seconds passed while Jimmy stared at the paperwork in front of him without seeing a word on the pages, listened to the floor squeaking with DeWayne's rocking.

"I was really hoping you'd be a little more enthusiastic about helping out your old neighbors, Brother James."

"I can't risk it, DeWayne. You boys are into too much heavy stuff. We could lose everything! Just a whiff of something like this and our whole house of cards comes crashing down, just when everything's going crazy. What if the banks, our advertisers, even the listeners, got wind of something like that? Damn! Don't ask me to get into something this dirty!" Jimmy knew his voice had taken on a pleading tone, cracking in exasperation and fear. He couldn't help it. "Please. Do this with somebody else and leave us alone!"

George whirled around to face him again.

"Shit, Brother James. It seems like to me you're into the cesspool waist deep already. I'd hate for the wrong people to find out where all that cash you were flashing at the closings in Nashville and Atlanta and Dallas really came from. And exactly who it was that busted up that newspaper bastard in Dallas when he crossed us that time."

The sudden sneer that crossed George's face was chilling. The temperature in the room seemed to drop noticeably.

"Oh. By the way. You'll be hearing in a few minutes about a really terrible thing that happened last night down there in Houston."

Something sharp seemed to penetrate Jimmy's gut then, twisting and grinding like a knife, swiping his breath in the process.

"Houston?"

"Yeah. Too bad, too. That big old tower that K-Rock broadcasts from? They should have kept a better watch on the guy wires on that thing, what with all that salt air and stuff. A couple of the wires must have had the anchor bolts rust clear through. Whole damn thing's just a pile of scrap iron now. They're lucky nobody was killed!"

Jimmy's face burned like fire while the rest of him was taken by a sudden cold shiver. His mouth was open, but no words came out.

"I hear their transmitter and the building it was in are flatter than a flounder. They're gonna be back on the air in a day or so, I imagine, but with about as much power as that lightbulb in your desk lamp there. They might as well stay signed off for all the good it'll do them. And with that rating book just starting and our new station giving them some new competition and all, it's a damn shame. A real tragedy."

Jimmy Gill managed to stand then, his hands held outward in

questioning desperation. DeWayne's face was set hard as concrete, the evil serpent's grin frozen on his lips.

"It wouldn't do for them to take too close a look at the damage, though. Especially with the pictures I got of our man doing some late-night maintenance work out there. I'd hate for them to connect that awful accident with the new owners that just come to town." He paused for effect, letting the implication sink in, twisting the knife another turn. "I'll give you a call with the exact stations we wanna start in with and you can get the ball rollin' on this end. I imagine you know what to do."

He was slithering toward the door now, but turned suddenly, obviously to leave one more pregnant thought with Jimmy Gill.

"Oh, and tell that hillbilly-singer gal-friend of yours to be careful out there on the road. Accidents do happen, you know."

Chapter 28

A trio of persistent mockingbirds were singing their hearts out from their perch in a persimmon tree down by the church. The fussing and cawing of a playful flock of crows somewhere off in the distance was the only other sound Jimmy Gill could hear. The air was still and warm, the sun out beyond the shade of the big elms so bright it was almost blinding. He was sitting on a sixty-foot-long, hand-built picnic table, his feet propped on the bench that ran its length.

The wooden tables were used for "dinner on the ground" and cemetery decoration day and other special days at the nearby Holiness church. Jimmy Gill sat there in the shade of the elms, with the mockingbirds for a choir, the crows doing all the preaching, while he drank a warm beer and let the calmness of the moment wash over him.

Twenty feet away from where he sat, at the edge of the cemetery, the graves of his mother and father were barely discernible in the high weeds and twisted vines and piled-up pine straw. Most of the other plots near them had much bigger markers. They boasted colorful pots of flowered plants placed there carefully by remembering family, probably on the most recent decoration day. Or on Father's or Mother's Day. Or on a birthday counted even after the particular loved one had long since quit having them.

But his folks' tombstones were simple flat slates tenuously balanced on a chipped cement base. Their names had been crudely chiseled in, and were now almost erased by the elements. It almost seemed as if the weather and the undergrowth had tried to take away any proof of their existence. Only a wild dogwood sapling rooted at their heads adorned the neglected graves.

He couldn't imagine what had brought him to this calm, quiet spot, just up a hill from the Tennessee River. What unknown force had left him with red clay mud on his three-hundred-dollar shoes and yellow pine dust streaking his custom-tailored pin-striped suit. Here in an elm grove a million miles from the clutching grasp of the business that was about to stifle him, threatening to claim what minute sanity he had left.

The company airplane had been over in Memphis for its annual inspection for three days. The only commercial flights out of Nashville were booked solid with country disc jockeys fleeing their annual convention. So, on an impulse, he had decided to drive his new car down to the Atlanta stations for some meetings, the way he and Detroit had once done a hundred years ago. He would use the time out of reach of the office and the car's mobile telephone to think about where the hell it was that he was headed. He never thought he would detour through a country church cemetery, though.

Detroit had reluctantly offered to ride down with him, but he had already lined up appointments with equipment vendors all day. They would be clamoring to sell them more studio equipment for the new satellite channels, and decisions had to be made soon. Detroit had finally decided that he would have to take the early flight out of Nashville the next day to join him so he could get everything done that had to be done.

No matter, Jimmy thought. It would be good to be alone with only his own thoughts holding him prisoner for a few hours. Without Dee. Even without Cleo.

God, he was dizzy! Whipped silly from all the whirling, grinding meetings with accountants and bankers, putting together the stock offering for Wizard Satellite, the new company that would actually own the satellite channels. Conferences where a nod of the head or a decision made too quickly could affect millions of invested dollars and people's lives and careers, too.

He had managed to keep the satellite programming company separate from the radio stations, partly to shield it if his wild idea somehow went belly-up, and partly, he had to admit, so the windfall would be mostly his if it hit as big as he suspected it would. If the television idea came to pass, he could fold that into the public company, too, with money easier to raise with a stock offering when and if the time came. He was satisfied that Dee, Lulu Dooley, Greta Polanski, and Clarice George were well cared for with the radio-station business. They were making far more money than they could ever have dreamed, thanks to him and his vision. Now, with the satellite venture, it would finally be his turn to cash in big-time.

The radio formats and the future cable-television channels were his baby. His ideas. He should be the one to reap all the rewards.

His head still ached and his stomach knotted painfully every time he thought about the grilling, the probing, the paperwork of taking the venture to a public stock offering. That's another reason he had been smart to keep the radio business separate. It would never have stood up to the scrutiny of the bankers, the underwriters, the attorneys, the accountants, the government. Especially with the latest involvement with the George twins.

Now that it was all about to finally happen, and despite the reassurances of those who were supposed to know, Jimmy was still teetering on the ragged edge of panic. All that was left was to stroke the group of underwriters a little more, satisfy a few more gut-wrenching questions from the feds, and it would be done. The radio channels were a success already. The first cable channel, Satellite Super Store, could be up on a bird in a little over a year, beaming bargains to millions, all in plenty of time to hit and build a viewership before Christmas shopping started that season if all went well.

"Not that any of you care," Jimmy said to a couple of thrushes playing in the dust of a fresh grave nearby.

The ride down I-24 from Nashville had helped his mood immediately, just as he had suspected it would. He watched the gossamer early-morning fog lifting from roadside pastures where Tennessee walking horses ran free. The worries were left behind with the mist as he drove the winding freeway ribbon up the side of Monteagle Mountain.

The air was clean and cool when he pulled off an exit and into a truck stop on the mountaintop for coffee and a stack of syrup-covered flapjacks. The friendly banter between the waitresses and the truckers was so free and simple and uninhibited it reminded him of a good pop song. The words weren't deep or profound, but the music of their voices made him feel happy. Their only worries were the size of their tips and whether the customer wanted the breakfast steak rare or well done, where to go to dodge the speed traps and how to best skip the truck scales.

The waitress pouring his coffee was named Rita. At least, that's what it said on the plastic name tag over her breast. She was a little too skinny, but attractive in a rough sort of way.

"Honey, the way you ate those hotcakes, I'd say you could use another half dozen."

"Oh, no, thanks."

"On the house."

She was giving him a look that was familiar, but he couldn't quite place it. Then it came to him. Though not nearly as intense, it was still the same look he'd seen in the eyes of girls on the front row when he had gone on stage to introduce Paul Revere and the Raiders or Neil Diamond in concert. Or in the faces of the women who'd come to the backstage door and promise anything . . . *anything* . . . if he could just get them in to meet the Rolling Stones or Lynyrd Skynyrd.

"Tell you what. I could use three more after all. And maybe another cup of that coffee."

She smiled, winked, and was back in a minute with the pancakes and coffee.

"Look, mister. I don't want you to think I'm being pushy or nothing, but your voice sure sounds familiar. Are you a singer from Nashville or something?"

"You listen to the radio?"

"Lord, yes. All the time."

"What stations?"

"We get a bunch of them up here on top of the mountain. But mostly the River from Nashville. It's my favorite one."

"You ever hear of Brother James?"

Her hand flew to her mouth and she shrieked so loudly the whole truck stop turned to see who had been pinched on the ass by which truck driver.

"I knew it! That voice . . . well, I'm so pleased to meet you in person. I'm Rita. Rita Thornburgh."

"Glad to meet you, Rita. You know, I haven't been on the air in quite a while. I'm really flattered that you remembered."

He caught himself. He had inadvertently lowered his voice, the disc jockey coming out in him instinctively. Rita looked around her, as if checking for eavesdroppers. No one was sitting in either of the booths on each side of his.

"God, I don't want to seem loose or nothing, but . . . uh . . . I get off work at nine. My husband is gonna be at work, and if you wanna go to my place and talk or . . ."

For an instant, he shocked himself. He was on the verge of accepting her offer. Lord, what was he thinking? But it had been a while since someone had recognized his voice. A damn long while. And it felt just as good as it always had.

"Look, honey, I'd really love to. But I've got a roomful of people waiting for me down in Atlanta. Maybe next time I'm through here, I'll take you up on it, Rita."

She smiled a disappointed smile, produced an order pad for an autograph, and then was gone to another impatient customer. He left her a ten-dollar tip.

As he fell off the back side of Monteagle Mountain, past the runaway-truck escape ramps and the gaudy fireworks stands that occupied every crossroads, he surprised himself once more. He suddenly swerved to take a deserted-looking exit that fed down onto a narrow, two-lane, patched stretch of blacktop that would eventually lead him to the bench in the cemetery. He had no idea then where he was going, what his immediate destination might be. Or why such a side trip was worth the risk of being late to the crucial pending business in Atlanta.

He only knew that he was winding through doorknob-shaped hills, past rusty mobile homes propped precariously high on wobbly stacks of cement blocks. He had to brake for coon dogs sleeping lazily in the middle of the warm roadway. He knew, too, that he was completely lost and was aimlessly searching for anything familiar. The miles and minutes had been slipping away like ill-spent money when he suddenly realized he had been off the interstate, blindly navigating through these stunted hills for an hour already, and still had no idea of where he was or where he was going or what he was looking for.

When he hit the next high spot, he tried and managed to get a dial tone on the car phone. He called Atlanta, lied that he had had car trouble, and postponed their noon meeting until late afternoon.

He had just wrecked the schedules of a dozen highly paid pencil pushers, but for some reason, he didn't care. He was the boss, after all.

Certainly, he couldn't have told them what he was really doing. He couldn't even explain this impulsive detour to himself, let alone a roomful of land sharks in expensive suits.

Finally there was a half-rusted-away road sign, almost covered with honeysuckle vines, but it pointed the way to some road whose number seemed familiar. Then an obscure landmark caught his eye. A light came on. He realized exactly where he was.

The town was totally different from the hazy way he remembered it. The shack he had lived in when his parents died was gone. Some kind of junky metal-fabricating factory in a Quonset hut now claimed its spot. The one-room school had been replaced by a convenience store and a gas station. He stopped, filled the gas tank, and bought a six-pack of beer.

The little town was so dilapidated, so lacking in anything warm or familiar or of home, that he suddenly was left empty, saddened by the absence of anything that he remembered being a part of. It was clear. Jimmy Gill no longer had any roots in this ramshackle place.

That decided, he turned the car around, took the river road, skirted the shore of the Tennessee River for a half mile, and sped back toward Chattanooga and the interstate highway that led to his postponed meeting. He had seen all he wanted to see. There was nothing more there for him.

But as he rounded a sharp curve, lost again in thoughts of business, he suddenly caught sight of something painfully familiar. He was going so fast that he shot on past it a half mile or so before he came to a turnaround. Then he had to wait for a truck loaded with paper timber logs to creep by before he could backtrack.

And there it was, the rock church house and the cemetery behind it, tucked back among the elms just as he remembered it from the last time he had seen it. Exactly as he had watched it fade away into the river mist like a bad television picture the day he and Grandmama had moved away to Birmingham.

He had to search awhile for their graves. Quite a few people had died since they had, apparently. The additional plots had all been crammed together in a tight patchwork, and many were marked as poorly as he eventually found his parents' to be.

But finally, there they were. They slept in the afternoon shade of the elms, near the wooden picnic tables. He could almost picture the crowds of families gathered here so close to their dead, laughing, praising, enjoying lovingly cooked food spread for all to sample on these rough tables. He could almost see the families wandering from one grave to another by memory, depositing flowers of love, prayers of hope on each one. But now, the place was deserted, ghostly still, near deathly quiet. Just him sitting alone on the bench, the crows preaching and the mockingbirds singing.

Then a gentle breeze from down toward the river kicked up a few clouds of red dust. The wind sounded like voices harmonizing in the branches of the elms, humming a sad, sad song. He imagined for a moment that he was able to hear voices talking to him from their graves. The chattering of the dry leaves, scurrying along the dusty ground, seemed to be fussing at him, too.

Oh, God! He had only had two of the beers. What was wrong with him? A spastic shiver shook him violently. Then there was another voice. A real one. Someone speaking words out loud. It took him a moment to realize they were coming from his own mouth.

"You didn't leave me by your own choice, did you?" he had suddenly asked, questioning the vine-choked graves, the singing trees.

But the graves were silent. The trees answered him with only another low, sad moan.

"Daddy, I know what you said after you fell into that damned saw. You knew the last of your life was spilling out of you then, but you coughed up love for your wife and your baby boy with your last breath."

The leaves hissed for him to go on. That they were listening to him.

"Mama, I understand you, too. How you drifted, rudderless, to a fast life you wouldn't have chosen otherwise. I know it was only out of pain and loneliness. That you were only searching through your drunken haze for him. You never meant to abandon your boy-child or your mother. And you certainly never suspected you would die the way you did."

He couldn't believe it. He was talking to a pair of cold, dead gravestones. And tears, hot tears, were boiling from his eyes.

But suddenly, from somewhere so deep inside him that he had never suspected it was there, a fierce white-hot anger overtook him like a vicious fever. The words were suddenly harsh, acid.

"You ignorant, illiterate redneck trash!" he screamed to the washed-out markers, first his father's, then his mother's. "You, with no more ambition beyond your two dollars a day, breaking your back, shuffling through sawdust. And you, nothing but a damnable slut, a whore. Your mourning nothing more than an excuse to turn your back on your son and mother until the sorry life your were leading caught up with you like a well-aimed bullet." He stomped the wooden bench at his feet, daring the jabbering leaves to talk back to him now. "I wasn't a damned thing to either one of you. Just one more hindrance in the middle of your dreary existence! How dare you! How dare you bring me into this world, then ignore me, abandon me!"

Jumping from the table, he took three big steps and kicked his mother's headstone as hard as he could. Then, ignoring the pain that shot up his leg, he sent Daddy's marker tumbling with another sharp boot. Each one shattered like glass as it landed on the hard-packed red earth.

Standing between their dim graves, clenching and unclenching his fists, Jimmy Gill let loose a scream so loud that it echoed off the church two hundred feet away and sent a startled covey of quail fluttering into the brush at the far edge of the cemetery.

"Listen to me for once! Go on! Leave me alone for good, damn it! I can do it myself! I didn't need you! I never needed you! I don't need anybody! Stay away from me! Stay away!"

For the first time that he could ever remember, he was crying out loud. Huge tears rolled off his cheeks and fell into the dust like summer rain. His shoulders quaked, his feet stomped in anger, fired by frustration and long-denied grief. Dropping to his knees between the two of them, he now spoke quietly through his bitter sobs.

"I'm somebody now despite the both of you! You didn't count for anything at all when you were here. Just the work, the drinking, the dreariness. Now I've made everyone listen to me like you never would. Millions know me. Millions more will. I'll be there with them in their cars, in their living rooms, inside their heads. They'll watch and listen, laugh and cry when I tell them, buy what I show them, eat and sleep and talk and make love when I let them. I got here without you and I'll go on without you. Stay there in hell or wherever you are and . . . leave . . . me . . . alone!"

He grabbed the biggest piece of broken tombstone and hurled it into the weeds and vines along the border of the cemetery, then sent another one tumbling down the embankment toward the swift brown water of the river. Then others went sailing across the highway into a pine thicket. Finally, when only two small pieces of the headstones remained among the straw and weeds, he picked each of them up and looked at them through what was left of his tears, turning them over with his fingers.

But then, for some reason, he chose not to throw them. Instead, he slipped them into his trouser pocket.

Without even looking back, he stumbled among the plots and markers and flower bouquets, back down to where the Cadillac was parked. He jumped in, cranked it up, jerked it into gear, and stomped on the accelerator, spraying clods of red dirt and pinecones as he gunned the big car away from the cemetery as fast as it would go.

Halfway down the driveway to the church, he slapped the rearview mirror askew, just in case there might be a temptation to glance backward. He didn't dare set it straight again until he was on I-75, halfway to Atlanta.

Chapter 29

Jimmy Gill didn't even have to look up when he heard the hesitant knock on the doorframe of his office. And he knew exactly what the expression on Detroit's face would be.

"Jimmy, I've been wondering how long it would be before you told me, but I guess you haven't had the time. What's the deal with us buying these dinky little low-powered AM stations?"

It was the third time Detroit had brought him this question, but they always seemed to get interrupted before Jimmy was forced to conjure up some kind of a believable answer. Besides, Dee had been so busy working the bugs out of the radio satellite network that Jimmy had been able to avoid giving any kind of explanation to him so far. As president of the company, Detroit still had to sign off on the formal offers to purchase properties, and, for once, he had read the damned things before he signed them. He was, of course, wondering what Jimmy was buying and why, especially when it was something so far off the game plan for growing the group.

"Simple, Dee. I don't think we should give up on AM radio just yet," he answered weakly, pretending sudden interest in a ten-page list of figures and columns he held in front of him.

"Yeah, maybe if they had some power and a decent dial position, like Birmingham and Atlanta and Dallas do. But five hundred watts with a directional signal at fifteen-forty on the dial in New Orleans? A damn kilowatt daytime-only station on thirteen-ninety in Miami? Ain't no way those things will ever do anything, Jimmy. Hell, they are like a lightbulb! And you have to tune the dial all the way to the glove compartment just to find them!"

"Uh, there may be good use for those things. Power companies using the subcarriers for remote control of some kind," Jimmy ad-libbed. He had read something about such a thing somewhere in one of the trades. "They could be valuable for that."

"Daytimers? Not a chance. What about remote-control use at night if our little dud stations are off the air? No way. You could have asked me about—"

"Look, damn it!" Jimmy half rose from his chair to snap at him. "Let me decide what's best for this company. I know what needs to be done and I'll damn well do it without any unsolicited advice from you. You worry about keeping the transmitters on the air! We were off for two hours in Louisville last week and I still haven't seen a written explanation from you or—"

The intercom on the desk buzzed loudly to interrupt his tirade, as if right on cue. He sat back down hard and glared. Detroit glared back for a few seconds, then sadly shook his head, turned, and stalked out of the office.

Sammie told him it was line two. Code blue. That meant it was someone he would want to talk with.

"Jimmy?"

It was Cleo's voice, warm, wondering, too far away, on the other end of the telephone line.

"Yeah."

"Boy, you sure sound happy to hear from the only woman you love!"

"Sorry, baby. It has been one helluva week here at the radio ranch."

"Tell me about it?"

He rarely did anymore. Even when she asked. Even when it involved their co-owned stations. No need to bother her with it all. He was making her enough money that she shouldn't have to worry about it anyway.

"Nah, it's just business, Cleo. I gotta make some decisions. It may be time to cut out some deadwood around this place."

He bit his tongue. He had said more than he intended. Luckily, her mind was on something else. She had not caught the implication.

"Well, I've got an announcement to make that you may or may not want to hear. But being the legendary bigmouth that I am, you're going to have to hear it anyway."

"If it's good news, I'm game. If it's not, please send me a damned telegram."

She was quiet for a moment, apparently hesitant about how Jimmy would take whatever it was she wanted so badly to tell him, especially considering the mood in which her call had found him.

"Okay. Here's the deal. I've got concert dates booked through the middle of December. And when I finish those, I'm finally pulling the plug. Laying off the band. Selling the bus. Coming in off the road. Growing up and running away from the circus."

"Cleo! That's fantastic!" He almost shouted the words, and she could tell that he actually meant them.

Jimmy had juggled his schedule a few times to try to match hers, taken the company airplane and met up with her on the road somewhere. But it was always such a whirling rush for both of them. His mind was usually back with the empire he was building and hers was on sound checks and collecting money from shady promoters. Their time together was always like a blurred series of wonderful but rudely interrupted dreams.

And even when she was home between tours, she seemed to always be entangled in something. If she wasn't in the studio or trying to write songs she was on the phone dealing with agents and record-company cranks and demanding radio stations. His thoughts, too, were usually wavelengths away from where their bodies physically were.

It was no surprise to Jimmy that she was reeling it in. The thrill of performing on stage had long since deserted Cleo Michaels, and she readily admitted it to him and herself. She had long ago grown weary of the cigarette smoke, the impossible hours, the look-alike faces in the audience, the endless roadways that seemed to mark her life by exits and rest stops. And she had often talked of spending her time finding and producing new artists, writing more, and pitching her new songs and the existing catalog to producers and singers. Or she could help him run the Dallas stations. They were half hers anyway. It wasn't the need for money that had kept her pushing so hard for so long. Her music publishing company alone could keep her lifestyle luxurious.

And now she had found someone she loved more than the vagabond lifestyle. Jimmy Gill had been the final thing she needed to explode into her life to bring her to the inevitable decision. Telling him had been the one thing she had not quite figured out how to do until now, and she was pleasantly surprised he was taking it so well.

"You really think it's fantastic? I was afraid that . . ."

"God, yes, Cleo! I'm selfish enough to want you here in town with me all the time. So I can call you up for some soul food cookin' or to ravish your naked body any time of the day or night."

There was a brief pause from her end of the line then. He could hear the roar of big trucks passing by whatever roadside parking spot she was calling from.

"I thought maybe, with me finally settling down, we could . . ." Her voice had changed so suddenly that even Jimmy noticed it. It hardly sounded like Cleo's at all, except maybe in one of her saddest songs. But then, before she could finish the thought, she stopped again, took a breath, and she was back. "I haven't been ravished in so long I'm not sure what goes where. And anyway, what makes you think you'd have any more time for us then than you do now, Mr. Wizard of the Wind?"

It was her newest pet name for him. She had named him that when he had told her about his first impressions of the magical goings-on in the field behind WROG back in Birmingham. She had even laughingly threatened to write a song with that name about a man who loved his damned old radio more than the wonderful woman who loved him.

"Just don't roll that Silver Eagle into a canyon before you can get your butt back to Nashville. I'll show you some free time! You'll be begging for mercy, Miss Michaels."

She laughed that enchanted laugh of hers and started telling some tale about something one of the band members had done in Oxnard. He tried to listen to her, to act as if he were really interested, but all the lights on his phone were blinking, someone had put another stack of pink message slips under his hand, and Sammie was now standing at his door, waving her arms and mouthing the words "Richard's here."

Richard Graffeo was now Wizard Broadcasting's number one legal counsel. He knew more about how the rigmarole they had created was slung together than anyone else, including James Gill.

Now he had to help Jimmy untwist the corporate mess that had been made in ignorance in the mad scurry to get a signal on the air in the first place.

Jimmy motioned for him to shut the door and take a chair while he abruptly finished the call with Cleo. He wished her well at the Academy of Country Music Awards that night, promised to be watching on television, and told her he hoped she'd win her usual bushel basket full of statuettes. His mind was already racing ahead to the business at hand though, and she seemed to sense it, and then was gone.

He had hung up before he realized he had not told her again how glad he was about her decision. Or even that he loved her. He told himself that he'd make it right when she got home. And he half noticed that the sad note had crept back into her voice again when she said, "Good-bye" and "I love you, Jimmy."

There was business to do. He stood and shook Richard's hand.

"I need to restructure the radio-station company, Counselor. Wizard Broadcasting."

Richard Graffeo needed no warm-up. There was no need for small talk with him. He was instantly at full stride, with no prattle about the weather, football, or politics.

That's one reason why Jimmy liked him so much. Sometimes he felt as if he had already used up most of the words that God had allotted him for this lifetime. He had foolishly wasted so many speaking into microphones over the years. He could appreciate someone else who avoided throwing them away needlessly.

Graffeo was all business. He probably slept in his double-breasted suit, his briefcase for a pillow. He was totally serious, painfully straight talking, always able to hit the bull's-eye with his dartlike questions. And he had the ability to read his clients, as well as his opponents, like an open book.

"Trouble with the darky, huh?" he asked as he settled deeper into the office chair and unhinged his valise.

"Look, Rich. I'm trying to do some new business with the Georges, and Detroit is going to fight me every inch of the way on it. I don't know why. Lately, it seems like he is constantly standing in the way of everything I want to accomplish. His goddamn aunt is convinced he should be running the whole company just because he's got 'President' printed on his business card, so now she's pissed at me, too. And when I need something signed or voted on so we can get some important business done, Greta Polanski and Clarice George are out of pocket at some charity thing or traipsing across the country on some damn fool trip. I've made them all rich and they just go along their merry way, while I try to make this top spin all by myself. And frankly, I'm of the opinion that it's getting too big to try to run it the way we have been doing it."

Jimmy knew he didn't need to tell Richard why. He simply had to lay out what he wanted done. Then Richard would tell him precisely how it should happen. But he couldn't help trying to sell the attorney on the reasons for what he was about to ask him to do.

"Jim, you trying to convince me or yourself?"

Jimmy chuckled softly. On target again, Mr. Graffeo.

"Look, Rich, we've got about everything liquid tied up in the satellite radio network, and I've borrowed until I'm blue to add the new formats. We'll want to do the television channels soon, too. All of these ventures will be a license to print money within five years. You've seen the business plans. Hell, you wrote the prospectus, for God's sake. But it's going to be touch and go for a while yet. We have some very frightening things we may have to do to keep it together. I don't want the old women getting the vapors when they see some of the things I'm going to have to do to make this airship fly. They don't have a clue about business. And I sure as shit don't need Detroit Simmons throwing his figurehead title around and getting in my way all the time because it doesn't all fit into some kind of algebraic formula that he can cipher out with a calculator. Lord knows I love the son of a bitch! And he could build a transmitter from scratch with chewing gum and fishing line. But the bastard doesn't know beans about running a company."

"How quick do you need it done?"

Damn, the son of a bitch was cold! No argument, no questions. Just "how quick?" Jimmy was once again glad that Richard Graffeo was on his side.

"Month or two."

"You don't need all these minorities on your letterhead to get broadcast licenses now, you know. You're big, Jim. The new Federal Communications Commission's not as hard-assed as the last one either. Thank God for a Republican president. You can buy and sell anytime, anywhere, as long as you hang on to the properties for three years. You know the rules. And with all the money and the preferential interest rates and all the deals these banks are throwing at you, you absolutely have to be trading up right now while you can. It'll all swing the other way someday. Always does.

"Let's see, you already have yourself and Cleo on the board, and I assume you can control her. The twins' mama will do what they want her to do. You only need one more vote."

"Jerry Morrow."

The man who had helped put the River into profitability as sales manager now ran several of the stations. Jimmy knew he would do whatever he wanted him to. Except stop buying and wearing those horrid striped and plaid sport coats. Jerry was thriving on the power that bringing in so much money can give a man. He would kiss anybody's ass to be elected to the board of directors of Wizard Broadcasting.

And, just in case he needed it, Jimmy also knew the names and apartment numbers of both of Morrow's mistresses. The other board members wouldn't be suspicious. They would see it only as a well-deserved perk. Hell, Detroit had even suggested it himself a few years back.

"Here's how it'll work, Jim. We can give Mr. Simmons some kind of title and he'll assume it's a promotion, kick you up to CEO . . ." Graffeo quickly planned the entire coup out loud.

As he talked, Jimmy realized that he had developed a sour feeling in his midsection, where his ulcer often ached. But he blamed it on the hastily eaten omelette he'd grabbed at Maggie's Diner well before sunup that morning. He knew what he needed. Cleo. She could help him eat right.

". . . and if we can get Simmons to swallow this, it will be a breeze," Graffeo was saying.

"Hey, if you can't draw it on a damned schematic diagram, he'll never figure out what's happening until it's done. It's best for him, Dick. We'll make him far more money this way than he ever dreamed of without nearly the responsibilities. He can go on back to his transistors. . . ."

"You're selling the sold, Jim," Graffeo growled, with a look that said, "Let's get on to something we haven't decided already, okay?"

They talked more of specifics and the paperwork needed, of the progress of the public stock offering for Wizard Satellite, of the cash-flow situation for the companies. But Jimmy was distracted by the queasy ball in his stomach that wouldn't go away. Then finally, when Richard felt that he had said all that needed to be said, he jumped to his feet, shook Jimmy's hand, and was out the office door, off to begin the execution of the plan that could change the complexion of the company forever.

Jimmy stood stiffly and fought a sudden wave of nausea. Shit. He didn't have time to be sick right now. Too much to do.

Slowly, he ambled over to the window and surveyed his collection of satellite dishes that were visible on the office building downtown. They looked like giant mouse ears. He could also see the corner windows on the top floor that would soon be his office. They would be moving the entire operation there in a few weeks, claiming three floors for the rapidly expanding company.

Jimmy stood at the window for ten minutes, ignoring the work that waited impatiently on his desk. The stomachache had finally gone away as he enjoyed this view of a part of his empire he could actually see. The rest of it was mostly air. Invisible signals racing through the ether like fleeting ghosts. But there, on top of the building, was tangible proof that he had built something new, different, revolutionary. And he was only beginning to conquer a world no one could see or feel. A world of ether and spark.

As he watched and thought and planned, he idly rubbed together the two jagged slivers of broken tombstone that he kept in his trouser pocket.

Chapter 30

He had never avoided a confrontation in his life, but Jimmy Gill had no desire to face Detroit Simmons the morning after the board meeting had been completed and the changes approved.

They had spent the first hour as they usually did in such meetings, with charts and graphs unveiled on an easel, shimmering images cast on a screen from an overhead projector, and huge stacks of documentation lurking close beside the coffee and juice and pastry that rested on the conference table in front of each director. The manager of each station came in, laid out his own good news in turn, and told them all how great things had gone with their individual properties so far that year. The accountants used the overhead projectors and dozens of slides and still more paperwork to tell the story of the programming network's spectacular growth, and how the television plans would eventually pay off, though most of those on the Wizard Broadcasting board had little to do with that side of the business.

Wizard Broadcasting now had purchased and was running eleven stations in six cities. Wizard Satellite was broadcasting four different formats with over three hundred affiliates pulling the programming down from a geostationary satellite circling the planet twenty-two thousand miles above the Northern Hemisphere at the exact speed of the earth's rotation. Each of the board members was duly and fittingly amazed by all the figures and projections, charts and graphs, pictures and slides, ratings and billing information, cash flow and inventory-management systems.

Jimmy knew Lulu Dooley and Clarice George didn't understand any of it, and that Greta Polanski, for her part, didn't understand much English at all, much less the language that was being spoken that morning around the massive table in the company's new conference room in the rich new office suite atop the glistening high-rise building.

And he knew, too, that these people were not really clear on what the corporate restructuring that was being proposed actually meant. And they understood even less after Richard Graffeo ran through the deal in a mad rush of legalese.

The procedure took two minutes to accomplish.

The George twins had told their mother to vote with Jimmy Gill, no matter what. She didn't really pay much attention to what was happening anyway. She had tickets for the Grand Ole Opry that night. She simply said, "Yea" when Jimmy pointed at her. The secretary dutifully recorded the vote.

Detroit sat quietly throughout the entire meeting, his head down as if studying all the papers in front of him, or examining the fine grain of the blond wood in the new conference table's shiny top. He knew "chairman emeritus" wasn't much of a functional title, but he could count votes as well as anyone. He had long since realized it was a done deal. And he had purposely avoided asking Jimmy about it. Somehow, he had convinced himself that it was not what he thought it was. That Jimmy would never do anything like that. On some level, he had hoped that it would all be made clear at the meeting.

Well, it was clear all right. And Detroit still couldn't believe it was happening.

When the vote came to Dee, he whispered, "Nay." Then he nodded to his aunt to do the same thing. She did, with her lip jutted out and a go-to-hell look in her eye when she looked in Jimmy's direction at the head of the massive table. The secretary made two marks in the other column on the sheet of paper in front of him.

Mrs. Polanski voted nay also. But she had looked confused when Lulu nudged her. She still had no idea what was going on.

Three nays. One yea.

Cleo had signed her paperwork in front of a notary in Pueblo, Colorado, and mailed it back without even reading it. She trusted Jimmy to vote her proxy the correct way. He did. And his own vote was tallied, too.

Jerry Morrow's appointment to the board of directors had passed unanimously earlier. Now Detroit Simmons knew why the time had come to finally reward the man for all his work and why Jimmy Gill had at last seen fit to propose it. Morrow gave a heartfelt "Yea," and it was over.

The secretary said, "The motion is carried, four to three." There was no other business. The meeting was adjourned.

After the meeting broke, Detroit loitered for a moment under the spectacular new chandelier in the lobby. He had intended to wander back to his new office with the big windows and maybe spend a few minutes at some busywork until his aunt and the other ladies were ready to go to north Nashville for dinner. But just then, Jimmy and Richard Graffeo walked out of the conference room, smiling and shaking hands. The attorney merely nodded and discreetly kept on walking toward the elevator lobby when Detroit pulled Jimmy aside.

He couldn't help it. He had to say something and say it now, before the words festered inside him any longer. When he spoke, it was more with sadness than anger.

"I remember when you fired the sales manager in Louisville over the telephone for practically nothing, Jimmy. And the day you fired that morning disc jockey while he was in the middle of his show and they had to get the engineer to play records until they could call somebody else to come in and finish the program. And I was there the day you cut loose the whole sales staff in Houston because they couldn't meet some silly, impossible quota, all to make a point to the rest of the chain. But I never thought I'd see the day you'd fire me like this. Through some damn lawyer and a stack of paperwork and a rigged vote."

"Dee, I didn't fire you. You're still my main man! We just have to streamline the way this puppy hunts or we're gonna get outfoxed in the major markets. Everybody's going to get the same money cut as before, probably even more. We're going to have to take Wizard Broadcasting public very soon to raise the kind of capital we need to grow. And it'd be tough on Wall Street with the way we were structured. With the lack of business experience at the top. And when we go—"

"Jimmy, you don't have to use your redneck analogies on me or come up with all the bullshit reasons. I know you better than anybody except maybe Cleo. And we are both worried about you. You're changing. You're getting away from the things that got you and me into this business in the first place. Take a step back, Jimmy, before it's too late. Look at yourself. At Wizard. Don't let the power and the greed blot out the magic of this medium, man. It's too special to mess it up."

A couple of the satellite jocks walked past them then and nodded respectfully. Jimmy waited for them to get out of earshot before he spoke, his voice barely in control.

"Look, you better come down off your high horse and . . ."

But Detroit Simmons had already turned and was walking away slowly, ignoring what might be left of James Gill's carefully rehearsed sales pitch. He let the door slam behind him when he stepped into his new office and workshop with all the new electronic toys lined up on the shelves, wall to wall. He stood with his hands in his pockets at the big window with the wonderful view of the Cumberland River and downtown Nashville. He sadly watched the quickly disappearing sun as it fled the western sky, looking for a place to hide from the darkness for a while behind the distant brushy mountains.

Chapter 31

James Gill had never been to Miami before. It was not bright and sunny as he had expected. Everything about his arrival was foreboding, threatening. Dark storm clouds gathering out over the Atlantic Ocean waved an unfriendly welcome to him as he brought the Cessna King Air in from the west, over the Everglades, and touched down hard at Miami International Airport with a series of jarring, bouncing hops. A hostile head wind and a few rattling splatters of hail on the windshield kept his attention riveted on the nose wheel and the plane's instrument panel. He had no chance to admire the palm trees and the sea of red tile roofs that stretched off into the distance toward Biscayne Bay. This was not going to be a sight-seeing visit anyway.

It felt funny not to have Detroit Simmons in the copilot's seat next to him as usual. He missed him. The flight had been extra long and lonely with only the chatter of the aircraft radio and the drone of the engines to keep him company. And Dee had become a damn good pilot, too. Much better than Jimmy could ever hope to be. He still scared himself sometimes. It was good to know Dee would be there to get him out of trouble if there was any.

But Dee rarely traveled with him. In fact, he hardly spoke to Jimmy unless he was forced to by the necessity of business. Sometimes Jimmy would catch him down the hall or through his office door, simply standing there watching him as if he was trying to read Jimmy's mind like one of his electronic instruments. He mostly kept to himself in his workshop. He would cryptically explain what purchases they needed to make or technical things they needed to do in terse, stunted memos, written in sullen pencil on the back of his old "President" letterhead. Jimmy strongly suspected that the choice of stationery was for effect, too.

Detroit didn't even go with him to Atlanta when they closed the sale on the pip-squeak AM in Homestead, just out of Miami. It was the first time Jimmy had done a closing without him. But it was just as well, since he didn't have to explain to him why DeWayne George was there, too, hovering greedily over the proceedings like a buzzard sizing up roadkill.

Jimmy parked the plane near the executive hangar and told the attendants to gas it up because he would be back quickly to try to fly out ahead of the storm.

"Better hurry, man," one of them warned. "She's coming on in pretty quick. We hear that they'll be shutting down the airport soon."

God knew he had better things to do than fly half the night to beat a tropical depression into this muggy city. But there were things going on down there that scared the hell out of him, things more frightening than some gusts of wind and a few drops of rain. His name was on the license of a radio station that was being run by a psychopath, an outlaw doing God knows what under the banner of Wizard Broadcasting.

Jimmy knew DeWayne George wouldn't level with him if he came right out and asked him what was going on down there. He finally decided he had to go find out for himself. He had told Cleo he was flying down to look at another property that they might be interested in buying. He left word for Sammie that he was going to be away on business for a day or so. Then he drove to the airport and filed a flight plan that took him directly into the mouth of a thundering Gulf Stream squall.

The automobile rental agency had only small foreign cars left on the lot. Local residents had rented everything else to flee northward, away from the storm in case it should decide to become a hurricane. With nothing else to choose from, he was stuck with a tiny Toyota with no air-conditioning. There was just enough rain falling in spits that he had to keep the window cranked most of the way up to stay dry, and it stayed hot and humid inside the boxy car. The blustering weather blew the damned thing all over the highway, too. He had to fight the toy car's steering wheel hard-

er than he had the stick of the King Air on the airport approach
into the head wind.

Then he got himself half-soaked in a quick downpour when he
stopped at a convenience store to get directions to the station. The
man behind the counter spoke only broken English. Jimmy knew
no Spanish. They reverted to hand signals and gestures until the
clerk finally understood where Jimmy was trying to go. He grinned
and pointed to the south, along Highway 27, toward a hazy swamp
and a bank of swirling, boiling storm clouds.

After driving along about three more miles of arrow-straight
blacktop, past scrubby pines and saw grass and brackish standing
water, Jimmy finally spotted the squatty hundred-foot-tall tower
he had been looking for. Near it, a pastel-painted concrete-block
building hid among the brush and peppertrees. A rusty sign next
to the drive was mostly hidden by undergrowth. The station's call
letters painted on the front of the building had faded away to almost nothing, long since chased away by the weather. The narrow
dirt driveway that led to the studio building was rutted and full of
mudholes. Wet limbs slapped both sides of the car as he inched
cautiously along into a muddy clearing that passed for a parking
lot for the station.

Some radio station. Nine-thirty in the morning on a Monday,
a business day, and there was not a soul in sight. Not another car
was parked in the oyster-shell-littered lot except for his Toyota.
There were no lights on inside the building. A yellow bulb above
the small porch at the entrance was turned off. The front door
appeared to be locked tight. Bushes and small trees almost completely covered the entranceway. It looked as if it had not been
used by anyone in years.

Jimmy had tried to listen to the station's weak signal ever since
he had climbed into the Toyota at the airport rental lot. He had
fought with the steering wheel while twisting the radio's knob until he finally found it, almost lost among the high numbers and
wavering voices on the far right side of the dial. Its audio sometimes sank completely below the deafening waves of electrical
noise and static crashes. Then, when it would fade back in more
strongly, it would suddenly be blown away entirely again by Spanish jabbering or a wheezing Pentecostal preacher from a nearby
station.

He knew immediately that it was DeWayne's station, though. Technically, Jimmy's station. It was rebroadcasting the familiar programming from the Wizard Rock Network. But the station didn't break a single time for the optional local commercial positions. It simply allowed the carefully timed fill-in music to roll on and on until the rest of the network joined back up.

And when the mandatory cutaway came up, the station was silent for three minutes and ten seconds while everyone else on the network filled the void with local commercials. To Jimmy's ears, that sounded like an hour of silence. The damn station was on automatic pilot all the way. No jingles except those on the network. No promotional announcements but the network's. No local deejay. No commercials at all. Only the weak, muffled, tape-recorded voice of DeWayne George giving the legal identification at the top of the hour in his sleazy redneck accent. That was the only identification of what the station's call letters were for anyone who might be listening and at all interested.

At least that much of the operation was legal. They were doing the legal identification near the top of the hour. Small comfort.

The rain slackened a bit as he carefully parked in the deserted lot, looking for a spot where he wouldn't step into sandy mud or dark brown standing water up to his ankles. He climbed from the car, parted the bushes, stepped up onto the porch, tried the front door, and confirmed it was not only locked, but nailed closed. The fire marshal would love that. He peered through the dirty windows and saw nothing but junk office furniture, ancient electronic equipment, and mounds of trash and papers piled on everything and stacked on the filthy floor. It was all covered with a fine sheen of dust, as if it had been entombed, undisturbed, for centuries.

Weeds grew knee high around the sides of the building. Paint peeled from the mildewed wood trim around the windows. Green moss and small trees sprouted from the roof tiles and broken gutters.

Jimmy stepped high as he left the porch and walked around the side of the building that seemed to be the least choked with vegetation, but his suit pants were immediately sodden and his legs were snatched and snagged by briars and thistles. A cooling vent fan, probably for some kind of small transmitter, exhaled warm, dusty air out a louver at the side of the building and into his face. Except for the whoosh of the fan, there were no other sounds or signs of life. But at least that showed there was electricity to this place and something electronic inside that was creating heat.

In the distance, a flock of egrets soared on the wind gusts at the edge of the overgrown field where the tower stood precariously. The rusty structure looked rickety and unsure, as if the blustering wind could easily have its way with the thing if it really wanted to. He thought he could almost see it swaying with the gale.

In the other direction, low, approaching storm clouds bumped the horizon, kicking up sparks of lightning. The worst of the weather was coming on quickly now, threatening. He needed to find someone quickly, learn what he needed to learn, and get back on his way.

He called "Hello" several times, but the undergrowth and wet, nervous wind swallowed his voice whole. Nobody answered.

A back door to the building was also locked, though not nailed. He tried it but couldn't force it open. Then he found a rear window that was opened slightly, apparently for ventilation. It was not bolted. It took some effort to raise the window, since its casing was swelled tightly from all the moisture and it had been almost glued into place with rot. But he managed to get it shoved up high enough to allow him to slip his slender body over the sill and to step into the small, dark room. Inside, the transmitter hummed and a small speaker on a shelf softly played the rock music beamed down from the satellite and retransmitted on the air.

Jimmy stood straight up as soon as he was sure of his footing. He swiped at a sneaky spiderweb that tickled his cheek, and tried to get his bearings in the dense gloom. The room was lit by only a few status pilot lights from boxes that blinked on equipment in a rack. The little daylight that had made it through the storm clouds struggled past the filtering of the filthy, rain-streaked windows.

The air in the room was hot, still, heavy. For an instant, he felt that this must be what it felt like to be in a crypt.

Something flashed. Immediate thunder. Then the rain began to fall heavier outside. The wind whipped around the corner of the building, and he thought he could feel the whole place shudder.

He noticed then that none of the meters on the transmitter seemed to be working. There was no remote-control equipment in the rack. Damn! This station was illegal as hell. The FCC would pull the switch on it if they came in for an inspection. But Jimmy suspected the technical shortcomings were minute compared to what else might be going on there.

Just then, he thought he saw a shadow dart quickly to his left. He turned to see who or what it was. Maybe a movement at the window. Someone coming. Or a bird, one of the egrets, trying to get in the open window to the warmth inside.

Suddenly, quick as a bolt of lightning, a million stars exploded inside his head. There was only an instant of spiky pain at the base of his skull. A sensation of falling, falling.

And then, nothing but warm, sticky darkness, washing over him like a hot, violent rain.

Chapter 32

J eemy? Jeemy Gill? You okay?"

The raspy, nasal voice was swimming around out there some-where in the middle of the swirling, painful darkness, almost washed away by the sick, roaring noise.

"If old En-reeky had done his job the way he was supposed to, you'd be floatin' out yonder in the flats with the sharks and the jellyfish by now, buddy. You're one lucky son of a bitch."

His head didn't feel so damned lucky right then, and he was having trouble even opening his eyes or making his mouth work to ask what the hell was going on. The eyes seemed to be glued shut by white-hot pain and what was apparently dried blood. His mouth tasted something metallic.

Someone was trying to wipe his face with something cold and damp and most likely filthy. But at least he was alive.

He was able to see that he was flat on his back in the middle of the dirty floor, looking up at the spiderwebs on the ceiling of the room he had entered through the window at the back of the radio station. There was more light in the room now. Somebody had switched on the bare bulb that dangled overhead. And someone with a familiar face was becoming a little clearer through the pain-ful smog. Then he could make out the features. The goofy grin. It was Duane George who squatted there next to him.

Jimmy Gill was thankful that it was Duane George and not his twin, DeWayne. Another man, smaller and much darker than Duane, and infinitely more sinister looking, hovered dimly in the shadows in the fuzzy, out-of-focus distance.

"En-reeky figured you wasn't no DEA agent, what with all the hollerin' you was doing coming around the building out there. And you sure ain't dressed like no burglar. But he's supposed to kill graveyard dead anybody that tries to break in out here. Anybody. You are one lucky son of a bitch."

Jimmy managed to sit upright with Duane's help, but his head seemed to want to fall off his shoulders. Duane continued to jabber on endlessly as a strong wave of nausea threatened to overthrow Jimmy's stomach.

"He decided on his own that if you turned out to be one of Garcia's men, me or DeWayne would want to have a little talk with you before he turned you into shark bait. That's the only thing that saved your life, Jeemy. You are one lucky son—"

"Damn it, Duane! What's going on out here? What kind of scam are you bastards into? And who the hell is Garcia?"

Oh, Lord, it hurt to talk. And by his last words, he had quieted down to a weak whisper.

Duane George stood then and took a couple of steps backward, partly from the force of the angry questions, but mainly because at that very moment, like punctuation on the last question, Jimmy Gill vomited all over the twin's expensive alligator shoes. When he had finished heaving, Duane was again kneeling next to him, concern on his unshaven face, wiping Jimmy's brow again with the cool, wet, dirty rag.

"You are gonna be okay, now, Brother Jeemy. Sit back against this wall now. Take it easy. Garcia's the one who controls most of the coke trade around here. Me and DeWayne and some of our friends are already taking a big chunk of his business away from him, and he don't even know who we are or where we are yet. That damned old Cuban never even seen us coming. And with this here radio station to make sure all our runners are in the right places, we . . ."

The bile left on Jimmy's stomach threatened to erupt again and he retched involuntarily. Then, slowly, he pulled himself back to his feet, teetered on the brink of toppling over for a moment, and finally staggered over to the rear window, the one he had crawled through only a fractured skull ago. Then he realized that the roar in his ears wasn't so much from the knock on the head. It was the thunder that seemed to roll constantly, the pounding of huge raindrops on the roof of the building, and a gale that now doubled over the trees that grew wild around the station. Thankfully, the cool, damp wind helped revive him and blew some of the cobwebs from his head. He caught a handful of water from a torrent that poured from one of the broken gutters and washed out his mouth and then splashed another handful into his face.

When he turned back inside, Duane was standing awkwardly, apparently not sure what to do next. Enrique seemed to have his mind made up already. The man had cold death in his eyes.

"Duane, I don't really want to know any more facts about all your dirty business down here," he said. The words were weak, almost lost in the wind and the clamor of the downpour outside. He had made up his mind. They would have to kill him if they didn't want to answer his next question. "Just tell me one thing, please. What do you mean about the station and the 'runners'?"

"Well, Jeemy, that's the beauty of what you and DeWayne done with getting in here with a radio station for a front business. Old Garcia never knew where we was comin' from, see? And we're able to put little commercials out over the air that sound like real commercials to anybody else that might be listening. But they really tell our people exactly where the deliveries are gonna be made and when. Even boats and airplanes coming in off the Atlantic and the Gulf of Mexico can find out where to land or dock. Or if we have got word of some kind of trouble we can steer them away until it's all clear. Hell, Jeemy, I'm surprised we don't have any ratings 'cause there are times I know we got half of Little Havana listenin' in to us!"

Glenn Frey's "Smuggler's Blues" was pounding out from the speaker in the corner of the dusty room as Jimmy stood there, his throbbing head held back out the window once again, letting the cooling rain try to chase away the sick ache in his stomach. The damn song was the perfect sound track for what was happening there, in his bailiwick, under the banner of the company that he and Detroit Simmons had built, with a government license that had his name right up there on top of it.

"Maybe we ought to get you to a doctor, Jeemy. You still look kinda peaked around the gills there, buddy."

"No. No, Duane. I'll be okay. That is, I think I'll be okay."

But James Gill, the president of Wizard Broadcasting, wasn't actually feeling okay at all. And it wasn't necessarily from the blow on the back of his head. He knew at that very moment the exact feeling a drowning man must know as he clutches for air but grabs only seaweed and salt water instead.

Detroit Simmons had been soldering the same transistor onto the same heat sink for the last fifteen minutes, and he was sure he had burned up the component's delicate innards already.

"Damn it, Jimmy Gill!"

He had uttered the same curse a dozen times since he had started to try to work on the power supply, but only the shop walls were there to hear him. He couldn't remember when anything or anybody had frustrated him more. Detroit knew it was simply because he loved Jimmy Gill like a brother. And he had not yet come up with a way to stop the son of a bitch from ruining everything.

That morning, Jimmy had flown off to Miami without telling him or anybody else the truth about where he was going. Detroit had had to quiz a buddy at the airport flight service to find out that much. He had a strong suspicion who Jimmy was going to see. He just didn't know why. And whatever it was, there would certainly be short circuits and flying sparks that Detroit Simmons knew he couldn't fix with a pair of pliers and a volt meter.

Finally, frustrated, he dropped the soldering iron, stepped to his desk, typed a few strokes on his computer keyboard, found the number he wanted on the screen, and picked up the telephone and dialed.

It rang a dozen times, throbbing, like an out-of-control heartbeat.

"Come on, Cleo. Answer," he said between each of the fluttering rings.

But the voice that finally came on was not Cleo's. It was some recording telling him that the mobile phone he had dialed was not in service, to please try again later.

Detroit gently replaced the telephone in its cradle, walked to the window, and gazed across the tops of the buildings below to the mountain south of town. He could just make out the new strobe lights that winked at him along the length of the River's tower. Their tower. His and Jimmy Gill's.

That reminded him of the day he and Jimmy had crossed the sage field and Jimmy had made his stupid climb up WROG's spire. And Detroit remembered how he had fled in panic when they had been caught, deserting his friend, leaving him to the mercy of gravity and Charlie McGee, the angry, spitting little engineer.

"Not again, Jimmy. Not again," he told the darkening sky outside his window. And he meant it.

Chapter 33

Business was business, after all, and there was plenty of it to do. Duane and DeWayne George and the frightening mess that Jimmy had flown into down in Florida had to be put aside for a while. First, though, he had to try to ignore the blinding headache from the whack on the head while he piloted the King Air back on the hairy trip home through the remnants of the tropical depression. But Jimmy almost welcomed the buffeting he took. The rough ride kept his mind on the airplane's lurching stick and balky foot pedals and off the snake pit he had stepped into. He listened to the near panic in the voices of the other general aviation pilots he heard on the radio. The noise didn't help the ache behind his eyes though.

Even when he got back to Nashville and finally, thankfully stepped down onto solid, nonbucking ground at the airport, he had little time to put into play the plan he was starting to formulate. There were plenty of other towering mountains for him to climb.

James Gill and the rest of the Wizard team played the National Association of Broadcasters convention in San Francisco exactly like a well-tuned guitar. The massive exhibit booth was built in the shape of a dollar sign. Richard Graffeo had found out who had to be bribed to make sure they were the centerpiece, right in the middle of the Moscone Convention Center exhibition floor. Beautiful models had been hired to distribute packets of information and sample tapes of each of the satellite channels. Some of the packages contained gift certificates for free merchandise from network sponsors and some held varying amounts of cash.

Everyone who asked for one got a genuine "Wizard Magician's Kit" to take home to the kids. That was Graffeo's idea, too. "You want to get to a guy, do something nice for his kids," he had preached over and over.

Detroit Simmons had his own wing of the booth to welcome the station engineers, a place where they would find someone who spoke their language and could explain the algorithms and circuitry that the networks would employ to make the sound pristine and the switching flawless. A couple of times, Detroit paused in his pitch to watch Jimmy through the glass partition, but they had no chance to talk. There was work to be done, more questions had to be answered, more lines and circles had to be drawn on the easel in his cubicle.

Richard Graffeo worked for Wizard full-time now. He was being groomed for COO. At the convention, his primary job was to bring by and introduce to Jimmy all the people who had been hired to finish putting the satellite channels together and on-line, people who had been ordered to build them solidly from the ground up.

And Graffeo also had the responsibility of rounding up and bringing in all the key decision makers in the most crucial radio groups, the people that they wanted to attack most viciously with their well-honed sales pitch. They did come by, new employees and prospective clients, in an almost constant procession, while Mr. Gill held court at the convention headquarters hotel's penthouse suite with the spectacular view just over his shoulder of San Francisco Bay and Marin County past the Golden Gate.

He had been supplied with painstakingly researched index cards for each person. The cards told Jimmy each person's wife's and children's names, his favorite pro sports teams, even his drink of choice. And Jimmy dutifully impressed each of them when he would interrupt the conversation about the Dodgers or the Knicks, get up, and mix each of them exactly whatever it was that he preferred to swill. Head man of a major new radio programming network bartending for his honored guests!

New employees were proud. Prospective clients were amazed.

"Piranhas, Jimmy. Every single new guy you've hired is a goddamn killer," Graffeo had said, almost giddily. "Bastards who would eat their young to win. You could go to war with these guys. Hell, you will be going to war with these guys! Shit, you already have gone to war with these guys!"

It was the first time he had ever heard Richard Graffeo display any emotion at all. It was actually a bit frightening, like seeing a hungry tiger wandering the convention floor.

The last night of the broadcasters show, Saturday night, they put the chief executives of every serious group or station in the United States and Canada and several foreign countries on a Red Line ferryboat over to Alcatraz Island. Then they fed the captive audience such vast quantities of prawns and guacamole and Swedish meatballs and served up so much Jack Daniel's that a second-rate dog and pony act would have looked like high-class entertainment to them by the time the evening's party was up and rolling.

Somehow, Richard had found out which ones of them wanted hookers for the rest of the evening, which ones wanted limo rides to church the next morning, and which ones wanted both. At the same time, he managed to convince each of the unsuspecting victims that he was the only one getting such royal treatment from those great guys at Wizard.

James Gill gave his brief presentation from a small stage set up under the stars in the old Alcatraz prison's exercise yard. Giant television monitors banked behind him played scenes shot in the new studios, clips of the disc jockeys at work, and examples of the stock commercials for affiliates to run on their local television stations. As the images flickered on the upturned faces, a gentle fog rolled in over the bay between the island and Fisherman's Wharf. The entire function was taking on an almost surreal feeling by then.

With the cold microphone caressing his lips as he spoke, Brother James flashed back for a moment. He could almost imagine that he was back on the airwaves once again. On the radio, talking to an unseen audience that would remain hidden from him out there in the thick mist. He unconsciously dropped into his deepest radio voice as he recited the carefully memorized script with the powerful inflection and practiced salesmanship he had used thousands of times before on so many commercials, between so many records, on so many radio stations. He closed his eyes and he was on WBHM or the Super Q or the Fox or 92 Rock, and he had the listeners mesmerized, hanging on his words, allowing his velvet voice to carry them away, listening to him and him alone.

There was no DeWayne George then, no engineers union, no

payroll to meet, no sulking Detroit Simmons, and no FCC to mollify. There was only Brother James and his audience out there in the mist.

Then, when the time was right, he dropped his voice yet an octave deeper for the closing clincher, and he could feel rather than see that mouths were open throughout the audience. It didn't matter that the people in the audience had been temporarily swallowed up by the fog as well as his sales pitch; he knew that he had scored, that he had their attention, that they were listening.

Brother James also knew that no matter how well fed or how drunk or how impressed they were with these magical surroundings, how captured they might be by his vocal magic-wand waving, they would still be expecting the other shoe to drop, to hear how much Wizard was going to demand from them to put its wonderful programming on their stations. But that was his closer. Unlike every other radio network in the business, Wizard was proposing paying station operators a set monthly fee based on their ratings in exchange for minimal commercial time on the network they chose to run. And they would even pay the stations a bonus for ratings plateaus. The station owners and operators could be automatically making a profit the instant they sent Wizard's programming down their signals to listeners' radios! They would be partners in the networks' success!

The awestruck executives had had just enough time to realize that James's offer was serious, that it contained no hidden catches, when he raised his hands to quiet the murmuring out there behind the mist. It was time to bring on the evening's musical entertainment, just as the thickest of the fog passed on by, as if prearranged by the magicians at Wizard.

Cleo Michaels was as wonderful on stage that night as he had ever seen her. He had to force himself not to look at the writhing, dancing audience of drunk media executives as he walked among them, shaking hands and allowing them to pound him on the back like a long-lost friend. Jimmy knew exactly how these men would be looking at the woman he loved. He didn't want to see that in their eyes.

She danced and swayed, sang happy and sad, hot and sultry, cool and mellow. She pulled loose every emotion she could wrench

from each song, then reached somewhere deep inside herself for
still more. Somehow, she was able to get that passion across to the
audience. That's why she was so good. Every person in the crowd
felt as if this beautiful woman was singing just for him.

Jimmy thought he heard her dedicate one of her songs to him,
but he couldn't be sure. He was in the middle of a group of executives from Taiwan and trying to understand what they were saying. When he finally turned back to the stage she was into some
rocking country song and doing a wild dance with the guitar player
in her band.

They only met for a brief moment after she finished her third
encore. He had more hands to shake, so they had time for only a
few much-too-short embraces, a couple of deep kisses, a quick reading of the tiredness in each other's eyes. Between the kisses, she
told him matter-of-factly that she was off to Fresno for an afternoon county fair performance the next day, then back to Sacra-
mento, and on to Reno. She was going to say more, probably give
him the rest of the tour itinerary, but he closed her lips with his
own again before she could.

When he broke the kiss again, he checked her eyes as she kept
her face turned up to his in the dim light. That's when he realized
that there was something different about her tonight. Something
he had missed when they first held each other, as the fog drifted
past and the party swirled on around them. The way she stiffened
ever so slightly when he pulled her to him. A faraway look in her
eyes. Something he couldn't quite put his finger on. He assumed
it was fatigue. God, didn't she see how hard she was pushing
herself? Did he have to write her a memo to get her to go ahead
and quit this madness?

"When are you gonna slow down, Cleo? When you drop dead
on the bus?" he asked, but she didn't answer and pulled quickly
away from him, turned her back, and walked a few steps away.
Jimmy checked to make sure no one was watching them. Someone
might have misinterpreted and thought they were having an argument.

But then she turned back to him and walked back closer. Her
eyes were clouded even more then and she paused a long beat
before snapping at him in a voice he had never heard from her
before.

"How dare you ask me that. We need to talk, Jimmy. And we need to talk soon."

"I'll catch you on the phone—"

"No. I mean we need to really talk. About you. You and me. The company. Everything. Dee and I—"

"So that's it. He's still pissed at me and now—"

"No, Jimmy. Don't say anything else. Not here."

"Okay, maybe the end of next week we can hook up somewhere. Or the weekend."

She smiled and it, too, was a smile he had never seen on her wonderful face before. Her voice was just as chilling.

"I'll have my people call your people."

And then she was gone.

He didn't have time to think about what had just happened. No time to figure out what the hell had come over her. Jimmy checked again to make certain no one had seen her performance. Then it was time for him to leave the island, too, to go with Richard Graffeo to take the heads of five large radio groups to a private dinner at a swank Nob Hill restaurant. Later, with no time at all scheduled for sleep, there was a breakfast meeting with a Hollywood studio president who wanted to pitch them some idea.

Then they had a contract-signing brunch at the Mark Hopkins with the guys from the fulfillment house who would handle the 800-number calls from direct-response advertising. That had been Detroit's idea: fill any unsold commercial positions on the networks with offers of records or merchandise that listeners could order.

They already had the flight plan filed to swing the new company Learjet through Omaha on the way back to Nashville. There they would tour the fulfillment company's warehouses and telephone-bank facilities and nod and grin a lot. The deal had been done already. The visit was window dressing.

But first there was a luncheon meeting with the team who would be putting the staff together for the all-news channel. And then they would head back to the convention exhibit floor to finish out the show, count the signed agreements that were stacking up in the booth office, shake hands one more time with anybody and everybody who extended one their way.

Detroit had tried to get him aside a time or two during the

convention, but there certainly was no time for that. It was big-picture time. But if Detroit had gone to Cleo and tried to make her an ally in his war with Jimmy, then they had even more to talk about than Jimmy had thought. They had been friends too long to let personal shit interfere with business.

"Handle whatever it is the best you can, Dee," Jimmy had said, trying to hide his growing irritation.

"Jimmy, we need to talk about—"

"Soon as we get back to Nashville. I promise." Someone was waving at him from behind Detroit. Someone important. "Jerry? Jerry Partain? How *are* things at the number one station in Cleveland these days?"

And he was off again. Dee had no choice but to watch him dance away.

There would be time for Dee and his technical stuff later in the week. Time to head off whatever ambush he and Cleo were cooking up. Time for sleep then, too. No time for trivia or rest now. There were deals to cut. Contracts to sign. An empire to build.

By noon Sunday, thankfully the last day of the show, James Gill had completely lost his voice for the first time in his career. He had to squeak his instructions to the convention crew. Had to squawk a "well done" to Richard and his staff. Had to whisper a quick "I love you" to Cleo when he finally made her answer her mobile telephone some time Sunday night. Jimmy was calling her from a pay phone in the airport lobby. Cleo was in the bus somewhere on a stretch of highway south of Bakersfield, far enough out that her telephone was barely making it back. Jimmy had only wanted to tell her that he loved her and to be careful, but she didn't seem to want to hear it. Instead, she quickly picked up right in the middle of the conversation they had left hanging backstage at the Alcatraz party.

"Jimmy, I told you this doesn't need to be a telephone conversation with you in some booth somewhere and with me in the middle of nowhere. Dee and I have been talking . . . ," she started to say, but a burst of static almost washed her voice away.

"Yeah, honey. Dee says hi. He flew out a few minutes ago, I think."

". . . the way things are going, we're just worried . . ."

There was a loud, screeching voice on the page speaker directly over Jimmy's head calling urgently for someone and he couldn't hear the rest of what she was saying.

"Yeah, things are going great, honey. We nailed down a lot of business out here. Look, I've got to run. . . ."

For some reason, after he hung up, he couldn't remember exactly what they had said to each other during the hurried one-minute conversation. He only remembered returning the phone to its hook and running fast to catch up with a wildly gesturing Richard Graffeo and sprinting through the cool drizzle for the airplane as it waited impatiently on the tarmac to whisk them out over the bay and off into the busy skies for some other place they had to reach as quickly as possible.

Once in the air, as the sleek plane hurtled into the darkness, he struggled to recall exactly what their destination was. But his mind was as muddled and dense as the Alcatraz fog had been.

It was funny. Just before he sank into a fitful sleep, he could easily remember where he had just been. But he had no idea where he was going.

Chapter 34

Detroit Simmons knocked gently, tentatively, on his door, then entered the office at his wave. Jimmy had almost forgotten about their aborted talks at the trade show. He now figured that Detroit was only there to bring him some purchase that needed approval or to mention someone he wanted to hire. At first, he thought about simply sending him on his way, telling him to please, if he would, put it all down on paper instead, do a memo, and he'd look at it when he got a chance.

Tomorrow. The next day maybe. Next week at the latest. Promise.

Jesus! He certainly didn't have time to humor the man. He had stacks of paperwork to hammer on, financial reports to try to decipher, a dozen life-or-death decisions to be made. There were rulings from on high that had to be handed down before lunchtime to keep some people from blowing their gaskets.

But for some reason he didn't send Detroit away as usual. Maybe he felt guilty about turning him away at the show. Or maybe, on some level, he knew now was the time to get on with what he had been thinking about doing. He motioned Dee to a chair and finished up his telephone conversation. Yet another chat with the head man for the new religious channel they were building for the satellite network. Just at that moment, though, he couldn't quite remember what the bastard's name was. He called him "buddy" as he dropped him from the line and said his sincere good-byes. Jimmy had learned he could usually get away with such familiarity if he only used enough of his residual southern accent to soften it.

It had been, Jimmy realized then, at least a month since he had spoken more than a few broken sentences to Detroit Simmons.

"Lord, Dee! I'm damn sorry. It seems like I'm in the middle of a cyclone most of the goddamn time nowadays."

"You're going to wear yourself to a nub, Jimmy. Some of us are worried that you are just gonna keel over one day. There has been a lot going on lately and we've seen the way you're pushing yourself."

"We've all been working hard. We can slow down soon, though. You'll see."

"Maybe so. But you ought to take it easy now. Start having some fun. Let some of these hard-ass guys you've brought in handle more of this stuff for you so you can enjoy what you've been building."

"Aw, it'll all slow down when we get these new radio channels launched. . . . another month it looks like, at the outside, for the hard-rock channel, another three or four months for Newsdial, and I've just found out that God's gift to radio is only about five months away from liftoff. Hey, how's your grandma and Lulu and them doing? I haven't talked with them in ages."

"Everybody's fine, Jimmy. Fine."

And just like that, Detroit started talking, hurriedly laying out some of the things that were on his mind, as if he was afraid it might spoil if he talked too slowly. Or as if he expected Jimmy might stop him midsentence, slap him with a sudden dismissal, and send him on his way, as was his custom lately.

But Jimmy didn't. He listened to every word. The phone rang once, twice, a third time. Jimmy made no move to pick it up except for an involuntary flinch and uncharacteristically let the new voice-mail system get it. Detroit plowed on. Told him of his concerns for Jimmy's health. His sanity. How he was afraid the alliance with the Georges was going to come back and bite like a caged bear. How Cleo was just as worried about him for all the same reasons. And how she was afraid she was losing him to the tornado that his life had become.

When Dee stopped for a breath, Jimmy fired right back at him and the give and take between them was wonderful, as clean and honest and unpretentious as their boyhood chats along the creek bank and in the sage fields. There were no titles. No incorporation papers between them. He avoided discussing the Georges, though. He was still chewing over that piece of gristle.

Several times they laughed wildly with each other when they coincidentally recalled a common memory or suddenly realized they had reached some beautiful common ground that had been there between them all along, hidden by work, passion, or stubbornness. Anyone passing Jimmy's closed office door would have thought two lunatics had taken charge of Wizard Broadcasting. But they both recognized that it was that old familiar laugh of joy that always came with every discovery they had ever made together.

Detroit had that same old look in his dark brown eyes. The look that he had when he first put together Jimmy's junkyard bicycle or when he patched together a car sound system for the George twins or wired up some kind of thingamajig box with blinking lights and a wailing siren in the back room at WROG. Patching up the rift that had grown between him and Jimmy Gill was clearly his latest project.

Along the way, they actually stood and hugged awkwardly, and both ducked to wipe away a tear or two without the other one seeing. The phone rang another couple of times but neither of them seemed to hear it. The sun was well below the lip of Jimmy's office window, but time had stopped for them quite a few minutes before. The hour didn't matter. Neither did the blinking red light on the telephone or the stacks of paperwork on the desk. They had more talking to do.

Jimmy admitted to Dee that he had not listened to more than a few seconds of the programming on any of their stations in months. That he had no idea how the cable radio programming sounded coming out of the speakers in the dashboard of a car. That he had heard no radio at all in so long. And that he missed it. Oh, God, how he missed it.

"Everything's sounding great, Jimmy. You know I won't lie to you like some of them. You've hired some good folks who love radio to do it and they are doing it right, just like you would if you had the time. The new black music channel is right on target and the hard-rock format is going to go great. I just reworked the audio chain in the Louisville station a few weeks ago and it's sizzling . . . louder than anything else on the dial, but clean and pure as it can be. And it's totally legal, too. Those other stations up there are doing some serious head scratching, trying to figure out how I'm doing it. I've got the circuitry at the patent office now. We can make some money on it someday, I think. And we did a transmitter upgrade in Birmingham and that thing is causing cancer in five states now! I'll show you some tricks I came up with when you have time. We can do it at all the FMs for next to nothing. Just a few parts and some fine-tuning. And wait'll I tell you about . . ."

His eyes sparkled as he talked, his face bright—he was back in his element, talking wizardry and radio magic. Jimmy tried to hold his smile, to share the mood, but there was too much he wasn't saying. He didn't have the heart to tell Dee that the stations in Louisville and Birmingham were going to a broker to start shopping them around, looking for a buyer, within a week. Several of the others would follow in a few months. Wizard Broadcasting had put offers on the table for two stations each in Los Angeles and Chicago. They simply had to spin the smaller-market stations to raise the acquisition capital to go big-time. And with the FCC's station limits, they had to make room for the AM stations they would be forced to accept to make the deals work. Not to mention the money they had to raise to help with the staggering investments for the satellite channels.

The conversation eventually lagged, dead air hanging between them finally. Detroit dropped his head as if exhausted while Jimmy pretended to study a spreadsheet in front of him. He knew Detroit Simmons well enough to know that he was changing moods again, probably from light back to dark if he gauged correctly. Some kind of deep observation or question would soon follow. He steeled himself. After a long moment's silence, Detroit spoke again, quietly, the joy and fun and abandonment of the last half hour disappearing like a fading radio signal.

"Look, I know a lot more than you think I do. I know you're about to cut those two markets loose from the chain, Jimmy. Birmingham and Louisville. It's hard to keep something like that quiet. We've already had tire kickers through both of the facilities and I know they aren't insurance people, like you told everybody they were."

"Dee, we've got to grow. And to grow, we've got—"

"I know, Jimmy. I'm not as dumb a nigger as you sometimes think I am. Maybe I'm not the figurehead president of Wizard anymore, but what I want to know is why you don't sell those little AMs in Miami and New Orleans instead. They're not making a dime and you know it. They never will. There's absolutely nothing we can do to upgrade them. Louisville and Birmingham are both sounding great. People fly in from all over the country to listen and tape them and go back and try to duplicate what you're doing with them. And they are making money like crazy. Besides that, there are lots of bright, dedicated folks in those stations who will get shot when they change ownership. Always happens without fail. You know that. And there's something else about Birmingham that may not be practical and measurable. We started this long, strange trip there together! I can't believe you're gonna throw that away just to go big-time."

Jimmy spun around in his chair so he wouldn't have to see Dee's face anymore and walked quickly to the office window. He could survey a hundred square miles of middle Tennessee from this vantage point at the top of the steel-and-marble bank tower. And since the trip to Miami and to the San Francisco convention, he had done quite a bit more of that between urgent phone calls and demanding memos. It helped him avoid hyperventilating, or losing what tad of breakfast he might have grabbed that morning on the way to work.

He liked to look down there. The broadcasting company that Detroit and he had built from a crazy idea would, sooner or later, touch practically every one of those people who scurried around on the streets and highways below. All the people who lived in the houses and apartments stretching away into the distance. The millions and millions more that were beyond his eyesight but well within the reach of the electromagnetic waves that he, James Gill, had caused to be created, and that his best friend, Detroit Simmons, had conspired to push out into the ozone.

Jimmy smiled at his own thin, sallow reflection grinning back at him from the darkly tinted window. Sometimes he still had the almost overpowering urge to jump up and down in front of this floor-to-ceiling pane of glass, waving and screaming at all the people who scurried around down there. Do whatever it took to make them look up at him. Make them notice him. Listen to him.

"I couldn't sell those damn pip-squeak stations in Miami and New Orleans. Not even if I wanted to, Dee."

He waited for Jimmy to go on. By then he had stood up himself, had leaned forward, braced against the desk, his stance begging for more information, ready for whatever the story might be. Even if it was what he was afraid it would be. He finally spoke to Jimmy's back.

"Okay, I'll bite. Why not?"

And then Jimmy slowly, reluctantly, turned away from the towering, seductive view and looked at his only friend. He walked back to his desk, and then quietly began to talk. Slowly, completely, he spun for Detroit the whole sordid story. Of the Georges and their "legitimate" business venture. Of Garcia down in Miami and his grungy counterpart in New Orleans. And of DeWayne's threat to spill the beans about the seed money if anything ever happened to get in the way of their grand scheme.

The intercom on his desk blared twice while he spoke, but he ignored it. The telephone pealed another couple of times but he made no move to answer it. Not even a flinch this time. Sammie knocked on the door a couple of times and called his name, finally pushed it open and gave him a mean look, but he yelled at her as politely as he could to please shut the door and leave them be.

Finally, Jimmy told Detroit about DeWayne's threat against Cleo, and about the look in the twin's eye when he had told Jimmy to tell her to be careful on the road. Detroit's face fell even further when he heard that.

Finally, the story was finished. Detroit was quiet as he sank back into the office chair and tried to think logically about all Jimmy had said.

Then, suddenly, he sat up, pounded the desk in anger with his balled-up fist, stood and stalked back and forth across the length of the massive office, marched in circles for a while until the rage had subsided enough for him to be able to talk again. He flopped heavily back into the chair, slumped, and finally stared up at the high ceiling and the dangling chandelier over Jimmy's desk.

"Jimmy, you know I love you. As much as I would have a brother if I had been blessed with one. And you know that I really do appreciate all you've done for me."

Jimmy held up his hand to try to stop him, to give him his share of the credit, but he marched on.

"I'd probably be welding wrought-iron furniture together like my granddaddy or doing some dirty work in the mills down in Birmingham if it wasn't for you. If you hadn't been so pigheaded about everything all along the way. You had the vision. Not me. And my aunt would most certainly still be cleaning up for folks, being a maid like she had always done. Same thing for the rest of them, too. All the ones you've brought along on this wild little ride and have made the better for it. You fooled a lot of folks, Jimmy Gill. The ones who thought that all you were was a high school dropout, a midnight-to-six disc jockey, and a plain old white trash redneck to boot."

He looked at Jimmy across the desk, checking for signs of offense, but Jimmy had sunk deeper down into his own office chair, tired from all the revelations he had just shared, his feet propped amid all the crucial papers and screaming figures now laying ignored on the desk. He, too, watched the ceiling and listened for once to what someone else had to say.

"But look what you built, Jimmy! Goddamn! Just look what you have done! Sure, you had to take some shortcuts. There was no way you could have pulled it off without the Georges' money. I know I screamed like an old woman when you first proposed it. But just look. You did it. Oh, and I'd like to think I helped just a little bit."

Jimmy looked down at him quickly.

"Damn, Dee! There's no way I could have done anything without you. Right now, you and Cleo are the only people in this world that I love, and I've shut you completely out and she's two thousand miles away singing to a bunch of drunks in some honky-tonk while I'm here getting neck deep in a mess that just might get her killed and cost you everything you've built!"

Jimmy didn't know where the tears came from so suddenly. So uninvited. So unexpected. He had never dreamed that he had so many. But they burst out of him like a downpour. For the second time in a year, he was squalling like a baby. Only this time, there was somebody else there to see him crying. Not just a flock of crows and couple of ghosts in a cemetery by the river.

Detroit was up immediately, his arm around Jimmy's shoulder, quiet, but comforting in his silence. Finally Jimmy stood and wiped the remaining tears with the initialed cuff of his custom-tailored dress shirt; then, embarrassed by his sudden letting go, he returned to his favorite place for contemplation, staring out the office window.

Below, on the Cumberland River, a tugboat shoved a barge loaded with coal upriver at a brisk pace, angry white water churning at its stern. The long, thick shadow of the building in which Jimmy stood fell directly across the muddy stream, cast there by the late-afternoon sun. It seemed to put up a dark, impenetrable barrier to the boat's progress, but the boat simply plowed right through the shade, shoving the barge even faster, and left the black shadow of the solid building diffused and shimmering in its frothy wake. He hardly noticed that Detroit now stood beside him at the window, watching the tug.

"You know what, Jimmy Gill? Sometimes things we see as impossible obstacles to overcome aren't really so tough after all. We only have to try to push on and think our way through them. Maybe what we need to do now is to sit down and get busy rigging up something that will get the job done."

And even over his own sniffling, above the renewed buzzing of the intercom on the desk behind them, the screaming of the telephone, and more of Sammie impatiently pounding on his door, Jimmy Gill was sure he could hear the wheels beginning to spin inside Detroit Simmons's head.

Chapter 35

You know what, Jimmy? I hate to sound melodramatic, but I don't think you love me anymore."

The cold matter-of-factness of Cleo's long-distance voice left him stunned. A harsh metallic echo on the telephone line surrounded her words and made them rattle and snap like brittle ice.

"But Cleo, I—"

"You ought to listen to yourself sometime, Jimmy. Look at how you are. Look at how you allow me to get just so close to you. Then you seem to suddenly wake up or something and shove me away like I'm trespassing on posted territory. Look at how you wrap yourself in a cocoon with your work so nobody can get near enough to you to reach you. Not even me. Why won't you let me love you, Jimmy? What in hell are you so damned afraid of?"

He was silent then, with only the hum of the phone in his ear. He didn't know what to say.

"Good answer, Jimmy. Damn good answer. I've got a few days off. Some promoter went bust and canceled out on us. I'm going to hole up somewhere and think awhile. Probably cry my eyes out and eat way too many chocolate-covered cherries or something, too. I do that when my heart is breaking, you know. No, on second thought, you wouldn't know, Jimmy Gill. You wouldn't know. Maybe I can write some and that'll help me work it out. Figure out some way to touch you. Hopefully, I can decide if I really want to try anymore. You know what? Sometimes talking to you is exactly like trying to talk back to the radio!"

Again, he was silent, not sure what words to say to convince her how much he loved her. Needed her. "I love you and I need you" somehow never occurred to him. Fine damn communicator he was!

"Jimmy? Are you listening to me? Maybe right now would be a good time for you to do some serious thinking about us, too. That is, if you care."

And with a loud, terminal click, she was gone.

The call had come out of the blue, a shock in the middle of one of the most fantastic days Jimmy had enjoyed in months. Of course, they had hardly spoken to each other in over a week. When they did, her voice was hoarse and tired from the grueling final leg of the tour. He usually was distracted, his mind more on stock offerings and profit-and-loss statements. And it seemed like years since they had held each other. He could hardly remember what she felt like lying close to him, what her voice sounded like when she was there in the same room.

The distant coldness of the telephone usually left him silent, not sure what to say to let her know how much he missed her. Or else he ranted on and on about stupid business drivel that he should have known she didn't care to hear. He let her tell him what was happening on the road, in the shows, at the radio stations she visited for interviews. But he knew that even she could tell, over the thousands of miles of wires and microwave links and telephone relay stations that were stacked up between them, that his mind was blitzing back and forth from her to company business. That kept her from getting to what was really bothering her until that last call.

Now, just that quickly, with the breaking of the long-distance telephone connection, Jimmy Gill faced the inevitable. He had known all along Cleo Michaels was too good for someone like him. One day she would wake up to realize who and what kind of man he really was. And then she would run away from him as fast and as far as she could.

Somewhere deep inside, he had always harbored the thought that he should drive her away from him first, spare her before she was hurt even more, make the unavoidable easier for her. And maybe that was why he had stayed so quiet on the telephone while she spilled her raw words. Even when his throat ached to speak and his heart burst from loving her so much.

Soon. Soon he could have her back, in person, and most of the blackness that had been occupying his mind would be past. Then he could tell her how he felt. Or maybe not. Maybe she was gone for good. Maybe he would never say what he needed to say to get her back. Before it ate him whole, he tried to shake the call from his mind and turn back to work.

Richard and the team that had headed up the stock offering for Wizard Broadcasting were ecstatic. The stock had flown out the door and was already up several points.

"Three or four holding companies I've never heard of bought most of the shares in a hurry," Graffeo reported. "The underwriters couldn't believe what you've built down here without borrowing money through conventional channels. But you've got control of the whole shebang now, Brother James. And lots of cash to throw at some more properties anytime you are ready. Just keep those stockholders happy 'cause if they ever get their noses out of joint, they can get together and fire you and me both!"

Now that the radio stations and satellite programming networks were public, Jimmy somehow felt a huge pressure lifted off his shoulders. With a management team in place, maybe he could once again spend time thinking of creative programming and music. Of making magic out of nothing but thin air and sound. Talking with Detroit about his technical ideas had fired Jimmy up for more innovation and less financial manipulation.

But for the first time, he was having some doubts about his ambitious growth plans. He wasn't so sure they should spend all that available cash on new properties. Maybe they should take what they had accumulated already and concentrate on making them the best they could be. That had been Detroit's suggestion, and Jimmy had to admit that it was sound.

When Cleo called, Jimmy had been immersed in a project that had him tingling all over. But there had been no way he could have told her what it was. He had long ago decided to shield her from all that was happening with the Georges.

That morning, with Dee looking on, he had personally placed the licenses for the puny AM station in Homestead, Florida, and for the one in New Orleans into a brown manila envelope along with a handwritten note. Then he prepared to overnight the package to the Federal Communications Commission in Washington, D.C. It was the first part of his and Detroit's plan. He was simply going to turn the licenses back in to the commission and wash his hands of them.

He'd tell the board of directors and the stockholders eventually in some dull prospectus that he was only cutting loose a couple of nonprofitable facilities in depressed markets. The others who would have to know about what he had done would find out soon enough on their own.

The power companies in each city had already been notified to pull the electric meters outside each transmitter as soon as possible. A couple of college broadcasting departments would soon receive a windfall donation of old AM transmitting and studio equipment. For Sale signs would go up in front of the grimy little block buildings in both cities as soon as contracts could be signed with real estate companies there.

The Wizard Rock Network was about to lose two of its marginal affiliates, and the man who had started the whole thing was happy about those developments. The rest of his crumbling life would have to wait a few more days.

Chapter 36

Jimmy Gill couldn't shroud his feelings behind the veil of work. He kept hearing the sound of Cleo's voice underneath everyone else's on the telephone calls he took. Her words kept washing out the printed ones on the reports that he tried to study the balance of the day.

Finally, frustrated, he left the office early, out before eight o'clock for the first time in as long as he could remember. He steered the car toward Cleo's place that night instead of his own lonely house, partly out of habit, but mostly out of a need to be somewhere that he could feel closer to her for a while, in a place that bore her touch, her feel, her scent.

He tried to call her a couple of times, but there was no answer on the portable phone she kept in the Silver Eagle bus. He tried his own answering service several times but there was no message from her there.

Her agent had no idea where she had run off to after the show dates had been unexpectedly canceled. He said that she had sounded tired when he last spoke with her, though. She had said that she intended to find someplace quiet and dull to rest up for a week. The band and crew had gone on to Phoenix without her to wait for the next show.

"Is everything okay?" the agent asked him.

"Sure, as far as I know. She said the tour has been going gangbusters."

"I mean between you two. I've been booking Cleo for ten years and I've never heard her like this."

There was suspicion, blame in his voice.

"Aw, I think everything is okay. It's just the big change coming up. Pulling back isn't easy for her, you know. Everything will be fine."

Wishful thinking, Jimmy thought. Sometime since her call and now he had come to a momentous decision. Maybe it had been the finality of her words, or maybe finally forcing the issue with the Georges had made him want to set things right with her, too. Whatever it had been, he had decided to finally let go, to commit to her, to let her know how much he loved her, to open up to her as he had never done with anyone else except Detroit Simmons, and to let the chips fall where they may. Let her fulfill his expectations and drop him once and for all, or accept him with all his flaws. That's what he would tell her, point-blank—if he didn't change his mind by the time they spoke and shove her away again.

And he had some plans of his own to tell her about. Plans that had to have been bubbling close to the surface of his psyche for a while to so easily come to the top after his heart-to-heart with Detroit. He had decided to pull back a bit himself, and to actually get back to those things that had kidnapped him into the broadcasting business in the first place. He had not enjoyed what he had been doing for a long time now. He was finally ready to admit to Cleo, to Dee, and, amazingly, to himself that he wanted to take pleasure in some of what he had worked so hard to achieve. He wanted to be able to do a show on the air again, and to have time to actually listen to the stations for which he was responsible.

There was one other thing he needed desperately to tell Cleo. Something so dark he had trouble even thinking about it. He needed to warn her to watch out for DeWayne George. And especially after what he and Dee had done that afternoon and what they would do tomorrow.

But he couldn't find her to tell her that either. Lord, where was she? Why didn't she call?

That night he went to Cleo's house as he often did when his missing her became something close to an obsession. He rehearsed all he would say to her in a rambling monologue to the walls of the mansion. He sincerely told the furniture how he felt about her. How much he needed her. How hard he would try to be the kind of man she deserved. But the walls and furniture couldn't answer him.

When he wasn't lecturing he was pacing, trying to think of

some other way to get in touch with her, hoping against hope that the telephone would peal and it would be Cleo on the line, laughing, joking, being her wonderful self. Or that he might suddenly hear the rumble of the tour bus outside and she would simply show up, run to him, grab him, not let him go.

Eventually, without his really intending it to, his nervous marching took him over to the old upright Zenith radio. It had stood there in the corner all alone, watching him striding back and forth like a caged cat, ranting like a loon. He reached out and gently touched the cool mahogany of its cabinet, felt the smoothness where Cleo had shined the wood to a glow with furniture polish and love. The speaker cloth was soft when he stroked it. He could smell the electric aroma of the radio's internal parts.

The On switch clicked loudly when he twisted it, snapping at him loudly in the silent, empty living room. And then he could hear the growling hum as the transformer sent electricity to the filaments of the radio's tubes, just as he had in the floor of his bedroom back in the duplex when he had first turned the box on. It almost sounded as if the radio was chiding him for being gone so long, for ignoring it as he had.

Then the tubes warmed and began to conduct the electrons, which did their job of amplifying through the speaker the sound that had begun to fade in as if from some great, mysterious distance. There was something so comforting and familiar about it all, the sounds, the smell, the warmth, that Jimmy at once began to feel better.

Then something strange happened. As if right on cue, as if the station the radio was tuned to was playing it just for him and him alone, the song he heard from the Zenith's speaker was one of Cleo's: the new single from her latest album. He had heard it only once before, and then quickly, half listening to a tape she had shoved into a cassette deck one day and made him stop and hear. But it had certainly not affected him then as it did now.

He trembled as the vibrations from the speaker and cabinet softly tickled him where his body leaned against it. Instinctively, he hugged the box tighter, as if it were a living thing, as if it were actually Cleo here with him now, singing to him. He pulled closer to the radio's warmth, placed his cheek against its top, and felt the power of her wonderful voice run through him, the gentle pulsing of her fingers on the guitar strings as she stroked them, pulled the tear-shaped notes from them.

Then there were the words of the song she was singing in a voice full of sadness. Jimmy had never listened to song lyrics. When he was a jock, he had spent the time the song was playing getting the next one ready and cued to spin, or preparing whatever wit or wisdom he was going to share with his audience when the record was over. He could still recite the length of time from beginning note till the first vocal of hundreds of records, their exact running time, even the color of the record label, but he hardly knew any of the words of the songs he had played over the air all those years.

But this time, the words to Cleo's song grabbed his heart and squeezed.

> *"Loving without touching, listening without hearing,*
> *Saying those same words you didn't mean before.*
> *How can I reach you, become a part of you,*
> *When you won't let me love you anymore?"*

She had tried to sing it to him on the phone several times while she was writing it, but it had been an especially busy time for him. He had only taken the trouble to give her some kind of quick approval and rudely steered the conversation some other way without even thinking of how important it might have been to her for him to listen to the words of a song. Words that were more important to her than usual.

It had been only another country song, after all. Maybe a hit. Maybe only filler on the back side of an album. But now, he realized it was much more. It was a song she had written for him.

The guitars and voices swelled to a finish and Jimmy was left weak and wounded. The disc jockey on the radio kicked off some wild and woolly Texas two-step song and Jimmy viciously twisted the volume control back to Off before the mood was ruined.

Then he ran to the shelves along the back wall of her living room and found a copy of the new album, still clothed in its protective shrink wrapping. He almost ripped the cardboard apart as he tore the disc from its cover and slung it quickly down on the turntable. He listened as the song filled the room again, this time in stereo, sounding all the more as if she were there with him. He kept a hand on the nearest speaker, again to feel her voice as much as to hear it as she sang. Then he listened to it again and again, letting the words beat him, punish him with their power and hurt.

Crying and almost exhausted, he let the needle stay in the groove and track through the rest of the album side, then automatically reject and start over again at the beginning. Over and over, the song and the rest of side one, at least twenty times through.

Jimmy Gill spent the rest of the night on the floor next to the speaker, clutching the pillow from her bed to his aching heart, as Cleo Michaels sang the songs again and again, just for him. Finally, maybe too late, he was listening to her.

Listening as she begged for his returned love in every verse.

As she pleaded for his heart with every chorus.

By necessity, Cleo had mastered the ability to disguise herself so she was rarely recognized. No makeup, an old scarf, some dimestore reading glasses and she could become as anonymous as she needed to be. No one really expected Cleo Michaels to be checking into the Motel 6 in Morro Bay, California, with one cheap, battered suitcase, or to be ordering the Mexican omelette for breakfast at Pepe's Eat and Run just off the freeway exit ramp.

She had disappeared several times before. Pulling in her horns had worked every time so far. It was the cheapest and surest therapy she had found. This latest excursion to solitude had been no exception. She felt better already, just lying there next to the ocean in the middle of a deserted beach watching the unmoving monolithic rock in the bay.

She had gotten past kicking herself for laying it on the line to Jimmy on the telephone instead of waiting until they could be face-to-face, but the son of a bitch frustrated the living hell out of her. He could be so wonderful most of the time, so warm, so real. Then other times, he threw up a wall so thick and impenetrable he might as well have been yet another voice on the radio, talking but not listening.

"Buenos días!"

She jumped, startled, and quickly sat up on her towel. She had not noticed anyone else on the beach. But the man who had spoken had passed on by, walking quickly, waving something flat and metallic above the sand in front of him as he made his way down the beach. A metal detector.

He was an older man, dark skinned, in short pants and a golf shirt, with a broad Panama hat shielding his face from the sun. Had he recognized her? Apparently not. She watched him until he disappeared around the curve of the beach before she lay back down and breathed easily again. She didn't want anyone, and especially Jimmy Gill, to find out where she was.

Cleo had already decided what she had to do, just not exactly how. After her last couple of shows, she would lasso the hardheaded so-and-so, tie him down, and they'd have their own private little rodeo. Whether Mr. James Gill wanted to or not, he would have to listen to what she had to say. They would finally talk it out, finally come to some kind of understanding. They'd have to decide once and for all if the haphazard waltz they had been doing with each other was worth continuing. If so, they would both commit and let the band play on. If not, they would dance away from each other.

God, she hoped she could make him listen. Why was it so hard to make him listen?

The voice on the radio told her it was "ten minutes leaving eleven o'clock" and her stomach confirmed it. An enchilada platter from Pepe's was calling her name. Even the screeching of the terns ferrying between the beach and the harbor rock seemed to be urging her on to something hot and spicy and disgustingly fattening.

As she gathered up her towel and radio and started back to the rental car on the roadway at the edge of the beach, she half noticed movement a hundred feet down the way, behind the only other car parked anywhere in sight. It was the man with the metal detector, his trunk up, apparently having trouble putting away the instrument. For an odd instant, Cleo thought she could see the man watching her from under the brim of the big Panama hat. But then his head was down, hidden by the trunk lid, trying to fit the long handle and bulky body of the metal detector into the narrow compartment.

No, he doesn't recognize me, she thought. But it's nice that even the old guys are still checking me out. Um, maybe I'll have the tamales instead.

Putting the rest of her life into some semblance of order had made Cleo Michaels as hungry as a wolf.

Chapter 37

The regular weekly conference call with the station managers had been under way for ten minutes or so. Jimmy was half listening. His mind was two thousand miles away from all the loud talk of billings and quotas and capital budgets. But he was forcing himself to listen, to grunt occasionally to let the rest of the guys know he was still there on his end of the telephone lines. Then Sammie burst into the office, almost in a panic.

"He's here! He's out there right now," she stage-whispered, and pointed back toward the lobby. "And he wants to see you 'right damn now.'"

Even in her whisper, she did a perfectly believable imitation of the oily, grating voice of DeWayne George.

"Sam, would you please send them on their way, honey?" he said, half covering the mouthpiece with his hand so the others on the line could still hear him. "I'm spending lots of the stockholders' money and the managers' time on this conference call."

She looked at him as if he had lost his mind. Had he not told her to interrupt anything . . . *anything* . . . if DeWayne George showed up?

"I know, Jimmy, but it's DeWayne. At least I think it's him. I can't tell those two apart. Anyway, he says it's a matter of life and death that he sees you right now. That's what he said. Life and death."

She looked pale. Jimmy shuddered. Naturally, he had been expecting this confrontation, but now that it had blown into the building like a compact, slicked-down tornado, he wished there was some way to escape from this penthouse office and avoid the blowup, some way to dodge the storm that he knew was about to rumble through his big polished-oak double doors.

"Guys, I gotta cut it short," he finally said into the telephone, struggling to keep his voice on an even keel. "Y'all can carry on without me. Jerry, you run the meeting, please. Just sell lots of commercial spots and try to collect at least half of the money we're charging for them and I'll be a happy man."

They laughed politely as he hit the cutoff button, pausing a moment to gather his strength and click on a tiny switch that dangled from a set of wires under the desk near his knee. He then took several deep breaths and was about to rise and go out to the lobby to escort DeWayne back as any good host would do. Suddenly though, without warning, DeWayne filled the doorway like a black cloud, stepping inside the office without invitation and slamming the door behind himself with a sound like a close clap of thunder.

"DeWayne George! How's it hangin'?"

"Lissen, you skinny-ass blond bastard. What kind of shit are you tryin' to pull on me?"

DeWayne stood there, lightning flashing in his eyes, squeezing his thumbs, seething furiously. His words rattled like hail on a tin roof.

"What do you mean, DeWayne?"

"I just talked with Duane a little while ago. The goddamn power company shut us off this morning in Homestead and yesterday afternoon in New Orleans. They took the meters, goddamn it! And when I called 'em, they said the CEO of the fuckin' company ordered it done himself. And while I was checking on that, Duane called to tell me the FCC had called him. They wanted to make sure we weren't still broadcasting. That is, since the president of Wizard Broadcasting had turned in the goddamn licenses. Have you lost your damn mind?"

Jimmy didn't take time to breathe. He knew he couldn't stop to think now or he might cut and run for his life.

"They're my licenses to do with whatever I please, DeWayne. It's my name up on the top of them. And when I applied for them, I agreed . . . swore, in fact . . . to use those licenses to broadcast to serve the public interest, convenience, and necessity. That's what it says right there in the Communications Act of 1937. I don't see any way that your dope dealing on the airwaves serves the interest or necessity of most of the public in Miami or New Orleans. Nor the convenience of more than a criminal few either."

It was just the way he had rehearsed it. He might have been reading live commercial copy on the air. DeWayne took a step back, recovering from Jimmy's first shot, but he blew even harder when he spoke again.

"You're forgetting one important thing, Brother James. I'm the one that gave you the money to buy these and most of the other stations in the first place. I was there when it was convenient for you and provided you with one goddamn big necessity. Money. Cash money. Else you and the nigger would be back in Biloxi playing cowshit country records and screwin' fat girls."

"DeWayne, you'll get a package FedEx at the studio building in Homestead this afternoon with the exact amount of cash you put up for the two stations, plus twenty-five percent interest. If there's no one there to sign for it, the man will leave it on the porch."

DeWayne tensed slightly. Jimmy could imagine him mentally pulling another card from a deck to play. He fully expected it to be his trump card. It was.

"Looks like I'll have to let some people know where you got the money to start this little old company, Brother James. And how we used the new stations to tell our runners where the stuff would be delivered. The FCC would love to get that kind of information, I expect. Find out what kind of outlaw they been giving their precious licenses to."

"Exactly where did I get that money you're speaking of, DeWayne?"

DeWayne paused for an instant, not ready for the question.

"I loaned it to you, of course, you son of a bitch!"

"And did I pay you back? Every damn penny? And with extremely generous interest?"

"Yeah, but that ain't the point and you know it."

"What is the point, DeWayne?"

"You knew where that money came from. You knew all along that me and Duane was selling smoke and cocaine all up and down Alabama and Mississippi and Georgia!"

"Did I or anybody else associated with these stations ever sell any dope? Did Detroit Simmons or I ever actually see you or your

brother sell any dope to anyone? Did you not include with each
package of cash a tally of the money and a note from you with your
signature written on the letterhead of legitimate, functioning businesses that were incorporated and run under your and Duane's
names? Do I have any proof that you sold dope for the exact cash
money you loaned us to start the company? That it was anything
but the proceeds of completely aboveboard companies?"

"No, but—"

"Haven't you and Duane owned and run legitimate businesses
all along? Don't you have a used car dealership in Pascagoula? An
appliance rental store in Pensacola? A package delivery company
in Birmingham?"

"Sure we have," he admitted, but he looked at Jimmy warily,
probably wondering where he had gotten the information. "We
gotta have fronts to work out of. My competition could spot us
coming a mile away. Feds see us flashing the kind of money we
make with no legit business to generate it, they're on us like stink
on shit."

"Then how do I know that the money you loaned me and that
we so generously paid back in a timely manner, and with interest,
didn't come from the legal businesses you were running?"

"Money's money!" he practically shouted. "You know damn well
where most of that money—"

"And DeWayne, did I know anything at all about what you
were doing on the stations in Miami and New Orleans until I went
down there and saw it for myself? And almost got my skull fractured by one of your thugs for all my trouble? Did you tell me
beforehand?"

"Naw, and I wish Duane had kept his damn mouth shut when
you blundered in down there. Or that Enrique had finished your
ass off like he was supposed to do. That's what we pay him for."

George turned abruptly and paced back and forth across the
office then like a nervous cat, possibly thinking carefully about his
next angle of attack in the face of Jimmy's full frontal assault.
Maybe the animal even suspected he was sticking his paw into a
trap.

Jimmy simply sat there and waited to see what he spit out
next. He had no choice, but he had the impression no one had
bucked DeWayne George and that the experience was a totally new

one for him. Now, whether he wanted to or not, Jimmy Gill would find out if he'd back down like a beaten bully, or strike out viciously like a cornered animal.

It was the decision he and Detroit had reached two days before. Whether George fought back or slithered away, Jimmy knew he had to do what he was doing or they would be under his thumb from then on. There was no backing out of this now. He sucked up all the resolve he could muster and tried to make his voice go as deeply confident as he could.

"DeWayne, you can go on back to whatever gopher hole you crawled from. You can keep on doing whatever it is that you and your brother do for all your money and leave us alone. Or you can set off such a firestorm that you and me and Detroit Simmons and your brother and your mama and lots of others will get caught up in the whole mess and burn right along with us. Yeah, you might be able to bring me down. But all that you say you've built would be blown to hell at the same time. Hell, from the way you talk, I'd say you're as proud of your little empire as I am of Wizard Broadcasting. Look, DeWayne. You can back off right now, go on about your business, and we can all keep what we've built up. Nobody but you and me will ever know what happened between us. Or you can be a big tough bastard like the guys in the movies and push your little vendetta and we'll all suffer for it. Your choice, man. Your choice."

He had said his piece and his voice had only broken a time or two. He prayed that there was at least an ounce of rationality in DeWayne George's sick mind, that the psychopath was listening to what he had said to him. Jimmy searched for something in the man's twitching face that might show he had reached him on some level that he could understand.

But there was not a flicker of understanding or reason at all to be seen there. Instead, he only saw the mottled face of hate. It was almost the exact same face Jimmy had seen years before on DeWayne's father, Hector George, when he chased Detroit Simmons away from the duplex with his rifle, and the same dim face filled with vile loathing visible in the light from the dashboard of the old man's beat-up car as he plowed through Mr. Polanski's island of beauty back on Wisteria Street.

Jimmy's stomach sank. He had gotten adept at reading a man's intentions by his facial expressions and body language. It stood him in good stead when he was negotiating a deal or shoving some flunky to greater accomplishment. And Jimmy Gill realized then that he might well have just lost the most important deal he had ever attempted to bargain.

It was suddenly apparent that the bastard was going to stand and defend his own squalid territory. Do whatever it took to fortify his own bailiwick of ugliness. Defend it as readily as his old man had. Screw the consequences! Reason be damned! Nobody could be allowed to bring anything but hideousness and evil onto DeWayne George's block.

DeWayne paused for a second, apparently thinking, then stalked some more, suddenly stopped again, spun, slapped an expensive china vase from a table near the window, and methodically stomped its shattered pieces into shards of rainbow glass with the heel of his snakeskin cowboy boot. Finally, he tramped over to the desk and leaned across it, his face only inches from Jimmy's.

"I don't know if I can do that, Brother James. Let you or anybody else get away with fucking me like you have. I'm bringing in probably a third of the Mexican marijuana that's bought and smoked in Alabama and Mississippi. A big part of the cocaine, too. And I'm making progress every day against Garcia in South Florida and the Musso family in Louisiana and East Texas, and they don't even know who I am yet. But they will soon. By then, I'll have them by the balls. But you know what happens if they find out their worst enemy got buffaloed by some half-ass skinny disc jockey like you? That I'm weak enough to let you pull a stunt like this and get away with it? And they will find out. Somehow they will."

He spat in Jimmy's face as he forced out the words, stabbing him in the chest with a dirty-nailed index finger as he talked. Jimmy swallowed hard before he spoke.

"There's only one way they'll ever find out about what has happened between us, DeWayne."

"Okay, smart boy. You tell me how?"

He fell back and began to pace again as he listened.

"Well, if you decide to tell the Federal Communications Commission or the Drug Enforcement Administration or any law, you might as well buy yourself some prime-time commercial spots on the River and tell the whole world at the same time. The word's going to be all over the place in about a minute. Garcia and the others are almost certain to be wired in to the FBI and the DEA, so they're sure to know your name, address, and Social Security number as quick as somebody can get to a telephone after you spill your guts to the feds."

Then Jimmy paused, allowing DeWayne to mull over the logic of what he had just said. Slowly Jimmy stood, careful to not make a sudden move that might force the twin toward violence. Jimmy stretched as tall as he could, as if he were merely working out the kinks in tense muscles, but he was checking for something. Making sure, for his own peace of mind, that it was still there.

If he had only reached up to the chandelier that swung just above his desk, he could have touched the wireless microphone Detroit had put there. He could see it, strapped to a fourteen-karat gold candleholder, but DeWayne couldn't see it from where he paced. At least, Jimmy hoped he couldn't. Its weak transmitter had been rigged with a power amplifier and a heavy-duty battery pack. The remote power switch was taped to the bottom of Jimmy's desk drawer. He had barely managed to get it flipped on before DeWayne blew into the office like a gust of bitter wind.

They were making four copies of the tape. One was to be removed from the recorder and placed into an envelope just after DeWayne admitted that he had sold drugs and that he had used the radio stations in the course of his trade. It was ready to be delivered to someone who would take a great deal of interest in the nature of the twins' business dealings.

The other three tapes were still spinning away on the bank of reel-to-reel machines. Two of them would go into envelopes already addressed to Miguel Garcia and Dominic Musso, to be sent to them at their homes if DeWayne tried to push the point. Another copy would be put in a safe place.

The receiving and recording equipment were not physically in the bank building. Their conversation had been broadcast a long way that morning. Some little old lady with a police scanner in west Nashville could have gotten an earful if she had only been tuned to the right frequency, but it was a risk they had had to take. Jimmy had wanted the recording done as far away from the Wizard offices and studios as the battery-powered amplifier could fling their voices.

DeWayne stopped his pacing in front of the desk, then bent at the waist like a defensive prizefighter, balled his fists, and glared. For a moment Jimmy thought the twin was going to take a swing at him and pop him full in the face. He tensed for the blow, prepared to block it if he could, but he knew he would be no match for somebody like DeWayne George who, no doubt, had had his share of punch-outs.

But slowly, DeWayne dropped the fist and uncoiled, standing erect again. His face was tight skinned, like a lizard watching its prey. All color had left his features. Then he turned slowly, walked over, and opened the door without saying anything more, his shoulders slumping, the fight seemingly gone from him.

Suddenly, he stopped dead and spun back around. The look on his face sent a chill through Jimmy as the room seemed to immediately grow colder. The twin's voice was as raspy as scraped frost when he spoke:

"There are some things a real man can't let go by, Brother James. Double crossing is one of them. You are with me all the way or you are my worst enemy. That's all there is to it. I'll see you again soon, neighbor. I'll see you again real soon. But right now I got a craving to hear me a real pretty country song."

Chapter 38

Jimmy was relieved that Cleo was lost somewhere out there. Lost from him. Lost from her manager. But also, thank God, lost from the vengeful wrath of DeWayne George. Detroit said the same thing when he bolted through Jimmy's office door fifteen minutes after DeWayne had stormed out. Jimmy was still sitting in the chair, still trying to catch his breath, his body caught in some kind of a shivering fit. He had not moved since DeWayne had slammed the office door shut.

"It'll blow over, Jimmy. You were great. Man, what a performance. You scared him enough to keep him from doing anything stupid. Shoot, you even scared me a time or two. Once DeWayne cools down, he won't want to risk everything just to get back at you. We got what we need if he calls our bluff but we won't ever need it. You'll see."

But Jimmy Gill wasn't certain. The rabid-animal look Jimmy had seen on DeWayne's face just before he left could not have been relayed to Detroit by the amplified wireless mike.

"I don't know, Dee. Man, I wish she would call. I've got to tell her to stay hidden until he calms down. That's all. Did you get the tapes okay?"

"We got it all fine. That is, except for a few words when some citizens-band guy with a linear amplifier almost knocked the headphones off my head," Detroit said. He could see the concern on his friend's face and knew it wasn't over a few garbled words. "She'll be okay, Jimmy. It'll all be finished before she pops up again. The timing is right. You'll see. And then you two can set things right between you, too."

"From your lips to God's ear" was the only response Jimmy managed to come up with.

He swallowed hard and threw himself into the middle of the stacks of paperwork and the reams of computer printouts of ratings reports, working with a fury. Those who called him were amazed that he picked up so quickly, and doubtless noticed how his tone changed immediately to one resembling disappointment when he found out who was calling. Those unlucky enough to receive telephone calls from him that afternoon must have wondered why the boss was so cranky, so short, so stick-to-business. It wasn't his usual way. He almost always asked about the family or talked some football first. Only then would he bore in. But not that day.

Finally, when there was nothing else on his desk or on his mind to try to hide behind, he stood, stretched, and walked to the office window.

It was already approaching nighttime. He watched the twinkling lights of Nashville's Lower Broadway for a minute, but there was no peace for him in their impersonal glow. Instead, they seemed to be winking at him, as if they shared his secrets.

He finally turned and headed for the door, not certain where he was headed. Just out. Home, maybe. Cleo's house probably. Anywhere but the office.

But when he punched the elevator button to select the floor, it wasn't for the parking-garage level. His finger curiously selected one floor down, just below the offices, where the studios for the radio satellite formats had been built.

Jimmy had only been through the elaborate maze of small, sound-deadened rooms and past the walls filled with shiny, gleaming equipment a few times since everything had been finished. Even then, he only gave them half his attention, an approving nod. Detroit had done a beautiful job designing and building it all, bringing it in well under budget. Jimmy had not gotten around to telling him how much he appreciated it.

He realized that in the last few years, the rooms, the equipment, the people working away there had all become no more than liabilities or assets to him. Capital outlay or amortized investment. Income producers or drains on the budget. That's all.

After using his key to open the double-locked door, he stood in a small octagonally shaped lobby surrounded by huge double-glass windows, each allowing him to peer into studios dominated by immense mixing consoles, lit by soft track lighting and colorful blinking indicators for this and that technical monitoring equipment. The walls of each room were covered with soft gray acoustic foam and even the ceilings were carpeted. The control boards had dozens of knobs and switches sprouting from their upturned faces, while rows of needles danced with the music that was being shoved through them.

In front of each console, with their backs to him as they worked, stood or sat the disc jockeys, the men and women who were spinning out the programming on each of the networks. A speaker on the receptionist's desk in front of Jimmy was clicked to the country station. He stood there in the darkness and watched the announcer in that studio hunch his shoulders forward, wag his head wildly, and wave his arms animatedly in the air as he talked his way out of a hot country song, matching his mood exactly to the happy-go-lucky words and tempo of the music he had just been playing.

From his hiding place in the shadows of the lobby Jimmy could almost imagine the smile on the deejay's face as he happily presold the next song that was coming up on the eighty-six radio stations whose signals he was talking over at that very minute. Then the guy punched a big red button in the middle of the console that sent tape players spinning in each one of those stations, seamlessly spilling out some localized announcement with his same voice. The words had been scripted by the station and prerecorded by the deejay days earlier. But they were timely and localized, and delivered in the same pleasant, happy, lilting voice. There was no reason for the listeners in those eighty-six towns to think anything other than that this honey-voiced young man was right there in some studio in the radio station in the middle of their town, talking to each of them individually. That was just one aspect of the illusionary magic he was making in that tiny, cramped chamber, his theater of the mind.

The deejay watched a big stopwatch on the wall until he knew exactly when to begin talking live into his microphone again. He was saying something clever about an event that was happening in the national news that day, tying it in perfectly with the lyrics of the song whose instrumental opening had already begun thumping away under his monologue. Then, just as he had made the point he wanted to make, he popped a big green button in front of him. It would play another tape at each of the stations, one that spoke the call letters or slogans of every one of those stations in each of the far-flung cities. Again, it would perfectly match the announcer's real-time voice. Then the singer started wailing right on cue, as if he had simply been biding his time, waiting for the deejay to finish all he needed to say before he took over and sang the lyrics.

Jimmy smiled to himself and made himself a promise: When this DeWayne George mess blew past and a few more things were taken care of, he would once again push the elevator button for this floor, come into one of the studios, and sit in front of one of these microphones for a few on-air breaks. That would let him recover some of that old, familiar, magical feeling again. The feeling of climbing inside someone's head and making himself at home. Of using nothing but carefully inflected spoken words and prerecorded music to weave a beautiful, entertaining fabric.

Jimmy Gill watched the men and women work for a few minutes longer. He couldn't help it. He envied them deeply. Then, quietly, he slipped out of the studios and down to his car before he was noticed. He didn't want to intimidate these people with his presence, tongue-tie them if they saw they were under the gaze of the Big Boss. Jimmy knew only too well their paranoia, their insecurity, in this fragile business where on-air talent was only as good as his last rating book, only as strong as his quarter-hour shares.

The night was lonely, cold, and moonless. The sky was so black and dense the stars seemed to have to strain to create any light at all. Jimmy paused at the guard gate on the way out of the garage. He pulled the new Mercedes onto Lower Broadway and headed south, out along Franklin Road, where the mansions of country music stars mingled with those of old-money bankers and merchants. He supposed he was headed for Cleo's, but suddenly realized he did not want to go there this particular night. The loneliness and worry that were eating him from the inside out would only be worse in what amounted to their home together in those rare moments when they had been in the same place at the same time.

He turned around in the lip of her driveway and headed back

toward the downtown buildings. Before he got there, though, he turned right onto Demonbreun Street, guiding his car past the glaring souvenir shops and the gaggle of sightseers marching up and down in front of them. Then he steered down Music Row, where broken dreams haunted the sidewalks like tapped-out tourists. The feeling was so strong it brought him a shiver, like the chill of the night air.

The few visions and dreams that had been gloriously fulfilled were signified by the rich stone-and-glass buildings of the record-label offices and music publishing–company buildings, and by billboard signs congratulating various writers and singers for their most recent number one songs and the awards they had won. One praised Cleo Michaels for her recent Academy of Country Music trophy. She smiled down at him like a captured angel and he gunned the car past before his heart broke.

Somehow he found himself on the freeway, and eventually he ended up amid the ferns and falling water in a bar under the massive glass atrium of the Opryland Hotel. He was surrounded by eager tourists, sitting there sipping their warm beers and craning their necks, valiantly watching through the thick cigarette smoke, waiting impatiently for someone famous to amble past.

A pretty red-haired girl sang and played guitar on a small stage near one of the bubbling fountains. She tapped switches on a drum machine with her feet to change the tempo of the percussion that accompanied her medley of recent country songs the tourists were requesting. She reminded him of Cleo Michaels. He thought of young Cleo, earning her keep the best way she could before she could get her big break, just as this pretty red-haired girl was doing. But Cleo's dues had been paid in a much seedier place, in clubs at the end of some dark street downtown in Printers' Alley.

She had told him several times about how the apparent hopelessness of it all, the dead ends and hard work, had helped to steel her. Her struggle had made her appreciate more the battles she finally won. It now made it possible for her to walk away from all the visible trappings of her stardom without looking back.

Baptized in the fire of frustration back then, she believed it was now easier for her to simply turn and leave it all behind. She was satisfied she had proven to everyone, and especially, most importantly, to herself, that she was worthy of all that she had earned. Cleo had expressed those thoughts to Jimmy several times. He had not gotten the message.

And at that very moment, as he studied the bottom of his empty beer glass, the smoke swirling around him, Jimmy realized for the first time that her words had been meant for him. They applied to him as much or more than to her. And it was just one more bit of wisdom from the woman he loved that he had chosen not to hear. Another slingshot aimed directly at him that he had managed to completely dodge.

"Jesus, Cleo. That's what you were trying to tell me all along."

"What you say, pardner?"

On the bar stool next to Jimmy, a massive-sized tourist in a Conway Twitty baseball cap leaned closer to see what this slim blond-headed guy in the ritzy suit was saying. Jimmy hadn't even realized he had spoken out loud.

"Oh. I was just saying that she's pretty good. That gal there."

"Damn right she is! Better than lots of them that's making all that goddamn money squealin' and squallin' on the radio nowadays, I'll tell you. Nobody'll ever beat Loretta Lynn and Dolly Parton and . . ."

The redheaded singer kicked the drum machine with her toe again and whipped at the guitar strings with a clenched fist. The frets squeaked with the force of her fingers as they chorded, thankfully drowning out the tourist's tirade Jimmy had accidentally set loose. There was something familiar about the melody. The girl had launched into one of Cleo Michaels's signature songs.

It was painfully obvious. There was going to be no way Jimmy Gill could escape from her this night.

The singer's music drove him from the bar at a stumble before she had even started singing the lyrics he knew so well. As the fat tourist worked his way back to Kitty Wells and Patsy Cline. Before the cigarette smoke brought more tears to his eyes.

Before Cleo's own words could give him another vicious punch in the gut.

Chapter 39

As much as he wanted her to stay lost for a while, now, more than ever, he also wanted to hear her voice and know that she was all right. He wanted to warn her to keep her head down and to tell her he had finally heard what she had been trying to get him to listen to.

He rang her portable telephone number again and got a busy signal. He was not surprised. She had been having trouble with the hang-up sometimes not catching and leaving the damn thing off the hook, unnoticed for hours. She had fussed about the ridiculously huge charges she had racked up because of it, and the rundown batteries. Mostly, though, she was upset because its being off the hook might have kept Jimmy from being able to get in touch with her sometimes. He doubted she felt that way now.

Then, hoping that she might have tried to get in touch with him, he tried his answering machine at home again. Nothing but some telephone solicitor trying to sell him something. The answering service from the office had a half dozen urgent, crucial, earthshaking messages. None was from Cleo Michaels. Just more blazing fires he would have to stamp out first thing tomorrow morning. He felt his stomach fill with acid in dread.

Maybe it was the crushing tension, broken finally after the confrontation with DeWayne George. Or maybe the horrible loneliness and worry for Cleo had seized him in their vise grip. Or maybe it was only the bone-weary tiredness brought on by all the work that had avalanched on top of him the last few months. Suddenly he was so tired he could hardly step out of his clothes and fall across the unruly, unmade bed at his empty house.

No matter how deep and absolute the sleep was that overtook

him, no matter how intense the numb exhaustion, he was visited
as usual by a familiar dream that starred his dead mother and
one-armed father. Usually he would awaken, panting, exhausted,
and climb from the bed, get himself dressed, and drive toward the
office no matter the hour, knowing he was doomed to toss sleep-
lessly the rest of the night anyway.

But this night, amid the voices of the figures in the dream,
there was an insistent, shattering, ringing noise that threatened
to tear apart the fabric of the nightmare. Jimmy finally awoke with
a start to the pleading ringing of the telephone. He had trouble
locating it in the dark, and then realized his eyes were still shut.
It lay on the floor in a thin sliver of illumination from the night-
light in the bathroom.

"Cleo?"

He prayed it was she. Maybe simply saying her name instead
of hello would make it so.

"Jimmy? It's me."

Damn! It had worked. It was Cleo!

But her voice was different, heavy, as if filtered and twisted by
pain of some kind. And he could hear a noise that sounded like a
hellish wind rushing and roaring past her. She was in a moving
vehicle for sure, but it was certainly not the quiet rumble of the
tour bus he usually heard.

"Cleo! God, I've missed you. Are you okay?"

"Yeah, I'm okay, Jimmy." She was quiet for an instant, as if
swallowing something she didn't really want to. "DeWayne George
and I are taking a little ride, Jimmy."

The breath left him in a rush. He thought for a moment that
he had stopped breathing altogether. That he might not ever start
again.

"Cleo! So help me God, if he—"

"Listen to me, darling." Her words were deliberate, and he
could hear a tone in her voice begging him to, for once, listen to
what she was telling him.

Whatever you do, listen to me! she seemed to be saying. Goddamn it, for once, listen to me!

Jimmy struggled to blot out the panic and make some sense of
what she was trying to tell him between the lines. The rush of the

wind almost shrouded the words, but he listened. God, how he listened!

"The last cut on side two of the new album says everything I want to say to you right now, Jimmy. And I love you. No matter what happens—"

There was a sharp yelp from her that could only have come from pain. Then Jimmy heard the sound of the mobile telephone's receiver being ripped from her hand. The cruel, oily voice of DeWayne George took over.

"How ya doin', neighbor? How's Brother James this fine evenin'?"

"You hurt her and I'll kill—"

"What? You'll do what? Play me a request on the goddamn radio, Mr. Deejay? Spin one for ole DeWayne George and his little girlfriend while we are out ridin' around on this beautiful evenin'? While we are rockin' and rollin' to the sounds of Brother James on the radio?"

"What's it going to accomplish for you to hurt her, DeWayne? She doesn't have anything to do with what's between you and me."

"I know what you done, Brother James! I know you and the nigger have already gone and give a tape you made to the fuckin' DEA. I ain't dodged them bastards as long as I have without knowing everything that goes on with them."

Again panic spread throughout Jimmy like the cold breath of the devil. His five-page affidavit and a copy of the tape had been delivered before noon that morning to the Drug Enforcement Administration office in the federal courthouse on Broadway in Nashville. DeWayne George had found out about it before the day was over.

"Don't matter none, neighbor. I was going to invite Miz Michaels out for a nice ride anyways. Even before y'all screwed me. Me and Duane have had your old buddy Enrique keeping up with her whereabouts for a few days now, just in case we wanted to catch her act. But, hey! I ain't gonna kill her just yet. I'm gonna ride around and enjoy the cool air and the moonlight with her for a while. Maybe I'll show her some of the countryside. That'll give you some time to sit there and think about what her pretty little body will look like when they find it someday. And that will be a long time after I'm gone to some place where the sun shines all the time and the DEA can't touch my ass! And you, Brother James, get to look over your shoulder from this moment on. Maybe one day me or somebody who's loyal to me will put a knife blade between your third and fourth ribs. And somebody will make that coon partner of yours dance at the end of a rope like his kinfolk used to do when we knew how to keep 'em in their place."

Jimmy Gill's tongue was tied fast with dread and frustration. Words wouldn't come. DeWayne went on, half yelling to overcome the roar of the rushing wind.

"It wasn't the way I had planned to finish it out, Brother James. But I figure I've got plenty of money to last down there for the rest of my life. Oh, and neighbor? There is no use in you calling the law. You ain't likely to find me, not knowin' where in the whole country we might be right now. It is a big old country, ain't it? But we can still pick up one of our radio stations out here. Can't we, Miz Cleo Michaels?"

There it was. Amid the rush of the wind that changed pitch in the background as he sped up and slowed down the car, Jimmy could just make out the sounds of rock and roll on the car's radio. The sound of the Wizard network. Blue Oyster Cult. "Don't Fear the Reaper" was the song. The programming originated from downtown Nashville, ten miles from where Jimmy trembled in rage. But the madman could be listening to any one of seventy-five radio stations, practically anywhere in the United States. In the broad footprint of the satellite were seventy-five stations, all with their satellite dishes turned upward like massive hands cupped to giant ears to catch the signal.

"I'll call you back directly, Brother James. I want you to hear Miss Cleo sing a real sad song when I start to whittle on her a little bit!"

And he slammed the portable phone down hard with a horrible crash.

Jimmy shook even more violently now as he held the receiver tightly to his ear, hoping somehow that he could still hear them on the now dead line. Instead he was startled when the painfully loud dial tone replaced crackling silence.

Keep calm, he kept telling himself. Don't panic. Dear God, don't panic. He had to keep his head or he would lose Cleo for sure just as he had finally understood what it would take to get her back.

Pretend it was only another big deal coming down. Negotiating to buy another radio station. Closing a deal to sign a bunch of stations to a long-term contract. He could do it. He'd done it many times before, against big-time, stony-mountain odds. But if one of those deals fell through, what the hell? Nobody died. He simply regrouped and closed it some other way the next day.

Instinctively, he began to dial police emergency, but something stopped him. As if acting automatically, he fumbled through punching in Detroit Simmons's number and counted six, seven, eight rings. He had to be there! He needed him more than ever now!

Then there was a pickup, a sleepy fumbling with the receiver, the rattle of its being dropped to the floor, and finally an angry female voice spoke, spitting at him.

"Chris, he's already told you he'll fix it first thing in the morning! Work around it till then!"

It was Rachel with the irritated greeting, clearly upset with whoever she thought was calling Detroit about some technical screwup at the stations.

"Rachel? It's Jimmy. I'm sorry—"

"Jimmy? Damn, I'm the one that's sorry. I thought it was the night girl on the rock network with her headphones acting up again. She's already called—"

"Please, honey. Let me talk with Dee. Quickly."

"Something wrong, Jimmy? Are you okay?"

She must have heard the ache in his request, the knife-edge fear in the way he was pleading for Dee. She didn't wait for him to answer her questions and had Detroit on the line in a second.

"What's up, Jimmy Gill?" He was sleepy voiced, but the concern Rachel had conveyed to him was there, too.

"DeWayne's got Cleo. I don't know how he found her. I didn't even know where she was. He knows we spilled everything to the DEA. He says he's going to . . ."

And he lost it. He cried into his free hand.

"Jimmy! Jimmy! Listen to me, Jimmy!"

He barely heard Dee's yells buzzing from the phone receiver

over his own gasping sobs. But he put the telephone back to his ear while he wiped away his tears with a crumpled corner of bed-sheet.

"Damn it, Jimmy! We gotta keep it together if we're going to figure out how to get her back. Did you talk to her? Where are they now?"

"I don't know, Dee. I could hear the rock network on the car radio but that could put them in any one of six dozen places."

"They were in a car, though? On a car telephone?"

Jimmy was amazed Detroit could think so clearly, having just been rudely jarred awake in the middle of the night.

All Jimmy could do was sit there on the edge of the bed, stunned by the horror of what that animal might do to the woman he loved so much. Detroit had more questions.

"Could you hear any noises you recognized, any sound that might give us any idea where they were? Anything on the line that might sound like long-distance noises . . . an echo, static or something? We don't know where Cleo was going to be at all, do we? Did she say anything that might be a clue?"

Jimmy shook his head to all the questions, as if Dee could actually see him through the miles of telephone cable. And then, through the haze of horror, something clicked in Jimmy's mind.

She had said it to him as clearly as she dared. She had begged him to hear her.

But what was it? What had she said to him that she so desperately wanted him to hear?

Last cut on side two says all I want to say. . . .

Last cut, side two!

"Hold on, Dee! I've got to listen to a record."

No doubt Detroit Simmons was sitting there in the dark, making that slack-jawed "Man, he's crazy" look. Jimmy dropped the telephone, sprinted to his record shelf, and rifled through all the discs, searching frantically for Cleo's newest album. It wasn't on the shelf. Not in the stack of records littering the floor. Not piled with all the promotional copies of other albums resting on the dining-room table, where they usually went unheard these days.

He hadn't listened to music in months. Only side one of her album the night before. At her place. But where was his copy?

Then, there it was, waiting for him on the dusty turntable. He had meant to listen to it ever since she had given him a copy. He had been too damn busy.

The power for the stereo system was always on. His hand shook as he flipped the disc over, lifted the tonearm, and placed it expertly in the groove on the last cut on the record. Then he ran up the volume on the amplifier and listened intently, praying out loud that her message would come through clearly to him. He hoped whatever it was, it would give him some kind of clue with which they could save her life.

He knew the song instantly. It was a happy up-tempo number with almost a bluegrass feel to it. She had tried it out on him when she was putting the finishing touches on it months before. She had written it, she said, when she had been on a lonely stretch of road "between somewhere and somewhere else" and had grown so homesick she had "cried musical notes and haunting lyrics instead of tears." That's why Cleo was such a great songwriter. She wrote the way she talked, in poetry that easily could be set to music.

Her words on the disc rang out strongly, mocking the happiness of the mandolin and the banjo that swapped licks with each other from opposing speakers. Her words sang of dew-washed mornings, mimosa trees strung like a necklace against the bosom of the nearby mountains, the mist that mellowed the sharpest bends of the meandering Cumberland River.

It was there. It was clear! Thank God! He only needed a few words of "Cumberland Coming Home" to divine what she was trying to tell him. He dashed back to the telephone and screamed at Detroit.

"They're right here, Dee! Right here in Nashville!"

Chapter 40

It was an awful moment when Jimmy could do nothing more than listen to Detroit as he silently considered the situation. He realized that even knowing that Cleo and DeWayne George were right there, somewhere in town, still might not be enough to save her.

Please have an idea, Jimmy was thinking silently to himself. Please help her. Finally, Dee spoke.

"We'll come up with something, Jimmy Gill. We'll come up with something. I promise you that. Get dressed and I'll be there in a minute."

Lord. He had nothing at all. DeWayne George called back as soon as he hung up with Detroit.

"You still up, neighbor? Man, you are gonna be a real bear at work tomorrow, ain't ya?"

"DeWayne, no matter what they get you for, it won't be as bad as murder. Let her go and then you can get going to wherever you're running to."

"Well, there's one little flaw in your logic, there, Brother James. If they do too much lookin', they might find out that me and old Duane have already had to kill off some folks. Could be they're getting close to us anyway and your little treason just pushed us into executing our getaway a little early. Hey, Mr. Dee-jay. Speaking of executions, you want to hear your little songbird yodel?"

He could hear a sharp slap and a quick squeal of pain. Jimmy groaned, hurting for her, and crushed the telephone with his hand as if he were going to squeeze it in half.

"It's all right, Jimmy," she yelled over the wind noise in the car. "He's not hurting me. He's only—"

"My, my, neighbor. She's such a fine-looking woman. I sure would like to hear her hum a little something in my ear while I played her like a bass fiddle."

"I swear, George, if you—"

"Now, now, now. I know your poor old grandma told you not to be swearing. Me and my new girlfriend, Miss Cleo Michaels, will be talking to you again in a few minutes, Brother James. We got some more sight-seeing to do right this instant. This is old DeWayne, signing off."

And again he slammed the portable phone down with a hard thunk.

Jimmy was pacing, panting, almost raving by the time Detroit Simmons slid his car to a sideways stop in the driveway of the house. Jimmy met him on the walkway out front and they embraced as loving brothers. It helped. Jimmy took some strength from the sincere, heartfelt hug. Then he told Dee about the latest call.

"You're sure he's calling on a mobile telephone? Not just saying it to throw us off?"

"Yeah. You can hear it. The road noise and static and all. And he says they are riding around."

"Do you have call forwarding on this telephone?"

"Yeah. I always send my calls to Cleo's place when I'm over there. Why?"

"Forward your telephone to my mobile phone number and let's get going."

He didn't ask more questions. Somehow he fumbled through punching in all the digits and then fretted that he might have missed some or misdialed in his frenzy. But Detroit wasn't going to take the time to redo the operation. It had to be right. They jumped into Detroit's four-wheel-drive utility vehicle and peeled out of the driveway. Once under way, Jimmy got enough breath to ask, "Where are we going?"

"A mobile telephone's nothing more than a radio transceiver. We can maybe do ourselves some foxhunting." Detroit pointed to a box covered with knobs and dials in the backseat of the car. A coil of cable was hitched to the box on one end, and the other went to an aerial of some type that was propped on the back floorboard. "We got a bunch of us ham radio operators who do this kind of stuff all the time. Sometimes just for fun. One of us will hide out in an unlikely place and the first one to find him wins. Or we'll track down somebody whose microphone switch has gotten stuck on. But sometimes they use it to catch thieves who steal their radios and are stupid enough to actually transmit on them."

Dee was obviously telling Jimmy far more than he wanted to know. But he could also see that Jimmy was dangerously near panic. He had to keep his mind off what might be happening at that very moment or he might lose him. Detroit steered the vehicle around a curve much too fast for any rational physical law of motion, teetering on two wheels.

Jimmy didn't seem to care. He only wanted to find Cleo. His eyes told Dee to break any law necessary.

"We gotta get to the highest place around here to try to pick up their signal when they call again. I suppose the River's tower site will be the best we can do on short notice," Detroit continued. "We have to try to home in on the signal being transmitted from their phone with the directional antenna. Not the repeater at the telephone tower that picks it up and retransmits it. The portable telephone has a transmitter that puts out only a watt or two of power at the most. It's gonna be hard as hell to pull that little signal out of the mud, even if they are within line of sight . . . a direct shot to the tower. And I'm not even sure of the frequency they use on those things exactly. But, damn! It's our only chance, Jimmy."

His face was screwed up with tension in the dim lights from the dash, and again, Jimmy Gill could almost hear the man's mind working.

"I got a ham radio buddy from WSM Radio who should already be climbing halfway up their FM tower in west Nashville with a walkie-talkie. And I got another buddy at Channel Thirty-two's stick up north of town in Madison. We are gonna do our best to triangulate the bastard!"

Just then his telephone, resting in its pouch between them, jingled to life, shocking them both as if a jolt of lightning had struck. Detroit waved him away from answering it until he could slam on his brakes and skew the car to the side of the road and kill the engine.

"Now get it. As far as he knows, you are still sitting at home, frustrated, stewing helplessly about this whole thing. But try to get him to call back later."

Jimmy took a breath, tried to calm his beating heart, and answered the telephone before DeWayne gave up or got suspicious.

"George?"

"Man, it's gonna be a shame to mess up such a pretty woman as Miz Cleo Michaels," the twin growled. "Lucky she's left us so many fine recordings to remember her by, ain't it, neighbor? Record company's gonna be rich selling all her fine material when she's a corpse."

Jimmy started to beg again, but DeWayne interrupted.

"Too bad I can't get you and your nigger tonight, too. But I suspect seeing this pretty thing lyin' dead in that casket will be worse than dying for you, won't it, Mr. Radio? Especially knowing that basically it was you that was the cause of it all."

DeWayne again slammed the receiver down, leaving Jimmy with his mouth wide open in silent anguish, with nothing to say at all. He could only pound the dash while Detroit grabbed his shoulder, popped the clutch, and kicked gravel as they sped on up the winding mountain road. They stopped only to open the padlocked gate, then climbed some more.

"He'll call back again," Dee said, as reassuringly as he could manage. He hoped he was right in assuming that DeWayne would want to goad Jimmy some more before he did whatever he was going to do to Cleo.

They jumped from the car as quickly as they could after Dee had skidded it to a stop in a circle of mercury-vapor light near the base of the massive steel tower, the same one he and Jimmy had visited on their first trip to Nashville.

There was no time for nostalgia now, though. Taking a small black box from a clip on his belt, Detroit pushed a button on its side and spoke into its front.

"Lacey, this is Dee. Do you copy me?"

"Yeah, Dee. You are a little scratchy," a tinny voice said from inside the box. "But I got you five by five."

"I can hear you both okay, Dee," another voice interrupted to say. "You're noisy but perfectly readable up here, too."

"Roger, Buddy. Thanks! I don't know about the batteries in this thing so I'll keep it short."

Jimmy found himself shivering again, as much from the cloy-
ing tension as from the chill night air on the mountaintop. From
somewhere inside the building, he could hear the exhaust fans
pumping cool air over their FM transmitter. And he could hear the
pulsing of some rock music from a monitor speaker. The frenetic
music seemed to provide a score for the whole adventure, making
it seem to Jimmy all the more like an unreal movie instead of a
true life-or-death drama.

Outside the building, there were only the sounds of crickets,
the squawking back and forth of Detroit and his buddies, the shrill
distant whistle of an L&N freight train, and the hum of light traffic
on the freeway several hundred feet below where they stood.

Jimmy felt useless, frustrated by his powerlessness to save
Cleo from this madman who held her, was hurting her, even as he
stood helplessly by in the middle of a patch of weeds on the chilly
top of a mountain. What could they possibly do to get her to someplace safe? What sort of radio-frequency miracle would Detroit be
able to pull off to help them find her before it was too late? Dee
seemed to anticipate the question before Jimmy even asked it.

"Here, take this, Jimmy, and we can get to work."

He had fetched the box with its length of cable and the aerial
from his car. He held out toward Jimmy the spidery antenna and
the pouch with the portable telephone in it.

"You've always been the one who was so damned quick to
shinny up towers. Well, climb up this one as far as you can get
before you play out of antenna cable for the monitor. When the son
of a bitch calls back, answer the telephone, keep him talking, but
look down toward me here at the bottom of the tower. I'll motion
you which way to point the antenna. That's the front of it there
with the smaller elements. Keep him on the line as long as you
can. We don't have much chance, but we don't have any chance at
all if he decides to get short-winded on us now. Please, God, let
them be somewhere between here and Madison and west Nashville, or else we are going to have to start this hunt from scratch
again."

He helped Jimmy sling the telephone satchel over his shoulder,
then clipped the aluminum antenna grid to his belt with a twist of
stiff wire, and opened the lock that held the gate to the tower fence

shut. Jimmy climbed upward, his face to the sky. Putting one hand over the other, stepping from rung to rung as fast as he could manage, he tried to get as high as he could before the telephone's ringer went off.

His hands were instantly wet with sweat. The tower ladder was slippery from dew, too. The dangling phone bag and the aerial he was dragging behind him made the climbing awkward. He almost lost his grip several times, banging his shins and knees painfully on the ladder rungs, grabbing for anything he could get his hands on. But he dared not stop to rest. He kept reaching for the next cross-member, then the next, pulling himself upward as hard and as fast as he could. He had no consideration for gravity.

And it felt so natural. As if he had done it many times before. Climbing. Pushing upward into the cold, damp darkness. As if he belonged there on the side of the tower as surely as the lighting beacons, coax cable, and transmitting antennas.

Then the aerial's cable grew taut. He was as high as he could go. Jimmy stopped his ascent and got as comfortable as he could, sitting on a rung, wrapping a leg around the ladder, locked on with the other leg gripping the tower leg, keeping one hand free to answer the telephone if it ever rang again and the other to rotate the direction-finding antenna.

As far as he could see from the tower, streetlights twinkled like distant ground-locked stars. The beginnings of a moon had risen over the hills to the east of town. A mourning dove called softly from a tree several hundred yards down the valley. Jimmy remembered the old superstition about the bird's mournful song meaning imminent death for someone when the singing was close by.

The air was still, but the night's coldness and the bird's eerie mourning caused his teeth to chatter and made him shiver. He tightened his hold on the cold steel tower. Thousands slept peacefully down there below him. None of them suspected the drama going on above them. None knew that there were two men up there on the mountain trying to save someone's life. Someone special who was moving among them out there, lost somewhere amid the blanket of blinking diamonds.

Forty feet directly below Jimmy, Detroit had spread a topographic map of the area on top of the gravel driveway. His only

illumination was from the security lights strapped to the transmitter building and the flashing beacon strobes stretched above
him on a leg of the tower.

Detroit was keeping busy, trying to think, doing his best to
keep his own hopes up. He knew what a long shot this was. Like
finding a break in one color-coded wire in a hundred-pair cable.
But it was the only shot they had. He looked up at Jimmy, clinging
to the tower somewhere up there in the darkness. He could hardly
make out his form.

Jimmy Gill, please hold on, he thought. Don't lose your grip up
there. I need you, buddy. I need you.

"I've got it set to scan all the local telephone channels," he
yelled up to Jimmy, then thought to himself, I only hope there's
not anybody else wanting to chitchat with each other this time of
night, or they might lock up the scanner. And I wish to hell we had
another thirty feet of coax cable. He still might not be high enough
for us to get a decent signal from them.

At that moment, Jimmy felt like he was plenty high, but he
knew, too, that it would be difficult to pick up the soft signal from
the mobile telephone. Several minutes had passed now since the
last call, and the thought had occurred to him more than once that
DeWayne George might have grown tired of playing his games,
and simply gone ahead and done what he had set out to do. That
Cleo was dead and George was on his way to some Caribbean island. Or that maybe he had driven by Jimmy's place to include
him more directly in his plan for revenge. Gone by and not found
him there where he was supposed to be.

Then, just as he was beginning to fear the worst, the portable
telephone on his shoulder sang so suddenly and so loudly in the
cold quiet that he almost lost his grip on the tower's ladder. He
barely managed to catch the wet, slippery antenna as it almost
tore loose from his grasp.

"Ringing, Dee! It's ringing!"

"Let it ring several times," Detroit shouted back up at him. "I
think I got him locked already. It's the only signal on the telephone
channels, thank God. Swing it slowly from due east to north to the
west while you talk to him. And watch me, Jimmy. Watch me!"

Jimmy clumsily pointed the antenna toward where he knew
the sun would rise soon. The tinge of dawn gray was breaking the

hold of blackness on that part of the night sky. Then, slowly, he began turning it back to his left, toward the north and downtown.

"Whoa! Back two hairs to the east!" Detroit yelled up excitedly.

Jimmy could wait no longer. The telephone had rung five times already. He fumbled for the receiver, almost losing in his frenzied haste the entire bundle off his shoulder and down the side of the tower.

"Yes? DeWayne?"

"What took you so long, neighbor? You ain't takin' a nap while your sweetheart's about to meet her maker, are you? Maybe you got yourself another sweetie already."

He laughed uproariously for Cleo's benefit. He was high, getting more and more wasted. His words were slurred. God knew what chemicals were driving him toward greater craziness!

"Take it out on me, you bastard. Leave her alone. She hasn't done anything to you. I'll come to wherever you are. I'll get in my airplane right now and meet you anywhere. Take me instead. Let her go."

Below, in the eerie blue mercury light, he could see Detroit talking as quietly as he could into the walkie-talkie, putting his ear to its front to hear the reports back from his buddies out there somewhere in the predawn darkness.

"Naw, I expect me or Duane'll come back for you someday after it all blows over. You never know when one of us is gonna pop up and visit awhile with you. We'll go by and see ole nigger Detroit, too. Just for old times."

"Do it now. I'll make sure Simmons will be on the plane with me. Both of us will come. Leave Cleo out of this. She doesn't know anything about our arrangement. Don't you see what a mess it'll be? She's such a big star, there'll be all kinds of—"

"All the better, Brother James. Some of them bad boys down yonder in South America will be wanting to make me king of my own country when they see what I did to the people who crossed me. Why, those folks respect a man who—hey! What the hell's that?"

The mourning dove that had been singing farther down the mountain had now lit on the side of the tower, fifty feet above where Jimmy clung. Wrapped up in trying to keep DeWayne talking and aiming the antenna, Jimmy had not noticed that the bird had joined him on the tower and begun calling to its mate across the valley. Calling loudly, sorrowfully.

Jimmy pounded the tower ladder with the heel of his hand as forcefully as he could without losing his grip on the crossbar. The bird fluttered away.

"It's only an old dove in a tree out behind the house. I took the call out on the patio. Trying to get some air . . ."

DeWayne was breathing hard into the mouthpiece. The rushing sound had stopped. He apparently had pulled over to listen more carefully. Messed up as he was, he would never have noticed anything if it had not been for the damned bird.

"Something don't sound right. Your voice, the phone, something is different. Hell, it's gonna be daylight in a little while anyway. The next time you hear from me, I'll be letting you listen in as Miz Cleo Michaels sings her swan song, neighbor."

Detroit was jumping up and down, waving, shaking his head "No!" Dear God, he had not had time to draw a good line on them! The next call would come much too late. They would never be able to get to wherever DeWayne and Cleo were by the time they were zeroed in on them.

Jesus, don't let him break the connection! Please don't let him go! Jimmy searched his mind desperately for something, anything, to keep him talking.

"DeWayne, wait! I've got another offer for you. I can get money. Don't hang up! Let's talk about this. . . ."

DeWayne had slammed the phone down brutally, cutting off all hope.

The call was over. They were gone. Cleo was gone.

Complete despair filled his soul then. Coldness seized his heart. He slowly banged his head against the tower leg in frustration. They had been so close, damn close, but she had finally slipped away from him.

He stared up the length of the tower, where the strobe lights blinked their eyes at him, probably within view of DeWayne and Cleo if they had only looked toward the mountaintop.

He slowly began the dreaded descent on the ladder. His mind was spinning, trying to come up with some solution, but despair was wiping out rational thought. They could go ride around, he supposed. Maybe accidentally run across them. There couldn't be much traffic.

But then, below him, he noticed that Detroit was animatedly speaking into and listening to the two-way radio, twisting knobs on the direction-finding monitor as if he could home in on a ghost signal that had long since departed the band.

"Jimmy! Wait! Climb back up and point that antenna about where it was when he was talking!"

He yelled so loud his words echoed off the nearby transmitter building, off the next mountain across the valley. Why the hell was he bothering? What was the use?

"He hung up, Detroit. It's gone. There's no reason—"

"No, Jimmy, the telephone signal's still there. The receiver is off the hook! He thinks he hung up but I can still hear him talking to Cleo. I can't make out what he's saying over the wind noise, but there's still a signal!"

Jimmy stopped his descent and quickly climbed back to where he had been nesting a few moments before. Then he lifted the aerial again and pointed it just to the left of the glow where the sun would be burning brightly in another hour.

"A shade more to the north!"

He swung it away from the predawn glimmer, ignoring the pulsing cramp in his leg and arm, caused by his death grip on the tower leg.

Detroit was drawing lines on the map, using a ruler for a straight edge.

"I-Forty, just coming past the I-Sixty-five split. That's where they are, damn it. I know where they are and which direction they're going!"

He waved for Jimmy to move the direction-finding beam again, a bit more back to his right, then spoke into the box at his mouth.

"They are on I-Forty heading toward the airport now. Let's go, Jimmy. Maybe we can catch up to them!"

Jimmy was perilously close to falling as he madly scurried down from the tower. And it was amazing that Detroit managed to keep from plunging the car off the hairpin turns as he pushed the thing back down the side of the mountain. He was taking each curve in a blind slide, skewing sickeningly in the loose gravel and dust while fighting the steering wheel, talking into the microphone for the car's mobile radio, and twisting the knobs on the monitor, all at the same time.

It was Jimmy's job to lean halfway out the passenger window, holding tightly to the direction-finding beam, trying to keep it pointed in whatever direction Detroit dictated. He almost flew out the window several times, but he locked his knees against the door and held on.

"Buddy's talking with Metro police, but they are flying blind without any way to hear their signal. And they don't know what kind of car DeWayne's driving. No way to find out. They are just gonna look for something unusual out there on the interstates east of town."

"God help us if he notices that the telephone's off the hook. We're dead if he does, Dee."

"Yeah," Detroit said as he sawed again on the wheel to keep them from careening into a big oak tree that guarded a fork in the dirt road. Then they were finally onto solid pavement, the car's tires squalling as he fought it through the curves much too fast. He gunned it down the freeway entrance ramp and onto the three-lane highway—still mostly deserted, an hour before the morning rush would come along to slow their chase.

"Still going east," Buddy reported from the scratchy speaker on the radio hanging under the car's dash. "Not going very fast, though. He doesn't want to do anything to attract the police."

"They've moved a few degrees off from where they were," Lacey next offered on the two-way. "The signal's picket-fencing, too. They may be off the freeway now, Dee."

"Roger that. Picket-fencing means it's fluttering rhythmically," Dee explained. "The signal's marginal. Lacey's right. They are probably on a surface street now. They'll be harder for the police to spot unless they accidentally happen upon them."

He turned quickly to look at Jimmy. Detroit had not meant to say anything now that might discourage him any more than he already was. He needed Jimmy to stay rational, to not give up, to help. But Jimmy's jaw was set firmly and there was something in his eyes that said he was solid. He would do whatever had to be done.

They took the ramp from I-65 northbound over to I-40 eastbound at close to a hundred miles an hour. Detroit gripped the wheel as tightly as he could to keep them on the road. Jimmy's job was to maneuver the antenna so as to keep the meter on the front of the monitor in the red zone, pegged against its post, indicating the strongest signal. And he had to make damn certain that the antenna was aimed directly at the place where DeWayne held Cleo.

They met a police car coming toward them, its blue lights flashing. Detroit blinked his lights at him and the cop blinked back.

Then, before Jimmy knew it, they had hurtled past the turnoff for Chattanooga on I-24, then the Opryland and airport exits off the freeway. They had zoomed past pickup trucks towing boats toward fishing on the Tennessee Valley Authority lake east of town. A couple of big trucks blew air horns at them when they swept past them at twice their speed.

But just then, Jimmy noticed that the signal meter showed full scale. It was pegged against the post on the meter, no matter which direction he turned the antenna.

Lord. Was the receiver broken? Had the rough trip down the tower and the wild driving busted something in the monitor or in the cable or antenna?

"Dee?"

Detroit looked at the meter quickly while trying to keep an eye on the highway and the traffic ahead. He reached over and thumped the meter with his finger. Still pegged hard. Then, as soon as he had steered around a creeping pickup truck, he clicked a switch on the front panel.

"Attenuator . . . makes the receiver less sensitive," Detroit said.

The needle had fallen to nothing. But then it rose again as Jimmy turned the beam directly out the right side of the car, perpendicular to the interstate highway.

"We're close. Damn close," Detroit said.

The next exit came up so suddenly Detroit had to lock the brakes and skid sickeningly in the loose gravel at the mouth of the egress, almost spinning around to face the way they had just come. Swerving dangerously, he somehow reclaimed control and slowed as they rolled up the ramp to a T-intersection. The antenna still pointed the way to the right and behind them.

"Percy Priest Dam," Dee read from a sign. Jimmy knew where they were. He and Cleo had been to the lake once. They had talked of putting a houseboat into its cool waters sometime, of having a place for escape on weekends. But it had only been a lark. They both knew neither would have the time to ever get the craft wet the way they were going, much less spend any time skiing, hiding, or making love in some secluded slough or cove.

It was a special spot though. The dam, visible from the interstate highway, held back an otherwise feeble and puny Stones River. It had backed up enough water to form a huge, beautiful lake that stretched in an arc around Nashville's southeast side.

Now, in the first light of impending dawn, the dam stood directly in front of them. The highway crossed the concrete wall in a narrow ribbon that headed back toward Nashville after winding through a series of isolated parks. Detroit had the presence of mind to cut off the headlights. Suddenly, he reached to kill the ignition, too, as they coasted into a small parking lot at the dam's edge. It was a paved-over area carved out just above the water of the reservoir for visitors to stop and view the water, maybe enjoy a picnic lunch on some nearby tables or cast a fishing line into the lake.

Jimmy and Cleo had parked there that one visit and made out.

"There's a car stopped about halfway across the dam, over against the drop-off side," Detroit pointed out, just as Jimmy noticed it, too. It was Cleo's platinum-colored Mercedes.

Then, from the monitor receiver's speaker, they could hear fumbling noises on the portable phone signal they had been following. There were curses, a cruel banging sound, and DeWayne George's drug-smeared voice.

"Goddamn telephone! Ain't working worth a—"

Then the signal disappeared. The meter on the monitor dropped away, but in a second it was back again, with the tweeting of tones as he dialed a number. Detroit reached to turn down the chatter on the two-way radio and click off the monitor receiver. He knew there would be feedback if he left the volume up when Jimmy pulled the telephone from its pouch and answered it. It began ringing two seconds later, as they knew it would.

"DeWayne, it's not gonna work," Jimmy answered, fighting to control the shaking in his voice. They were so close. So damn close.

"Nothing you can do to stop me now, neighbor. I got Miss Country Music right here on the edge of my knife blade. I want you to hear her strangle on her own blood when I cut her throat, Brother James. You hear me? I want you to listen to your woman die."

Slowly, quietly, Jimmy slid out the open door of the car. He ignored Dee's wild motions urging him to stay put, to wait until the other guys could give the police the bearings on where they were. Dee couldn't tell them precisely until DeWayne hung up.

But Jimmy ignored him. This was his score to settle. And there might not be time to wait. He couldn't risk it.

He started walking quickly along the roadway, heading across the dam to where DeWayne held Cleo hostage. In the distance, to his right, he could see traffic scurrying along the freeway. People were going about their early-morning business as if there were nothing at all wrong in the world.

Another blue-lighted police car zipped along the highway. But it was going the wrong way, toward downtown, away from the exit to the dam. Somewhere off to Jimmy's left, way in the distance, a solitary motorboat made its way along the lake's calm, hazy surface. It was a fisherman, probably getting ready to try his luck at hooking some crappie or bass with the first daylight.

"No, DeWayne. It's not gonna work the way you thought it would."

"Or maybe I won't cut her too bad at first, Brother James. So you can hear her scream when I drop her off this little bluff we got here. Hear her scream all the way to the goddamn bottom."

He laughed again. A phlegmy laugh. He was losing it. Whatever he was taking had made him even crazier. Bolder. He wouldn't be much longer about his meanness. His evil voice had been harsh and grating in the earpiece.

Jimmy heard Cleo crying quietly.

Then, he could see them clearly in the dawn's light. DeWayne was holding her around the waist, she with her back to him. He had a shiny knife at her throat. They were standing beyond and below the open door of her Mercedes, past the edge of the roadway that ran across the dam. Jimmy was sure there should be some kind of protective fence there. There was, but a gaping bite had been cut out. There would be nothing but open air down the long cement backside of the dam all the way to the small creek that was the Stones River. At the bottom were giant granite boulders that kept the land from eroding when the floodgates were opened. All of that, four hundred feet straight down from where DeWayne held Cleo.

"Might as well give it up, DeWayne," Jimmy said into the telephone's mouthpiece. He tried to be as forceful as he could. He knew DeWayne could hear him just as well across the short distance that remained between them as he could over the telephone.

"Where the hell are you, man?"

Then he turned and saw Jimmy walking slowly toward him along the dam, the telephone to his ear and mouth as if he still needed it to communicate. Even in the dim light, Jimmy could see the stunned look of shock cross DeWayne's twisted face. Strangely, a huge, leering smile took over, and Jimmy Gill felt the chill of the man's evil go cleanly through him like a blast of cold wind.

DeWayne took Cleo's telephone receiver away from his ear slowly, looked at it as if it had bitten him, then gave it and its case with its malfunctioning hang-up a quick toss over the edge. All three of them watched it twist and flutter as it plunged to the rocks below the dam. When it hit, it shattered noiselessly into dozens of pieces.

Jimmy kept walking toward them, letting the strap on Dee's telephone slide from his shoulder. He gently laid it down on the asphalt roadway, doing nothing sudden that might cause George to increase the pressure of the knife at Cleo's throat.

Jimmy realized he had no plan. He supposed he could only hope to stall the crazed twin until the police found their way here. Then it would all be over.

He only knew that short term, he had to keep the bastard from hurting Cleo. How, exactly, he wasn't sure.

"Damn, man. I don't know how you did it, but this little development just makes it all the more perfect."

"What do you mean, DeWayne?"

That would be the plan then. He had to keep him talking until some kind of real plan revealed itself to him, or until maybe the Metro police would come rolling up to save the day.

"You get to watch her go over the edge, then you can follow the bitch all the way to hell!"

Slowly, DeWayne reached into his belt and pulled out a pistol. He brought it to eye level and pointed it straight at Jimmy. Cleo struggled, but the knife at her neck brought a little blood and enough pain to cause her to catch her breath with a groan.

"Jimmy, don't. Stay back."

"Shut up, Miss Country Music. Come on with me, darling."

He dragged her down the short hill, even closer to the gap in the fence, his snakeskin cowboy boots slipping slightly on the loose gravel at their feet. DeWayne staggered, maybe from the narcotic swirling through his veins, maybe from the weight of Cleo Michaels. Both almost fell through the hole in the chain-link fence, and down. Down forever.

Jimmy screamed. Then he took a sudden, instinctive step toward them, to try to catch her before she went through and followed the crazy man down. Suddenly, the gun in DeWayne's hand barked.

Something hot and heavy slapped Jimmy Gill hard on the right shoulder and sent him spinning around and down to the ground in an awkward dance. Blood instantly pulsed from the tear in his shirt near the collarbone. Somehow, though, he managed to quickly stand again.

"One more step and you get to go first, Brother Jimmy. If I hadn't been smokin' meth all night, I might have got you the first time."

And as the first ray of sun slid along the length of the dam, Jimmy could see that DeWayne now stood with the toes of his boots at the very edge of the drop-off. Only the grip of his arm supported Cleo's weight over the chasm. One quick release. A second's relaxation. That's all it would take, and she would be spinning to the cold gray rocks below.

Time froze as Jimmy watched helplessly. The crazy son of a bitch was ready to drop her if he tried to get any closer to them. Or he would shoot him again. Or maybe both.

Jimmy closed his eyes. He tried to blot out the scene. All the sounds were amplified by the stillness of the air at sunrise.

He heard Cleo's soft whimper above the maddening drone of the motorboat, still buzzing along somewhere out there on the misty lake. Off in the distance, there was the reedy hooting of another solitary mourning dove. There was no doubt at all now about what the damned bird was heralding across the chilly waters of the reservoir.

Chapter 41

Cleo Michaels had dared to love Jimmy Gill. She had had the poor judgment to stay with him. And now it was almost certainly going to cost her her life.

DeWayne had been right. It was Jimmy's fault, after all. He should have shoved her away roughly long before this. But he had been too selfish. He had loved her too much.

"And you won't even get to kiss her good-bye, Brother James!"

DeWayne George seemed to have been reading Jimmy's mind. He was panting from the exertion of having to support Cleo's weight over nothingness. Breathing heavily from the chemical he had been ingesting. But his face was still split with an evil grin. He was clearly elated from the sheer mad control he held over her, over Jimmy Gill, over the entire situation.

Jimmy's head spun with sudden dizziness, the strength leaving his legs as if someone had pulled a plug and it was being quickly drained out of him. The pounding ache in his right shoulder seemed to be pulling him down toward the asphalt like a huge unseen weight. He tried to fight gravity, pain, weakness, terror, all simply to stay standing, to try to get close enough to do something to help save Cleo.

But he couldn't move. He was nailed to the same spot. His body was suddenly not obedient to his orders.

With no warning at all, a screaming, bellowing noise split the air with such force that Jimmy was knocked back two full steps and pushed down hard on the pavement. Startled, DeWayne staggered drunkenly, and, for an awful instant, almost slipped over the edge, almost let go his hold on Cleo and let her fall to save himself. But somehow he managed to spin back up the steep slope a few feet. He fell hard on top of her, looking around wildly for whatever had caused the deafening blast.

A set of air horns on a tall pole just above and behind where DeWayne and Cleo fell screamed a harsh, shrill warning. Jimmy was disoriented by the screeching, the pain, the dizziness, but he knew what the siren was. The horns were only the signal that the dam's floodgates were about to automatically open, dumping tons of water out of the reservoir into the gorge behind. They were designed to give fishermen near the intakes at the front of the dam a warning that they needed to move away, as well as to alert those who might be behind the dam to stay away from the rocks and the river's edge where the torrent was about to be set free.

Jimmy knew, too, that the blasting horns gave him the opportunity to seize on DeWayne's distraction and get to him. He tried to climb back to his feet, to lunge forward, but something pulled him back. He slipped down to his knees while some giant hand seemed to hold him in place, forbidding him to move. No matter how hard he searched, he couldn't find the strength to get back up. When he tried to brace himself with his hands, he keeled over onto his right side. When he rolled back over again, he could only get to his knees. He fought sudden vertigo to carefully balance himself on his haunches. The dam, the lake, the dawn sky all spun around him on their own axis, completely out of control. The horrible ache in his shoulder threatened to slap out of him what little awareness he had left and send him tumbling to his back again.

He had to help her. He couldn't.

He saw through all the spinning and whirling and creeping blackness that had begun to encroach on the edge of his vision that DeWayne George had managed to struggle to his own feet again.

He now straddled Cleo as she lay there in the gravel on the sharp slope, gasping to catch the breath he had crushed from her when he fell on top of her.

He frantically reached for her collar, trying to regain his hold on her as she squirmed and spun and tried to get away.

He grabbed at her, trying to shove her off the edge of the dam alive, without benefit of blessed death from his gun or his knife beforehand.

Finally, frustrated with the fight she was putting up, DeWayne took the gun and raised it back high over his head, then brought it down quick and hard. The butt of the pistol caught her directly behind the ear. Her struggling stopped then and she was still.

The blaring air horns covered Jimmy's weak screams. The wailing of the warning siren mingled with his weak, choked howling, knocking his words down, unheard.

Suddenly, warm, yellow morning sunlight got free of a row of trees across the lake and broke brilliantly across the dam.

There was movement of some kind, too, from behind the Mercedes. Quick movement by someone who should not have been there. Detroit Simmons stepped from behind the car into a patch of the sunlight, then edged gingerly down the grade toward the spot where DeWayne and Cleo had been struggling. He was spinning something above his head. Something square and dark and heavy was tethered to a long, black cord. He was whirling whatever it was like the homemade slingshots he and Jimmy had once played with in the woods behind the duplex in Birmingham.

Jimmy could see what it was: the heavy monitor radio that they had been using for the direction finding. He was swinging it on the end of a ten-foot length of the coax cable! The near end of the cable, the part that had been attached to the antenna, was wrapped, snakelike, around Dee's arm up the shoulder so he wouldn't lose his grip on it while he spun it around in a growing arc, playing out the cable a little bit at a time.

The weight of the radio was causing him to have trouble keeping his balance on the steep slope and in its loose stones. The force of the twirling, flying radio threatened to drag him right down to DeWayne and Cleo and maybe off the edge.

DeWayne once again grabbed Cleo's belt. He was dragging her dead weight back toward the hole in the fence. The gun was in his other hand, still aimed at Jimmy, making sure he no longer posed him any threat.

But something, maybe a shadow in the new sunlight, the whirring, whistling sound of the spinning radio, or a shoe scrape on the gravel loud enough to be heard over the din of the Klaxon overhead, made DeWayne turn suddenly and look up. He saw Detroit before Detroit had a chance to hit him with the whirling box.

It was all happening in slow motion as far as Jimmy Gill was concerned. Black borders were rapidly closing in on all that he was trying so desperately to watch. He did see the whirling radio strike

DeWayne's right arm solidly, hitting somewhere near the elbow and with more than enough force to break bones and to send the gun sailing into free air and down the dam's backside.

But DeWayne's anger, determination, and meanness, or maybe the dope he had been taking, let him ignore what must have been intense pain. It also gave him the quickness and strength to grab hold of the radio and its cable and wrap the cord around his own arm several times. And then he began to drag Detroit down the bank toward him. To drag him slowly, cruelly, crazily nearer to the edge of the precipice while he held Cleo with the other arm.

"Let go, Dee!" Jimmy screamed, and immediately realized that the weak words had hardly escaped his own lips, and that they had no chance of overcoming the clamor of the air horn. No one could hear him. And it wouldn't do any good to warn him anyway because the cable was wrapped so tightly and securely around Dee's arm that he couldn't let go, even if he had the time or wanted to.

Detroit wasn't even trying to resist DeWayne's hard tugging. He slowly allowed himself to be reeled in, dragged, sliding downward in the loose gravel, down the steep embankment closer and closer to the madman's knife blade and the edge of the dam.

And then, unexpectedly, when he was barely five feet away, Detroit suddenly pitched forward toward DeWayne, as if he had purposely taken a dive. He landed hard on his face, and began slipping and sliding directly toward the gap in the fence.

DeWayne fell backward with the unexpected slack in the tether, losing his grip on Cleo's belt. He dizzily staggered two, three steps backward, then teetered on the edge of the dam. Even in his rage, his drugged haze, he must have realized then that he was going over. He dropped the knife, waved his arms wildly in the air furiously seeking some kind of balance, then disappeared, screaming, into the smoky mist that was billowing up from the roaring water now pouring through the dam's floodgates.

Detroit was still sliding, and the weight of DeWayne George pulled him rapidly toward the brink. Detroit was now tied securely by the radio and coax cable to the man who had fallen over the side of the dam. He desperately tried to brace himself with his feet against the fence post next to the gap in the chain-link fence. It wouldn't hold long. DeWayne's weight dangling on the end of the cable dragged Detroit sideways, out over the edge, where there was nothing to grab.

All he could do was reach out quickly with the hand not caught in the coil of cable and try to wrap the arm around the post, hold on, and get enough leverage to support the heavy, struggling weight below him until he could somehow manage to unwrap himself from the cable. He was already half off the bluff, his face horribly contorted from the pain in his right arm and shoulder and the effort to hang on to the fence post with the other arm.

Still slumped on his knees, twenty feet away up the hill, Jimmy could hear Dee's grunts of pain, even above the ceaseless blaring of the air horns. He could see the sweat pouring from Dee's face as he fought to hold his grip. But he could also see that Dee was losing the battle a fraction of an inch at a time. DeWayne's weight and struggle as he dangled on the other end of the radio cable were relentlessly pulling Detroit over the edge after him.

When Jimmy struggled to get up and help him, he again fell flat on his face, unable to rise. He tried to slide on his belly. Maybe he could get to the bank and slip down it, letting the pull of gravity help him. Maybe he could give Dee just enough support so he could free himself from the coaxial cable. Jimmy's own strength was flagging. He couldn't even manage to work his way along the roadway toward the incline. He saw that he was leaving a broad stripe of bright red blood, shining wetly in the warm sunlight that now bathed the scene along the dam's top in yellow light.

Nothing he could do, no matter how deeply he sought strength, would make his good arm or his useless legs obey his commands. Just raising his head to look was almost more than he could manage.

Then there was someone else, sliding down the bank toward Detroit. Cleo was scooting along on her backside, her momentum almost taking her past Detroit and over the edge, too. Jimmy saw her grab the loose fence post as Detroit had also grabbed it to keep from falling off. It was clearly about to be ripped from the cement that barely held it in place. Cleo lay flat across the top of Detroit, held a handful of his shirt for leverage, and reached out over the emptiness. Then she began to hack away at the taut cable with a knife.

It was the knife DeWayne had dropped before he disappeared

over the brink. Its blade was red with Cleo's blood. She was sawing away on the coax as furiously as she could, as vigorously as she dared without upsetting the tenuous balance they had there on the edge of death. She tried to use her own weight and grip to keep Detroit from slipping any further.

They were slipping together now, sliding maddening inches at a time.

Jimmy saw that Cleo was leaning so far out to try to cut the cable, reaching so far down the length of Detroit's stretched arm, that any sudden tug from DeWayne would pull both of them over with him.

And they were so far over the edge that, even if Detroit was somehow hacked free, they might not be able to scramble back away safely.

Cleo was struggling, too, still stunned from the blow from DeWayne's gun, stopping now and again to shake her head clear of her dizziness. Jimmy was afraid she might drop the knife, lose consciousness altogether, and slip off the rim of the dam, her momentum dragging Dee with her.

As desperately as he wanted to crawl down and help, Jimmy could not even watch. He cried into the pavement, begged God for the right to at least be able to see her get Dee loose from the struggling DeWayne George. But he couldn't. He was no longer able to hold his head up, to keep his eyes open. He had to drop his face to the pavement, fighting to stave off the blackness that washed over him, taking away any hope he had of seeing Dee and Cleo get free and safe.

Or the chance of seeing the unthinkable.

And suddenly there was a silence so loud it was deafening. In his fuzziness, in the horrible black tension of the moment, Jimmy had forgotten the painful blaring of the warning signal that had been blasting away the past two endless minutes. And now the noise had abruptly disappeared except for its eerie echo rolling off across Percy Priest Lake like a fading sonic boom.

At that moment, another awful sound ripped apart the sudden quietness. It was a horrible siren of death, a falling, fading scream that was instantly lost, washed away in the roar of the rushing waters below the dam.

Sign-off

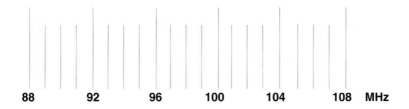

88   92   96   100   104   108   MHz

The day begins early, especially in summer, when the sun obeys the rooster down the road and comes up early. That means the morning deejay has to be ready to go well before first light, regardless of the time on the Big Ben on his nightstand.

But no matter the season, he hates leaving his wife's bed. Her warmth, her nearness, are such a comfort to him. Sometimes, in her half sleep, she clings to him when he tries to slide away, refusing to let him go from her. He has to tickle her for a release, then kiss her as an apology.

He always pauses to look in on Catherine as she sleeps quietly, a stuffed toy clutched close, even if he is running late. He is the boss, after all. He can simply reprimand himself. Besides, he has to allow time to marvel at her beauty, her brilliant yellow hair that's so long and full for a three-year-old.

She has her own radio that is never turned off. The glow from its dial is her night-light, and if he ever dared to switch it off, she would wake up immediately and turn it right back on, then fuss at him a bit before she slept again. Her record player hums quietly, too, spinning away in a far corner of her jumbled, toy-strewn world. It rarely stops turning.

He has to fight the urge to gallop over to where she sleeps and sweep her up and hold her close, nuzzling her neck until she erupts into giggles and hugs him back hard. No, he lets her sleep. He'll be back home soon and they can run and play then, with him being as much a child as she.

The mist is almost always rising from Lake Hampton as he pushes the pickup truck around the twisting, turning road girdling its shore. Then he crosses the dam that holds back the Okolona

River to form the lake. Cleo swears that children grow bigger and stronger near the water, just as oaks and elms do. She's probably right, he thinks. As he breathes in the smell of the deep water, it reminds him of his own growing up along the Tennessee River and makes him feel young again.

Just past the river bridge, he makes the quick stop each day at Jesse's Café and Bait Shop. Jessie always has a plastic foam cup of steaming black coffee ready for him, no charge. His wife, Vera, usually has him a hot biscuit with sausage or country ham inside, wrapped in waxed paper, and a song request or two jotted down on a paper napkin.

Usually, if the morning mist is not too dense when he makes the turn onto Route 22, he can spot the top beacon of the little tower just above the tree line. If he doesn't have to slow for an early-morning tractor, he can cut the engine completely and glide the last hundred yards. That spares the couple of farmers whose houses stand near the highway the noise of the engine when he downshifts into the radio-station parking lot.

Once out of the car, he usually pauses there in the gravel lot for a moment to once again breathe in the clean air and new-day smell. When he gets inside, he starts a pot of his own coffee brewing and turns on the switch for the tube filament voltage in the icebox-sized transmitter in the back room.

Then he is ready to sit down and shuffle through the twisting piles of wire copy that have moved overnight from the Associated Press. He culls carefully, tearing off the biggest news stories, the farm and market reports, the odd or funny stories called "kickers," the sports scores from whatever games are in season and of interest. He hangs them neatly on labeled hooks on the control-room wall, except for the weather report and hourly temperature roundup. Those are creased and propped against some switches on the front of the ancient control board.

The actual sign-on times for the station vary monthly with the time of the sunrise, earlier in the summer, as late as 7:30 in the winter. But there is always a little tingle in his gut when he first tosses the switch that sends waves of high voltage coursing through the old transmitter's dusty tubes. He smiles when the lights in the control room dim slightly from the strain of supplying all the electrical power needed to fire up the old box. Then he settles back into his chair and listens as the crackling static from the studio monitor speaker is replaced by the quiet hum of a strong signal. Soon, audio will be applied to ride piggyback out and over the air.

It's only a daytime AM radio station. Some call it "ancient modulation" since FM and its clear stereo signals kicked the mode off the top of the hill in the late seventies. And it only sends a modest thousand watts of radio frequency energy down a narrow one-inch-in-diameter stretch of coaxial cable. The signal moves along to a stubby two-hundred-foot tower that seems to sprout like a sweet-gum tree in the middle of a sage-grass field behind the little cement-block studio building. The station occupies a frequency somewhere on the high end of the AM band, up where the squealing heterodynes sound their siren calls, the gasping, wheezing preachers save souls, and the crashing static still jealously rules the domain on humid, stormy summer days.

But the little station is his. His and Cleo's. And it's on the wind.

The phone invariably rings just before he hits the button that starts the tape cartridge machine that plays "Dixie" for a sign-on theme.

"Is it gonna rain today, Jimmy?"

"Nope, Charlie. Not a chance today. Go ahead and get the plow out of the shed."

"I sure do appreciate it, Jimmy. Now don't forget to play me something by Tex Ritter."

"I'll do it, Charlie. You have a good day."

And then "Dixie" is playing on the air while Jimmy reads into the microphone all the legal sign-on stuff he has to say each day. He could record it once and not have to read it live, but he enjoys saying the words. Over the opening few bars of the first record, he leaves the microphone open while he takes a noisy slurp of his coffee right there on the air. Then he says a sincere "Good morning," gives the time and temperature, and gets out of the way for the singer and whatever the words are that he or she wants to sing. Words about love, life, happiness, sadness.

He plays whatever songs he wants to play or those his listeners tell him they want to hear. There are no long columns or tables of research numbers to analyze to hone the playlist down to the lowest common denominator. No "safe list" of music is sent down from some consultant somewhere, filled with songs that are supposed to be as good for Poughkeepsie as they are for Portland.

On this station, the Grateful Dead happily follow Hank Williams Jr. Michael Jackson yelps right next to Crystal Gayle. The Doobie Brothers share the air with Count Basie.

Any time the microphone is on, Jimmy still talks with his audience. Not at them. Not to them. With them. He puts some of them directly on the air over the telephone when they call in, and without benefit of a delay system of any kind. He trusts his listeners to keep it clean, and they haven't let him down yet.

He doesn't disappoint them either. He makes sure anybody listening will hear all the things he or she needs to know. He reassures them that the world didn't end or the Rapture come during the night as they slept. He lets them know if a slicker or short sleeves would be appropriate for the day. He brings them up to date on the news, the weather, the price of peaches at the Mississippi Farmers' Market. And he also tells them of the sale on seed at the Growers' Co-op Store in Corinth and the special on Spam at the Piggly Wiggly in Iuka.

One thing is for sure. When he tells his silly jokes or rambles on about something he thinks is important, he knows for certain that they are out there listening to him. WHOF is their entertainment, their information source, their best friend.

The listeners remind Jimmy of that everywhere he goes. At lunch at the café, they'll come right up and tell him how much they enjoyed the story he told that morning. Peggy, the waitress, will scribble down a request for the next morning's show on the back of his ticket. Baggy Morrison, the barber, will threaten to give him a buzz cut if he doesn't quit playing so much of "that old rock-and-roll mess."

Mickey Mashburn wanders into the studio just before nine o'clock in the morning. He's a part-time Primitive Baptist preacher, part-time radio-commercial salesman and deejay. He has done a midday gospel music show on the station since it went on the air early in 1952, forty years before Cleo and Jimmy bought it from its original owner. When he's not holding a revival somewhere or spinning Blackwood Brothers records on the radio, he sells commercial spot announcements for five dollars apiece, seven if they want him or Jimmy to do the commercials live instead of being recorded. Most of them do.

Jimmy Gill always moves the remnants of his show out of Mickey's way, cues up his first song on one of the ancient turntables, and almost reluctantly moves aside.

"Give 'em what they want, Mick."

"If the Lord's willin', I will, Jimmy. I sure will."

Later, Homer Davis will play country music for a couple of hours while he takes a long lunch from his day job at his law office in Booneville. Then a college student from Tupelo will spin rock-and-roll records (without the hard stuff, of course) until the sun goes down and "Dixie" comes on to wrap up another broadcast day at WHOF.

Sometimes, after his show is finished, Jimmy will spend a couple of hours with paperwork, or call on a few of his sponsors before he takes lunch at the café uptown. Maybe he'll try to sell some commercials to be run in the upcoming high school football play-by-play broadcast he enjoys so much doing. Or maybe he'll stop by the Massey-Ferguson tractor dealership and get on the telephone for a free live "cut-in" commercial on the air, just to show them how much he appreciates their business.

But he always calls Cleo first. He needs to make sure she's still there, that nothing has happened to her or the baby while he played radio. That's his greatest fear. That something or somebody will try to take them away from him.

She always puts her day on hold to listen to him. She postpones tending to the horses, fooling around in her little recording studio out back, or digging in her garden plot next to the barn. She understands how much he needs to hear her voice, how important it is for him to be able to talk nonsense with Catherine.

Once a month or so, they'll put Catherine in the car seat between them and drive up the winding back roads of north Mississippi and southwest Tennessee. Eventually, they meet up with I-40 and follow it on into Nashville like a trio of tourists. Jimmy never bothers to put on a tie, even then. He hasn't worn a suit anywhere besides church in four years.

Detroit Simmons is always glad to see them, even if he is in the middle of something important. He stops his chore and insists on spending the day with them. That's even though he and Rachel drive down to the farm often to spend the weekend. Even though they have their own bedroom upstairs at the house. They are Catherine's godparents. She named a couple of her favorite geese after them.

Wizard has continued to grow with Detroit at the helm in more than name only. The fallout from the mess with the George twins was minimal. Since Jimmy had voluntarily severed the connection when he learned what was going on, there was no lasting problem.

Jimmy could have stayed on if he had wanted to. The Securities and Exchange Commission hinted it might be best if he stepped down, but there was no pressure, really. Not from them. Not from the board of directors. Not even from the stockholders, who were so happy with their investment so far.

No, it was Jimmy's choice. Their choice, Cleo's and his, to pull back and let Wizard have its head.

Jimmy Gill had known deep down what was missing in his life, where things had gone wrong, even before the deadly showdown with DeWayne on the dam at Percy Priest Lake. Pride and stubbornness and the inertia of the roller coaster he had set in motion kept him from admitting it. Then, when the whole thing almost flew off the track, when he came so close to losing the people who really mattered, he finally realized that he had nothing else to prove to anybody.

Wizard had grown too big for him, had strayed much too far from the side of the business that he loved so much. He had found himself insulated from the magic that had pulled and tugged him into broadcasting in the first place. He craved the simple one-to-one communication between radio personality and radio listener. He finally saw that he missed it as much as he might have breathing.

Stations and chains of stations were run by accountants and regulators, consultants and researchers. It had to be that way. Too much money was invested by people who knew little or nothing about the broadcasting business, who were in it for the monetary return only. Some turned out to be good operators who hired bright and creative people to put an exciting product out over the airwaves. Others lived and died by the bottom line only, bought and sold stations for profit in the short term; and in the process, good people got hurt.

Detroit had hung on to the Birmingham and Louisville stations after all, pulled them off the selling block, and withdrew the offers for the stations Jimmy had gone after in the huge markets. The stockholders quietly questioned his strategy, but the profits were there already, their investments were sound, and they soon hushed. Detroit, Lulu Dooley, Clarice George, Greta Polanski, and the employees of the company had begun to gradually buy back all the stock anyway, and it will eventually return to being a private corporation again.

Cleo and Jimmy make more than enough from their shares to live comfortably, and all her music publishing goes directly to a trust fund for Catherine and their later children. Catherine Gill is already a wealthy young lady. The radio station they own isn't there for money. Jimmy takes no salary.

When they are back visiting in Nashville, Jimmy sometimes gets a twinge of feeling for the power he willingly turned his back on. When he walks through the studios at Wizard, he is reminded of the audience out there, the people listening to the programming that is being packaged and sent out from that special place. He can feel the creative energy that bursts from those padded, sound-deadened rooms.

And there's no mistaking the look he sees in Cleo's eyes when they drive down Music Row. She gazes out at the studios and record companies and booking agencies and he knows she misses it. But when either of them senses the other getting that feeling, they merely look at each other, smile, share a moment frighteningly close to telepathy, maybe kiss, and then move on without hesitation.

They both know they'll soon point the truck back toward home. And as soon as they top a certain hill just a few miles south of the Tennessee border, about the same time they can catch their first glimpse of the Okolona River, they will also be able to begin pulling their station's weak signal out of the mud and clutter of the high end of the broadcast band. Mickey will be playing a special request for one of the "sick and shut-ins" who lie alone in cranked-up hospital beds somewhere. Or he will send out a number to someone who sits in a wheelchair in a sliver of shade on a front porch, ear close to a radio, spirit buoyed briefly by the song he spins.

Or maybe it will be one of the late-afternoon pop songs breaking through the cacophony. They imagine some kid, maybe bouncing high inside the cab of a tractor, towing a plow across row after row in an endless field, his headphones taped over his ears so the jarring ride won't tear them loose. He'll be spitting dust, riding a sea of furrows, as the waves of music take him far away, to another place, another life.

They know that just across the river, up a narrow country road, in a grove of pines next to a field of sage, there is a small cinder-block building. Inside, ghosts hum and blue lights flash brilliantly in a couple of glass bottles caged in a metal cabinet. Magnetic energy is amplified and shoved along to the steel spire in the field behind the building, then spins out across the ether at the speed of light. Somewhere out there, it will be snatched from the wind by aerials, and radios will convert it all back to music and voices.

It's only a low-powered daytime station on the high end of the dial in a tiny town in north Mississippi. But inside that little cinder-block building, the wizard is still busy, still working his magic.